Praise for
Her Perfect Twin

"[A] masterfully orchestrated debut...Thanks to the author's ingeniously twisty plot...readers won't know the answer until the surprising and karmically satisfying final pages. This author is one to keep an eye on."

—*Publisher's Weekly* starred review

"Airtight, cat-and-mouse plotting with twists that will draw *Gone Girl* comparisons, this is a compulsively bingeable debut thriller." —*Booklist*

"Sarah Bonner's debut novel made my jaw drop. There are so many twists in this story, I never knew what was coming next. You won't want to miss this one!"

—Samantha Downing, *USA Today*
bestselling author of *My Lovely Wife*

"*Her Perfect Twin* is...perfect. Don't hesitate to grab this book and dive in. I promise you it's original, cleverly written, and guaranteed to keep readers guessing until the last phenomenal shocker on the final page."

—*Mystery and Suspense Magazine*

"If Sarah Bonner keeps writing novels like this, she will be a force in the future." —Red Carpet Crash

Also by Sarah Bonner:
Her Perfect Twin

Her Sweet Revenge

Sarah Bonner

GRAND
CENTRAL

New York   Boston

Grand Central Publishing
Hachette Book Group
1290 Avenue of the Americas, New York, NY 10104
grandcentralpublishing.com
twitter.com/grandcentralpub

Originally published in 2023 by Hodder & Stoughton in Great Britain
First US edition: September 2023

Grand Central Publishing is a division of Hachette Book Group, Inc. The Grand Central Publishing name and logo is a trademark of Hachette Book Group, Inc.

The publisher is not responsible for websites (or their content) that are not owned by the publisher.

The Hachette Speakers Bureau provides a wide range of authors for speaking events. To find out more, go to hachettespeakersbureau.com or email HachetteSpeakers@hbgusa.com.

Grand Central Publishing books may be purchased in bulk for business, educational, or promotional use. For information, please contact your local bookseller or the Hachette Book Group Special Markets Department at special.markets@hbgusa.com.

Library of Congress Cataloging-in-Publication Data

Names: Bonner, Sarah, author.
Title: Her sweet revenge / Sarah Bonner.
Description: First US edition. | New York : Grand Central Publishing, 2023.
Identifiers: LCCN 2023016009 | ISBN 9781538710036 (trade paperback) |
ISBN 9781538710043 (ebook)
Subjects: LCSH: Revenge—Fiction. | LCGFT: Thrillers (Fiction) | Novels.
Classification: LCC PR6102.O565 H474 2023 | DDC 823/.92—dc23/eng/20230403
LC record available at https://lccn.loc.gov/2023016009

ISBNs: 9781538710036 (trade paperback), 9781538710043 (ebook)

Printed in the United States of America

LSC-C

Printing 1, 2023

To Shelley
For being a brilliant mother-in-law
(and absolutely nothing like Geraldine!)

Part One
Murder

HELENA
2018

and

THEA
2022

Chapter One

My mother-in-law is already holding court in the dining room when I arrive to meet her for lunch. Just like every other Monday, regardless of anything else I might have going on. God forbid if I were to ever miss the bi-weekly torture session Geraldine subjects me to.

"You're late," she calls as I walk in, voice booming across the space. I glance at my watch—it's one minute past—and my heel catches in a gap between the flagstones causing me to stumble a little. "Drunk?" she asks, and her minions titter into their hands.

When I say I'm meeting her for lunch what I really mean is that I'm having lunch in her general vicinity. There are at least a dozen other women here, each an almost carbon copy of the others: perfectly coiffed hair, skin lined from far too many summers in the South of France, matching Brora cashmere cardigans. They are all wives of important people. Or at least people *she* considers to be important. The Grange is a very exclusive private members' club, with a stringent set of rules around who can—and more importantly who cannot—sip a cocktail at the large mahogany bar, eat a steak in the damask flock-wallpapered dining room, or stay in one of the handful of bedrooms each equipped with its own claw-foot bath. My husband's family have owned this club for decades.

"You have something on your dress," Geraldine wrinkles her nose as she gestures to an almost microscopic piece of fluff on my ribcage.

I pluck it off as I go to sit down and place it carefully on the napkin at my side. "Probably from the lining of my coat." I hate myself for explaining. I hate myself even more as I hold my breath to wait for her next criticism.

"You should be more careful if you're going to wear black." Her tone is clear: black is not appropriate for lunch. Black is for funerals and the weddings of women she loathes.

"I came straight from a meeting with a client."

She takes a sip of her water before she replies. "Yes, well I suppose it is *admirable* to have a hobby." Translation: she does not think it's admirable. She is just making sure she gets in her usual dig about me having a career. Taylor wives do not have careers. They have charities they support, husbands they look after, and—most importantly—children they coddle. And you thought 1950 was a lifetime ago. "But next time, please ensure you are dressed appropriately for lunch. There are important people here and I do not wish for you to embarrass me fur—"

Her last sentence is cut short as she notices the waitress hovering next to her, the large glass of wine in her hand dangerously close to sloshing over the brim as she bobs and weaves to avoid Geraldine's gesticulations.

"Just put the glass down you *stupid* girl," Geraldine snaps. I catch the waitress's eye and offer a small smile of encouragement. She looks terrified. I can't say I blame her. My best friend calls Geraldine "Smaug"—not to her face though, obviously—because she thinks she's a wealth-obsessed dragon. Geraldine is *also* a stuck-up class A bitch and she's rather prone to firing any member of staff at The Grange she deems "not up to par," despite the fact she's meant to leave the day-to-day running of the place to the manager.

As lunch continues, I find myself desperately trying to ensure conversation around the table remains in a territory I'm at least vaguely comfortable with, such as the weather or the new coffee shop opening in the next village. Edward and I have been married for almost six years now, so I'm well practised at staying away from anything political to avoid an inevitable argument, but I'm also trying to steer clear of anything baby related that might trigger Geraldine to bring up the subject of her lack of grandchildren. At least the food is incredible, and I have to confess I love cracking the burnt sugar on top of the world's smallest—and possibly most pretentious in a really quite fabulous way—crème brûlée.

After the dessert plates are cleared, I excuse myself and duck out of the side door of the dining room. Geraldine believes it is the height of rudeness to "check one's telephone in polite company," but I'm waiting on an important email from a potential investor. I pull my phone from my bag as soon as I'm outside and I'm ecstatic to find an invite for a lunch meeting next week to "discuss the finer details." My dream might actually happen and I almost prance around the corner to ensure I'm fully out of Geraldine's sight before I call to confirm. I nearly fall over a slim, blond haired young woman in the signature black skirt and bottle-green shirt of The Grange staff, sitting on the floor, smoking, who I realise is the same terrified waitress Geraldine was haranguing earlier.

"Shit! Sorry!" She leaps to her feet, grinding her cigarette butt with the block heel of the ridiculous shoes Geraldine insists the female staff wear with their uniform. "I...err...I was just..."

"Hey. It's OK. I promise I won't tell." I give her a smile. "But get one of the barmen to show you the spot on the roof. It's a much better place to hide from Smaug." The name flies out my mouth before I really think.

"Smaug?" She mouths the name back at me, but her eyes are dancing as she suppresses a giggle. "Like the dragon in *The Hobbit*?"

"My mother-in-law," I confirm with a raise of both eyebrows.

"Ouch."

"Yeah. Complete cliché, I know, but in this case it's true. The whole mother-in-law from hell thing. I'm Helena by the way." I extend my hand to her.

"Ella," she says. Then her face crumples, "I think she's going to fire me."

"That might be a blessing in disguise."

"Except that I have to pay my rent and this is the only job I could find. Maybe once I've saved a bit and I can buy a nice suit for interviews..." she trails off. "Sorry. You don't want to hear my problems." She lets out a shuddering sigh that should be melodramatic but instead seems... well, she seems vulnerable, as if she's balanced on a precipice and liable to fall at any moment.

"I could help you. I mean, we're probably not that different in size. And I have a wardrobe full of 'interview suits' that would work with a few adjustments. I'm a stylist." I say the last bit with pride, despite Geraldine's insistence that "shopping for other people is rather beneath the Taylors—people shop for us."

"Would you?" she stares at me, her whole face hopeful.

We are both five foot four, slim (well she's probably a ten and I'm a fourteen, but close enough); so similar in appearance it's like looking into a mirror back to 2005. Her long blond hair is glossy, falling in gentle waves down her back—although mine now requires over three hours in the salon every month to achieve the same look. Her skin has that effortlessly dewy appearance that requires no makeup and her teeth are white and perfectly straight (I'm a teeny bit jealous: no one tells you that your teeth move as you head towards forty and you find yourself googling how intrusive adult braces might be). "When you finish your shift, pop round, we only live down the road, on the corner, just before the *Welcome to Ofcombe St. Mary* sign. The Gatehouse, you can't miss it."

"Thank you!" She launches herself at me and wraps me into a tight hug as if we've been friends for years. "You're a life saver."

Back inside the dining room, Geraldine leans in to sniff my hair the second I slide onto my chair. "Fraternising with the staff, were we? Well, I guess you can take the girl out of Torquay but you can't take Torquay out of the girl. But really, Helena, you need to be more careful around smokers." Her expression hardens, her eyes piercing through me. "Especially if you're going to start IVF soon."

I stay silent, crossing my arms across my chest. It looks defensive but it hides the way I'm pinching the delicate skin on my inner arm, the bruising covered by the bolero I'm wearing. It's the only way I can stop myself from hitting her.

"Oh, don't give me that sourpuss look. You're hardly the only person to ever do it. Moira's niece did." Geraldine points to a small woman with blond hair so perfectly styled it looks like a helmet. "Moira!" The woman looks ecstatic to be singled out. "Your niece did the IVF, didn't she?"

"Oh yes. Six rounds in the end. Horrible process, but needs must."

"See," Geraldine hisses. "She did *six* rounds. And you won't even do one."

"Edward and I are looking at our options," I tell her, wishing we could drop this ridiculous charade. I do not want children and neither does my husband: we never have, our love for each other is more than enough, and we want to have careers and travel and freedom. I once asked Edward if he was upset that the Taylor name would end with him. He had smiled and gently chastised me that "continuation of the family name" is probably the worst possible reason for having children. His mother, however, is of an entirely different opinion and continues to insist I must be having trouble conceiving.

7

"I just don't understand why you haven't made an appointment yet. I gave you the number of that specialist who Cecily's friend was seeing. *She* just had triplets."

"I—" But my reply is interrupted by the sound of glass on concrete. A *lot* of glass. Ella is standing in the doorway of the dining room amidst a sea of glittering shards, a look of abject horror frozen on her face, an empty tray held vertically out in front of her.

"Oh, you *stupid* girl!" Geraldine exclaims. "Look at this mess!" Geraldine turns to her friends and rolls her eyes. "At this rate I'm going to have to find yet another waitress." She turns her gaze to me. "As if I don't have enough to worry about."

***

When Ella turns up at my house later that afternoon, frazzled and nervous, I immediately assume the worst.

"Did she fire you?" I ask, trying to sound sympathetic, pushing my rising anger to one side.

"Not yet," Ella's voice cracks as she talks, "but I think she wants to."

"What did she say?"

But Ella only shakes her head, dashing her hand across her face as if to hold back her tears. My heart breaks a little for her; she looks so vulnerable, so *young*.

I take a step to the side and motion for her to come inside the house. "Let's have a drink, OK? And I promise I will help you to find something else, something better."

"Why are you being so kind to me?" she asks.

I shrug. She'll probably assume it's to get back at Geraldine, and I admit that *is* part of it, but I just can't help but see myself in her. Once upon a time I was completely out of my depth, stuck in a place where the people around me treated me as if I were a second-class citizen. Ella and I have a lot in common.

"Follow me," I say to her, and lead her down the hallway and into the kitchen. It's my favourite room in the house; light grey cupboards and oak worktops give it a modern farmhouse vibe, and there's a large island with these fabulous bar stools. Although I'm not the most talented chef, I love to cook for Edward as he sips a glass of wine and we talk about nothing in particular, as if we are the only two people in the world.

"Wow!" Ella exclaims, turning slowly to take in the whole space. "Your kitchen is bigger than my flat."

"You should see Geraldine's place," I say quickly, doing what I always do when people assume we're wealthy, putting someone else in the spotlight.

"I bet that isn't any near as stylish as this," Ella replies with a grin.

"Let's just say her place isn't to my taste," I reply and then cover my mouth with my hand. "Don't tell her I said that," I add.

"Your secrets are safe with me. Now, are you going to give me the tour?"

I show Ella around the house and she *ooh*s and *ahh*s at the open-plan living and dining room, the walled garden with its pretty patio seating area, the three large bedrooms each with their own en-suite. "It was originally the gatehouse for the estate, but it's been expanded over the years," I tell her, "and then I redecorated when Edward and I got married and moved in. It was almost derelict before then."

We end the tour in the bedroom I predominantly use for additional storage. It is impeccably neat—my tidiness is a bit of a hangover from my boarding school days—with deep pile carpets, light oak built-in wardrobes and a fabulous purple sofa to add just the right pop of colour. "Now then. Let's find you an interview outfit."

***

Half an hour later, I've found the perfect skirt suit for her; classy and demure but with a clinging skirt that keeps the look feeling young enough for someone who is only just twenty-three. The only problem is a blouse, as Ella is blessed in a way that I am not and so all of mine gape unattractively. "How about I take you to this outlet place I'm a member of?" I offer.

"That would be amazing!"

"Great. Now, shall we have a sneaky cocktail?" I ask her. I'm enjoying her company and don't want her to leave just yet.

"Hell, yes!" she replies with gusto, and we head down to the kitchen. Her enthusiasm is infectious, she's so different to most of the other people in my life. Geraldine and her geriatric mean girls. Edward and his "rugger chums"—his term, not mine. Apart from Thea, all my friends are parents now, conversations dominated by school choices and screen-time limits. They've moved on from the baby phase, passed the toddler days, careering towards the tween years as I stay exactly where I've always been. I stand by the decision Edward and I made, but if I'm entirely honest I hadn't realised how much my life would diverge from the lives of my peers. Or that there would be some parts I would miss: no first words, first day at school, dance recitals, chess tournaments, their first love and first heartbreak. I've never told even Edward but I was pregnant once, but it wasn't meant to be. I would have called her Thea after her godmother and she would have been fierce and fearless. She would have changed the world.

"You must be so proud of your business." Ella pulls me back from the daydream. She's scrolling on her phone. "This is UH-mazing!" She turns her screen to show me what she's looking at. It's my Instagram feed. "You have like a hundred thousand followers. You're practically a celebrity."

"Hardly," I reply, but I can't help smiling while I busy myself by preparing us a Mojito. I try to avoid glancing at the alcove I use as a home office, the vintage roll top closed to hide the chaos of papers sprawled across it. And the hidden drawer stuffed full of the evidence of my notoriety.

"Tell me all about it," Ella begs, taking the proffered cocktail, curling her legs underneath her on the sofa.

"There's not a lot to tell."

"Really? I don't believe that for one minute."

"Well, there's this investor who is interested..." I trail off. "But it's early days and I can't really talk about it."

Ella applauds. "Brilliant. I'm in awe of you. It must piss your mother-in-law off, seeing you with this big successful business."

"Not quite... Geraldine is horrified that I suggest people wear *high street*." I do my best Geraldine impression and Ella snorts Mojito as she laughs. "Like where else do real people shop?" My mother-in-law only wears vintage Diane von Furstenberg wrap dresses; she has a whole wardrobe of them. Geraldine's functionally bankrupt, essentially living on money borrowed against The Grange, but she's very good at keeping up appearances. The late Mr. Edwin Taylor—my father-in-law—put all the cash assets in trust rather than leave them to his wife, or directly to his son. Which means there is no Taylor money unless Edward produces an heir. Edwin revelled in making everyone's lives as shitty as possible when he was alive and he just couldn't help continuing his sadistic legacy in death.

I drain my glass, pushing the thought of him from my mind. "Another Mojito?" I ask Ella, not waiting for her answer before walking back into the kitchen to prepare another cocktail.

"I'd love to, but I'd better run." She wrinkles her nose and sounds genuinely disappointed. "But I'll see you on Thursday?"

The question is accompanied by a raised eyebrow and hopeful smile.

"Absolutely," I confirm, following her into the hallway.

"Ooh, what's that?" She scoops a little envelope from the door mat and passes it to me. It's small, about the size of a postcard: *Helena* written on it in elaborate calligraphy. Did I miss it earlier, or was it delivered while we were sipping Mojitos? I try to peer round Ella, but it's almost dusk, the trees silhouetted against the darkening sky, offering the perfect place for someone to hide. A chill runs down my spine.

Is someone watching from the shadows?

"Thank you, Helena," Ella says, lifting the suit slightly. "For the suit and for... well, for treating me like a person."

I close the door behind her and look at the envelope in my hand, exactly like the others hidden in my desk. Inside is a simple white card, a single sentence written on it.

We all have secrets...but you're going to pay for yours

Chapter Two

2018
HELENA

We all have secrets . . . but you're going to pay for yours

Just a single sentence written in curling lettering on a plain blank card.

Just like the ones which have come before:

Secrets and lies ruin lives

Some secrets are buried deeper than others

How far do I need to dig before I find yours

I feel numb as I head back into the kitchen and the open bottle of rum. My hand is shaking as I pour two fingers into my glass and gulp it down, wincing at the taste of the salt I'd applied to the rim. I pour another shot, the sound of the bottle thumping onto the work service as loud as thunder in the silent kitchen.

Fortified with alcohol, I pick the card back up, turning it over in my hands. There is nothing else written on it except that one line.

We all have secrets . . . but you're going to pay for yours

The first note arrived just under two weeks ago, pushed through the letter box while I was upstairs. Sometimes when Edward is out—this time Geraldine had dragged him to dinner with some boring banker types she was hoping would invest in The Grange—I lock myself in the bathroom so I can pretend I'm not all alone in the house in the dark. The Gatehouse can feel so isolated, surrounded by tall trees that block the noise from the road and cast eerie shadows against the windows.

I thought it was junk mail at first, expecting to open it to find a flyer for a local takeaway, or a letter from an estate agency telling me they wanted to help sell my home. But then I read those five words, written in curling copperplate:

Secrets and lies ruin lives

I had frozen, staring at the words as the room started to swirl and shift around me. My feet turned to blocks of ice on the cold stone floor and all the blood rushed to my heart, beating a mile a minute. *Who had sent it? How could they possibly know?*

After a few minutes the spell holding me in place had begun to dissipate. I locked every door, every window. Lowered every blind. Drew every curtain. Tried to fight the overwhelming desire to crawl into the darkest corner of the house and hide there until morning. In the end, I went to bed, the covers pulled over my head, praying for the sun to rise and reveal this was all just a bad dream.

But the note was still hidden in my desk when I looked the next morning. And so I composed myself, put on a nice dress and some makeup, and went to the police.

The police officer was an attractive guy in his late twenties. He'd put the note in one of those evidence bags—you know, the ones that look like a glorified sandwich bag—and spent all of about twenty seconds looking at it before he handed it back to me. "And?" he asked, tilting his head slightly.

"And?" I replied, confused.

"Is this all?"

"It's a threatening note, sent to my home. Someone knows where I live."

"Right." He drew the word out. "It doesn't seem very threatening." He shrugged his shoulders.

I went back a few days later when the second note came. *Some secrets are buried deeper than others*

It was the same officer. "Back again?" He read the new card before sitting back into his chair. "Do you use social media, Mrs. Taylor?"

"Of course." I stopped myself from adding *who doesn't?* "I blog and use Instagram. For my business." I added that last bit hoping it would make him take me more seriously.

"And do you post pictures. Of yourself, your home?"

"Of course."

"Could someone have seen your address online? A stack of post in the background of you pout— err, posing, I mean."

"Well . . ."

"Because I think this is probably just someone messing with you."

"You think it's a prank?"

I didn't bother going back. Especially after what had happened to my friend Natalia.

Natalia Ormerod was a fashion blogger and Instagram star, one of the very first "non-celeb" people to hit over a million followers. Was. Past tense. Eighteen months ago she began receiving these anonymous notes. Day after day she would get them, week after week, month after month. She only showed us the first few. A year ago, someone hacked her Instagram account and uploaded photos onto her feed. They weren't explicit—Instagram would have deleted them if they were—but they pretty clearly showed Natalia with a guy who wasn't her husband. The next day her entire social media just vanished. We met through this group chat for "influencers," a bunch of us getting together so we'd feel less alone in an industry that is basically bonkers. She posted a cryptic message before leaving the chat: about wanting to be left alone to "rebuild" but that she wished she'd just given them what they wanted.

The rumour mill had gone into overdrive, but the consensus was that she was the victim of a reputation scam and had refused—or been unable, I guess—to pay the demands. So whoever was behind it had revealed everything. Her shameful secrets splashed across the internet for everyone to see.

For her husband to see.

I didn't tell Edward when the notes first started arriving. My husband is supportive and lovely and even helped me to set up my website back at the start of this crazy journey. But he also hates what he calls the "celebritisation" of my job, the way I have to give over a huge part of myself to appear approachable and real on social media. I get what he's saying, but I love that *I* get to help people, that my clients don't think of me as some faceless person hiding behind a corporate machine. He thinks I am making myself a target for weirdos and freaks. I knew that first smooth white card with those five perfectly written words on it would just prove him right. Plus of course he would worry and he has so much else on his plate right now. He's always tried to take my problems and make them his own, looking for a solution, for an answer. And then he would have started digging and eventually started asking questions. Questions I'm not sure I want to answer.

Questions like what secrets I might be keeping.

We all have secrets. But one of mine might break him. Might break us. So I just kept stuffing the notes into the little drawer of my desk, until they threatened to explode. I began to have nightmares where the drawer would fly open, the notes—in my dream there were literally thousands of them—raining onto every surface of the house, drowning me in little rectangles of card, cutting my skin to shreds, the blood staining the white.

***

His key scraping in the lock makes me jump. The card is still in my hand and I only just make it to the desk before he's inside.

"What a day!" he calls as he moves from the hallway to the kitchen. "You have no idea how busy things are. It's a fucking nightmare."

"Hmmm," I say, trying to slide open the secret drawer in silence. The note safely ensconced inside, I vow to forget about it. Plaster a smile on my face and have a glass of wine with my husband. I'm good at pretending nothing is wrong, I've had plenty of practice.

"Mum said you were a bit off at lunch earlier," Edward says as he settles on the sofa. He takes a huge swig of wine and watches me over the brim.

"Off?" I ask. Because what the hell does *off* actually mean?

"She's worried about us."

"No, Edward. She's worried about herself." I'm tired, a little drunk after the rum earlier and my mind is half concentrating on the notes tucked in the drawer of my desk. I am absolutely not in the mood to talk about his fucking mother.

"She wants what is best for all of us."

"No, Edward, she doesn't. She wants what's best for her. She's banging the babies drum louder than ever. You aren't the one who has to sit there while she makes not-so-subtle digs in front of her awful friends."

"I'm sure she isn't making digs."

"She is. Jesus, she brought Moira along today just because Moira's niece *had the IVF*." I mimic Geraldine, a nasty nasal quality to my tone.

Edward sighs and runs his hand through his hair. I stare back at him, waiting for him to finally agree to tell her the truth. But he doesn't. That would involve having a proper adult conversation with his mother, one he has avoided for years. "She thinks she's helping, H-Bear."

The way he uses our nickname while defending her makes me want to scream. "Why do you always take her side?"

"I don't." He almost sounds offended, like he doesn't see the same dragon I see; he sees some poor innocent old widow instead. "She just wants to be a grandmother. That's all."

He still thinks she wants a grandchild to coo over, that it would break her heart if she knew her only son was denying her that dream. He really can't see that a baby would simply be the key to unlocking all the Taylor money.

"I'm going to bed," I tell him, picking up my glass and heading to the kitchen for a refill.

"Night, H-Bear," he says softly from his position on the sofa. I don't answer, but I take a full bottle of Sauvignon Blanc from the fridge and go upstairs without another word.

***

He slips into bed, making the mattress buck slightly beneath me. "Are you awake," he whispers.

"Yes," I reply.

"I'm sorry."

"For what?" I hold my breath as I wait for his answer.

"I just want you to be happy."

I try to dampen my disappointment in him. All I want is for him to recognise that his mother is a bully. I just want my husband to take my side for once. "Good night, Edward." I keep my voice neutral. It just isn't worth fighting anymore.

"Night, H-Bear," he says softly, burrowing a little more under the duvet. "Love you."

"Love you, too," I reply, almost reflexively; the same words we always say in the dark.

Five minutes later he's snoring softly, but sleep evades me. You know how when you try not to think about something, it just gets bigger and bigger and bigger? It's only words on a piece of A6 card. Words can't hurt me.

We all have secrets … but you're going to pay for yours

But whoever is sending these notes *can* hurt me. Especially if they really do know the truth.

Everyone has secrets. But mine could tear my life apart.

At one a.m., I'm still wide awake. Edward has curled himself into a ball, taking most of the duvet with him. I debate stealing it back, but I know that would only wake him and at least he isn't snoring. The house is silent, the moon casting a grey glow in the darkness. Outside an owl hoots, a fox screams, and I curse them both for the racket they are making, even though they are hardly to blame for my insomnia.

After another five minutes I give up and pick up my phone from the bedside table, reducing the screen brightness so I don't disturb Edward or attract moths in through the open window. I fire off a stream of texts to Thea in a veritable bitch-fest about my mother-in-law. It's about seven in the evening in New York, so she'll still be at work, but it feels good to just offload into the ether, to alchemise all that fear into hate. I'm lucky my mother-in-law is such a justified target for it.

Thea is my "little sister." She's not actually my sister; we're not blood relatives, but she was also a scholarship girl at Ferndown, a few years younger than me, and I took her under my wing. There was a time when she was basically the only friend I had in that place and even two decades later and with over three thousand miles between us, we're still close.

I'm awoken at five by the dinging of a stream of messages from Thea, replying to my earlier diatribe. She is absolutely vicious in her response and I love her for it. I won't repeat what she wrote about Smaug verbatim, but she can be wonderfully creative in her use of expletives.

Just cut Edward some slack, she adds.

I wish he was on my side, I reply.

He is for the important things. And imagine having that woman for a mother...

I guess she has a point on that last one.

Buoyed by Thea's bitching, I decide to get up and follow her lead of an early yoga session. Thea left Ferndown with the best set of A-level results they had ever seen, was sponsored through her under- and post-grad studies at MIT and LSE and is now the youngest director of an incredibly prestigious hedge fund in New York. She lives the most regimented lifestyle I have ever seen, starting the day with thirty minutes of yoga at five a.m. and dividing the next nineteen hours into perfectly choreographed segments. It must be exhausting but she seems to thrive on it.

***

Three hours later and I'm starting to wonder if maybe there is something to this whole five a.m. yoga thing. I'm on fire; my To Do list complete, the house clean and tidy, the card still tucked away in the drawer, and I've barely even thought about it. I've even made Edward a breakfast of eggs Benedict with a side of fresh fruit, and I've brewed coffee properly, in a cafetière and everything.

"Are you feeling OK?" he asks, humour dancing across his face and eyes alive in a way I haven't seen for a while.

"Can't I make my husband breakfast?" I reply lightly, spearing a strawberry from his plate with my fork and popping it into my mouth. For a few delicious moments it feels like normal again. But then his phone rings and he jumps, his hand moving to swiftly cover the screen. But not before I see who is calling.

"Sorry," he tells me, standing up and moving to his study to take the call. Can't his fucking mother give us just one morning to ourselves?

Ten minutes later he's left for the office and the house is silent. I walk listlessly from room to room, waiting for inspiration to strike me on how to fill the day ahead. I have a ton of admin to do, but I've run out of steam after my flurry of earlier activity. Perhaps the whole five a.m. yoga session wasn't such a good idea after all.

I'm in the hallway, idly wondering if I should replace the gilt-edged mirror his mother gave us as a housewarming gift with something more modern like the gorgeous, burnished silver one I've been coveting after seeing it in the window of a designer boutique in town, when the doorbell rings.

"Flower delivery," a voice says—rather unnecessarily—from behind an enormous bouquet of roses and other flowers I don't have names for. They are already in a vase and I discover it weighs a ton as I take it from him, followed by an awkward few moments as I try not to drop it, before setting it on the floor.

"Nice place you've got here." He takes a step closer. He's probably late forties and looks like he works out, muscles visible under his rather tight T-shirt. "Lovely and quiet. No neighbours close enough to be a bother." He grins in a way that makes my skin crawl and takes another step forward, his dark eyes travelling from my face down to my chest.

"Honey!" I call over my shoulder into the house, the same way I've been forced to do more than a few times. "Can you come help?" I take a step back, careful not to trip over the lip of the door frame. "My husband's in his office," I say to the delivery guy pointedly.

His whole demeanour changes in a moment, the leering grin replaced with a pleasant smile. "Have a great day," he says and turns to leave. I wonder how many times today he will creep along that line between acceptable and entirely inappropriate.

I close the door and take a few deep breaths, willing my heartrate to return to normal. My fear begins to fragment, reforming into anger at the sheer fucking audacity of him! What gives him the right to stand on my doorstep and look at me like that?

Creepy delivery driver...so gross!! I text Thea.

Eurghhh. I'm sorry!! You should kick them in the balls, she replies immediately. She's had her own share of unwanted attention over the years, I guess we all have. *You OK?* she adds.

Yeah. He's gone. Balls intact unfortunately.

Be safe. Love you millions xx

As hoped, venting to Thea has made me feel calmer and I stoop to pick up the vase. The flowers are absolutely gorgeous, in all shades of red from the colour of fresh crimson blood to a deep burgundy like a fine wine. Thankfully my hair is behaving and my makeup is freshly applied so I set them on the counter and start taking photos of them, my smiling face appearing in a few selfies alongside the bouquet. Nestled in the foliage lies a small rectangle of contrasting white, but I ignore it as I pick the best photo.

Another happy customer? #blessed I post to Instagram, where almost a hundred of the loyal followers of @BigSister-Helena instantly like it.

I pluck the small envelope from its place in the flowers, *Helena* written on it in a fancy calligraphy by someone with a talented hand. I jump backwards as if the bouquet might be hiding a hand grenade. It must be a coincidence: florist cards are always written a bit fancy.

But it isn't a coincidence.

I'm watching you, Helena. I see who you are behind the mask

Chapter Three

2022
THEA

Armed with a coffee in each hand, I turn down one of the narrow side streets and use my elbow to press the buzzer on a bright purple door. The receptionist buzzes me in, the lock clicking before the door swings open. Jen is waiting at the top of the stairs, one hand already reaching for the cup with her name on it. She takes a deep slug, smacks her lips in satisfaction and performs a little shoulder shimmy.

"I think I might be a little bit in love with you," she says seriously, before her face breaks into a grin and her cheeks flush red. "Gosh, that sounded a lot less weird in my head!"

I take a sip of my latte to cover my own awkwardness; I'm not great at taking compliments, especially those which are more in jest. I know how I'm meant to act, that I should wink and make a quip, but it never quite feels right. Luckily Jen has known me long enough to ignore my lack of social graces.

"I need you to sign off the pictures," Jen tells me as we walk towards our desks. We both rent space in one of those shared office places. After spending my previous life in investment banking I needed to find somewhere with a buzz, the silence at home was giving me headaches. Jen is a social media consultant and so could easily work from home, but she's so chatty she would have driven herself mad if she didn't have people around her to talk to.

I steel myself as she pulls up the images onto her screen. I hate—and when I say hate, I mean truly abhor—pictures of myself. It's not that I'm unattractive, I know that objectively, but something happens to my face when there's a camera in my proximity, my features twisting in an inexplicable fashion. There are so few photos of me in the world, Helena used to make a running joke of it, saying I was her imaginary friend whose existence she could never actually prove. But Jen thinks a few shots on my new Instagram profile she's been helping me with will make me more approachable.

"Look, I feel the same way about pictures of myself," she says when she sees my expression.

"Do we have a picture of you as my new social media tsar?" I ask.

"You're the star of the show, Thea."

I groan loudly. "OK then. Let's use these two," I say as I point to the least objectionable ones.

Jen yawns and rubs her hand across her face. "Sorry. It's not because I'm bored."

"Late night?" I ask her.

"Just Mum, you know." She shrugs her shoulders, but the tiredness etched into her face belies her apparent nonchalance. "The home called just before ten to say she was refusing to settle unless I spoke to her." She takes a gulp of coffee. "Sorry. I'll be alright once the caffeine kicks in properly." I reach over to give her hand a little squeeze. She offers me a thin smile in return. "Thanks. Sorry, I don't want to be a downer, but I'd better finish up. I need to find a new commission this week or I won't be able to pay for Mum's extras; it'd break her heart not to have the hairdresser and the nail technician come in to keep her looking vaguely like herself."

"You know I'd help, if you need it?"

"I just don't know when I'd be able to pay you back."

"I'm not offering you a loan, Jen. Just one friend giving the other a gift to help her out."

"Thank you," she says and then suddenly hops up, wrapping her arms around me in an awkward sitting hug. "I don't know what I'd do without you," she whispers into my shoulder.

"Right then. I guess I'd better get on," I say, partly to get out of the hug which feels increasingly uncomfortable as the seconds tick past, but also because I have a ton of work to get through.

***

I bought the Harris Bay vineyard in late 2019. It's a completely gorgeous place, with a whitewashed colonial house converted into a restaurant and boutique hotel; all you can see is green for miles and miles.

"One day," Helena had told me when we were teenagers, sitting on the windowsill of her dormitory, feet dangling into the darkness below, "we'll live somewhere completely cool."

"Like where?" I'd asked her, taking a long drag on the cigarette and leaning even more dangerously far out of the window to exhale the smoke.

"I don't know. Like a posh hotel. Or a private island." She leant into me to take a toke. "Ooh!" she exclaimed. "How about a vineyard?"

"But you don't like wine," I reminded her. She was sixteen and drank vodka mixed with orange juice. I was fourteen and could just about stomach a sickly sweet Malibu and pineapple.

"That's just a technicality." She waved a hand dismissively. "It'll be fun. And we can hire hot guys to pick the grapes." She snorted with laughter and bumped her shoulder against mine. "Come on, Thea. Promise me we can buy a vineyard one day."

"I promise."

Helena never got to see Harris Bay, even though I know she had finally developed a taste for Marlborough Sauvignon Blanc. I bought it on a whim, a way to feel close to her. I think some small part of me thought it would squash the guilt that threatened to consume me. But it didn't work. Perhaps it would have done if I'd stayed in New Zealand, if I hadn't come to the UK and ended up locked out of NZ by the pandemic.

I try to push the thoughts of her aside and open my To Do list. The effect of Brexit, Covid and the looming cost-of-living crisis is leading to huge demand for cheap—but drinkable—wine from outside Europe. I'm importing huge quantities of the Harris Bay for restaurants, bars, and events companies. Business is booming. But this is definitely not the glamorous vision Helena had romanticised about; I don't think she dreamt of spreadsheets and meetings and late nights in the office, followed by evenings spent alone with a ready meal.

***

It's gone nine before I get home and I close the door gratefully behind me. But the scent of vanilla and coconut in the air almost makes me stumble. My rational brain knows that the cleaner came today and she must have used some kind of new product. But my mind's eye is in the Mirage hotel in Las Vegas, Helena at my side as I try to teach her the basics of blackjack.

It was her hen party. Or at least that was what we called it. In reality it was just the two of us having a riotous time, getting pissed on these huge novelty cups of sickly bright pink frozen Margaritas, people watching by the pool, playing cards late into the night.

"Why does it smell so good in here?" she had asked as we walked into the foyer of the hotel. She stopped dead—causing the couple behind to swerve to avoid her, tutting as they did so—before spreading her arms wide, turning in a slow circle with a beatific look on her face.

"Vanilla and coconut. They must pump it in to cover up the smell of smoke and stale beer."

She stopped turning and hooked a finger into her sunglasses, pulling them down to look me in the eye. "It wasn't an actual question, Thea."

I nodded. "Noted." I cleared my throat and tried again, this time with a level of joviality that mimicked her own excitement. "It's like Piña Coladas!"

She winked. "Now *that* sounds like an excellent idea. To the cocktail bar!"

Helena was always patient to point out when I had responded in a way that wasn't... well, she described it as *strictly within the confines of what other people would call normal*. If I missed that a question was rhetorical, or gave an honest opinion when the recipient really wanted someone to say "no, of course that dress doesn't make you look washed out." It was just one of the many things I loved about her. She never made me feel like a freak, and she helped me blend in. That was her special skill—making you feel like you belonged. Even if you were always the one on the outside, she would bring you right into the middle.

I order a pizza—extra pepperoni and triple jalapeños—and change into some joggers before heading to the living room. The house belongs to my godfather, but he's been living in Dubai for the past few years so I have the run of the place. It's not one hundred percent decorated to my taste—there's a little too much dark wood and a rather masculine ambience—but it's comfortable and I've never been much into interior design. That was always more Helena's forte; when she first renovated The Gatehouse she would send me a constant stream of Pinterest boards and photos from *Country Living* magazine.

I know it would be better for my back to sit at the desk in the study, but the hunter green wallpaper and bookcases full of dusty leather books remind me too much of Ferndown. So instead, I find myself sitting cross-legged on the floor of the living room, my laptop balanced on the coffee table.

Ten people have responded to the question I posted on Reddit. The subreddit */r/peoplefinder* is apparently the go-to place to find out how to track someone. Nine of the responses tell me pretty much the same thing: Google search, reverse image search, friends and family connections; none of the suggestions are any help at all. The last response is some guy wanting to know if I'm single because he's a veteran and a single dad and a good god-fearing man who would show me the respect I deserve. His avatar is the U.S. flag and he's undoubtedly a fake account, probably from a bot-farm in Russia. I post an update into the thread, thanking everyone for their super helpful suggestions and adding *If only Ella Hazelwood would contact me* 😄 I'm assuming she will periodically Google her own name—don't tell me you don't ever do this; the internet has made narcissists of us all—and come across my post.

I run through my own Google searches, not my own name, but the names of all the people who were part of Helena's life. The people she called her friends, her colleagues, confidantes and even casual drinking buddies. I check their social media profiles: Twitter, Facebook, Instagram, even TikTok. Nothing catches my attention.

Closing my laptop, I pick up the final slice of pizza from the box. It's cold, the cheese congealed into a solid shiny mass. There was a time I would have looked up the exact calorie count on the Pizza Hut website and calculated the precise distance I would need to run to burn them off. But that was back then, when my life made sense, when it had structure and meaning.

Now nothing really matters except finding out exactly what happened to Helena.

And bringing her killer to justice.

Chapter Four

2018
HELENA

I'm watching you, Helena. I see who you are behind the mask

The arrival of the note with the flowers was the catalyst I needed to finally tell someone. Surely the other ladies in the group chat will have some thoughts, even if they're bound to chastise me for not being more careful with putting my name and address online for anyone to find. And isn't the whole point of the informal network of bloggers and Instagrammers to be there to support each other? I mean as much as a bunch of women in competition with each other can—and they are the closest thing to colleagues I have.

I spend half an hour typing a single line and then deleting it, over and over again, unable to find the right words. Once it's said, I can't take it back. But in the end I just blurt it out.

Helena: I had a note.

Shaz: Note?

Helena: Like Natalia...

Charlotte: What, like a death threat? Or fishing?

Shaz: OMG! You did not?!

Tori: Oh, sweetie...Natalia was like mega huge. She had like a million followers. Honeybunny, I hardly think the same person would target you. You have like ten thousand ☹

I push my laptop away from me after I read the last message. Everyone knows Tori is a bitch, and I have almost a hundred thousand, thank you very much, but she kind of has a point. The general consensus of the group is that Natalia's notes were fishing for information and then the author found a chink in her life to exploit.

Maybe the note writer isn't targeting me because of @Big-SisterHelena.

I'm watching you, Helena. I see who you are behind the mask
What if they know about @PAGEFree?

It was just a joke at the beginning; a way to let off a bit of steam. Besides, @PAGEFree didn't exactly have a lot of followers on Twitter, I was basically tweeting into the void.

@PAGEFree. An acronym for Poise And Graceful Elegance. We had lessons in deportment at Ferndown and it was the only class Thea ever failed; the teacher was adamant she would amount to nothing given her shortcomings. "No! You must be better! Poise and graceful elegance!" she would screech at poor Thea who was trying not to giggle as the book slipped off her head for the second time in ten seconds. I thought it was kind of fitting as I eviscerated the great and the good who patronised The Grange, obviously anonymised and changed just enough so no one would ever know who I was talking about.

Trust me Mr. B, she knew you were rich and that is 100% why she started dating you #RealityCheck This was in response to this awful family friend, Rob Braithwaite, who droned on for almost an hour over dinner about how his wife Charlie "didn't even realise he was rich until they'd been dating for six months."

Being forced to wait in line like everyone else is not *persecution* #CryBaby One of Geraldine's cronies had been left flabbergasted when he tried to push to the front of the queue for a rollercoaster at Thorpe Park with his grandson. "It wasn't that they didn't seem to care who I am, it was the sheer joy with which they sent me to the back of the queue," he had wailed.

*Yes you do know how anyone lives on less than £100k pa,
you watch your cleaner struggle on far less #OutOfTouch* Two
women about my age were having lunch at the table next to me
and discussing their children's schools and future prospects.
"Arlo is going to be a doctor, or something professional at
least. How anyone can live on less than a hundred grand a year
is beyond me." Just ten minutes later, her friend expressed dis-
satisfaction with her cleaner. "Oh, you should try mine. She's
not cheap though; ten pounds an hour, which I think is rather
steep." She said it without a shred of irony.

It made me feel like I was getting one over on Geraldine.
You might have already realised that my husband's family are
dysfunctional at best, although I wouldn't really hesitate to
call them sociopathic. Geraldine is an awful human being,
but she does have one redeeming feature. She really does love
Edward, even if she doesn't always show it in the healthiest
of ways; prone to forgetting he's a fully grown adult capable of looking after himself, especially when it comes to his
allergies.

"You have your EpiPen?" she'll ask him every single time she
sees him, her hand out palm up, foot tapping out the seconds
until he produces one. "This expires in two months," she said
last time as she inspected it. "I'll make you an appointment to
renew your prescription."

"She treats you like you're still five years old," I told him
later that day once we were home.

"Better than being without one," he replied. He doesn't see
it—he doesn't see that it's just another way for her to control
him.

But however much I hate Geraldine, Edwin was far worse. To
the point that I almost felt sorry for her a few times. "Geraldine,
don't slouch," he would bark at her, rapping the back of her
chair with his walking stick. And he got worse once he got ill; it

was as if he felt he had carte blanche to just spew whatever shit came into his head at any moment.

"You're not what I'd hoped for Edward," he'd sneered at me, lying in the huge wooden bed of his bedroom. We were alone, the nurse had gone to fetch his prescription and Edward and Geraldine were getting some air on the patio below us.

"I'm sorry I'm a disappointment," I replied, trying not to rise to him.

"I should have been stricter with him. That bloody woman coddled him, made him soft. I should have made more of a man out of him."

"I'm sure you were plenty strict enough." I managed to keep my voice level, despite the abuse I know Edward suffered from his father over the years in the name of "ensuring he was a proper man," whatever that was even supposed to mean.

"Pfff. Evidently not." He waved a wizened hand at me, the skin almost transparent. "At least you'll be a breeder. Girls like you just can't help popping them out."

I should have walked away; he was on his deathbed, this might even have been the last time I had to visit the hateful old bastard. But I couldn't let it go. I leant in closer, my eyes on his, fingers gripping his wrist. "There will be no children. Edward is the last Taylor. No one else will be saddled with your legacy. It ends with us."

Edwin's eyes widened, I think in shock that someone was impetuous enough to use that tone with him. But then I watched as the words sunk in, burrowing into his brain through the fog of his drugs. He went through the full cycle of grief in front of my eyes: denial, a tiny shake of the head, almost imperceptible; anger, a flare of his nostrils; bargaining, a pleading in his eyes that I refused to react to; depression, the furrow in his brow deepening; acceptance, the relaxing of his features. He had closed his eyes and I had walked away, assuming that would be the last time I saw him. I should have stayed, I should have realised there's a reason it's described as a cycle because he went back round again and evidently settled on anger.

Edwin didn't die that day. He held on for another few weeks. Just enough time to get his lawyer to change the terms of the will, ensuring all the Taylor money was locked behind a condition of Edward's heir. Fucking bastard. He grinned a lipless smile at me as he gathered us around his bed to announce the changes. And then he was gone.

I didn't tell Edward what I'd done. We had promised we wouldn't tell Edwin that we didn't want a family. "Why upset a man who is going to die within days?" he said. I should have kept that promise.

The funeral was a predictably depressing and dour affair: a sea of old men in dark suits; their wives in almost identical black dresses, competing for attention only with their choice of hats and fascinators, although a few had even gone so far as to wear a veil.

Geraldine had played her part to absolute perfection: stoic and composed during the service and the first hour of the wake—held at The Grange, of course—accepting condolences graciously. But the mask began to slip as her gin consumption increased.

"Why?" she had keened.

"It really is a tragedy," her friends whispered around her.

An hour later I passed one of the smaller rooms, used for private dining functions and the sealing of business deals. Geraldine sat in one of the eight ornate gilded chairs clustered around the antique carved wooden dining table. One of her friends, Dinah, sat next to her, trying to calm her down.

"Why?" Geraldine's wail was so high-pitched I was surprised she hadn't inadvertently called her pack of hunting dogs.

"It was just his time."

"Not why did he die! Why did he do this to me?"

Dinah had obviously not yet been party to the full vagaries of Edwin's inheritance plan. "Do what?"

"He's left me with almost nothing." The wailing subsided into a sob.

"You have The Grange."

"It's a damn millstone. Money flows out, not in. I needed that cash."

"It'll all work itself out." Dinah's voice was placatory, but there was no sense that she believed what she was saying.

"You're an imbecile. It's all over. I just don't know why he did this. Why now?"

"Who would want you to suffer?" It sounded like such an innocent question, but it was laced with the desire for gossip.

"Susan." Geraldine spat out the name like a piece of gristle.

"Susan? He wasn't still..." Dinah sounded suitably horrified. Not that Edwin had had a mistress, but that he'd still been seeing her as his illness progressed.

"I bet it was her. Whispering poison in his ear. Bitch always hated playing second fiddle. If I find out it was her, I will rip her to shreds."

I know people often say they would kill someone when they are angry or upset, but they don't actually mean it. Trust me when I say that Geraldine meant it. If she found out it was all my fault, that I was the one who had made Edwin change the will, she would turn her venom onto me.

If only I'd kept my mouth shut. Then Geraldine would have all the money and she could swan around doing goodness knows what, probably find herself an attractive widower to entertain, and live the life she always thought she should have lived. And Edward and I would be free. Instead we're stuck in this purgatory, bound by obligation but not willing to budge, spinning lie after lie to avoid having any kind of serious conversation.

***

I've never told anyone what I said that day to Edwin. It's not that I'm ashamed; I feel zero shame at telling a dying man his legacy of being a terrible example of humanity wouldn't continue.

I wanted to tell Thea. I always want to tell Thea: she's the first person I think of when things go wrong. She's not one for hugs and cuddles and tears; she won't stroke my back and tell me everything will be alright. That's just not what she's like. She's never been like that.

When my very first boyfriend dumped me—for not wanting to lose my virginity to him, obviously—she found me crying in my dormitory. "Why are you crying?" she'd asked, hovering by the door.

"Lucas dumped me," I replied through the tears and snot.

"Why?"

"What do you mean, why?"

"Why did he dump you? He must have given you a reason." She was so matter of fact. "Oh, because of the sex thing."

I wiped my face on the sleeve of my blazer. "Maybe I should—"

But she interrupted me. "What you *should* do is realise you had a lucky escape. He's a dick who isn't worthy of you."

Sometimes I forgot Thea was a few years younger than me. It should have been me telling her not to sleep with boys to make them like you more. "But..."

"Eugh. Stop crying, wash your face and we can break into the upper-sixth common room for cakes."

"It's not that easy."

"Is crying over him going to change anything?"

"No."

"So, why are you crying?"

That was Thea to a T. As we got older she refined her philosophy: don't worry about the things you can't change;

it won't change anything. And don't worry about the things you can change; get off your arse and change them. Basically, don't cry on me, come to me when you're ready to fix your shit. With Thea a problem shared isn't a problem halved. It's a problem dissected into small enough pieces that they either cease to exist or come with a handy plan of action.

But that week after my—let's just call it a conversation, OK?—with Edwin, Thea was MIA—actually that's a little unfair: she was in the middle of nowhere on a ridiculous corporate retreat trying to convince her boss she was ready for a promotion—and I desperately wanted to offload. It wasn't just Edwin, Geraldine had cornered me a few days earlier at The Grange, her manicured hand gripping my arm so tightly she'd left a bruise as she told me in no uncertain terms that she wished Edward had married Cecily, the daughter of a family friend, despite them having never actually dated. Edward had laughed it off, saying he was sure she didn't mean it. When I showed him the bruise he'd said "oh, well you always bruise so easily," as if it was *my* fault that his mother basically assaulted me. "It was hardly assault, H-Bear," he'd said with laughter in his eyes, before heading to the golf course with one of his friends.

I obviously didn't use Edwin and Geraldine's names, but I used @PAGEFree to post a thread. A visceral rant into the ether, and I revelled in the freedom I felt as I stripped back the veneer of propriety I have worn like a suit of armour for so many years. I thought it would disappear into nothingness. But I must have struck a nerve. It went viral.

It is OK to say "no." To say "fuck this shit, it ends with me." My in-laws are the *worst* people, stuck-up snobs who think money and status and the continuation of the family name are everything. Mr. T: now you know your legacy is over. Ruminate on that from your deathbed #Confessions #ProbablyShouldnt-HaveSaidItOutLoud

I'm not going to pretend I didn't enjoy the validation that came from all the people who liked it, or added their own "horrible in-laws" story, or wished me well as a result. It was oh so cathartic.

But how difficult would it be to find out who @PAGEFree really is? I obviously signed up to Twitter with a random Hotmail account I created just for that, and I didn't fill in any of the details like location or my birthday. Could someone have linked me to it?

If Geraldine found out the things I told Edwin, she would know exactly why he changed the terms of the trust. She would know the current state of the family finances—and especially her own—was because of me. She's been looking for a scapegoat ever since Edwin died. She would kill me if she knew.

But what if Edward found out? We had made a promise to each other and I broke it because I was feeling petty and vindictive against a dying man. However much Edward hated his father, he still wouldn't forgive me. And for all I complain that he sides with his mother against me, I do understand his own impossible situation in all of this—or at least if I don't understand it, I recognise how stressful it must be for him. This stress that *I* caused. This stress caused by a situation *I* created, and one I have then lied about to cover up so no one knows what I did in a moment of weakness. Edward cannot find out.

***

That afternoon there is a card waiting on the door mat, *Helena* written on the envelope. My hands are shaking as I open it.

I know who you are, and I know what you told him

The knot in my stomach tightens. *What you told him:* they must be meaning Edwin.

I stumble into the kitchen, a disjointed film montage flickering behind my eyes: the look of pain in Edward's eyes when he finds out, the gaping hole of the loft hatch as he goes to get a suitcase, clothes and toiletries spilling out as he tries to stuff his life into such a small space, his face turning to stone as I apologise over and over and beg him to stay, the door slamming shut behind him as he leaves.

I slide onto one of the bar stools, gripping the note so tightly I bend the card. *I will not lose him.*

But what will they want to keep my secret?

Chapter Five

2018
HELENA

I wait for the next note. Surely they will announce their demands soon?

There is no note that evening.

Or the next morning.

I try to carry on with my life, painting on a smile and a veneer of pretence that everything's fine. But it's a façade that threatens to crumble at any moment.

I'm trying to catch up on some client billing when I get a phone call. For a second I wonder if it's them, deciding to call with their demands. But it's Ella.

"Hey," I say, half grateful for the distraction, half disappointed that my purgatory must continue.

"Hey, Helena. I was…err…well, I wanted to check you were still free tomorrow?"

"Of course. Are you OK?" She sounds like she's crying.

"Geraldine fired me."

"Bitch." I say it gently though and smile when I hear her small hiccough as she tries to giggle through the tears. "Why don't you come round here first thing and then I'll drive us both to the outlet place?"

"Yes, please."

"Let's say ten a.m. Oh, and Ella?"

"Yes?"

"Don't let her get you down. We'll find you something far better than The Grange."

"Thank you, Helena. You're a total angel."

I end the call and fire off a message to Thea. *Geraldine fired her.*

Despite the fact it's only six a.m. in New York, Thea replies straight away. *Bitch. Make sure you find her a better job, and then take her for celebratory drinks at The Grange.*

I smile at the message, creating a mental caricature of Geraldine's disapproval at such an action. But then there's a squeak of metal as the letter box opens, followed by a thud as something lands on the door mat. I jump from my seat, for the first time willing the appearance of a note, something that will tell me what I need to do next. But it's just a copy of the local parish magazine.

Deflated, I make a coffee and flick through Instagram for a few minutes. Half an hour later, I drag myself from the feed. Whatever else is going on I need to get these bills out to my clients.

Last week, an announcement appeared in all the major business supplements. It featured the incredibly brilliant, and fiercely competent, Ms. Sophia De La Croix, the new CEO of InterMutual Insurance and the youngest—and only female—member of their Board. All the papers ran with a full-length photo of her, in which she is impeccably dressed in a suit I selected for her. The compliments poured in on how kick-ass she looked, how she was changing the "face of the modern female workplace." I took so many calls from her peers about my styling services that I almost feel bad about billing her.

Half an hour later, I feel even worse about the bill when she calls me to finalise the details of the life insurance policy she's been organising for me. It probably won't come as any surprise that Edward has some kind of ridiculous family policy that pays through the teeth if he were to die. Not that I would see that money, of course, the policy's beneficiary is

Mrs. Geraldine Taylor. No, I wanted a policy that would protect my family if something happened to me, as you can bet that Geraldine wouldn't give a shit about my parents.

"I think you should take two separate policies," Sophia advises me.

"Two?"

"One that pays out to your parents. And the other that pays out to Edward."

"I think there is already a policy that pays out to Edward."

"You think?" She makes it sound like this is something I should know with far greater clarity. "You would have had to sign the policy."

"I signed a huge pile of stuff when we first got married," I reply, trying to remember if one of those was for life insurance. "But I was mainly focussed on the pre-nup to be honest." I say it as if it didn't bother me, as if it was normal to sign a document like that.

"Let me guess, you get nothing if you leave?" she says sardonically.

I laugh awkwardly. "Something like that." The joke is that there is nothing for me to get anyway, it's all in that trust.

"My ex-husband's family tried that shit on me too. Then I caught him shagging the au pair in our bed." She laughs. "Now I earn twice what he ever did. Karma's a bitch." There's a beat where she chuckles to herself.

"I'm sorry about your husband," I say.

"Believe me, walking in on him was the best thing that could have happened. Anyway," she drags out the syllables, elongating the A, "back to your policies."

"I just want to make sure Mum and Dad have something, you know."

"I totally understand. But here's the thing with families like yours. Like Edward's, I mean," she adds quickly. "They have this rather irritating tendency to want more."

"I'm not sure I'm following."

"Do you trust Geraldine not to come after the policy you intended for your parents?" She says it as if that is exactly what she assumes would happen, like it's a foregone conclusion.

"But if I name my parents in the policy?"

"Look, here's my advice. Take out a policy naming your parents. And then another one, for at least the same amount, naming Edward as the benefactor. I can pretty much guarantee his mother would contest your will and try to take the cash from your family, unless you make sure there is something already set aside for Edward."

"But..." I don't finish my sentence, but I'm not sure I can really afford two policies. The Taylors pretend they are wealthy, but it's all an illusion.

"Don't worry about the premiums. I can cut you a huge deal given how much help you've given me the last few months."

In the end we agree to an extremely generous amount for a pretty tiny monthly fee. "I guess Edward would have a lot to gain from a gentle shove at the top of the stairs," I joke.

"Oh, don't worry, no one actually kills their spouse for the money," she assures me. "We don't pay out if they do."

"Do they try?" I can't help myself, the morbid fascination in my voice is clear.

"Oh, you would not believe the stories we hear," she replies, and although we're on the phone I can tell she's rolling her eyes.

***

The next morning, a courier arrives with the insurance policy documents for me to sign. I'm still reviewing them when there's a sharp rap on the door. It's the kind of knock that makes your heart leap into your chest, the one favoured by TV policemen. But on my doorstep, dressed in skinny jeans and a cropped T-shirt, is Ella. She's brushed out her long blond hair and painted her lips a brilliant red. People will think we're sisters.

"Oh my God, thank you so much for doing this," she gushes as I motion her into the house. "You're an absolute life saver, you have no idea how much I need to find another job." She's earnest and cheery at the same time. I can't help but smile when I'm around her.

"Coffee?" I ask as I head towards the kitchen.

"Please." She stops in the doorway and motions at the paperwork I was reviewing spread over the kitchen table. "Did I interrupt you working? I can—"

"No, no," I jump in. "It's just something I have to sign." I sweep the papers into a pile. "Come and sit down and I'll get that coffee on."

"Wowsers," she exhales as she says it and I turn to see that she's staring at the top page. "Shit, sorry!" Her hand flies to her mouth. "I shouldn't have looked." A blush spreads across her neck and sets her cheeks on fire. She looks mortified.

"It's just a new life insurance policy." I laugh self-consciously.

"But . . . I mean, it's like over *two million pounds*." She whispers the amount, eyes darting around my kitchen as if looking for sneaky eavesdroppers.

"My friend cut me a good deal. It's not really that expensive." But even as I say it I realise that the three hundred pounds a month I'm paying for the policy is likely a huge amount for her. I've become far too used to the idea that needing to economise means buying Prosecco instead of Champagne and thinking twice before spending hundreds of pounds on a pair of shoes I'll hardly wear. I refuse to become like Geraldine, so far removed from the actual cost of things she genuinely describes herself as on the poverty line because her new credit card has any limit at all. When Edwin was alive they would think nothing of spending twenty grand on a week in a French chateau and she even spent fifty grand on a watch for him to wear in his casket. He is buried with a watch worth more than the average person earns in *two years*.

I don't meet Ella's eyes as I scoop up the papers and stuff them in a drawer out of sight. "Why don't we get coffee at the outlet place instead?" I ask, trying to cover my embarrassment. "Home coffee is never that good, is it?" I'm lying; my home machine makes a far superior cup than most baristas, but I'm suddenly conscious of how ostentatious that is.

There's a small outlet place just outside the city where I often take my clients. It's home to a number of normally expensive brands selling last season's designs at bargain prices. It's perfect for picking up classic pieces for a steal, especially as workplace fashion doesn't really evolve that quickly. Last week I found a fabulous Alexander McQueen blazer for a third of the price it had retailed at last year.

But I steer Ella towards the high street end of the complex, and we find an absolutely perfect top in Mango to go with the suit I already lent her; she's going to look like a total knock-out for the interview she's managed to snag tomorrow.

"What's the job?" I ask as we start walking towards the coffee shop for paninis.

"Oh, front of house for this little boutique hotel called The Lime Tree. It looks perfect." She grins. Then she stops dead and points a finger to where a gaggle of teenage girls is clustered around a pastel painted shopfront. "Oh. My. God!" she almost squeals. "They have a Lucille's!"

"Shall we skip the paninis and have cake instead?" I ask.

But she's already walking towards Lucille's. "They have a new range of cocktail flavoured cupcakes," she tells me over her shoulder as I follow.

Lucille's smells of pure sugar. My mouth starts to water immediately as I gaze at the display cases filled with iced confections. *A moment on the lips* . . . I can hear Geraldine's disapproval in my head as I contemplate the options. "Women should never be bigger than a size ten," she had told me the first weekend I met her. We were having what Edward had described as a "girly lunch" in The Grange. It was absolutely not the fun bonding experience with his mother he had made it out to be, especially as I'm a size fourteen. She has taken every opportunity to make digs about my weight since; I wasn't even immune on our wedding day. "Oh, aren't you brave to go sleeveless instead of a nice lace bolero to cover up those arms."

"I'm going to go for a Margarita one," Ella tells me, pointing at a cupcake that is more the size of a muffin, covered in a perfect mountain of pale icing, a slice of candied lime wedged into it.

It looks divine. And I love Margaritas, I miss them. "Two Margarita ones, please," I order for us, handing over the cash before Ella can object.

We take our sugary treats to one of the tables with its pastel striped tablecloth. The first bite melts on my tongue, the sweetness of the cake cut with a touch of sharpness from the lime zest, the icing is smooth and creamy, the sprinkle of coarse sugar offering up a tiny crunch. "Holy fuck that is good!" I exclaim.

Ella giggles. "It's the tequila. It really adds that extra layer to it."

"What?" I can already feel my panic rising.

"Tequila. In the icing. Not enough to get pissed or anything, so don't worry."

"There is real tequila in here?" My tone is sharp.

"Yeah. Is that a problem? Oh shit, you're not on meds or something, are you?"

"No. It's Edward." But as I say it, I can feel the terror sub-siding. Edward isn't here, nothing bad will happen, he isn't the one eating the fancy cupcake with its killer shot.

"Edward?" Ella asks.

"He's allergic. To tequila. Well, not just tequila. Bees, peni-cillin, molluscs."

"Like seriously allergic?"

"He almost died from a bee sting as a baby. He has one of those EpiPen things, but we don't take any risks." I can hear Geraldine in my mind, the way her voice rises an octave at even the thought of a possible contamination. I know it's serious, and I know she cares, but she puts me on edge about what could happen all the time. I look guiltily at the cupcake. I want to eat the rest of it, but I'm pictur-ing Geraldine's look of judgement. I push it towards Ella. "You'd better eat that."

"What happens if you eat it?"

"Nothing," I reply slowly.

Ella grins and shunts it back. "So just eat it and it'll be our little secret. You've already had some anyway."

"Promise you won't tell Geraldine."

"Your bitch of a mother-in-law?"

I nod in reply.

She laughs. "Oh my God! Is that why you won't eat it?"

"She's neurotic. Won't let anything Edward's allergic to even near The Grange. She'd kill me if she knew I was eating this."

"Your secret is safe with me." Ella gives me a conspiratorial wink. "Is she really as bad as she seems?"

"She's worse. She claws her way into all aspects of my mar-riage, undermining me, making me feel like shit." I take a huge bite of forbidden cake, but all I can taste is my own self-loathing, turning the treat to bitter ash in my mouth. I put the fork down, the joy gone.

Ella's face is full of concern. "You can talk to me you know. If it would help."

"Let's not ruin the day," I say. I want to rant and rave but I doubt Ella really does want to hear about my problems.

***

Just in case, I shower when I get home, putting the outfit I was wearing in the washing machine and cleaning my teeth three times. That should do it. I mean, it was only a teeny bit of tequila, it's not like Lucille's is putting whole shots of the stuff in each cupcake. I pour a glass of wine and knock it back, grimacing at the combination of tannins and toothpaste—even worse than orange juice—and wait for Edward to finish work.

He's promised me he'll be home at a decent time this evening; I need his help to prepare for a meeting tomorrow. There's so much riding on it, a chance to really grow my little business, make a real success of it. At seven thirty p.m. I call him, but his phone goes to voicemail. Has he forgotten me? Has something come up at work, or—and this is more likely—has his mother feigned some emergency that requires his immediate attention? My hurt at his behaviour morphs into anger and I pace the kitchen plotting his downfall.

Of course all I do—and I know it's petty—is order kung pao chicken for delivery, knowing it'll be too spicy for Edward and he'll have to settle for toast for dinner. I practise my pitch in the mirror as I wait for the food to arrive. Tomorrow could be the start of something monumental, an expansion of my style services and business coaching onto the actual high street. And with the backing of one of the most successful businesswomen in the West Country.

By the time the food arrives I've practised my speech more than a dozen times, but it still isn't perfect. I eat kung pao standing up in the kitchen and then start practising again. I know I should take a break, that I'm only winding myself up by picking holes in the pitch. But every time I pause, my eyes drift to the desk and my mind to the notes buried inside it. So I clear my throat and start the pitch again from the beginning.

Edward doesn't get home until ten thirty. His shirt is creased and untucked, hair mussed, and he reeks of cigarette smoke.

"Where have you been?" I try to control my anger as he almost stumbles over the doorstep. "Did you go out drinking?"

"I've been at work," he replies, shrugging off his suit jacket. "I'm sober."

"You've been smoking."

"I've been at the office since seven thirty this morning, Helena. I had a couple to keep me going through the evening." He sounds tired.

"You promised me you'd help me prepare for tomorrow."

"Tomorrow?" He runs his hand through his hair, messing it up even more.

"My pitch for Francine. Seriously, Edward."

"I'm sorry, H-Bear. It's just work. It's all a bit crazy at the moment."

"It's been a bit crazy for a while," I say, not really liking the nastiness in my tone.

"I know," he whispers and sags a little. "It'll get better." But I don't think it's me he's trying to convince.

He looks broken and my anger dissipates as I put my arms around him and pull him close. "I love you, Edward," I whisper into his chest.

He squeezes me tighter. "Love you too." He rests his chin on the top of my head and I feel him start to relax a little. "I'm sorry I wasn't here this evening."

"It's OK," I reply, even though it's not and we both know it.

His phone vibrates and we move apart so he can read the message. I'll give you three guesses who it's from. You won't need them all. "It's Mum," he says. "Reminding me to tell you she wants us all to meet that lawyer tomorrow."

"What lawyer?" I'm instantly on guard.

"Something about the inheritance." He shrugs as he puts his phone down and then turns towards the fridge.

"What about the inheritance?"

"No idea."

"Why does she want me there?"

"I don't know. You're a Taylor too, I guess. She said she wanted us there and that it was important. Something about knowing why Dad changed the will and getting it contested."

I think back to that last note.

I know who you are, and I know what you told him

What if I've had no more notes, no demands on what I must do to keep my secrets, because Geraldine already knows? Because whoever is writing the notes has already told her what I did and why Edwin changed the will.

Chapter Six

2022
THEA

I reach the front of the queue at Cafe Jardim and Ada's smile brightens my morning. "Morning chica!" This is her standard greeting, delivered with her Brazilian accent. "For you and Jen?" she asks as she picks up two takeaway cups and writes our names with a little flourish.

Cafe Jardim is little more than a glorified tuk-tuk, converted to house a barista-coffee machine and a display of pão de queijo—Brazilian cheese bread—and huge slabs of cuca de banana. Ada set up the cafe six months ago and she has developed something of a fandom among the hordes of Brightonites rushing to work through the Laines. Ada claims she's the Polish-born, adopted daughter of a Brazilian crime family. She says she named it Cafe Jardim as a dig at her adoptive family who lived in one of the wealthiest districts of São Paulo: Jardim Europa, and that she was meant to marry the son of a rival family in an effort to smooth fractious relationships. Instead she ran away with Daiki and found her way to New Zealand—that's where we met as they both worked at Harris Bay for a while—and after I came to the UK they decided to move here too.

I have no idea how much truth there is in Ada's stories, but I keep up the pretence that I believe them all. I once asked her if she was worried people were looking for her. "No one is looking for Ada Ikeda, darling," she told me. "They are looking for a plastic princess who dyes her dark hair white-blond called Francisca Adriana Marcia Oliveira. I am not her anymore. We all have secrets. You just have to learn how to cover your tracks." Then she raised an eyebrow and looked directly at me, eyes flashing with humour.

But this morning, before she hands me the cups, she squints, taking in my puffy red-ringed eyes and sallow skin. "You look like shit."

"Thank you for the compliment," I reply.

"Up late again?"

I shrug. She knows I've been spending too many evenings on my laptop. "I think I'm close, Ada."

"You're sure this is a good idea?"

I nod. There is no other way. I take the coffees. "I promise we'll have drinks soon, OK?"

"I just hope you know what you're doing."

Jen is already in the office when I arrive, engrossed in her work and nodding along to whatever music she has pouring into her headphones. She jumps as I place the coffee next to her.

"Cake?" I ask, handing over a paper bag already partly transparent from the butter Ada uses in the recipe. Low in calorie these cakes are not.

"You're a total angel," Jen tells me, taking the bag and breathing in the scent of warm banana cake. "Let me..." her voice trails off as she twists to reach her handbag.

"Ada's treat," I tell her. "She's like a drug pusher, getting you hooked on her gear for free before jacking the prices later."

***

"Thea?" I jump as Jen starts walking across the office towards me, and quickly minimise the screen I'd been looking at, replacing the Your Big Sister blog with an email from a client wanting to discuss a bigger discount. "You OK?" she asks me, a look of concern crossing her face.

"Of course." My voice comes out a little too high, a little too reedy.

"Sure?" She shifts to look at my screen, reading the email I was apparently so absorbed in.

"Sorry," I say, injecting some faux cheeriness that sounds ridiculous. "I was miles away!"

"I just wanted to ask if I could borrow a tenner." She looks sheepish. "My bank card is in my other handbag." Her words are fast, as if she's wanting to get the whole sentence out, one she's spent a long time turning over and over in her mind as she built up the courage to approach me. "Mum has an appointment with the specialist and I'd like to be there. If possible. But I don't have enough cash with me for the bus fare."

I had been working here at Q—yes, I'm aware that it's a ridiculous name for a shared workspace—for less than a week when I found Jen sobbing in the toilets. I'm not great when people cry on me; I'm the kind of friend you go to when you want practical advice and a plan of action rather than hugs and sympathy. But I steeled my nerves and forced myself to coax her out of the bathroom, feeding her tea and biscuits as her tears turned to hiccoughs and she told me her mum was seriously ill, had been for a long time.

"Thea?" Once more she says my name like a question. I must stop zoning out.

"Of course, Jen." I smile and fish out a ten-pound note from my wallet. "You know it's always OK?"

"I don't want to assume, or take the mickey."

"I know." I smile once more. "Shall we go grab some frappés?" I need to get out and get some fresh air for a little bit. I love the office space, with its high ceiling and large windows, but I get claustrophobic being inside anywhere for too long and the office is starting to feel a little too warm. "My treat."

"I couldn't..." she starts to say but then I pull out two fully stamped loyalty cards for the iced coffee place down the road. I learnt a while ago that Jen hates to feel indebted but freebies don't count. She relaxes and nods.

I've been there, the one who couldn't afford the things the others had. In my case it was skiing trips and private French tutors and brand-new uniforms. "Fuck them," Helena would whisper, "who wants a pony, anyway?" Helena couldn't afford those things either, but she never let them know it upset her.

***

That evening I find myself back on the floor of the living room, yet another pepperoni pizza leaking grease through the box as I spend my hours online.

But at nine p.m., when I log on to Reddit, I find a message waiting for me. The username is a stream of numbers and random characters and I immediately assume it's just a bot. I open it, expecting to find some opening missive calling me "dear" as seems to have become the fashion.

Secrets and lies ruin lives

Just five words staring at me from the white screen. The exact same five words that were written on a piece of card pushed through Helena's letter box. I click into my photos on my Mac, all organised into folders, and scroll to the one labelled HELENA MURDER. She sent me a picture of the first note and my breath catches in my throat as I bring it up, her perfectly manicured nails clear in the picture—she was always so impeccably well turned out, so different to my own nails almost bitten down to the quick.

My finger traces the outline of the words in the photo: *Secrets and lies ruin lives*

I stand up, wincing at the way my left foot has gone to sleep because of how I've been sitting. I hobble over to the drinks trolley that Uncle Jed bought for an extortionate sum and was always so proud of, and pour myself a Lagavulin. The whisky burns as I swallow it, causing my brain to fire back into action.

This is it. The sender of this message knows something. I return to my spot on the floor, placing my glass on the carpet next to me. There is another message:

Some secrets are better left buried

I consider my reply for a moment, but there is only one question I want to ask: *Who are you?*

I'm no one. But I'm warning you. Leave this whole sorry thing alone

I sip my whisky. Leaving this alone is the last thing I'm going to do.

Chapter Seven

2018
HELENA

I'm about to blow it. I'm about to take the most important opportunity of my whole life and fuck it up because I can't get those notes and my mother-in-law out of my head. Every time I try to explain something to Francine, I feel the cool hand of a stranger on the back of my neck and have to snap my head round to try to catch them in the act.

"Air-con?" she asks after the fourth time I spin round to come face to face with nothingness.

"Oh...err..." I stammer.

"Are you sure you're OK? You seem a bit jittery." She is looking at me in that cool and detached way that is probably why she's one of the most successful businesswomen in the country.

"I'm fine." I take a sip of water, willing my hand not to shake as the liquid touches my lips. Get a grip, Helena, I admonish myself. At this moment I wish I was more like Thea, able to compartmentalise my life, put things in little boxes so the edges don't bleed into one another.

"I need to know you can do this, Helena."

"Of course. Absolutely." I cringe as my mouth continues to form pointless additional platitudes. "Yes, indeed. All good. Completely fine." Francine owns a whole host of day spas and such. She wants to help me to open an actual space; part shop, part hairdresser/nail salon, part classroom. A place where women can come for advice on fashion and beauty and learn new skills and meet other women. However, that is not the end of this. In three weeks we're going to present the business idea to her own financial backers in the hopes they'll invest in an ambitious programme to bring a Big Sister Studio to every major city in the UK. One space in Exeter sounded like a dream come true a few months ago when Francine and I first met. Now, I'm standing on the cusp of heading up a multi-million pound business. It's terrifying. "There is a lot riding on this," Francine says, her nails singing as she taps them against her wine glass.

I need to focus on this meeting; it's too big and important to fuck up. And I am absolutely not prepared to lose this opportunity. Your Big Sister was my brainchild after a few glasses of wine on the train back to Exeter from London. I was sitting opposite a woman who was crying on the phone to her mum about an interview that had gone badly. "Oh Mum! That job was my ticket out of Newton Abbot!" she'd sobbed, until we'd gone through a tunnel and she lost signal.

She looked so bereft, so miserable, that I did something I wouldn't normally even dream of doing. I passed her a little pack of tissues and then dug two miniature bottles of Merlot from my bag. I waited for her to blow her nose before I pushed one of the bottles and a plastic cup towards her and said, "You look like you could use a drink."

That tipped her over the edge and the sobbing turned into bawling. I sat quietly, sipping my own wine, letting her cry out some of that frustration and anger and disappointment. Eventually she wiped her eyes, blew her nosé and took a huge swig of wine straight from the bottle. "Thank you."

"Shit day?" I asked, before I laughed. "Sorry! That was a stupid question!"

"The absolute pits!" Her accent was strong Devonian, the same accent my parents were so very proud of. Such a contrast to my own: I sound like a BBC World Service broadcaster from the 1950s; regional accents were not permitted at Ferndown.

"Want to talk about it?" I offered.

"Oh, you don't want to listen to me," she replied, ending the sentence with the traditional "windsucker" intake of breath that marks someone out immediately as having lived their whole life in the shadow of Dartmoor. I raised a single eyebrow—a talent I'd discovered at university and one I deployed regularly—and waited. "I thought I'd aced the interview, I practically danced out of the office." She grimaced at me as she remembered. "I had a little celebratory cigarette and then thought I'd treat myself to a posh sandwich for the train home."

She paused and took another swig of wine. "They were behind me in the cafe queue. I don't think they'd seen me." Her voice broke. "Sorry," she grimaced again and flapped her hand in front of her face as if that would stop the blush that blazed across her cheeks at the memory. "They were laughing about me...Said I sounded like a 'yokel' and that I should 'get back to the farm with my cheap suit'!" She motioned to her outfit and half wailed, "I thought I looked good."

I kept the smile on my face as I looked at her more objectively. Now, cheap suits don't need to look cheap—there are some great brands I recommend to my clients—but this one did look it, you could almost see the crackle of static electricity when she moved; her blouse was the wrong colour, making her look washed out and was definitely the wrong size, gaping slightly around her bust; her nails were unpainted and all different lengths, the edges nibbled at like she was a nervous rabbit. But you could tell she'd gone to a lot of effort: her handbag was new, her hair had been recently cut. "I could tell you they're bastards and you're better than them," I said, keeping my voice soft and gentle, despite the harshness of the words I was about to say. "Or I can tell you the truth and you can let me help you?"

She opted for the harsh realities and so I gave her a rather damning analysis of her outfit and her nails. And that, although her new handbag was actually rather lovely, it didn't match the shoes she was wearing. I bought another couple of wines to soften the blows I'd inflicted on her. Then we swapped numbers.

A few days later, she came to Exeter and we went shopping. The new suit I chose for her was a dark grey, the skirt just below the knee and fitted enough to look a little sexy when paired with the classic high-heeled leather courts I managed to find in a sale. The jacket was boxy, balancing out the slimness of the skirt to give her a killer silhouette and I picked out a bottle-green silk blouse that highlighted her eyes. A dark plum lacquer finish on her nails and a short makeup tutorial from the girls on the Clinique counter and she was set. The next day, she went back to London for an interview with her company's biggest rival. She smashed it.

"You should do this for a living," she told me. "Help other hapless women to look the part, be like the big sister doling out advice on being a proper adult."

"Personal shopping?" Edward had scoffed a little when I told him my idea.

"No . . . well, that would be part of it. It's more of a full service thing," I tried to explain, but the idea was still too ethereal to pin down properly. I was a writer, writing copy for a load of rather dull magazines. "What about a blog?" My eureka moment. It was perfect, something I could do around my other work, a way to maybe find some physical clients, charging for the service I'd offered Josie from the train for free.

"That sounds more like it," Edward said. I think he realised he hadn't been the good, supportive husband before. He even helped me to set up my new website and introduced me to Instagram, it was still pretty early days for it back then. @BigSisterHelena gathered steam and it took less than a month to reach five thousand followers.

The blog was even more successful than my Instagram as I wrote a series of articles giving advice on "adulting." Instead of using the term to talk about the banality of adult life, I reframed it as a shorthand for the transition from feeling like a clueless twenty-something into a composite professional woman and all-round female powerhouse. I talk a lot about imposter syndrome, and "faking it till you make it" and a whole load of other things. It's more than a fashion blog, although the endorsement deals and sponsorships mainly come from the clothing and footwear partners I've developed relationships with.

The rest of the meeting with Francine passes in a blur, and somehow I'm able to pull it off. As we stand to leave the table, Francine thrusts out a hand. "To a very profitable future," she says as I shake it. Then she pulls me into a brief hug. "You remind me of myself, Helena."

"Uh, thank you," I reply, assuming it must be a compliment.

"I have a very good feeling about this."

My excitement over the success of the meeting is shattered the moment I find Geraldine's racing-green Jaguar in the driveway of the house. Why is she here? I feel myself starting to cycle through all the possible reasons for her to be in my house. Is she waiting for me? Waiting to confront me?

I pause on the front step for a moment, using the little window in the door as a mirror to smooth down my blond hair and wipe any stray mascara from under my eyes. I let myself in, cursing Edward under my breath for letting his mother have a key.

She's in the kitchen, I can just make out her shadow. There's a sound of rustling and then the slamming of a drawer. "Is that you, Helena?" she calls out, as if it isn't my house and my kitchen she's snooping around in.

I take a deep breath and slip off my heels before I walk towards her. "Good afternoon, Geraldine." I try to keep my voice level, try not to allow even a trace of my fear that is bubbling beneath the surface.

"I was just popping round to make sure you remembered our appointment with the lawyer."

"Of course. I thought we were meeting at The Grange?" I'm scrutinising every move she makes, every word she says. Does she know it was all my fault? I don't think so. She hasn't clawed my eyes out yet.

"Well. You know how forgetful you can be."

"I haven't forgotten." How could I possibly have forgotten?

"Perfect. Then you can drive us up the road." She smiles at me, but her fingers are creeping towards the drawer she was snooping in, evidently making sure she closed it properly.

Fuck this. "Did you find what you were looking for?" I ask, looking directly at the drawer.

"Just checking the date on the spare EpiPen."

Of course she was. It lives in the drawer below the cutlery. Not in the drawer where yesterday I popped the paperwork for the life insurance policy. She's never been able to resist having a nosy around, even if she always denies it.

We meet the lawyer at The Grange, in the very same room where I overheard Geraldine wailing after Edwin's wake.

"I want to contest the trust." Geraldine doesn't bother with even the most basic of pleasantries.

"We've discussed this already," the lawyer, some senior partner who is no doubt costing a fortune, tells her. "There have to be suitable grounds in order for a successful case."

"I believe he wasn't in sound mind when he made the changes."

"We have already looked at that as a potential angle." The lawyer sounds tired, or possibly just bored.

Geraldine sighs theatrically. "Well, what if he was under duress?"

"Duress?" Edward asks. "You think someone forced him to change it? Why would anyone do that?"

"Men do not just cut their widows out, Edward. Or impoverish their sons."

"Do you have any grounds to make such a claim, Mrs. Taylor?" the lawyer asks. "Any idea that he met with someone in the days leading up to the change who may have influenced him?"

I swallow and try to make myself invisible.

"The only people around him would have been family. Or staff," Edward replies. I hate the way he says staff, it sounds so impersonal.

"Would anyone in the family benefit from the changes?" The lawyer sounds like he is really struggling to care all that much.

"That's not the point," Geraldine replies. "Someone said something to him to make him *ensure* no one in the family benefitted."

"So he changed the will to be—"

"He changed it to make me suffer," Geraldine interrupts him. "Someone who hates me did this. And I want you to figure out who so we can get the trust dissolved."

"I really don't think that will—"

"Make it happen." Geraldine is talking to the lawyer. But she's looking straight at me.

Chapter Eight

2018
HELENA

Rationally I understand she can't know I was the one who goaded Edwin into changing the will. If she did, she would not be able to keep her opinion of me to herself, she certainly wouldn't make passive aggressive inferences and loaded looks. But although she doesn't know, I have to caveat that with *yet*. She doesn't know *yet*. And I have to make sure it never happens.

We all have secrets...but you're going to pay for yours

I will pay whatever it takes. I just hope all they want is money.

Edward and I don't often talk about money. We have a joint account we use for the day-to-day stuff; bills and food and weekends away. We both pay in an amount each month from our respective businesses, and if there is anything left over it gets automatically transferred at the end of the month to a savings account for bigger treats like holidays. We call it the Lux Bucks fund, because it allows us to do fancy shit.

Now, I wouldn't say I've been hiding my income from him. Not specifically. But there was a time about two years ago when I logged into our savings account and discovered it was basically empty.

"Soooo..." I'd said to Edward that evening, "do you have anything to tell me?" I was buzzing, assuming he'd booked us a surprise getaway.

"About?" he asked, his face blank.

I did a little shimmy. "Where are we going?"

"What are you talking about?"

My excitement waned. "You haven't booked us a trip?"

"No. Why would you think . . . Oh." He ran his hand through his hair. "You looked at our account." It was a statement.

"Yes. So . . . ?" I waited for him to answer.

"Mum had a bit of an issue."

"What kind of issue?"

"I don't know. I didn't ask." He shrugged, but it was obvious he knew he'd done something wrong by the way he refused to look directly at me.

"You didn't ask? You just gave her all the money. *Our* money."

"She's my mum, H-Bear. Don't be mad at me. I hate it when you're mad at me."

That night I slept in the spare room, determined not to forgive him, hoping perhaps he would learn that he couldn't put her above me. But when he brought me a cup of tea in the morning and told me he was sorry and that he would never do it again, I'd forgiven him immediately.

I didn't forget though, and I opened my own savings account, squirrelling money into it every month, more and more as my business grew. I have almost twenty-five thousand in that secret account. I just hope it's enough to buy my way out of this mess.

Edward goes back to the office after the meeting about the trust and I leave Geraldine getting drunk with her cronies at The Grange.

This evening was meant to be a celebration. I was going to take Edward to that fancy Brazilian place in town that opened last month and serves steaks as big as a dinner plate; we were going to toast the fact that somehow the meeting with Francine went well, drink Champagne to the promise of an exciting new adventure. Instead I'm pacing the house on my own worrying about my mother-in-law. Does this ever end? Or will she hang over my marriage forever, like a spectre?

My phone rings. It's Ella. "So, how did it go?" she asks me, the second the call connects.

For a moment I think she means the meeting with the lawyer, but then I realise she's calling to ask about Francine. "Well, I think," I tell her.

"Eek! I'm so pleased for you. Congratulations!"

She sounds genuinely excited. And then I remember her own big meeting today and guilt floods me. I would've totally forgotten if she hadn't called me first. "How was the interview?"

"I fucked it. Royally."

"I'm sure you did—"

"I called the interviewer by the wrong name. Then my mind went completely blank when they asked me why I thought I would be suitable for the job."

"Oh."

"Yeah. Exactly. Anyway, I'm sure you and Edward are off out to celebrate your big news, so I'll let you go."

"Actually . . ." I trail off. I probably don't want her to feel sorry for me, like I'm this sad older woman whose husband works all the time and doesn't have any friends to celebrate with. But I don't have any friends to celebrate with. Fuck it. "Edward has to work this evening. Do you fancy a quick drink?"

"I'm unemployed and penniless," she says, completely deadpan.

"My shout."

"Oh. I couldn't, Helena. You've been far too generous already."

"Honestly, it would be my pleasure. All my friends are too busy shuttling their kids to ballet or gymnastics or football practice." No one tells you about this element of being childfree, how one by one all the people you might ring for an impromptu trip to the pub, or for dinner, or because you managed to snag some great last-minute theatre tickets, will disappear from your social calendar.

"Well...only if you're sure. An evening out would do me the power of good. Just so long as you don't want to go to The Grange," she jokes.

"I promise we won't go to The Grange. There's a fabulous little gin bar in town."

Ella is waiting for me outside when I get to the bar. It's the same thing Thea always does. For a moment I wish it was Thea I was meeting instead, but that feels mean and ungrateful to Ella. Besides, it's two in the afternoon in New York and no doubt Thea is chairing some ridiculous meeting and making everyone else in the room feel decidedly stupid in comparison.

"So, what are we drinking?" Ella asks me as she loops her arm through mine and leads me inside.

"They do some pretty good gin and tonics," I tell her as we approach the bar.

"Deal." She waves at the barman. "Two of your strongest gin and tonics, please."

"Any preference on gin?" he asks, motioning behind him to the vast array of options.

"Oh gosh." She shoots me a plaintive look and for a moment I'm reminded of how young she is. "Is there really that much difference?" She sounds more than a little out of her depth.

"Are you kidding?" the barman says.

"Well, how about you let us taste a few to see what we like?" She says it so innocently the barman instantly starts to prepare some drinks. With his back to us she turns to me and gives a huge theatrical wink. It was all an act: she's basically just pulled the oldest free drink trick in the book.

An hour later we've sampled more gins than I can count and I'm starting to feel a bit tipsy. And a bit bad for the barman, who's still trying to teach Ella why he personally prefers Tanqueray to Bombay Sapphire. The bar has started to fill up with actual paying customers, so I suggest we pick a gin and take them outside onto the patio so our barman can get some work done.

"He's kind of cute," I tell her as we sit down.

"Who? The barman?" She wrinkles her nose.

"No?"

"He's just not my type." She shrugs. "Besides, we're out to celebrate your amazing meeting and drown my sorrows about my awful interview, not pick up guys."

"But you're single?"

"Yeah. Just not really looking, you know. Plus," she says loudly, "it wasn't me he was interested in." She nudges me.

"No way."

"He is totally into you." She gives me a salacious wink. "What? You're super hot and that dress is fire."

I look down at the fitted black dress I'm wearing. "I did think it might be a bit..." I make a face. "You know, like I'm trying too hard."

"You look amazing. Edward's a very lucky man." She chinks her glass against mine in a toast.

"I think I'm the lucky one," I say.

She makes a face as if she's about to be sick, before she laughs. "You are just too sweet. I'm not sure I'd be feeling lucky having to spend so much time with Geraldine though."

"I sometimes wonder if I did something terrible in a past life. You know, something really, really bad. So my punishment is to find love in this life, but then have to deal with Smaug forever."

"You can't choose who you fall in love with," she tells me.

"And you can't choose your family," I add.

"I'll drink to that," she says drily.

"Do you not get on with yours?"

"Let's just say that I probably did something terrible in a past life too." Her voice says she's joking, her eyes say she isn't.

"Do you want to talk about it?"

"No." She's emphatic. "I want to drink shots!"

I haven't drunk shots since I was a student, lining up £1 Apple Sourz in little plastic glasses; I can instantly taste the synthetic sweetness on my tongue. But now I have a credit card and this place has a pretty extensive list of shooters for us to try.

***

I get home just after midnight, the hallway spinning slightly as I close the door behind me. There are no lights on so either Edward is already in bed, or he's still at the office.

I almost miss it, the little envelope on the door mat. It wasn't there when I left, it must have been delivered while I was out. The handwriting on the front is different, the fancy calligraphic hand replaced with more of a scrawl.

I carry it to the kitchen, careful not to make too much noise in case Edward is asleep. Inside the envelope is a card, three words written directly in the centre:

Hi there @PAGEFree

I drop it on the counter, feeling my legs buckle slightly beneath me. They know. This isn't just someone fishing, hoping I'll pay up for a random threat. This is real.

Immediately sober, I pick the card back up and turn it over. There is something scrawled onto the other side:

£10,000. In cash. Time and place to follow.

Chapter Nine

2022
THEA

"Morning, chica!" Ada greets me, already reaching for a cup for my coffee.

"Morning," I reply, with significantly less vigour.

"Oof." She makes a face at me. "You look like shit."

"Thank you," I reply.

"It's not mean if it's true." She shrugs.

This has always been her logic and I can't say I disagree with her.

"I think I'll pop an extra shot in yours, OK."

It isn't a question and so I stop myself from answering. "Thank you," I say instead.

"Late night, again?"

There's no one behind me in the queue, but I lean closer to Ada just in case. "I had a message."

"From who?"

"Anonymous. Basically telling me to cease and desist."

"Ooh." She claps her hands together and starts making the drinks. "Do you think it's real?"

"Real?"

She turns from the coffee machine to look at me. "As opposed to some kind of hoax."

"I think so."

"I think it's time you got some help," Ada says, placing the coffees in front of me. "Surely your social media guru can help you figure out who is sending the messages? You can't do this on your own."

"Not yet. I want to see what else they have to say first."

I spend the morning trying to concentrate on preparing for a big pitch with a potential client, but I can't help checking my Reddit account every five minutes. There are no new messages.

Forcing the anonymous DMs from my mind, I give myself a spritz of Coco Mademoiselle and attempt a final—and thankfully flawless—run through of the presentation.

"You've got this," Jen tells me with a wide grin.

"I'm glad you have faith in me," I reply as I gather my things.

***

I'm beaming when I get back to the office. "You, me, fancy Champagne in that posh hotel bar by the library," I say to Jen.

"It went well?" she asks.

"Harris Bay is now in a partnership with Hermann's."

"Whoop!" Jen exclaims. "Ooh, does this mean we get a discount on fancy holidays?" she laughs.

This isn't the first time we've had this conversation, and we both know that even with a huge discount Hermann's is out of reach for everyone but the super wealthy. They want to sell luxury trips to the Marlborough vineyards and a tasting experience in their office for their clients. The estate in New Zealand will definitely appeal to the Hermann's client base—after all, I chose it based on what Helena (who booked her honeymoon with Hermann's) would have wanted. The mansion at the centre of the property has a crumbling genteel charm and the new boutique hotel I've got planned, complete with a helipad and a Ayurvedic spa, will certainly be popular. Plus there is Betsy, the portly vineyard Labrador who Helena would have adored, and who I think will have rather universal appeal.

The Hermann's CEO had seemed genuinely excited for us to work together, even giving me the business card for an old friend of his who manages a place in the South West.

"Derek's always looking for new suppliers, even if the owner can be a bit sniffy about new world wine." He rolled his eyes. "Give him a call and tell him you come highly recommended by me."

Jen jumps at the chance to go somewhere fancy to celebrate. "Especially if you're paying." She grins at me. I wait for her to rummage around on her desk to gather her stuff. You have never seen anything like the state of her work station: piles of files, empty coffee mugs, a tangle of charging cables. She opens a drawer and I catch a glimpse of even more chaos as she tries to find something, eventually pulling out a lipstick and holding it aloft like a prize. "Ta da! Posh bars need posh lippy." Another minute passes as she hunts down a compact mirror—spoiler, it was buried under what looked suspiciously like the takeaway container her noodle soup came in, *four* days ago. It's a wonder we don't have rats in the office—and applies a slick of brilliant red to her lips. "You ready?" she asks me, as if it wasn't me waiting for her.

The bar is busy, especially considering it's a weekday, although it's probably because of the huge terrace they opened a few months ago. One of the only Covid benefits has been this move to al fresco dining and drinking, something I'm a huge fan of. There are a few guys taking up one of the long picnic tables who are happy for us to perch with them.

"We're celebrating my brilliant friend," Jen beams at them, pointing to the bottle of Taittinger in its silver ice bucket.

"So are we," the taller of the three tells us. "Harry just had a baby."

One of them blushes, outing himself as Harry. "Obviously I didn't personally have the baby," he adds.

"And your wife doesn't mind you being out drinking?" Jen asks innocently, her face turning to a scowl as the guys start laughing. "What?" She looks at them and then at the guy Harry is pointing at, walking towards us carrying a tray laden with colourful shots.

"Let me introduce you to Jacob. My husband," Harry says.

Jacob and Harry are adorable, regaling us with stories about their journey to become parents via a surrogate in the U.S. "We're flying out tomorrow evening. We'd wanted to be there for the birth, but it turns out our daughter decided to arrive over a month early."

Toby, the tall one, keeps buying us shots and I'm surprised that I'm having fun. I can fake it like the best of them, years of observing what everyone else does has made me a bit of an expert at looking like I'm enjoying myself. People who don't know me often describe me as the life and soul of the party, but it's normally an act and I spend the whole evening wishing I was at home in my pyjamas. But this evening I'm enjoying letting go for just a little while. I have a feeling things are going to get quite complicated soon.

"So, do you ladies work together?" Jacob asks.

"In the same shared office," I reply. "Q?"

"Ooh, fancy!" Harry says, with a whistle between his teeth.

"Thea helped me get through 2020," Jen says with a mock shudder. "And 2021, which wasn't much better."

"With all the lockdowns and restrictions during the pandemic we helped keep each other sane," I elaborate.

"Plus, Thea is a very good wingman," Jen adds.

"Am I?" I ask, surprised at this moniker.

"Well, you stop me from dating too many *complete* disasters!" She laughs and clinks her glass against mine. To be fair, she does seem to have a thing for entirely unsuitable men, not that she normally listens to me.

By nine p.m. I can barely stay upright, almost falling over as I weave my way to the ladies room. Jen is faring a little better. I guess that's one of the benefits of being younger. "Let's go and get you some food," she suggests. "There's a Five Guys over the road." Toby, Jacob and Harry try to convince us to stay, but Jen is right. I need to eat something and soak up some of the Champagne and vodka and that purple shot that smelt like my grandmother's handbag.

The burger is the perfect balance of grease and cheese, the chips hot and salty, dunked in a huge mountain of mayonnaise squeezed from about ten of those stupid little packets. Within minutes I'm feeling a lot better, the room no longer spinning. I dig in my bag for a mint to chase away the last traces of that parma violet drink that's still threatening to repeat on me, my fingers closing around a small rectangle.

"What the…" I say as I pull it out. It's the business card for the CEO's friend: Derek Matthews is written across the front. I didn't bother to look at it before, but now I flip it over. The image of the Palladian style building is printed on the back in shades of grey and navy blue, the curve of the upper balcony distinctive. The Grange. I squint; in the top corner I can see the small window she used to climb through to sneak cigarettes on the roof away from her mother-in-law's critical gaze. Four storeys from the ground and no safety rail. The papers said it was an accident waiting to happen. But I've never believed she fell.

"You OK?" Jen's hand is warm on my arm, pulling me back to the cacophony of noise around us in Five Guys. "You look like you've seen a ghost."

I hand the card to her. "Who is Derek Matthews?" she asks.

"The Hermann's CEO thought he might be interested in my wine."

"Isn't that a good thing?" She hands it back, barely even glancing at the picture.

I open my mouth to tell her about Helena. But the timing isn't right. "Just a bit of a blast from the past," I hear myself say instead, a nonsense sentence, and put the card back in my bag. "I should get home."

"Aww! I thought we could get more drinks now you have some burger in you." She pouts a little, trying to make me laugh and acquiesce.

But all the joy has gone, replaced with a cloud settling around me and the demon on my shoulder whispering that I'm a terrible person. That I should have been there for her. That if I'd been a better friend I would have seen just how much danger she was in and found a way to stop it from happening.

I saw a therapist—briefly anyway—after she died. I was in New York and therapy was like getting coffee; everyone did it. I worked with someone whose dog was in therapy for Christ's sake.

"Why do you think it was your fault?" they had asked when we finally had the breakthrough that I was carrying all this guilt.

"I could have stopped it." I'd shrugged; it was pretty obvious.

"Why do you think you could have stopped it?"

"If I'd been there I would have seen the warnings."

"What do you mean by 'there'?"

"I mean physically there. In person. Standing in front of her and all those poisonous people in her life. I would have known what was going to happen."

"And why weren't you physically there?"

"Because of work. Because I've been so busy building this big career that I forgot to build an actual life. I didn't even make it to her wedding. I never met her husband, or saw their house, or was introduced to her friends." The tears were rolling down my face, the guilt and shame physically pushing me down in the chair, suffocating me. "I even missed the funeral." That last sentence came out as a whisper. "What kind of friend does that? I loved her—love her—more than anyone in the world and I failed her."

"You need to forgive yourself," the therapist told me.

They were wrong. It wasn't personal forgiveness I needed. I needed the truth. And then I would make the person responsible pay for what they did to her. Revenge is far sweeter than absolution.

***

I'm woken from a deep sleep by my phone beeping with a notification. A message from Reddit.

Please stop looking I'm begging you

It's the same number that sent me the last message and I've been waiting for them to send another. I sit up and tap out my reply. *I need to know what really happened.*

You really don't. Leave it while you can

I have spent almost four years getting here. I am not going to leave it. I repeat the same question from before: *Who are you?*

There's no immediate reply and eventually I get up and go to make some coffee. I've been patient for so long, but I'm itching to move forwards. Eventually my phone beeps.

A friend

Of mine? I reply.

Of hers

The answer I was hoping for.

Chapter Ten

2018
HELENA

It's not even six a.m. when I wake up, but I can tell the bed beside me is empty. He didn't come home until I was already fast asleep, the combination of alcohol and relief that the note writer had finally voiced their demands pulling me into a veritable coma. Did he even make it to bed? I creep a foot tentatively to his side, trying to determine if there is residual body warmth, any hint he slept there at all. The sheets are cold in that almost damp way that expensive cotton feels and I pull my foot back to the warmth of my own side.

A grunt, followed by an expletive, floats up the stairs towards me. He's probably trying to make himself a coffee; he never listens when I try to explain to him how to use the machine. With a sigh, I drag myself out of bed and go to help him.

"You OK?" I ask from the doorway, watching him raking his hands through his hair in that way he does when life doesn't go how he expects it to.

"Fucking machine."

"Can I help?"

His eyes are bloodshot and his jaw clenched. "Please, H-Bear. I have a ton of stuff to get done today and I need some caffeine."

"Sit." I point at one of the bar stools and smile as he obeys like a chastised child. "Espresso?"

"Please."

"What time did you make it home in the end?" I keep my voice casual.

"About one."

I pass him his coffee and he drinks it in a single gulp, like it's sambuca.

"Another?" I ask, taking the cup from him.

He nods and I turn back to the machine to make it. "I'm sorry, Helena." He's quiet and I almost wonder if I misheard him over the hiss of the machine.

"For what?" I reply, not turning round to look at him. I want him to be honest with me about what is really keeping him out so late—is the business in trouble? I don't know, how would I know?—and he sometimes finds it easier to open up when he doesn't have to make eye contact.

"For not taking you out last night. For being distant and stressed and never here because I'm always at the office. And if I'm not at the office, I'm thinking about work, or schmoozing potential clients. It'll get better soon, I promise."

"I know," I reply simply. There isn't really anything else to say to such an empty platitude. He obviously doesn't want to tell me any details so I'm just going to have to trust it's one of those cyclical troughs all companies go through. The thought of handing over £10,000 to a stranger skitters across my mind, but I squash it down. That money is mine, funds Edward doesn't even know about. He's not expecting me to be able to help bail him out. I will hand it over to the blackmailer and then this will be over so I can play the supportive wife.

I arrange my features into a smile and turn round, sliding the cup towards him. "Perhaps you should hire someone to help you."

"I can't afford to get another architect in."

"What about an assistant? Someone to help with preparing your client information and booking appointments, sorting out your travel arrangements."

"A PA?"

"Yeah. Thea always says hers is an absolute life saver."

"OK. That sounds like an excellent idea." He grins and then reaches out to pull me towards him. "You really are amazing," he whispers in my ear, sending a shiver up the back of my neck.

"If I help you write an advert for that PA later, could I tempt you upstairs?" I ask him, pressing my weight into his lap.

His groan catches in the back of his throat.

"I'm going to take that as a yes," I say, sliding off his lap and taking his hand to lead him upstairs.

***

The sun streaming through the bedroom window wakes me, Edward's arm draped across my stomach and one of his legs pinning mine. It's gone ten and I know we need to get up and get ready for Rob's birthday party, but it's been so long since we spent the morning like this.

I roll slightly so Edward and I are face to face, stroking my hand down the muscles of his back. He opens one eye and squints at me.

"Please tell me it's five in the afternoon and we've already missed the party," he says softly, a smile curling the corner of his mouth.

"Afraid not. There's still over an hour until it starts."

"Hmmm. An hour you say?" He raises both eyebrows. "Any suggestions on how we could fill the time?"

"Well, we need to get ready."

"That'll take five minutes at most." He pushes himself onto his elbow, his gaze travelling down my body.

"And we need to write that job advert."

I can see him considering the options and then his eureka moment. He reaches for his phone and hands it to me. "Find a generic one we can tweak."

"And what are you going to do?" I ask.

But he's already shuffling down the bed. "This," he says with a huge grin, kissing my inner thigh.

***

Now, to be fair, the idea of an afternoon on the terrace of The Grange, sipping Pimm's from an oversized glass adorned with mint and curls of cucumber does have a certain appeal. However, it's Rob's birthday party so the company is going to be dreadful. He's a friend of the Taylor family—I think his father and Edwin went to school together or something—and he's been a constant feature of my life since Edward and I began dating. However much I try to avoid him, he's always there. He and his wife Charlie. Who doesn't laugh; she brays, like an actual horse. And who looks down that expensive equine nose at me as she touches my stomach and asks if Edward's mother is disappointed that she's *still* not a grandparent.

"Helena! Edward!" Her shrill voice pierces the small gathering in front of us as we arrive on the terrace. Charlie is like every girl I hated at school. The ones who thought they were better than the scholarship kid in the second-hand uniform that was still so expensive it almost broke my parents. I spent most of my school career trying to ignore the girls like Charlie, staying as far away from them as possible in the hope they would leave me to my studies and that elusive place at Oxbridge. It's almost ironic that I married a man so steeped in that world of wealth and privilege that I find myself at The Grange on a Saturday afternoon with Charlie fucking Braithwaite. Worst of all, she doesn't know the truth of my circumstance, that I wasn't born into my place at Ferndown School for Girls. She thinks I'm *just like her*, that we are *two peas in a pod* and laments that we didn't both go to Cheltenham. *It would have been so totally super!*

The first glass of Pimm's hits me in exactly the right spot, the zing of cucumber offsetting the sweetness of the lemonade mixer. "Cucumber vodka, darling," Charlie tells me with a conspiratorial wink. "It's strong though, so pace yourself! Can't have you falling over." She doesn't add *again*, but the inference is there.

An hour later, the stall swims in front of me as I go for a pee. In my head I can hear Charlie's prim voice, *"Pace yourself."* I don't think I'm ever going to live down the fact that I got a little too tipsy one time. I don't know how long I spend in the bathroom, but Geraldine is waiting for me when I leave.

"Charlie was worried about you," she says in my ear, fingers gripping my upper arm.

I squash my urge to twist from her grasp and run back into the safety of the bathroom. I hadn't thought she'd be here this early. She tends to arrive a few hours into an event, making sure everyone knows when she has arrived like she's royalty gracing us with her presence.

"I'm fine!" My voice sounds singsong in my ears. "Charlie didn't warn me there was extra vodka in the Pimm's."

"Well, I suggest you have some water and sober up a bit."

"I was already on my way to get a Diet Coke." I hate myself for justifying my actions to her.

"I'll come to the bar with you," she says brusquely. No doubt wanting to check I don't slip some Jack Daniel's into it. As if I'd be that stupid.

The rest of the afternoon passes in a haze, punctuated by staccato moments in which I catch sight of my husband chatting and laughing, apparently great friends with everyone at the party. I know it's at least partly an act, and when we get home he will tell me how he hates the way they treat me. But you'd never know it from watching him. Most of the Taylors' friends and relatives ignore me, still thinking of me as the pariah who ruined everyone's plans by sinking my claws into poor unsuspecting Edward. I find myself drifting around the periphery of the party, a glass of wine practically glued to my hand like a security blanket.

Charlie buys Champagne to toast her husband's birthday, filling my glass to overflowing, forcing me to catch the overspill in my mouth before it's wasted on the grass beneath my feet. My head is still spinning from the Pimm's with extra vodka, and the rum I sneaked into the Diet Coke I'd promised Geraldine was going to help me sober up. But I don't really care anymore.

A few metres away from me, I watch Edward chatting to Rob. He laughs at his jokes as if Rob is the funniest man alive, eyes dancing, leaning towards him so he doesn't miss a moment of the humorous anecdote Rob is sharing. I turn to see if there is anyone else I can talk to, feeling like the shy kid on the first day of school all over again.

Geraldine is sitting at the head of the largest table on The Grange's patio, every seat taken as her clique hangs on her every word. She's telling a story as she looks from face to face of her cronies to ensure they're paying her their full attention. I drift closer until I can hear what she's saying.

"Such an incredible selection. Honestly, I wouldn't dream of shopping anywhere else," she says. "Imagine having to slum it in Waitrose!" One of her hangers-on blushes. "Oh, Joyce!" Geraldine exclaims. "I'm so sorry, I didn't even think." Her tone suggests that of course she had thought. "I'm sure you'll be back shopping at Kenworth's soon."

Kenworth's is the so-called purveyor of fine foods who charges an extortionate sum for imported cheeses and other delicacies. A few months ago, Geraldine ran up a huge bill that Edward was forced to settle on her behalf. She's meant to be economising, but it sounds like she can't help herself. Just so long as Edward doesn't bail her out again.

I drift away from Geraldine's table, my eyes hunting for Edward. It can only have been a minute ago I was watching him and Rob, but now I can't see him anywhere. A gaggle of younger women, Rob's sister and her friends, glance over at me before turning back to each other. I hear a giggle from them and my hackles rise at the thought they are whispering about me.

That's it! I've had enough of pretending to be enjoying myself when everyone basically ignores me; I'm going to find Edward and make him take me home. I march over to Rob, now sitting at a table with Charlie; he eyes me dubiously as I approach.

I've never liked Rob; he has always seemed so, what's the right word? Self-righteous? Pompous? The kind of man who will drink a £250 glass of whisky but refuse to tip the barman who served him.

"Where's Edward?" I demand as I reach him, holding out my hand to steady myself against the back of his chair.

"I dunno, probably gone to the bar?" He shrugs his shoulders. "You're hardly offering him scintillating company right now." There's a sneer in his voice and unconcealed pity in his eyes.

"What's that supposed to mean?"

"I think you might have had one glass of celebratory champers too many," he tells me, waggling his finger towards my face. "You know alcohol is terrible for women who are trying to conceive. Especially at your age." He leans in closer to me, glancing to the space behind me, checking there is definitely no one close enough to hear him. "You remember all that trouble you caused?" He pulls back so I can see the smirk on his stupid chinless face. Edward was supposed to marry Rob's cousin, Cecily—not that they had ever dated or anything, but it was always what both families had assumed—until Edward brought me home to Exeter one

Christmas and caused a furore. I've never been allowed to forget it. Rob's smirk hardens. "Cecily is pregnant with her third, you know."

Cecily would have been the perfect wife for Edward. She would have smiled and charmed her way around this crowd, safe and secure in their shared histories and impeccable breeding. I bet she would be sitting right next to Geraldine at the head of her table, basking in all the attention.

I can feel the tears prickling the back of my eyes; I've definitely had too much to drink and too much sun. I don't belong here. I don't even bother to say goodbye. No one is going to miss me.

Chapter Eleven

2018
HELENA

My eyes are smarting as I walk home from The Grange, I couldn't find Edward so I left him there; perhaps eventually he'll notice I've gone. Rob's words rattle around my head. He didn't say it, but I knew exactly what he meant. Cecily would have made sure Edwin's inheritance trust wasn't an issue. She would have produced the expected heir and a spare, even if that wasn't what Edward wanted. Obligation and expectation trump desire. Or at least that's what Cecily would have told him and the whole vicious cycle would have begun again.

I send a text to Thea. *Cecily is pregnant again.*

Bet Smaug is livid, Thea texts back. *I suggest you revel in the fact you aren't by drinking a bottle of her Sancerre.*

I laugh out loud. Geraldine insists we keep a case of this stupidly expensive Sancerre for the odd time she pops round for dinner. It costs almost a hundred quid a bottle and it's not even that good. Give me a ten-pound bottle of New Zealand Sauvignon Blanc any day. But I follow Thea's advice and open the Sancerre, sending her a picture message. She texts back a thumbs up emoji.

I pour myself a particularly large measure, using the balloon glasses we are meant to use for red wine. "Why yes, Mrs. Taylor, I am aware I'm using the incorrect glassware, thank you very much," I say to the silent kitchen, imagining that half-snarl, half-smile Geraldine wears whenever I'm around her. I know it's a cliché, the whole "my mother-in-law hates me" thing, and trust me, I hate myself for it. Arghh! How many times have I wanted to wipe that look off her face? Give her a piece of my mind, or a hard slap across the cheek, or swing an empty Sancerre bottle with just a little more momentum than would be strictly necessary.

As if she knew I was thinking about her, she calls me. "Did you really cause a scene at The Grange?" she asks, clipping her words.

"What?"

"Pardon," she corrects. "Rob said you had too much wine and screamed at him in the middle of the garden. In. Front. Of. *People.*"

"I didn't scream at him," I say carefully. What the actual fuck? Did Rob ring my mother-in-law to dob me in like we're fucking children?

"Well. He said that you did. He's worried about you."

"He's worried?" I splutter.

"He thinks that maybe you should see someone. You know, a professional. Even though *that* kind of thing isn't really the Taylor way." She lets out a long and decidedly disappointed sigh. "But I suppose we need to do all we can to avoid future outbursts."

"I'm fine," I tell her. "He's blowing everything out of proportion."

"Well. Just make sure it doesn't happen again. If you want to make a scene, you do it in private."

Did you ring Geraldine? I message Rob. I know I should let it go but I'm just so goddamn angry.

I couldn't find Edward and I was worried you might do something stupid, he replies.

Fuck you. I call him. "Where is Edward?" I ask as soon as he picks up.

"I don't know. Last time I saw him he was heading up to the roof with one of the Dumbarton twins."

I don't give him the satisfaction of asking which of the Dumbarton twins my husband is sneaking around with. "Just tell him to call me as soon as you find him." I don't wait for him to reply before I disconnect the call.

I've not even drunk a quarter of my glass of Sancerre before Edward barrels through the door, red-faced as if he's been jogging.

"Thank God you're here!" He wraps me into a hug, spilling wine onto the kitchen floor.

"I couldn't bear it anymore. So I came home." He's squeezing me so tightly I can barely breathe. "Edward . . ." I push back against him slightly and he releases his grip.

"I was having a fag with Martin—he wants me to buy into some super dodgy pyramid scheme, I'll explain that in a minute—and then I came back down and Rob said you'd screamed at him and left."

"Martin?"

"Martin Dumbarton. You know Martin." He looks confused.

"Rob told me he'd seen you sneaking about with 'one of the Dumbarton twins.'" I do the air quotes and raise my eyebrows.

"Is that what he said?" Edward laughs, but there's an angry edge to it. "Like it was Charlotte, I suppose?"

Charlotte Dumbarton is a thirty-three-year-old retired Victoria's Secret model turned philanthropist, and the daughter of one of Geraldine's distant cousins. She is literally the hottest woman who has ever set foot in The Grange and I don't envy her one bit. Every man wants to seduce her, and every woman wants to keep her the hell away from their husbands. Like she would go near any of them with a ten-foot barge pole.

"You know I only have eyes for you." He takes my hands and looks at me earnestly.

"I know." Whatever flaws my husband may have—like having a mother from hell—I have never thought for a moment he would cheat on me. It's just not his style.

"So what was the problem with Rob?" he asks, taking a step away from me so he can look me in the face properly.

"Nothing." I slide my gaze away.

"Helena."

"Alright. It was just the usual. Blah blah blah, you should have married *Cecily*." I draw out the syllables, mimicking the rather grandiose way she always says her own name. But we both know I'm using mimicry to hide the way every mention of her reminds me I will never really fit in, will never really be accepted by his peers.

"I didn't want to marry Cecily." He's matter of fact. This isn't the first time we've had this conversation.

"She's pregnant again, apparently."

"Ahh. Mum said something too, makes a lot more sense now."

"We could—"

"Not yet." He cuts me off.

"You didn't let me finish."

"I know you want to tell Mum that we're choosing this. And I hate lying to her, and putting you in such an awkward position, but she's having a really tough time of things. I think it would break her."

"I didn't mean tell her. I meant we could..." I leave him to fill in the gaps of what I'm trying to say.

"You want to have a baby?" He sounds puzzled.

"No. Yes. Maybe. I don't know." I take a deep breath and try to order my thoughts so we can talk properly. But all I can see is Cecily's sneering face as she hands a gurgling blonde baby—Edward's baby—over to a smiling Geraldine. I don't want to live on the outside, I don't want to be a pariah everyone ignores. I want to belong. But I don't say this to Edward. Instead I say, "Everyone seems to think it's what we should want."

"But it isn't," he says. "Is it?" He sounds unsure, as if he doesn't know how to broach this.

"Maybe..." I start, but trail off, still trying to put into words the pictures crowding my mind. Parties and school fetes and recitals and lunches and family holidays. "I just don't know anymore, Edward." I twist my hands together. "What if it's what we *should* do?"

"You want us to have a baby out of obligation?" He sounds almost disappointed. In me. It breaks my heart.

"No, I..." I take a step forwards, reaching up to touch his cheek.

His gaze softens. "Is this about Mum?" he asks.

I shake my head even as I want to say *Yes! Of course this is about your mother. And your friends and the whole lot of them who treat me like I'm nothing.* "It's just hard sometimes."

"I know it's hard. But we can't have a baby just to make things easier. Or to satisfy some stupid inheritance. Or to make my mother happy." He smiles sadly at me.

"I know I'm being ridiculous..." I start to say, even though I'm not sure if I *am* being ridiculous.

"H-Bear?" he says softly, forcing me to look him in the eye. "My father had me because that was what you did. He had no right to have a child, no paternal aptitude, no love to give. I will not bring a child into the world to satisfy the misguided expectations of other people."

"I know. Just sometimes those other people can be..." I grope for the word.

"Complete and utter dickheads?" His voice rises a little, the skin around his eyes creasing as he tries to stop his smile breaking.

"I was going to say 'surprisingly persuasive' actually."

"Helena," he sounds solemn, serious. "I love you. More than you will ever know. And all I want is for you to be happy."

"For *us* to be happy," I correct him.

"For *us* to be happy," he concedes gently. "Do you think having a baby would make you happy? All the nappies and sleepless nights and pressure to give up your job? Not being able to travel, or go for dinner on a whim?"

I look at him as he parrots back to me all the things I've said over the years. Then he pulls me closer, his lips next to my ear as he whispers some of the things I haven't said, however many times I've thought them. "Do you think my mother's meddling would make you happy? Arguments about boarding school, and what sports they should do, and why we aren't teaching them toxic gender norms?"

"I don't think that would make me happy, no," I say into his chest.

"Me neither." He pulls me even closer and we stay there for a few moments, wrapped around each other. "And what if I was like him?" He says it so quietly it takes me a moment to process what he's said.

I pull away and look at him. A single tear runs down his cheek and I wipe it away with my thumb...When we were first married he told me about the kind of man Edwin was and it devastated me to hear it. Now he stares at me, painful memories hidden behind his deep brown eyes. "You are *nothing* like him. *Nothing at all*." I am vehement.

He nods, but his eyes say he doesn't really believe me.

"I'm sorry," I say eventually. "You know we're on the same page with this. It's just sometimes...sometimes it all becomes a bit much..." I let out a long breath.

"I do understand, Helena," he tells me. "And I know how much harder it is for you. That you're the one who bears the brunt of everyone's questions."

"I can see them looking at me, wondering what's wrong with me."

"There's nothing wrong with you."

"I know. I think tonight was just a step too far. Fucking Rob."

"He really is the worst," Edward says. I don't correct him that actually the worst by far is Geraldine. It's probably not the time or the place. "But we'll be alright, H-Bear. We can get through anything. Together. Besides, one day they'll all stop asking." He raises an eyebrow so I know he's only joking.

I swallow, thinking about the notes and the money I'm going to hand over to keep my sorry little secret from my husband. "Do you think your mum will ever forgive us for not unlocking the trust?"

"I genuinely don't know. Maybe one day. And it is a lot of money."

It's a complete understatement from Edward. It isn't a lot of money. It's ALL the money. Without the trust, we will eventually have to sell The Grange—the club doesn't turn a profit and we can't afford the upkeep—and the main Taylor house which is mortgaged against it. I come from nothing, taught to make my own way in the world, to work hard and hope it paid off. But Edward comes from privilege, the kind most people can't even imagine. He will find the adjustment far harder than I will. Geraldine will find it near impossible.

***

Later that night I'm lying in bed, listening to the softly snuffling snore Edward does after a few drinks, playing that conversation over and over in my head. Edward is right, we can't bring a life into the world for the wrong reasons, especially for money.

Is that what Geraldine did? She must have known what an awful father Edwin would be and yet she had a child anyway. Did she have Edward to secure her own financial future?

I'm just about to drift off when I'm suddenly hit by a vision of Geraldine, standing in my kitchen, her sticky fingers digging through the paperwork I had stuffed into a drawer. The paperwork for the life insurance policy that would pay Edward handsomely if something were to happen to me. Money he would no doubt share with his darling mother, settling her bills in Kenworth's and wherever else she wanted to shop.

I sit bolt upright and Edward huffs beside me. I thought she was looking guilty because she was spying. But what if the guilt was because she's planning something else?

If she'd create life for money, would she destroy it? Sophia, CEO of Intermutual Insurance, told me no one ever kills their family for the life insurance.

But she has never met Geraldine.

Chapter Twelve

2022
THEA

Jen slaps a leaflet on my desk with a flourish. I look up to see her grinning, eyebrows waggling. "Free yoga!" she exclaims, her emphasis heavy on the word "free."

"I don't really do yoga." I used to, once upon a time. I told everyone it helped keep me grounded, kept me sane. Now it just gives me too much time to dwell on all the things I don't want to think about.

"And?" She shrugs and then taps the leaflet with her manicured nails. "Did you not hear me when I said it was free? C'mon! I thought we were going to get our money's worth?" Her eyebrows waggle again, her grin somehow widening even further.

Ever since the owner of Q—the rather unfortunately named Seymour Cox—announced an eye-watering rent rise, Jen has been obsessed with squeezing every last penny out of the place. If there's anything free to be drunk, or eaten, or squirrelled from the shared stationery cupboard, she's there at the front of the queue.

"Half past seven?" I ask her, squinting at the details of the class. "In the morning?" I raise an eyebrow at her. I'm a lark, up at five and most productive before lunch. But I don't think I've ever seen her arrive at the office until at least eight thirty.

"It'll do us good. Just promise me you'll bring super strong coffee!" Her hands are clasped in front of her, eyes begging but with a hint of mischief.

"Alright!" I give in. She punches the air and blows me a kiss over her shoulder as she runs to answer her mobile which is now blaring with Ed Sheeran's "Bad Habits."

Five minutes later, my email pings with a notification. Jen has sent a link to a fashion blog, some piece entitled "How to maintain your professional integrity, even in down dog!" She's added a little note: *apparently the key is to make sure your colleagues don't see your knickers. Completely life-changing advice right there* 📷

I click through to the blog. Ultimate Adulting. Some sisters from Hertfordshire who hadn't even waited for Helena's memorial service to finish before trying to take over the remnants of Your Big Sister. Like a pair of well-dressed hyenas picking over the carcass. They had spent most of the service posting photos of themselves in oversized hats and even more oversized sunglasses. They barely knew her but they acted like she was a relative. #HeartBroken. #HeavenHasGainedAnAngel. I would have throttled them if I'd been there. I damp down my rage at their overfamiliarity which threatens to edge out my own self-loathing that I wasn't there. I paste a smile on my face. "Thanks, Jen," I call across the office.

"It's some women writing about how to be better adults and how to behave in the office," Jen sneers. "They advocate deodorant, shaving your pits, and making sure your leggings aren't see-through." She rolls her eyes. "But I thought some of the other ladies might need the tips." She grins and points towards Dee who runs a homeopathic beauty company and doesn't believe in any form of hair removal. I'm a bit surprised at the bitchy undertone of her comments; aren't Gen Z all about body acceptance?

I scroll through a couple of the other posts on the blog, one about the perfect English garden party making me click through to the main article.

"Make sure they know you're the boss, not the spouse." Pictures of women in floaty floral dresses and wide-brimmed hats (what they called "spouse chic") are juxtaposed against women in a range of semi-fitted, structured shift dresses in shades of deep teal and dark plum, paired with killer heels and leather handbags. "Always make sure your bag is big enough for a laptop, not just a compact mirror and lipstick," was the advice. Helena would be horrified by how dull Ultimate Adulting was; how it had taken everything she had worked so hard at and distilled it into this mundane bullshit. One of the reasons Helena was so successful was the way she demonstrated how achievable her advice was for everyone: no matter your budget, or size, if you preferred a suit to a dress, or you struggled to wear anything other than flats. These sisters had thrown out all the nuance and inclusivity in favour of demanding a cookie cutter look. And they advocated Helena's greatest bugbear: heels for somewhere you'd be standing on grass.

"You can't wear that," she'd told me, taking in my plain black skirt suit and stilettos I had bought specially for my graduation ceremony.

"Why not?"

"Because you look like a banker."

"I am a banker, Helena," I'd replied, gesturing to the already packed suitcase behind me, all ready to whisk me to Singapore to start my career with J.P. Morgan.

"That's not the point. Today is a party, a celebration of what has already been, not what will be." Luckily I'd been staying in her flat for the past week, all my own stuff already in storage for my big move. She disappeared into her room and I heard the sound of coat hangers screeching against the wardrobe rail as she went through her own clothes. She reappeared with a dress with a full pleated skirt and structured bodice, and a pair of ballet flats.

Everyone commented on how gorgeous the dress was, how the neckline looked perfect with my gown, and how genius I was not to wear heels as all my classmates sank into the grass with every step.

I scroll through a few more of the blogs, getting more and more annoyed at how they were pissing all over Helena's legacy. She deserves better than this. I stop scrolling. Yes, she deserves better than this. What she deserves is justice. It's time for me to move forwards to the next step.

I need to know who the so-called friend who messaged last night really is. Luckily for me, I just happen to know someone who is a bit of a whizz with social media.

"Jen?" I say it like I'm apologetic to interrupt her work, even though I can see she's just aimlessly scrolling Instagram.

"Thea!" She turns to beam at me.

I pull my chair over so I can sit close enough to avoid the rest of the open-plan office hearing. "I have a favour to ask you."

"Anything."

I take a breath. "You're pretty good at social media and stuff, right?"

"It's my business. And I've freelanced for you?" She sounds puzzled, like perhaps I've lost my mind a little.

"I know. It's just…this is a bit different." I stop and chew the inside of my cheek for a moment. "I've had some DMs."

She leans closer to me. "DMs?"

"From an anonymous account, one of those with just a few letters and a string of numbers."

"If they are saying they have videos of you enjoying some *onanism*," she accentuates the word, "that's masturbating to you and me," she says quickly before adding, "it's a scam."

I grimace. "It's definitely not that. I want to know where the DMs are coming from, who's really sending them."

"OK," she grins. "That sounds like the kind of thing I can help with."

"How about you come to mine this evening? I'll get pizza to say thank you."

"Deal."

***

Jen arrives exactly on time, ringing the doorbell at seven p.m. on the dot.

"Jesus Christ, Thea!" she exclaims when I open the door. "I didn't realise you were *this* minted." She waves an arm at the curved façade of the townhouse, the cream paintwork immaculate and the black ironwork details gleaming in the evening sun.

"It is a beautiful house," I say, motioning her inside. I don't tell her that it technically belongs to my Uncle Jed, who is letting me stay while he entertains wife number four at his villa in Dubai.

"Is it just you living here?" she asks as we move towards the kitchen.

"Yeah," I answer as I get out some wine glasses and pour her a huge glass of Sauvignon Blanc. I pour sparkling water into my own; I'm just not in the mood for wine this evening.

"Well we both know my efforts to find a suitable husband have been rather lacklustre." I laugh; it's a bit of a running joke that both our love lives are doing badly. Not that I've been actively trying to meet someone. Jen, on the other hand, has been on a string of dates with some completely inappropriate men, coming into the office with tales of guys who turn out to be at least a decade older than their pictures suggested, or who think socks and sandals is an acceptable footwear combination.

"Well, you're still doing better than me," Jen says, taking a long drink of wine. "That guy with the crazy ex-girlfriend tried to get back in touch."

"No! Even after the whole window incident?" The ex had climbed through the window of his bedroom the first time—and only time, obviously—Jen stayed over.

"Yep." She shakes her head. "You know, you should let me update your dating profile for you. Get some pictures of you in this amazing kitchen to entice in some more talent."

"What, like try to get some sort of . . . what would be the male equivalent of a sugar baby?"

Jen laughs. "It might be fun."

"I think I'll pass for now."

"Your loss." She shrugs and downs the rest of her glass. "So, you wanted me to look at these DMs?"

I nod and hand her my laptop, open on the messages from my mystery *friend*.

"OK, so this @Anon5971205 is a username generated by a computer programme. It's basically like putting on a mask. Whoever is sending these messages is logged into their own account, but the software shields their real username from you and uses this one instead."

"You're really good at this," I say, but instantly regret the surprise in my voice.

"Just because my business isn't exactly flying, doesn't mean I'm not good," she replies curtly, looking up from the screen as if to challenge me to say something more.

"I didn't mean it like that, Jen. And you know I think your social media optimisation is amazing—I wouldn't have hired you to work on the Harris Bay stuff otherwise."

"Sorry," she says. "I'm just a bit touchy at the moment. Things haven't really picked up yet." Jen manages social media accounts for influencers but a lot of them went quiet during 2020 and still aren't back to where they were. I get it though, no one wanted to see rich people spending lockdown in their luxury villas while the rest of us sat at home in the rain.

I pour her another glass of wine and use my phone to order some pizza. The delivery driver is going to be thoroughly confused when he has two boxes to hand over, instead of my standard single lonely one.

***

An hour later, Jen finally gives out a little "whoop."

"Have you got something?" I ask, pushing away the pizza box and wiping my greasy fingers on a piece of kitchen roll.

"Yep. I have a name. The person sending these messages is called..." she narrows her eyes as she looks at the screen. "Ella Hazelwood." She turns to look at me, not even a flicker of emotion on her face. "Do you know her?"

"We've never met, but I feel like I know her very well."

Jen breaks eye contact, stands up and stretches. "How about we have another drink and you can tell me what's going on?" She says it gently, as if she already knows this is going to be a long and emotional conversation.

I pause for a few moments, as if trying to decide where to even start. "In 2018, my best friend was killed. Everyone said it was an accident. But I know it wasn't."

"You think she was *murdered*?" Jen sounds shocked, forming the word as if it's a foreign language she barely knows.

"Yes. And I think Ella knows what really happened. I need to persuade her to talk to me."

Chapter Thirteen

2018
HELENA

On Monday, I kiss Edward—who is leaving for the office before the sun is even fully risen to get all his work done—goodbye and do something I very rarely do. I make a cup of tea and I go back to bed, relishing the quiet of the morning, turning my pillow over so the cold side caresses my cheek.

I find it impossible to relax though, my mind churning through the events of the weekend and fucking Rob's stupid party. There are two pictures I keep snagging on: Geraldine at the end of her table making Joyce feel small for not going to Kenworth's, even though I know Geraldine can't afford to shop there herself; and Geraldine riffling through the kitchen drawers and finding the life insurance policy I've taken out for Edward. She wouldn't even think about it. Wouldn't dream that she could get her hands on all that money if she...I'm being absurd. I know that—it's one thing to think it in the middle of the night, but in the cold light of day it sounds ludicrous, farcical.

I text Thea: *Being a neurotic fool. Tell me to get a grip.*

It's two a.m. in New York but she replies anyway: *Get a grip.*

I read the three words in her voice; hearing her deadpan delivery and seeing the look of slight castigation on her face. It isn't the first time she's told me to get a grip. I feel instantly calmer.

I get another text, expecting it to be another Thea-ism. But it's Ella.

Back on the job hunt this morning, send me luck!

Anything interesting so far? I reply.

Not much out there. Might have to look further afield, move to Bristol or something ☹

I take a gulp of my—now almost cold—tea. I don't want Ella to have to move away; I like spending time with her and despite the age gap it feels like we could be friends. And God only knows how hard it is to make new friends as an adult. Another message comes through from her.

I hate to ask, but do you know anyone who's hiring? I can waitress and I've got a little bit of office experience. Sorry if this is super awkward 😬

Enough office experience to be a PA? I text back. Because why doesn't Ella work for Edward?

Sure. If you help me polish up my CV ☺

Meet me for coffee?

In an hour at Sebastian's? I need caffeine and pastry

Ella looks amazing when she walks into the cafe, dressed in a simple pair of jeans and a plain grey T-shirt, a stack of coloured bracelets at her wrist for a pop of colour. Her blond hair is braided into a fishtail over her shoulder. She has that effortless beauty that looks good in any style and skin so smooth it's like she's had ten hours sleep and a green smoothie for breakfast. Her smile widens as she spots me and she waves. We order coffees and pains au chocolat.

"So?" she asks, looking at me expectantly.

"So, I was thinking you could work for Edward."

"Edward? As in your husband, that Edward?"

"He desperately needs a PA. Someone to help him stay organised, sort out his appointments and client dinners and help him with paperwork."

"Do you think he'd hire me? I don't really have any experience as a PA."

"Oh, you'd be fine. I'll work some magic on your CV. Make you the perfect candidate." I waggle my eyebrows at her.

She pauses for a moment, shredding her pain au chocolat in front of her. She sounds serious when she finally speaks. "I appreciate you thinking of me. Don't think I don't. But what if I'm not very good at the job? I could, I don't know, like mess things up horribly."

"Edward is working all hours," I tell her. "He just needs someone to help relieve the pressure, so he can concentrate on the stuff he's really good at."

"Only if you think I'd be OK?" She looks so earnest, like she's desperate for my approval, even though I was the one who suggested it in the first place.

"I think you'd be brilliant," I tell her.

Ella pauses for a moment and then breaks into a grin. "OK! Let's do it! And thank you, Helena. I don't know what I'd do without you."

"It's nothing," I say with a shrug. "It's what friends are for."

***

Two days later, Edward stays at home long enough in the morning to eat breakfast.

"You seem a little happier this morning, sweetie," I say as I watch him slice a banana onto his granola.

"Well, your excellent job advert went live yesterday morning and I had a great application by lunchtime. She seems ideal and so I'm going to interview her today."

"Oh," I reply. "That's great news." We decided it would be best for Edward not to know Ella and I are friends. Well, it was her suggestion. Although she was happy for some help with her CV, she didn't want to get the job as a favour, and I fully understand that. Respect it even. And she might not have been a PA before but she had a ton of previous experience we could match to the job advert: she's an absolute shoe-in.

***

Geraldine calls me that afternoon, just as I'm waiting to hear from Ella about the interview. "Edward hired that tart I fired from The Grange."

"Who?" I reply, feigning complete ignorance.

"That blonde one. *Ella*." She says the name like she's talking about something unsanitary.

"Oh?" I reply.

"You didn't know?" Did she really call me to gloat that she knows more about Edward's life than I do?

I check the time, the interview probably only finished ten minutes ago. "I haven't spoken to Edward all day," I reply. "He's at work." I add that last bit pointedly; she really needs to stop pestering him during office hours.

"I'm furious with him." She's really not; she thinks the sun shines from her only son's arse. "He should have asked me what I thought before offering her the job." She clips the vowels and I detect a slight undercurrent to her words. Perhaps Edward's crown is slipping slightly. I can't help but smile a little at the thought of even the tiniest wedge between them. "I'm just hoping she's a better PA than waitress."

"I'm sure Edward knows what he's doing." I tuck my phone between my ear and shoulder to pour myself a glass of Sauvignon.

"Huh! She's probably spun some line about what she can do."

Oh shit. I pause with my wine glass mid-way to my lips. Is that why she's calling me? Because she knows I helped Ella to apply?

"Are you listening to me, Helena? Isn't that what all the young ones do these days? You can't trust any of them."

I take a sip of wine and decide to brazen it out, crossing my fingers behind my back that she's just being a bigot. "Of course. Sorry. I'm sure Edward will have checked her credentials. And I'm sure she'll be fine." I take another sip of wine.

Geraldine snorts. "I highly doubt it. These youngsters all think they're God's gift because some teacher once told them they were special. You know how it is these days. I heard that awful new academy school in town gives out awards just for turning up. Those kids are going to be *bitterly* disappointed when they enter the real world."

Is Geraldine…moaning? With me, like we're friends? This is just bizarre. "It certainly wasn't like that at Ferndown," I chip in. I can't help but want to impress her and the fact that I went to an exclusive boarding school is about all I have in my arsenal.

"Of course not. All that money the parents pump in comes with a certain expectation of standards. Not that your parents contributed, mind." Well that was short-lived. She just can't help herself from bringing up my scholarship status. "Anyway, I've got to go. At least the girl is pretty enough to give Edward something to look at, even though she'll mess up the filing. Silver clouds and all that. Don't forget the charity auction on Friday. I expect your attendance."

She hangs up without so much as a goodbye and I stare at my phone. She shouldn't still be able to shock me after all this time, but did she really just say that Edward hired Ella as something pretty to look at? She *is* pretty of course—in fact she's more than just pretty, which always sounds a bit of a non-compliment to me, like describing something as *nice*, or *pleasant*—but letching over the young PA isn't Edward's style.

Edwin was a letch. He'd had a string of affairs, and I'm sure had ended up paying out to settle a few harassment claims over the course of his own career. Edward wouldn't dream of following in his father's footsteps.

My screen lights up, a notification from Twitter. @PAGEFree has a DM from an account with a handle that seems to be random letters and numbers: @KP1256790.

£10,000. The Northernhay War Memorial. Tomorrow. 11am.

I message back. *How will I recognise you?*

Don't worry. I know exactly who you are.

I take a gulp of my wine. Of course they know who I am. I just wish I had any idea who they are. I click on the handle name to bring up their Twitter feed, but it's empty; they've never tweeted, or commented, or even liked anything. @PAGEFree is the only account they're following. A complete dead-end.

Whoever this @KP1256790 is sends me a stream of messages, directions for what to do tomorrow. The steps to ensure the handover looks like nothing more than two friends meeting in the park.

Buy a coffee and a sandwich from a coffee shop on the way.

Recommend Queen's Bakery by the station as they use paper bags.

Put the cash in a padded envelope and then the envelope in the sandwich bag.

It feels so practical. So impersonal.

But so very real.

Chapter Fourteen

2018
HELENA

I know this is going to sound ridiculous, but what *does* one wear for a clandestine meeting to hand over a huge amount of cash to a blackmailer? Sorry, I don't mean to be flippant, I'm just trying not to think about the reality of this situation. There is far too much at stake here.

We're meeting somewhere public, which might not be busy at eleven a.m. on a random Thursday, but the weather forecast for tomorrow is sunny and so there will definitely be people around: walking dogs, strolling with toddlers, having picnics on the grass around the memorial. I'm not worried that I'll be attacked, or kidnapped, or physically harmed in any way.

But what if it isn't enough? What if they don't keep their side of the deal? It's ten thousand pounds, I tell myself. It's a *huge* amount of money, more than a lot of people earn in a year. It *has* to be enough. I feel a little sick as I think about what else I could spend it on, but it'll be worth every penny to keep my secrets safe. I take a deep breath to try to calm my nerves. I'm sure Thea has a trick, some kind of breathing exercise to still the demons. I should ask her for more details next time we speak.

I haven't told her about the money. She wouldn't approve of me paying up. And of course then I'd have to tell her about @PAGEFree and I think she'd be disappointed in me. Not for writing that stuff in the first place—she'd get a kick out of that—but because I managed to get myself caught.

No, I'm just going to go to this meeting, hand over the money and trust that is the end of it.

***

I've followed the steps exactly, the cash in a padded envelope and then in a paper bag from the Queen's Bakery, sitting on top of a club sandwich on granary. If anyone sees me it'll just look like I'm handing over lunch. The last thing I need is to look like I'm dealing drugs in the park.

They're late. It's now five past eleven and I'm starting to get worried. Worried they won't show up. Worried that this is all some kind of scam and they are sitting with Geraldine at this very moment, telling her everything. Or that they are sitting in Edward's office, showing him my Twitter feed, that he's learning my betrayal from some nameless, faceless stranger. Or that I got the time, or the place, wrong and they will think I'm not going to pay up and it will all come crashing down anyway. Would they give me a second chance, or if I blow it, is that it? Game over. The loss of everything.

But then I feel someone slip onto the bench next to me, the wood bending slightly under their weight. I don't know what I'd expected but he's huge, probably six foot five and weighs as much as a rugby player. His handsome face breaks into a smile. "Hi Helena," he says. "Sorry to be a few minutes late. Did you bring me some lunch?" His voice is almost accent-less; he could be from literally anywhere.

"Err. Yes," I stammer slightly and hand him the paper bag.

"That's very generous of you," he says, looking inside. "My favourite." Then he stands up and turns to face me, almost blocking out the sun. "Hopefully this will satisfy my appetite." He winks and walks away.

I stay sitting on the same bench for almost half an hour. His demeanour has confused me. He seems so normal. So innocuous. The kind of guy you might try to set one of your friends up with. Not the kind of guy who is trawling the internet looking for people to blackmail. Something in this whole set-up doesn't make sense. But I can't put my finger on it.

I'm still thinking about the giant of a blackmailer that evening when Ella calls me. For once Edward isn't working, but he's not at home, he's gone to The Grange to oversee the set-up for this charity auction Geraldine is planning. I had to feign a headache to get out of going too.

"How was your first day?" I ask her. Edward hadn't wasted any time in asking her to start. Especially when he confided in me that she'd asked for a salary far lower than he assumed he'd have to pay.

"It went well," she replies, but there's an edge there.

"Really?"

"Yes. Edward is lovely," she says quickly. "And the job isn't that hard. I think I'll be good at it."

"But?" Because I can tell from her tone there is a but.

She sighs. "I err . . . it's kind of awkward . . ."

"Just tell me, Ella. Please."

"It's just . . . is the company in trouble?" She sounds like she's wincing as she says the words.

"Trouble? Like financial trouble?" I ask.

"I took a call from a guy he had subcontracted some work to; this guy hasn't been paid for months. And then there was an email from his accountant about an outstanding balance on his professional services account. I assume that means he hasn't paid him either."

"Shit," I whisper under my breath and sit down heavily at the kitchen table. There's a bottle of Merlot in front of me. I was meant to be saving it for when Edward got home. I pour a glass and take a long slug.

"Are you still there, Helena?" Ella asks gently.

"Yeah. Sorry, I just..."

"You didn't know?"

"No, I didn't."

"It might be nothing. I'll see what else I can find out, OK? Just try not to worry about it. I'm sure it'll all be fine." She doesn't sound convinced and neither am I. If he's not paying people what they are owed there is definitely an issue.

I think guiltily of the £10,000 in cash I handed to a stranger in a park. How much is that relative to the hole Edward's trying to climb out of? For a brief moment my anger flashes: why hasn't he told me he's in trouble? I could have helped him. But even as I think it I know that given the choice again, I would still pay the ransom. I would risk his business to keep my secrets safe and my marriage intact. The shame is almost unbearable.

***

The charity auction is to raise funds for the construction of a local children's hospice. Whatever faults I may find in my mother-in-law, I can't say that she doesn't do a lot of good for the community, even if her intentions aren't one hundred percent altruistic. She is hoping this evening will push the project over the finish line and allow the developers to begin work. Her target is fifty thousand pounds, enough to convince the charity to name the hospice after her: it's lucky she has rich friends.

Geraldine has spent two months rallying her contacts in the area, persuading business vendors to offer up lots for the auction: a luxury stay at the Fullcroft Manor Hotel, a VIP tasting experience at the Michelin-starred The Hope and Hero, a helicopter flight over Dartmoor with a gourmet picnic. Geraldine has even offered a one-year membership for The Grange—but the ten thousand reserve she's put on it ensures only the "right kind of person" can afford to win.

I did offer a consultation and shopping experience with Your Big Sister, but Geraldine turned me down. "You're so generous, Helena, but these ladies don't need to work, let alone need someone to tell them what to wear," she said with a condescending smile. When I messaged Thea to tell her, she replied *Bitch! But it's her loss. And at least you don't have to style her stupid friends.* That had made me feel a little better about the snub.

My duties tonight are basically non-existent. Geraldine has roped in the local auction house to run the whole thing, and a team dressed in smart polo shirts embroidered with the company logo are milling around talking about the lots on offer. The usual Grange staff are on hand to ensure everyone is well lubricated, the distinctive bottle-green of their uniforms weaving among the guests as they serve flutes of Champagne.

"A drink, Mrs. Taylor?" one of the waiters asks me politely.

"Thank you, Benji," I reply, as I take one and sip it gratefully.

"It's a Piper-Heidsieck 2002 Rare," Benji tells me, repeating the name of the vintage like an automaton. He's obviously been instructed to tell everyone what they are drinking.

"It's very nice," I say. I mean, it *is* very nice. I also assume it's phenomenally expensive. I take another glass just to spite Geraldine.

***

The room is starting to fill up with Geraldine's wealthy friends and acquaintances and I employ my usual tactic of hovering in the corner close to the bar and the door to the kitchen. I chat occasionally with the waiting staff as they exit with trays of canapés and a never-ending stream of Champagne, and periodically check my phone. I'm hoping it looks like I'm helping to coordinate things, that I'm working and so no one tries to engage me in conversation.

It works like a charm for at least an hour and most of the guests ignore me, until, of course, Rob and Charlie arrive. She's wearing a floor-length beaded dress—completely over the top for the occasion in my opinion—and makes a bee-line towards me. "Helena! Oh isn't this such a smashing event!" she exclaims loudly. "Isn't Geraldine such an amazing woman? Organising all this on her own."

I smile noncommittally.

Benji arrives with canapés. "What are these?" Charlie demands, as he presents the platter to her.

"Mushroom and truffle tartlets," he replies.

Charlie screws up her face. "I don't want vegetarian rubbish. Bring some meat ones." There is no "please," or "thank you," just a demand and a flick of her wrist so Benji knows he's dismissed. I shrink into myself a little, hoping he doesn't think I'm as rude as she is.

Charlie turns back to me, placing her hand on my arm, her rings glittering in the light from the ceiling chandeliers. "Now do tell me what you and Edward have decided to bid on. A little healthy competition is always good for a charity auction!"

"Oh, you'll have to wait and see when the bidding starts," I say, hoping I sound enigmatic. My plan for this evening is to put in a few early bids for the items I know will go for astronomical amounts; that way I'll appear generous, but can then win something cheap. I can't afford to throw money around, the £10,000 hole in my finances is taunting me, especially with Ella's revelations about Edward's business. But it sounds like Charlie is going to try to ruin my evening.

The auction begins at nine thirty, once the guests have drunk a huge volume of Champagne and the platters of canapés have been reduced to a few sad-looking morsels. We all gather in the main room of The Grange, where a small stage has been set up, paddles at the ready. I am allocated paddle number 9. I surreptitiously take a photo of it and send it to Thea with the message: *I take it 9 is a bad omen somewhere?*

She went through a stage at school when she got a bit obsessed with symbolism and she messages back immediately: *Ouch! The number 9 is bad luck in Japanese culture as it sounds like the word for suffering.*

That figures, I reply.

As expected, Charlie swoops in on my bid of two hundred pounds for a hamper of local goodies worth no more than seventy-five.

"Five hundred pounds!" She raises her paddle with aplomb and gives me a wink across the room. I let her win it, cursing her under my breath. That was my chance to get out of here without spending a fortune. And yes, I know that isn't very charitable.

The next lot is the very last one of the evening, a pair of matching leather passport holders from some fancy gift shop in town. "Shall we start at a hundred pounds?" the auctioneer asks.

I raise my paddle. I have to win this lot or Geraldine will have something to say about my lack of participation.

Charlie raises hers. "Two hundred," she calls out.

"Two hundred and fifty," I counter.

She shoots me a look and grins. "One thousand pounds!"

For fuck's sake! "One thousand, one hundred," I say, with significantly less enthusiasm than Charlie.

"One thousand, five hundred." She accents the *five*. Rob lets out a little "whoop" next to her, like she's done something wonderful, rather than offer to pay thirty times what the item is worth.

I'm about to raise my paddle when I decide to say *screw it*. So what if I'll face Geraldine's wrath? I can always just write a cheque for five hundred quid and call it a simple donation.

The auction ends and the guests start to mill around again, congratulating each other on their generosity.

"I paid seven thousand for a weekend at the Atlantis Bay in Mazzaro," a guy in salmon trousers tells the man in a mustard sports coat next to him.

"Well," his companion exclaims loudly. "We paid twelve for a week in the most charming chalet in Verbier."

Jesus, the kind of money changing hands this evening is obscene. I remind myself that it's for charity and decide to head off the whole "I didn't win a lot" situation and go to find Geraldine. But I can't spot her in the main room where the auction was held as I weave through the crowd. I head out of the door, cross the main entrance hall and take the corridor lined with some of the smaller rooms, often used for private dining and business meetings between members.

My footsteps are muffled by the burgundy carpet, so thick my heels sink into the pile. Framed pictures of hunting scenes adorn the walls, interspersed with various trophies from over the years: the eyes of a large boar seem to follow me as I walk past.

There's a slightly musty smell in this part of the building, too many decades of closed doors and cigar smoke being puffed into the air as the men of the family intoned their wisdom to their friends. I shiver as a puff of cold air crosses the back of my neck; I swear the place is haunted, but Edward always tells me I'm imagining things.

A loud bang from inside one of the rooms behind makes me jump and I whirl around, half expecting to see an apparition of an ancient ancestor sail past me. Another bang follows and I creep back down the corridor, holding my breath to keep as quiet as possible. I don't want whatever is behind that door to hear me.

But I recognise the raised voice as I pass: "You can't keep doing this." It's Edward, his tone exasperated.

"But it's for charity." The other voice is unmistakably Geraldine. "And stop banging those trays, they're solid silver."

"I know it's for charity, Mum. But we can't afford it." Did he just say *we*?

"Oh, pfft! Of course you can. It's only a bit of Champagne for heaven's sake. We raised over sixty thousand this evening, Edward. Mainly because everyone had a few glasses of fizz before the auction."

"It wasn't fizz!" Edward's voice rises higher. "It was a Rare 2002 Piper-Heidsieck!"

"It won a Masters Medal," she replies huffily.

"It's hundreds of pounds a bottle! And you expect me to pay for it."

"You can call it your donation," Geraldine says with a bitter edge. "Your wife failed to make a serious bid on any of the lots."

"Mum. I cannot afford to keep bailing you out. You have to start listening to me and start being more sensible. We just don't have this kind of money."

"Of course you do." She really isn't listening to him.

"No, Mum. I've given you everything we can spare." How much has he been giving her? But then his next sentence turns my blood cold. "I've given you more than I should." Is that why he can't pay his suppliers?

"You're being dramatic, Edward."

"No. I'm not. This ends now, Mum. I'm putting my foot down."

"OK." Geraldine sighs so loudly I can hear it through the door. "I promise I'll be good in future. I'll just have to use some of the donations to pay for the Champagne."

"That's stealing."

"You're not leaving me any choice, Edward."

"Alright. I'll pay for the Champagne. But this is the last time."

I slip away from the door, cursing them both under my breath. Edward for giving in as usual. Geraldine for putting him in that situation yet again. I need to know just how much trouble he's really in.

I wait for Edward to tell me about the Champagne bill, but he doesn't even mention it for the rest of the evening. I'm just about to bring it up, admit that I was eavesdropping and tell him this has to be the absolutely last time he bails her out, when my phone vibrates with a message.

Yesterday's lunch proved to be the perfect appetiser. Now it's time for the main course. £15,000. Monday. Same time, same place.

£15,000! *Another* £15,000? I feel sick, bile filling my mouth. I can't pay him that kind of money. Especially not now I know about Edward. My fingers hover over my phone as I debate what to reply.

Are you ignoring me?

You know what happens if you won't pay?

Shall I tell your husband or your mother-in-law first?

I stare in horror at that third message. My fingers form a reply without my brain registering the words I'm typing. *But what if I don't have that kind of money?*

Do you think it's a coincidence I'm asking for the same amount you have in your savings account?

How can he possibly know that? The answer comes in seconds:

You should be more careful on public wifi ☺

Fuck. Fuck. Fuck.

You're boring me. Let's make it £17,500. I'm sure Edward will lend you the extra.

Chapter Fifteen

2022
THEA

Despite spending last night relaying my fears over Helena's death to Jen, the morning dawns bright and sunny, as if the darkness has been scrubbed clean. I don't need to take the car to the office and so I walk into town along the seafront, breathing in the salty air. I used to spend my holidays from school by the sea with my Uncle Jed. He's not my real uncle, more like a godfather, the one constant of my adolescence. The scent of the ocean on a calm summer morning makes me feel safe, like I'm living back in a time when the world still made some sense.

I'm still thinking about last night—the concerned look as I told Jen all about Helena, her promise to help me if she could—as I try to figure out if you can see through my slightly threadbare leggings, arse in the air as I peer through my legs at my reflection in the mirror behind me. Suddenly Jen pushes open the door to the "recreation and meditation zone," as this room is called.

"Please tell me there's coffee before I literally die!" she exclaims, ignoring my ridiculous position as her eyes sweep the small space in search of caffeine. I straighten up and point at the little recess in the wall behind me where I have already deposited her a cup so strong you could stand a spoon in it. "I can't believe you convinced me early morning yoga was a good idea."

I scoff. "This, young lady, was all your doing."

"I fucking hate past-Jen," she tells me.

"Oh yeah, past-Jen is a complete taskmaster."

"Complete bitch, more like." Her serious expression suddenly drops and she laughs throatily, so close to my face I can almost taste the coffee on her breath. "Alright," she says and then pauses to drain the last dregs from the paper cup, "I'm ready for this shit. Let's get this show on the road!"

The class is full; ten of us squeezing into the studio, all wanting to take advantage of the freebies. Despite being advertised as for beginners, the class is surprisingly hard and I'm struck by the terrible realisation that my years off the mat have been unkind. There's a strange tightness in my hips: when the rest of the class is sitting, legs stretched out to each side and bodies almost touching the floor, my knees are bent and my fingertips barely graze the mat in front of me.

"And breathe," the instructor—one of those inordinately perky women in the world's tiniest yoga shorts—is saying as she presses herself even flatter.

"Who does she think I am?" Jen hisses under her breath from next to me. "Does she think I'm a human pretzel or something?"

But by the end of the class, lying on the ground in Savasana, a peace settles over me, the sound of ten other people inhaling and exhaling slowly, and I remember the way I used to feel during my early morning sun salutations in New York, even if it was only for a few minutes each day. That perfect stillness, the stolen moments before I got up, took a shower and began another rigidly planned day in my carefully constructed life.

***

It's not even lunchtime when Jen comes to my desk. "I've been doing some research, a little digging," she whispers.

"Digging?"

"Into the person who was sending you messages. The one your friend knew. Ella Hazelwood? Come to my desk so I can show you."

I follow her, balancing awkwardly on the corner of her filing cabinet. She looks at me like a disapproving parent. "For someone who is obviously so clever, you can be a little odd sometimes. Get a chair!"

I do as I'm told and roll mine over to nestle next to her. "What have you found?"

"So, Ella Hazelwood is originally from Oxfordshire." Jen pulls up an Instagram account in Ella's name. "She wasn't one for socials, has basically just this Instagram account and it is *sparse*."

"You're sure it's the right Ella Hazelwood?" I ask, squinting at the profile picture. It's a cartoon avatar with blond hair rather than a photograph.

Jen rolls her eyes. "I'm not an amateur, Thea. Yes, this is the same Ella who was friendly with your Helena. From the looks of her Instagram, she posted a few times during the summer of 2018." Jen shows me the little squares on her wall: a pair of drinks with fresh berries adorning the glasses, a picture of the outside of a rather fancy looking office building, a name tag with her name and the logo for The Grange. "Any idea on the office block?" Jen asks me.

"Taylor Architectural." I point at the sign listing the building's occupants. "Edward's company. Helena got Ella a job as Edward's PA."

"Cosy," Jen says.

"She was always trying to help people. Ella needed a job after she was fired from The Grange and so Helena found her one."

"Shall I contact her?" Jen asks. "See if she'll talk to us?"

"She's told me to leave it alone."

"She sounded scared in her messages to you. But maybe if I contact her, someone neutral, she might talk to me instead."

"It's worth a try," I say.

***

The next morning, Ada asks how things are going as she makes my coffees.

"Jen found Ella," I reply. "Well, an Instagram account for her anyway."

"Interesting." Ada draws out the word a little, as if she's deep in thought.

Ada knows all about Helena, and that I think she was murdered, and that I believe Ella is the key to finding out exactly what happened. A few months after I bought Harris Bay, Ada found me in the wine-tasting room after the guests had left for the afternoon.

"You OK?" she asked from the doorway, not wanting to interrupt if I just wanted to be alone.

I was slumped on a stool, an empty bottle in front of me. I opened my mouth to tell her that I was fine, but instead this low wail escaped my lips. It took us both by surprise. Most people would have run a mile from their drunken wreck of a boss crying on her own at the end of her shift, but not Ada. She made us both a coffee, pulled up a stool and waited for me to talk to her.

The guilt had spilled out, the way I blamed myself for Helena's death, how I was convinced I could have saved her if only I'd taken the time to pay her more attention. Ada let me get it all out of my system, and then she looked me in the eye. "You have two choices. Number one," she held up her index finger, "you let it go, find a way to forgive yourself and move on with your life."

"That simple, huh?" I tried to make it sound like a joke, but it didn't sound very funny.

"I never said either choice was easy," Ada replied. "Or number two," she held two fingers up in front of my face, "you accept you're too late to save her and you turn that anger and pain into finding who killed her and you bring them down."

"Revenge?"

She nodded.

I felt something inside me start to awaken. "Revenge," I repeated, this time without the question.

She nodded again.

Two weeks later I moved back to the UK and she eventually followed with her husband, Daiki, who found his paramedic experience in huge demand. "I think you're going to need to see a friendly face occasionally," Ada told me. "And I make a mean cuca de banana; the Brits will love it."

Ada drags me back to the present as she puts the coffees down in front of me. "You're sure it's definitely the right Ella she found?"

"Yep. Photos from Exeter, of Edward's office, even the name badge for when she worked at The Grange."

"Interesting you never found it before."

"I'm assuming she'd taken it offline or something. She was the one sending me the DMs."

"Hmmm. Will she talk to you?" Ada asks, her eyes meeting mine.

"Well, she told me to leave it all alone in the DMs. But Jen thinks she can get her to talk," I reply.

"Like a middleman?" A flash of amusement lights up Ada's face.

"Exactly," I confirm.

"Well, here's hoping," Ada says and makes a show of crossing her fingers on both hands. "Oh, and I've just baked a fresh batch." She hands me a paper bag, the warm scent of sugar and banana coiling into my nostrils.

At the office, Jen devours the cake in about three bites. "Ella replied to me," she says through a mouthful.

"And..." I cross my fingers.

"Well, she started by telling me to leave her alone."

"Oh." I slump backward in my chair.

"Ah! But..." Jen says, leaning forward a little, "then she sent me another message. Asking who I was and what I wanted."

"What did you tell her?" I sit up a bit straighter.

"I told her the truth. That I'm your friend and you think something bad happened to Helena. She definitely knows something. And she definitely shares your view that it wasn't an accident."

"She thinks Helena was pushed?"

"She didn't say that explicitly. She was super cagey about any details. She just said the circumstances were suspicious. But that she doesn't think you should dredge up the past. I think whatever happened, she's scared there'll be some kind of fallout and she'll end up involved. I get a feeling she's really frightened."

"But I need to know what happened." I hear myself and blush, I sound like a whiny twelve-year-old. "Sorry, I just..." I take a deep breath, like my first J.P. Morgan mentor taught me to, and I feel myself calm instantly. "I've been trying to find out the truth for so long. Ella is my best chance at finding out what really happened. I can't just let it go and walk away. I need her to talk to me."

"Look, Thea. How about you let me try again. I can be pretty persuasive," Jen says, a flash of darkness behind her eyes.

"What are you going to do?" I ask, brow furrowing as I try to read her expression.

Jen laughs and rests her hand on my shoulder. "Nothing dodgy. Or not too dodgy anyway, I promise. Just trust me, OK?"

"OK," I reply, and then I smile at her. "Thank you. For everything."

"What are friends for?" she replies.

It's such a seemingly innocuous phrase, but I'm forced to turn away before the tears prick the back of my eyes. I was the friend who stood by and let this happen to Helena. Who left her all alone in that place with no one to talk to, no one to share her worries and her fears with. Friends are meant to be there when you need them. Not on the other side of the ocean, too wrapped up in their own lives to care.

Chapter Sixteen

2018
HELENA

There's a spring in Edward's step as he lets himself into the house on Monday evening. "Good day?" I call from the kitchen.

"The best!" he exclaims and presents me with a small box tied in orange ribbon.

"Are these..."

"A client sent them and I know they're your favourites." Inside the box are nine exquisite artisan truffles which are literally better than an orgasm.

"Thank you." I kiss him on the mouth before pulling back to look him in the eye. "So, how are things with the new PA?"

"Ella? She's brilliant."

"You know your mother thinks she's pretty." I raise an eyebrow so he knows I'm teasing.

"Are you jealous, Mrs. Taylor?"

"No!"

"Oh my God." He laughs. "You are! I can see it in the way your mouth is twisted up."

He used to say it was my "tell" when we played poker with his friends. Back in the days when they welcomed my company, back when they assumed I was just a girlfriend, a temporary distraction before he married some exceedingly suitable girl called Cecily.

"My mouth is not all twisted up," I retort, a smile spreading across my face. I don't have a tell, my poker face is impeccable. But I would always let his friends beat me at cards, my way of trying to curry favour with them.

He leans casually against the kitchen island. "OK. She is pretty. You've probably met her at some point, she waitressed at The Grange for a bit. Anyway. She's very good, perfect CV!" I smile inwardly. I put a lot of work into that CV.

He moves behind me, snaking his arms around my waist. "You know I only have eyes for you," he says into my hair.

I lean back against him and he kisses my neck. I try not to think about the £17,500 hiding in my desk with all the notes.

***

He's already waiting when I arrive. Just standing there, staring up at the figure of Victory with her laurel held aloft, the dragon beneath her foot. There is something beautifully evocative about the war memorial, and it seems almost incongruous as a place for our exchange.

"I thought you might not come," he says as I approach him.

"You didn't give me much choice."

He inclines his head slightly to acknowledge my point, then looks at the paper bag in my hand. "How did you explain the extra £2,500 to your husband?" he asks, his tone casual, as if we're just having a friendly chat.

When I don't answer him, he laughs and puts out a hand the size of a dinner plate. "You are very kind to bring me lunch again," he says loudly as a group of school children in bright blue uniforms pass us.

"I trust this will be enough to curb your appetite." I sound far more confident than I feel.

He grins. "These food analogies are wearing thin."

"Well hopefully we won't see each other again." I keep my tone neutral, but inside I'm desperately praying to every possible iteration of God that this is it, that he'll simply take all my savings and leave me alone.

"We'll see," he says and starts to walk away from me. But then he stops and swivels on his toes back to face me. "So if you didn't ask your husband for the extra £2,500, where did you get it? Is there another savings account I don't know about?"

"There is nothing else." I try to keep my voice from shaking.

"Hmmm. Well, we'll see." He turns away and walks off. I can hear him humming under his breath.

I had to take £2,500 from our Lux Bucks account to make up the payment. There's barely anything left so if I take any more Edward will definitely notice. And if he starts asking questions about the money all of this will be for nothing.

£27,500. That's how much I've handed this stranger. It's more than most people earn in a year. Surely he can't expect me to find any more? A huge sum, but I had to pay it. After all, what price would I put on my marriage, on the man I love more than anything in the world? But that's it now; it has to be enough. There is no more.

I walk around the city, barely taking in my surroundings, my mind still whirring with the possibilities of future demands. I can't get the man out of my head and that "well, we'll see," as he walked away. His nonchalance somehow makes the exchange seem even more threatening, more ominous. *Could* I get my hands on more? I suppose I could take out a loan, or pay myself a bigger dividend from the company. But it has to stop somewhere. He can't just keep demanding more and more.

It didn't stop for Natalia. The thought hits me as I stand outside John Lewis, looking at the window display of Le Creuset casserole dishes. I lean against the window frame, willing the dizziness to pass, the buzzing in my ears to fade. I can hear Thea's voice on the wind: *deep breaths. Panic is pointless.*

I need to speak to Natalia, find out exactly what really happened to her. And if it was even the same person behind her notes and mine. There's only one problem, she's ghosted the entire influencer community and so I have no way to contact her.

For fuck's sake, why is the universe conspiring against me like this. I want to scream with frustration. I can't even ask Thea to help me track her down—she does have some pretty good skills at finding people—as it's still the middle of the night in New York.

Without even realising, I find myself wandering around John Lewis, fingers stroking the vibrant teal of the Le Creuset I had promised myself with some of my savings, but now can't even dream of buying. Listlessly I take the escalators back down to the ground floor, walking a loop around the store. I weave through the handbag section, trying to give the Clinique counter in the centre a wide enough berth. I'm not in the right mood to chat to the ladies who've helped me with clients needing pointers on their makeup.

In the stationery department, I debate upgrading my battered Filofax to a new slimmer style. I know it's a bit old-fashioned, and that I'm only thirty-five, but yes, I still use a Filofax. Not for everything, a lot of my day-to-day meetings I just put in my calendar on my phone, but I tend to record important things. Like birthdays and addresses so I can make sure I send a card.

Holy shit.

I pull it from my handbag, and flick towards the end, turning the pages over until I get to "O." Natalia Ormerod. Two years ago she invited a few of us to a birthday party. I didn't make it in the end—and in all honesty I'd assumed she'd only invited me out of obligation—but I did make sure to send her a gift. And diligently recorded the address, just in case.

***

Natalia lives just outside Shere in Surrey. I think the village was where *The Holiday* is set, all perfect chocolate box cottages and quaint touches like old-school post-boxes and tiny antique shops full of potential treasures.

Her house occupies a corner plot, and what it lacks in size it certainly makes up for in charm. Exposed beams criss-cross the white-painted façade, and the wisteria surrounding the porch is enjoying a second flush. I'm about to lift the heavy knocker when the door flies open.

I barely recognise her.

Gone is the tan and the hair extensions and the false eye-lashes. Gone is the yoga wear to show off her six-pack and the heavy makeup with the perfect smoky eye. She looks, well, like a regular person instead of a doll—Thea once described her as a prototype sex robot, which may have been accurate but was pretty mean.

She recognises me though and goes to slam the door in my face. I instinctively put my hand out to stop it closing. "Please, Natalia. I need to talk to you."

"Why?" She sounds defensive.

"Just please let me in." I lift the bag I'm carrying, stamped with the name of a patisserie I passed in the previous village. "I bought doughnuts."

"Ha! The old me would never have eaten doughnuts." She has a point, but I'd taken a chance that a year away from Insta-gram might have mellowed her a little.

"Will the new you?"

"You belong to a part of my life that no longer exists." She goes to close the door on me again.

"Secrets and lies ruin lives," I say quickly and she pauses. "You had the same notes." I don't phrase it as a question. "I'm being blackmailed and I think it's the same person who came after you. I need to know where it ends."

She sighs and looks behind her, into the house. Then she steps towards me, pulling the door closed behind her. "I have worked hard to rebuild my life," she says, her voice thick with exhaustion. "They do not need to be reminded of the past."

I nod. "I understand."

"Tell me about your situation."

"Anonymous notes, written in calligraphy, hand-delivered to my house."

"Mine were posted," she says. "Can I see the ones you've been sent?"

I pull it out of my bag and pass it to her. The wind almost catches it, but she grabs hold of it tightly.

"Hmmm. The handwriting looks a little different, but perhaps the writer is more practiced now."

She moves as if to hand it back to me and I physically recoil. That can't be all she's going to say. We lock eyes and I stare at her until she huffs slightly and turns her attention back to the card. She flips it over and runs her finger over the embossing on the back. "Same brand. Common as shit, but I guess you already know that. Look, I didn't keep mine so we can't compare properly, but I'd say it's the same person."

I offer her a grim smile of thanks. "How many notes did they send you?"

Natalia shrugs. "Ten? Twelve, maybe. I ignored them to start with, assumed they were just someone trying to get a reaction."

"Until they started to get specific?"

"Yeah." She looks around her, as if to check the front door is still closed. "They . . . they knew things. *Private* things. And they had proof. Photos." She blushes and then whispers, "Videos." She glances at me, a question in her eyes.

But I'm not sure if she's asking if they have footage of me too, or if I saw the stuff they released of her. I answer neither. Instead I ask, "What did they want?"

"Money." She shrugs and laughs without even a trace of humour. "What else?"

"How much?"

She picks at her thumb nail. "Too much. Have they made demands to you yet?" She turns the questions on me.

I suppose it's only fair I answer, so I nod. "Twice."

"Have you met him? Very tall. Huge even. Disconcertingly attractive." She looks at me and furrows her brow for a moment. "Charming, even when he threatened to tear your life to pieces."

"Yeah. Definitely the same guy." I take a breath. "What happened, Natalia?"

She sighs, and sits down on the porch steps, motioning for me to sit next to her. She wraps her arms around her calves like a little kid, her face mere inches from her knees. "I paid when the first demand came through," she says softly. "What else was I meant to do?" She glances at me and I offer her a thin smile of encouragement. "I left the cash in a bag on a bench in the park like they told me. I thought it would be over then."

"But it wasn't?"

"The next demand came a couple of days later. For even more this time. I paid again, even though it was everything left in my savings account." I swallow audibly and she turns her head to look at me. "I take it our stories are the same so far?"

"Yeah," I reply, feeling a heavy blanket of dread settle across my shoulders. I want to run away, pretend this isn't happening, but I need to hear what happened to Natalia, what will happen to me. "Please," I implore her, trying not to crumble. "Tell me how it ends."

"Oh, Helena," she says, sympathy written across her face and colouring her words. "I gave them everything I had and it still wasn't enough. The next demand was for even more. When I said I couldn't pay, they told me to take out a loan."

For a moment hope fills me. I have good credit, I'll be able to get a loan.

But then it's dashed. "I took out the loan," Natalia says. "This time I met him in person, handed it over." She looks completely wretched. "The next day they released the footage anyway."

"But you'd paid?" Am I missing something?

"It didn't matter in the end." She stands and offers me a hand to help me up. "Go home, Helena. Whatever they have on you is going to come out eventually. Perhaps you can find a way to minimise the impact." She reaches out and squeezes my shoulder. Then she turns and walks back into the house, closing the door behind her and leaving me standing frozen on the porch.

I feel numb as I drive back to Devon, barely acknowledging the world around me. Eventually I pull into a lay-by and buy some strawberries from an elderly gentleman and his yellow Labrador who have set up a little stall to tempt tourists. "Some fresh fruit will help put a smile on your face," he says kindly.

I take the punnet and sit on the grassy verge, looking out over the endless rolling fields in front of me. I can hear Natalia telling me it'll all come out eventually. Is she right? Or is there still a way I can stop this? It can't possibly be over.

I wish Thea were here. She'd know what to do; she'd break it down into potential outcomes and probabilities and action plans. But she's half a world away and I'm all alone.

The air is warm and still. Peaceful.

The calm before the storm.

I shiver, sensing the tempest building behind me.

Chapter Seventeen

2018
HELENA

I paint a smile onto my face as I turn into the village of Ofcombe St. Mary and head towards home. I'm just going to pretend that everything is fine, that everything is just how it has always been. Thea always tells me not to worry about the things I cannot change and so that is what I'm going to do.

It might seem childish, like I'm burying my head in the sand and hoping it all goes away. But what else can I do? There isn't any more money. And even if there was, it didn't stop him from spilling all Natalia's secrets. The clock is ticking on my life, counting down to the day it could go up in smoke.

I'm holding on to a tiny nugget of hope, so small I might only be imagining it. What if Edward dismisses it, calls bullshit on this guy and the secrets he claims to be privy to? Could it be possible, or have I become completely delusional?

Edward isn't home yet and so I make a start on dinner. I'll make one of his favourites; steak and creamy dauphinoise potatoes and asparagus baked with garlic. I don't know if I'm trying to make the most of the days or weeks we have left, or if I'm hoping that playing the perfect wife will help convince him of my innocence.

His key scrapes in the door less than ten minutes later and I make sure to check my smile is still intact as he comes into the kitchen. "Something smells good," he says, wrapping his arms around me and dropping a kiss on my lips. I lean into him, losing myself in the scent of him, in his solidness. I feel safe, as if nothing could hurt us. But the moment is shattered by the obnoxious ringtone of his mobile. "Sorry," he says pulling away from me. "I need to take that."

Of course he needs to interrupt a moment with his wife to answer his mother's call. He leaves me slicing potatoes for the dauphinoise, but the vigour with which I wield the knife results in something more akin to wedges. I take a breath and try to cut them more thinly. I want this evening to be perfect.

"That's a lot of potatoes for one." Edward leans on the door frame, trying to thread a cufflink through the cuff of the clean shirt he's put on. I turn to him, clutching the knife harder as I take in his appearance. He has slicked his hair back, and he's wearing the suit I found in a little boutique that makes his arse look like a peach. Dior Sauvage wafts towards me.

"You're going out." It's not a question.

"It's Mum."

"Of course it is." I don't like the bitterness in my tone, but this is meant to be *our* evening. Just the two of us. Hot tears of frustration prickle the corners of my eyes.

"I'm starting to get really worried about her, Helena. She's consumed with getting the will contested." He puts a hand up to stop me from talking. "I know she's always been a bit obsessed about it, but this feels different. She keeps saying she knows someone got to Dad. Keeps saying it over and over."

My blood turns cold as I remember what the man said in his first few DMs. *Shall I tell your husband or your mother-in-law first?* Losing Edward isn't the only risk. I try to swallow my fear as I ask, "What does she mean by got to?"

"As in, someone convinced him to cut her out and make it impossible for us to get the money. As in someone twisted him against her."

"Does she have any proof?" I can hear my heart hammering in my chest as I fish for any information that might reveal if

Geraldine's just crazy and paranoid or if someone is already talking to her. About me.

He shrugs. "She says she will get it. She's convinced it's someone close to her." He runs his hand through his hair. "I think she's heading towards the edge." He pauses for a moment and stares at me, a wild panic in his eyes. Then he whispers, "I'm afraid she might do something stupid."

"She wouldn't hurt herself, surely?" I say.

His face twists as he struggles to control his emotions. "I don't think so. But I'm worried she might hurt someone else. I've never seen her like this, Helena." I take a step towards him, desperate to fold him into my arms and tell him everything's going to be OK. "She scares me," he whispers. I stop moving, frozen to the spot as his words hang in the air between us.

The oven beeps to announce it has reached the right temperature for the dauphinoise and it breaks the spell holding us in place.

"Right, I'd better go," Edward says, stepping around me towards the door.

"Would you like me to come with you?" I don't want to, but I'll support him however I can. And for as long as he'll let me.

He shakes his head. "She said she just wanted to talk to me." I must make a face without realising because he adds, "Don't take it personally, Helena. Please." That last word sounds almost plaintive and guilt stabs me in the gut that I'm the one who is really responsible for all this mess. "Apparently she has someone she wants me to meet."

"About what?"

He smiles sadly. "I have no idea. But I have a feeling it's linked to this whole trust thing."

I follow him. I don't feel good about it, so spare me your judgement. But what if it's *him*? What if he's decided that he doesn't need to debate if he should tell my husband or my mother-in-law first, realised he could kill two birds with one stone and tell them together. I need to know who Edward and Geraldine are meeting. And if it's a six-foot-five behemoth determined to destroy everything.

Edward heads to The Grange; I don't think Geraldine knows anywhere else actually exists. But it has a distinct advantage for my snooping.

Dinner service in the restaurant starts at seven p.m. and I know that Jamie, the person ostensibly employed as the manager, will be front of house greeting guests and making sure everyone is comfortable. Especially if Geraldine is there this evening, he knows it wouldn't be worth her wrath if he didn't schmooze when she's holding court. I let myself into his office. There are no access controls; it's a private members' club so it's not like the place is crawling with strangers. "It's private to keep the riff-raff out," I remember Geraldine telling me once, when I had the audacity to suggest it was opened up to the public in order to improve profitability.

But there are some CCTV cameras dotted about. Some of them are in the guest areas—sorry, *member* areas, hearing the correction in Geraldine's clipped tones—designed to ensure she's always the holder of the best gossip, and knows exactly who has been meeting whom. The other cameras are in the staff areas. Geraldine doesn't trust people she considers to be below her. "Most people will steal if you give them half a chance," she has told me pointedly on more than one occasion.

I can see her on the screen, sitting at the bar with Edward, one bony hand resting on his arm, the other wrapped around a wine glass like a claw. She turns to look at someone who is still out of view of the camera, her face breaking into a saccharine smile I'm not sure I've ever seen her wear before. She certainly didn't look like that on our wedding day when she watched her son marry the love of his life.

I scan the bank of screens in front of me, looking for the same scene but from another angle. There. But it isn't a hulking man weaving through the tables towards Geraldine and Edward. It's a woman, dressed in a simple, yet phenomenally expensive—I can tell it's Roksanda from the neckline—silk dress. She's maybe a few years younger than me, rail thin but in a way that suggests a chef and personal trainer, her blond hair in a perfectly neat chignon. She isn't Edward's dream woman. But she is every inch the wife Geraldine dreamt of for him.

Geraldine hugs her—hugs her!—and then plants a kiss on each cheek, before taking her hand to turn her towards Edward. I can't hear what she's saying, but it's obvious from Geraldine's body language that she's making a gushing introduction.

I watch as Edward smiles—the handsome smile I thought he reserved for me—and reaches out to shake her hand, before changing his mind and kissing her cheek. He touches her back as they walk towards the table in the centre of the restaurant. She laughs as he says something she obviously finds amusing.

I can't watch anymore. Geraldine has lured him to The Grange with her batshit behaviour and is now, what? Setting him up? Or at least trying to. This has nothing to do with the will. But I have no idea what she's trying to achieve.

Back at the house, Ella rings me. "Are you OK?" she asks, concern in her voice. "You sound kinda fierce."

"Geraldine," I say, the name imbued with my anger and frustration and too many years of trying to keep everyone happy and always—*always*—failing.

"Uh-oh. What did she do now?"

"I think she is trying to set my husband up with a woman. The three of them are having dinner together at The Grange, all nice and cosy."

"Helena." She sounds serious. "You know that sounds...well, don't take this the wrong way, but it sounds a little irrational. I know Geraldine is terrible, but even she wouldn't try something like that, not practically on your doorstep."

I pause for a moment. "I know it sounds like I'm a paranoid mess. But I know what I saw."

"Did you *spy* on them?"

"There's CCTV in the restaurant. I slipped into Jamie's office."

"You broke into his office?"

"Of course not. It's not like he locks it or anything."

There is silence on the other end of the line.

"Are you still there?" I ask her.

"Yeah, sorry, I was just thinking. So, even if Geraldine *is* trying to play matchmaker, Edward isn't going to do anything."

"No..." but I can't stop thinking about his hand on the small of her back, the way she laughed at his joke.

"I think you just need to, you know, make sure he knows exactly what he has at home." She clears her throat as if saying it has made her feel more than a little uncomfortable. I suppose he is her boss, after all.

***

Despite it being almost midnight by the time Edward gets back, I'm still going to initiate sex with him. Ella's words ring in my ears: *make sure he knows exactly what he has at home.* But I can't help but feel that I'm living on borrowed time, trying to save something I'm going to lose anyway. As soon as he knows about @PAGEFree, as soon as he sees that viral tweet about his father and my vow to Edwin that his hateful genes end with us, he will leave me because I breached his trust so completely. He will leave me and walk straight into the arms of the woman in the Roksanda dress. Geraldine will whisper in his ear that she is the kind of woman he should be with, the epitome of the Taylor wife.

I've spent the last hour preparing and I don't want my efforts to go to waste just because he's even later than I expected. I've gone full on: matching thong, bra, and stockings. Killer stilettos. Hair brushed out into gentle waves down my back. The pièce de résistance a spritz of the sultry perfume he used to say made him hard in seconds.

He doesn't call out when he comes through the door. From the upstairs landing I hear him put down his keys, hang up his jacket and take off his shoes. The bottles in the door of the fridge clink as he opens it, the sound sending a frisson up my spine. If he's getting himself a drink, I may as well have that last glass from the bottle I brought upstairs with me. The Prosecco is still cold, the condensation on the glass almost makes the crystal slip through my fingers before I down it.

I'm careful as I totter down the stairs, trying not to roll my ankle in the heels, fingers gripping the banister so tightly my knuckles turn white. The space between the bottom step and the lounge door looks wider than it should, yawning in front of me like the long walk to hell. I almost fall as I navigate the space, managing to catch myself on the door frame and picking up one leg to make what I think must be a rather alluring pose in the doorway. I clear my throat to get his attention, proud of the way I recovered from the near fall, my heart hammering in my chest.

I feel almost invincible.

But the look on his face as he lifts his eyes to me is not one of unbridled lust. "Jesus, Helena," he says and puts his glass down on the coaster, hauling himself to standing.

"What?" I ask quietly.

"You're pissed."

"So?" My voice sounds like a squeak in my ears. I clear my throat and start again, lowering my pitch to something more seductive. "I thought we could," I raise an eyebrow. "You know."

He sighs, the same way my father would sigh when I was naughty as a child. The sigh that carried the weight of his disappointment. "It's gone midnight. I've just got back from dealing with Mum all evening."

"I could help you relax." I perform what I think is a sexy wiggle, but I'm forced to grab the door frame again to stop myself falling.

"Look, H-Bear. I've had a long night and I'm completely knackered. I just don't have the energy to deal with..." he trails off, picking up his drink.

He was going to say *to deal with me*. My husband has spent the evening with someone else and now he's pushing me away. "Don't you want me?" I feel my cheeks redden as I realise I said *me* and not *to*, which would have sounded considerably less desperate.

He sighs again. "H-Bear. Sweetheart. You're pissed as a fart. You can hardly stand up straight." His voice softens. "What's brought this on, eh?"

"It's nothing," I say, but tears begin to form as I turn away from him. "Just forget about it." I grip the banister hard as I walk back up the stairs.

He doesn't follow me.

I sit down carefully on our bed and slip my feet out of the stilettos, then exchange the sexy get-up for plain knickers and an old T-shirt. There was a time when he wouldn't have even dreamt of turning me down. A time when he would have jumped up off the sofa and thrown me over his shoulder in a fireman's lift to carry me upstairs. Or pulled me onto his lap right there in the living room, groaning in his desire for me, whispering that he had to have me or he would burst.

The threads holding everything together are weakening. I'm going to lose him, I can feel it.

I let the tears come.

Chapter Eighteen

2022
THEA

I don't know how well you know Brighton, but it's an amazing place to live, especially towards the end of the summer when the weather is still good but the tourists have begun to thin out and the queues reduce to a more manageable level.

My favourite thing to do here is to stroll along the seafront while I take a lunch break, keeping watch on all the crazy wonderful people who live in this little liberal enclave on the south coast. All around me are a mass of people: teenagers on skateboards as if it were still the nineties; groups of students just starting the new semester at the uni—I think there are two universities in the city—and finding their feet; middle-aged couples who haven't quite fully grown up yet—it is perfectly normal to find a forty-something guy with a man bun in a pair of tie-dye harem trousers—even though they hold down serious jobs in the City during the week.

In front of me is an older couple, they must be at least in their sixties, holding hands as they walk along the promenade, the one on the left in the most garish shirt I've ever seen, his husband in much more muted tones. They stop to say hello to a tiny little sausage dog being walked by a tween and I swerve to walk round them.

I almost miss her. I'm too busy looking at the adorable way the Wiener has rolled onto his back to accept a tummy rub from one of the guys. She's dressed more casually than usual in a simple pair of jeans and a plain grey T-shirt, no makeup, hair in the kind of fancy plait I've never been able to master.

She's coming out of a shop, one of the ones that sells sweets and ice creams and little pictures of the derelict pier against gorgeous hued sunsets, a blue-striped plastic bag slung over her wrist.

"Jen!" I call as she turns to walk away from me. "Jen!" I call again as she continues to walk and I hurry to catch her up. I rush forwards at a half-run and tap her on the shoulder, expecting her to be wearing headphones or something.

"Oh, hey!" she says as she whips round and eyes me suspiciously. "You OK? You look kinda..." She grimaces. I'm assuming I'm bright red from trying to catch her up, and I can feel a sheen on my forehead. I should never have given up running.

"I was calling you," I say, trying to catch my breath.

"Oh, sorry! I was miles away!"

"You must have been. I was literally calling your name right behind you."

"Sorry! Just having one of those days."

"Is your mum OK?" I ask.

"Mum?" For a moment she looks confused, but then she papers on a smile. "She's about the same, still calling me at silly hours in the night if she can get to the payphone." Jen hefts the bag on her wrist. "She asked me to get some fudge and stuff." She yawns and wipes the back of her hand across her mouth. "Sorry, I'm just exhausted."

"I get it," I tell her and cock my head a little as I take in the shadows under her eyes, the slight stoop in her shoulders, the chips in her nail varnish. She really does look knackered. "How about I take you for lunch? My treat."

She pauses for a moment and I assume she's going to turn me down, make some excuse. But eventually she nods and her face breaks into a smile. "Thanks, Thea. I could do with a few hours of feeling normal." She laughs. "Whatever normal means."

"Shall we go somewhere with a decent wine list?" I ask.

"Or beer and chicken wings?" she asks hopefully.

"BrewDog?"

"Now you're speaking my language," she says, taking my arm.

***

On Monday morning, I head into the office extremely early, determined to catch up on some of the work I should have done over the weekend. Instead I'd spent Saturday drinking through almost the entire BrewDog tap list and Sunday nursing the worst hangover I've had since Helena took me to a student house party when I was still only sixteen.

"I'll forge your release form for the weekend and then you can get the train to Bristol," Helena had told me. "I'll pick you up and then we can go to this party. It's going to be insane!"

"But what if I get caught?" I was going through a phase of being a fastidious rule-keeper, too afraid of punishment to risk such a huge infringement.

"That's part of the fun," Helena promised me. "Please, Thea. Live a little. Otherwise I feel too guilty about leaving you at Ferndown."

"You're three years ahead. You couldn't have stayed at school," I replied matter-of-factly.

"I'm not being literal, Thea. Just come to the party and let's have some fun. Please?"

In the end I'd got extraordinarily drunk and was so hungover I almost missed curfew when I returned to Ferndown on the Sunday. But I got there in the nick of time. "See," Helena said, when I rang to tell her, "I told you it'd all be fine." And it was, until I got to evening registration and then let loose a stream of bright blue vomit all over the shoes of my house mistress. Even a decade and a half later I can still smell it, acrid and sweet at the same time.

Luckily, I'm now an adult and so at least I can layer coffee over the remnants of the BrewDog hangover still lingering more than a day later. This is the shit no one tells you about getting older—two-day hangovers are a scourge of adulthood.

Jen rolls into the office at eleven a.m., wearing oversized sunglasses and with an air of absolute exhaustion. She comes straight to my desk. "We need to talk," she says.

"Err. Ok." I have no idea what this is about, but it doesn't seem like she has good news for me.

We duck into one of the small conference pods. They've been designed to be confidential, the shape of the upholstered roof created to absorb the words spoken inside. "Ella is gone." She hisses as soon as we're both inside the pod.

"What do you mean, gone?" I ask.

"I mean she's removed all her social media. I found a Facebook for her, but that's gone as well."

"But she was the key. She's literally the only lead I've found in months and months of searching."

"Are you really serious about this?" Jen asks.

"Of course. Why?" I take a step back and angle my head slightly to look at her. "What do you have up your sleeve?"

"An address. We could just go and see her? It's maybe a two-hour drive."

"I'll get my keys."

The address Jen managed to find is in the small town of Amesbury in Wiltshire. It's a pretty nondescript place, with a small high street consisting of a handful of shops and a Wetherspoons. We take a wrong turn and end up on a road out of town that opens into the countryside.

"Stonehenge Road," Jen says reading a road sign. "Ooh, we're really close. You know I dated this guy once who thought

Stonehenge was a landing port for ancient alien spaceships." She peers at the screen of her phone. "Yeah, this is definitely not right. We should have turned right at that last T-junction."

I turn around and we head back into the town, eventually pulling into a close of semi-detached houses. "Isn't Ella like your age?" I ask Jen.

Jen shrugs. "Close, I guess. Why?"

"Well, this feels so suburban. The kind of place you would live with a young family. Not if you were a single twenty-something."

"She knew Helena four years ago," Jen says. "She was single then, but she could be married with kids by now."

I have to concede she has a point. My own life is hardly recognisable compared to the summer of 2018. Actually, even *I* am hardly recognisable; ditching the rigidity of my investment banker routine means I've gained a—welcome—stone, my hair is longer and doesn't shine like silk from two-hundred-dollar treatments every few weeks, my nails are unpainted, and I haven't worn those horrible 20 denier black tights—pantyhose my American colleagues would call them—in years.

"Besides, there's a block of flats up ahead, I think it's one of those."

But when we scan the list of buzzers there is no Ella Hazelwood listed. "What number is she meant to be?" I ask.

"Twenty-eight."

I look again. "Twenty-eight is someone called J. Gill. Where did you get this address?"

"It was in the background of one of her pictures on Facebook. There was post on the side and so I zoomed in," Jen explains, sounding defeated. She pushes the buzzer for number twenty-eight.

"What are you doing?" I sound horrified. "You can't just randomly ring someone else's buzzer!"

She rolls her eyes at me and presses it again.

"Hello?" A man's voice floats from the intercom.

"Hi." Jen adopts a super-friendly singsong voice. "I'm looking for an old friend. Ella Hazelwood?"

"No one called that here, love. Sorry."

"You're sure?" I ask.

"Trust me, I think my wife would be pretty livid if there was another woman living here with us." He laughs. "But we did only just move in. Perhaps she was the last tenant?"

"How long ago?" I ask. I hate prying, accosting someone in their personal space goes against everything I believe in—I mean, there is nothing worse than random people turning up at your door without warning—but it's over a four-hour round trip and I don't want to leave with nothing.

"We moved in about a month ago," he replies. "I've not had any post for an Ella Hazelwood, but she could have set up a redirection. It might be worth chatting to the letting agent? It's OpenHouse in town."

Back in the car, I take in a deep breath and release it loudly. "What a waste—"

"Shhh," Jen says before hissing, "I'm calling the estate agent."

I keep quiet, listening as a disembodied voice on the other end says, "OpenHouse, how may I help?" in the cheeriest voice I've ever heard.

"Oh, hi," Jen replies, her voice as smooth as treacle. "I'm really hoping you can help me." She sounds like charm personified.

"Of course. Are you looking to rent?" chirps the voice on the other end of the line.

"Actually, I'm looking for someone. My baby sister, she was one of your tenants, but..." Jen drops her voice a little, imbuing it with concern, "this is kind of delicate. It's just we haven't heard from her for a while and I'm getting worried. I don't suppose you have her new address on file?"

"I'm afraid we can't give out information on our tenants." The voice sounds a little less chirpy now it's obvious Jen isn't a potential sale.

"She's my sister."

"Sorry." Although she doesn't sound particularly apologetic.

"Bitch!" Jen says as she stares at her phone. "She hung up on me."

I slap my hand against the steering wheel. "Fuck's sake. It's a total dead end."

"Well..." Jen trails off. "I mean..."

"What?"

"You really want to find out where she lives, right?"

"Of course I do."

"Because there is a way." Jen shifts in her seat a little. "But it's not necessarily strictly above board." She says that last sentence quickly.

"What are you saying?"

"Look, Thea. Just promise you won't judge me, OK?"

"I promise."

"So, I'm good at social media stuff. And I can design a mean website...But, well, let's just say that my skills go a little deeper."

"Just spit it out, Jen."

"If you want me to, I can probably hack into the letting agency's files and get her forwarding address. But only if you want me to."

"You can do that?"

"Given that you sound impressed rather than horrified, shall I take that as a yes?"

Chapter Nineteen

2018
HELENA

I wake up with a pounding headache and a terrible sense of fore-boding. What did I do last night? But before I've even opened my eyes it all comes crashing back. Edward's rejection, the look on his face as he watched me trying to seduce him. Shame swirls through me, chased by the heart-breaking memory of the way he had smiled at that woman in the expensive dress.

I can tell the bed is empty next to me and I listen for sounds of movement from the rest of the house. But it's completely silent, Edward must already have left for work. I'm glad. I don't want to face him.

Memories of what happened earlier yesterday start to form around the rough edges of my hangover, flashes of despair and fear and anger and frustration, followed by roiling waves of nausea as the inevitability of my fate presents itself in increasing clarity. I'm going to lose everything. It's only a matter of time before my carefully constructed house of lies crumbles around me.

I open my eyes to check the time and notice Edward has left me a glass of water and a packet of ibuprofen on the bedside table, along with a cereal bar, and a Post-it telling me not to take ibuprofen on an empty stomach. He has signed the note *Love you H-Bear xxx*.

The gesture feels like another punch to the stomach. I don't want to lose him. I can't lose him. I contemplate getting out of bed but can't muster the energy. Perhaps if I stay in bed for long enough, all my problems out there in the big wide world will solve themselves. If I pretend there's nothing but me and the duvet I'm wrapped in, it will all just go away.

But the incessant ringing of my phone on the bedside table seems determined to remind me time continues to march on no matter how hard I wish it would stop. Eventually I can't ignore it anymore.

It's Brenda Jenkins—one of my least favourite clients— insisting I meet her in an hour for a coffee and what she calls "a strategy session." There are rumours swirling around her company that her boss is thinking of early retirement and she wants to make sure she's at the top of the pile of potential replacements. She's one of my most lucrative clients, but also has this huge chip on her shoulder and is convinced the only reason she isn't already Managing Director of EuroValet is because she's a woman.

I don't have the strength to deal with her right now. I feel like I'm falling apart, unravelling as everything around me begins to crumble. But I can't let her down and so I drag myself through the shower and head into town to meet her.

"Are you even listening to me, Helena?" Brenda is staring at me. "It's basically sexual harassment." She sits back and huffs like an over-privileged French bulldog.

"Do you mean sexual discrimination?" I ask.

"Whatever. It's not right, whatever you call it."

I resist the urge to give her a reality check. To tell her the truth is that she's just not that good. She has a limited grasp of financials and is a terrible public speaker. It also doesn't take a rocket scientist to figure out she's probably an awful person to work for. You can tell a lot about a person from the way they treat the people around them and Brenda's habit of clicking her fingers at bartenders—and refusing to say "please" and "thank you"—speak of a woman so far up her own arse I'm surprised she doesn't fall over.

However, whatever the truth about why she won't get her promotion, at least it won't be because she doesn't look like an MD. Whatever else is happening, I can't afford not to do a good job. Can't afford to risk the business. I take a gulp of coffee, wishing it was laced with a fortifier, before I give Brenda the advice she pays me for. "You need to wear a medium grey structured dress, just below the knee, slash neck, heavy wool. With a cropped jacket, black tights—20 denier only—and a pair of heels—black, not too shiny, but not suede."

"I was thinking of this suit." She shows me a hideous trouser suit on her phone. It's double-breasted and screams 1980s fat-cat banker.

I try to keep my cool as I hand her phone back. I don't have the capacity to deal with her petty problems and I just want to get this meeting over with. "Understated elegance is what you want. Go for the dress. That one in the window of Whistles on the high street would be perfect." I see her open her mouth to argue with me, but then I spot someone who looks just like Ella walking past the window. Perhaps she's out running errands for Edward.

I slyly tap out a text to her under the table, Brenda still droning on. *I'm in town. Can you sneak out for a coffee?*

It is definitely Ella, as she pulls out her phone and then texts back *Snowed under in the office* ☹ *Edward is a harsh taskmaster* 😄

She looks around her and then lights a cigarette. I feel the itch at the back of my skull. I gave up smoking—publicly at least—when we got married, but sometimes I'm struck by a craving so bad I feel as if it has coiled around my brain, squeezing everything else out.

"I'm talking to you." Brenda is tapping my coffee cup and staring at me.

"Sorry." I come down to Earth, but my eyes are still on Ella. She lied to me. She said she was in the office, but clearly she's not. Why is she lying? What is she hiding? God, I sound so paranoid.

"You promise me the dress rather than the suit?"

"Yes." Jesus, I can guarantee I'll have to ring her later when she has another wobble. "Look, I've got to go," I say and grab my iPad, phone, and notebook, stuffing them into my bag as I stand up. "You'll be fine, Brenda," I tell her without conviction as Ella pushes off the window and turns to walk away. I might be being ridiculous, but I need to know why she's lying. "Call me if you need anything," I almost yell as I stumble away from her and push open the door to the cafe, determined not to lose sight of Ella. I want to know where she's going, what she's up to.

I follow her, staying far enough back there is no chance of her seeing me. She ducks down a side street that pops out just in front of a fancy looking day spa. She starts to pace, obviously waiting for someone.

I don't know who I was expecting to walk around the corner, but it wasn't him. His huge frame is further exaggerated next to Ella, there must be well over a foot difference in their heights.

I duck behind a car like some kind of criminal, praying that neither of them has seen me. Why is Ella meeting the same man I've been paying for his silence?

She hands him a padded envelope and he smiles at her. I can't hear what they are saying, but they both laugh. Does she know him? Surely not. But . . . the thought hits me like a sledgehammer . . . what if she's here because of Edward? What if he's been blackmailing my husband as well?

Ella walks away from him, turning back to offer a brief smile and a casual wave. She looks relaxed, almost happy. Or is it relief I see in her posture? Relief that she is walking away from the rendezvous. Surely Edward wouldn't put Ella in this kind of situation, he's far too much of a gentleman to do that. Unless I don't know my husband at all.

I follow Ella as she walks through town. What did she give him? Waiting until we're in a busy area—so she doesn't think I've been following her—I call out, "Ella?"

She spins round, her mouth in a perfect shocked "O."

"I *thought* it was you!" I exclaim and take a few quick steps towards her.

"I was just on my way back to the office." She looks nervous. But then she clears her throat and squares her shoulders.

I tilt my head to one side as I look at her. She's wearing a cute tea dress, with a sensible pair of ballet flats, a skinny belt clinching her cardigan at the waist. She looks like a teenager. Surely Edward didn't send her to meet that man. I feel suddenly exhausted, all the stress of the last few weeks compounding to bear down on me at this exact moment. I almost collapse with the weight of it all.

"Hey," she says, reaching out to steady me. "Hey. Let's go sit over there. OK? On that little wall."

"I saw you," I tell her, every last ounce of my energy forcing the words from my lips. "With that man. Did..." but I can't finish the question. I sink to sit uncomfortably on the narrow wall.

"You...you followed me?" She looks shocked for a moment, before turning away so I can't see her face.

"Ella," I say softly. "What does he want from Edward?"

"Edward?" She turns back to me. I stare up at her. "What does Edward have to do with anything?"

"He didn't send you?"

She looks puzzled. "I don't know what you're talking about."

A motorbike passes us and she visibly blanches at the noise. I take her hand, pulling her gently to sit down next to me. "I know who that man is." I say it softly. "Please tell me what he wants with my husband."

Ella looks at me for a moment and then she laughs, but it sounds hollow, false. "He's been blackmailing me." She says it quickly, almost under her breath.

"He's been blackmailing me too," I reply.

"Shit, Helena. That bastard."

"How much have you given him?" I ask.

"Everything I have." She sounds wretched. "He asked for five thousand, but I could only give him two. He said it might be enough, but he has to think about it."

"What does he have on you?"

She blushes, a deep scarlet spreading up her chest. "Photos." It's barely a whisper.

"What kind of photos?"

"Seriously?" she replies. "What kind of photos do you think?"

"Oh."

"What does he have on you?" she asks, and I can see it on her face that she's wondering if he has compromising pictures of me as well.

"Not photos," I say.

"Worse than photos?"

"Yeah."

"Shit. How much have you—"

"A lot more than two grand," I interrupt her.

"But he's leaving you alone, right?" When I don't answer she repeats, "Right?" with more dread.

"I don't think he's finished with me, no."

Her face perfectly mimics the torrent of emotions flowing through me.

"I think I'm going to be sick," Ella says.

***

Ella calls me the next morning, and I snatch up the phone, desperate to know if she's alright. Or if she's heard any more from our mutual "friend."

"Is everything OK?" I ask. "Is it him?"

"Him? Oh no. It's just...I..." Something in her tone makes me sit up. "Look, I'm in the office so I can't talk properly. Come and meet me? I'm going to take my lunch break at midday."

We meet in an Italian restaurant not far from Edward's offices. Ella is tucked in a booth right at the back. We order some pizzas, and then Ella turns to me, her demeanour serious.

"So. Erm..." she clears her throat. "I..." She takes a piece of blond hair and wraps it round her finger. "It's just...It's about Edward."

I don't trust myself to speak so I wait for her to elaborate.

"Look, it's probably nothing. I'm sure it's nothing. But it just seemed kind of an odd thing to be printing. You've been married for like *ever*, right?"

"Six years in two months."

"He sent it to the printer by my desk by mistake. Came rushing out before I could see what it was, all super cagey, and grabbed the sheets."

"What was it?"

"Well. He thought he'd got away with it. Getting to the document before I could see what it was. But he's not that savvy, is he? With technology?"

"Not really." He never has been. He didn't even get a mobile until he graduated and that was in 2002.

"I don't think he had any idea there's a reprint button. So I waited until he went back into his office and just printed another copy." For a moment she looks really pleased with herself, but her expression turns serious again.

"What was it?"

"Sorry. So, at first I didn't really know what I was looking at. I mean, I'm not exactly a genius, some of it went right over my head." She takes a long drink of water, her eyes refusing to meet mine.

"Please tell me, Ella. However bad it is."

"It was your pre-nup."

I take a sharp intake of breath. The pre-nup was Edward's parents' idea. Well, it's not like I was bringing any assets to the marital table. Edwin and Geraldine had the whole thing drawn up, then sat me down in the library to sign it. Yes, the Taylor family home has a library, and I don't just mean a bookshelf in the corner like normal people, I mean a whole room dedicated to dusty leather-bound tomes no one has read for a hundred years. Geraldine still lives in the house, despite it technically belonging to Edward; he was hardly going to kick her out when she was widowed, was he?

I never talk about the pre-nup unless I have to. I'm too embarrassed, too ashamed they bullied me into signing something so . . . well, it's downright insulting. All these terms about what happens if the marriage collapsed because of something I had done, and all the rights I would lose if I ever tried to walk away because of something Edward had done. But I couldn't tell Edward how I felt, and besides it wasn't as if the pre-nup was ever going to be needed. All newlyweds assume their marriage will last forever.

"Why would he be printing out your pre-nup?" Ella asks softly, but the look on her face belies the fact she already knows exactly why a man might be looking at his pre-nup. "You don't think..." she looks stricken, her eyes wide.

I look away. The truth is I think Geraldine is trying to push us apart, showing him the alternative life he could live. One where his mother and his wife are friends, where the future is secure. And I have a horrible feeling she's starting to make him think this replacement might not be unattractive.

Chapter Twenty

2018
HELENA

Early the next morning, Ella sends me a photo message. It's a picture of an email addressed to Edward. For a moment I wonder how she got it, but of course he would have given his PA access to his emails.

The email is from Jonathan and McCarthy Associates, specialists in family law. I scan the subject line: Marriage Dissolution Estimate.

They have sent my husband an estimate of how much it would cost to divorce me.

I stare at the picture, barely believing what I'm seeing. Did he ask for this? He can't possibly have done. It doesn't make any sense. I zoom in on the picture.

Dear Mr. Taylor, Further to your request . . . I stop reading. *Your* request. It's addressed to him. Bile rises to the back of my throat and my mouth fills with saliva. I pull out one of the kitchen stools and sit down heavily.

Edward wants a divorce.

The brave mask of normality I've been trying to wear for so long starts to slip. I can feel a sob building and I finally let it erupt, a huge tear plopping onto the screen on my phone. It magnifies the corner of the image and a number with far too many zeros.

I dash my hand across my eyes and wipe the screen on my dress. Then I read the letter properly.

They have basically told him he owes me a fortune if he wants to leave me. Apparently the pre-nup isn't particularly watertight and I'd be entitled to a fairly big sum if he decided to file for divorce. Big enough that he would have to sell The Grange to pay me.

We at Jonathan and McCarthy Associates would highly recommend you do not proceed with the request for a dissolution of your marriage at this time. For a brief moment I feel my heart soar, perhaps there is a way to solve this, to persuade him to stay? But then I read on.

In the spirit of completeness, we have also calculated the potential cost of a marriage dissolution in a range of alternative situations. If filed by Mrs. Taylor, clause 35c would apply and the resulting payment would be significantly smaller. However, the most cost-effective scenario would be an "at fault" claim against Mrs. Taylor. For example, if you could provide evidence she had acted in a way that caused detriment to yourself.

Edward has been offered three choices: sell The Grange to pay me what I'd be entitled to, make me file first, or uncover something I've done that is bad enough to allow him to walk away for free.

Something like lying about my involvement in his father's will. Like broadcasting my secrets—albeit anonymously—on Twitter. Like paying a stranger £27,500 to keep quiet. I feel like there's a noose around my neck, tightening millimetre by millimetre as time ticks on.

I go to close the image, but then I notice the date on the email. It wasn't sent today. It is dated four weeks ago.

The day before I received the first note.

Secrets and lies ruin lives

Ruin lives . . . And destroy marriages? But surely Edward isn't a part of this whole mess? Surely he isn't behind the notes?

I've spent the last few days obsessing that he will find out my secret and leave me. But what if I've already lost him? What if my perfect husband doesn't love me anymore and has been planning on leaving me for weeks? Even longer than that, maybe? I've been so busy catastrophising about my blackmailer unmasking me that I've ignored the real question: who is the blackmailer and who are they working for?

My tears have evaporated and I'm left feeling hollow, like a shell discarded by a hermit crab when a better home has presented itself. It's not even ten a.m., too early for alcohol, but my eyes flick surreptitiously towards the fridge and the cold white wine nestled within it. *No!* I admonish myself for even considering it and walk over to the coffee machine instead.

The machine hisses ominously and dispenses a stream of muddy brown water that is most definitely not the espresso I asked for. I swear under my breath, pour it away and try again. This time barely a dribble of liquid comes out.

For a moment time hangs suspended.

The clock ticks.

The kitchen tap drips.

And then I break, a river of expletives gushing from my mouth as I scream at the stupid bloody cunting bastard of a fucking machine. I pick up the ridiculous miniature cup that cost me £25 for a pair and hurl it into the butler sink where it shatters into a million pieces.

How have I been so stupid? So naïve? My rage turns to shame that I've been so wrapped up in my own problems I've missed the obvious. Geraldine has spent years meddling in my marriage, dripping poison in my husband's ear, dreaming of the moment she can usher in a more suitable wife to take my place. Is the woman in the Roksanda dress the first potential replacement she has introduced Edward to? Or is she just the latest in a long line of temptations dangled in front of him before he takes the bait?

Fuck this! I will not live like this. I will not live with a cheating bastard for a husband. And I will not go down without a fight. I owe myself that much. There's a scythe hanging over my head, just waiting to drop with the whisper of my wrong-doings, but even so I don't deserve this. I don't deserve to lose everything.

I need to get out of the house, away from all the things that remind me of our life together, the souvenirs from a decade spent in the pursuit of each other's happiness. I drive into the city and head to a cafe. Once ensconced on a sofa with a latte and an almond croissant I find myself navigating to Edward's Instagram page. He rarely posts, just the odd picture of him out drinking with his rugby friends, or his golf scorecard. His last post was liked by a @PersephoneEtherington and I click on her profile. The woman in the Roksanda dress.

Persephone? The irony isn't lost on me. The Greek goddess was Queen of the Underworld following her marriage to Hades, but she was also the goddess of fertility. The woman that my mother-in-law is pushing onto my husband is named after the fucking goddess of fertility! If it wasn't so tragic I might even laugh.

Most of Persephone's pictures are horribly generic: fancy food, cocktails on a bar, the ubiquitous sunset on a beach that could be anywhere in the world. I scroll down until I find a picture of three smiling women in ski gear, the mountains reflecting off their goggles. "With my Surval Montreux sisters." I read the caption out loud. Surval Montreux is a stupidly exclusive Swiss boarding school. Persephone's parents must be absolutely loaded. One of the girls at Ferndown transferred there for sixth form, and I remember some of her acolytes squealing in excitement as she described the facilities and the fancy school trips, the collective gulp as she told them just how much the fees were. Seventy grand a year, in case you're wondering. A few more pictures down is one of her flanking a bride in a puffy white gown. *Congratulations to the happy couple. #WaitingForMyOwnPrinceCharming*

God, I need something stronger than coffee. I make my way to one of my favourite little bars; it's tucked away off the main area of shops, just far enough out of the throng that people won't just wander past, but still stylish enough that if they did I could claim I was meeting a client. They also have a pretty extensive cocktail menu and I'm in the mood for something bitter and fucking strong. "I'll have a Cointreau Cosmopolitan, please," I tell the nice barman, Elliot I think his name is, although it's not the kind of place where they put the staff names on a badge.

"Of course," he says to me and my stomach does a little flip-flop. There's a gleam in his eye, a touch of a smile at the corner of his mouth. God, I've missed someone looking at me like that. "Anything else I can get for you, Miss?"

When was the last time someone called me "Miss"? Not "ma'am," or "Mrs"? He raises his eyebrows slightly when I don't answer him, lost in a fantasy that brings a bloom to my cheeks as I return to reality. "Sorry." I shake my head a little to clear the image of him on his knees in front of me and clear my throat. It comes out as something more akin to a low growl and my blush deepens. Jesus, where did that even come from?

"Pull up a chair while I mix that Cosmo." I look back at Elliot; his smile is that lazy type, only ever offered by a man who knows exactly what you are thinking and revels in it. "Unless you don't want to keep me company?" The mock pout and hint of petulance in his tone shouldn't be sexy, but I can't help myself.

"Well, I wouldn't want you to be lonely, would I?" I reply and slide onto one of the luxuriously upholstered bar stools.

My hand brushes his as I pass him my credit card. His eyes widen as they land on my rings adorning my left hand. For a moment I wish I'd taken them off; surely he'll shut off the flirting now, and I'm kind of enjoying myself. As if I'm not really me anymore, as if I've left the real world behind.

"So, what brings you in here before lunchtime?" he asks, leaning his elbows on the bar, his eyes on mine as I reach for the cocktail he's just prepared. Is it really still so early? "Work? Or pleasure?" He elongates the vowels as he says "pleasure," rolling the word around his mouth as I take a sip of the drink. I swallow carefully.

The cocktail is divine. The sour of the lemon juice cuts through the sweetness of the Cointreau, with the vodka bringing warmth to the back of the throat. It's also strong. Really strong. And by the time I've drunk three of them I'm feeling a tingle in my fingers and a loosening in the tightness across my chest. Elliot—if that's his name, I still haven't actually asked— has continued his patter of flirtatious banter and I'm feeling warm and attractive and almost glowing.

"Another one of these please." I motion to the once again empty cocktail glass at my elbow, steadying myself against the polished bar.

"Are you sure that's a good idea?" His voice is less flirty now, more nervous, concerned perhaps. I don't know, it's taking more of my concentration than it should to maintain an appropriate posture.

"Of course," I say, trying to keep my tone light.

"One more," he says as he turns to reach for the Cointreau.

I go to the bathroom, wipe a streak of mascara from under each eye and run my fingers through my hair, smoothing down a pesky bit that was sticking up a little.

When I make it back to the bar, Elliot isn't there. There's a door at one end, marked STAFF. It's propped open. That must be where he is.

I pop my head around the door, and spot him reaching up to grab something from one of the shelves that run around the top of the room. His T-shirt rides up so I can see the base of his spine, the dimples covered by a soft blanket of downy hair. I want to stroke it.

"What the hell!" he shouts, spinning round to face me. I stand my ground, heart thudding in my chest. I wait for him to realise we're alone. Alone in a confined space. "You can't be in here," he says, trying to take a step back from me, but there's nowhere for him to go.

"Really?" I reach a hand out for him again. *Fuck you, Edward. And fuck you, Persephone.*

"It's a staff area," he tells me.

"I know," I whisper and take another step forwards. *Fuck you both. I can play this game too.*

I reach up to touch his cheek, my hand landing more heavily on his skin than I'd been intending. "Oops." I giggle. "Sorry."

He takes my hand in his and smiles at me. I wait for him to lean in, imagining the feeling of his lips on mine, the urgency and the longing, the shift as his passion takes over and he can't help but push me back against the little desk, hands finding their way under my dress. But the kiss doesn't come, the look in his eyes isn't unbridled lust.

"Look. You're a lovely woman." His voice is soft and gentle, his hand holding mine away from his face. "But I think you need to go home. Before you do something you'll regret."

"I won't regret it," I say and push myself against him.

He slips away from me, leaving me standing against the wall and he backs away further. "I'll call you a taxi."

"Oh, don't fucking bother." I'm suddenly angry, cheeks flaming at the pain of his rejection. "I wouldn't want you to do me any favours for fuck's sake. You tease me all day and then...what? Hmm?"

"Hey." His hands are up as if to placate me. "Let's just get that taxi, OK?"

"Fuck you!" I scream in his face, pushing past him, desperate to be out of there before the tears fall. And they will, I can feel them building, held back only by the magic of water tension. I knock over the stool as I grab my bag and jacket. *Serves you right if I make a mess.*

"Hey," his voice rings out across the bar as I stumble outside, momentarily surprised to discover it's still broad daylight. The numbers on my phone swim a little, but it's only four p.m.

I spot sight of myself in the mirror of a shop. I look like shit. Perhaps I should go and get a coffee and sober up a little. I can already feel the start of a headache as my body begins metabolising the alcohol from that last cocktail. I need caffeine to combat it. Then I'll be fine in half an hour.

The double shot latte is served in what can only be described as a bowl and I sip it greedily as I will the pain in my head to dissipate. It takes almost an hour and the addition of a double espresso to the mix, but finally I feel strong enough to walk to the taxi rank. I'm going to go home and have some food and maybe a shower. Then when Edward gets back we are going to sit down and have a proper conversation.

I need to know what is really going on. I can't go on like this, with both of us lying to each other and sneaking around. If our marriage has a future—which I want more than anything in the world, however unlikely that seems as I sit here—we have to be honest. I need to tell him the truth about his father and @ PAGEFree, and he needs to tell me about Persephone. We can get through this.

Buoyed with my conviction, I settle back into the leather seat of the taxi, half closing my eyes as the driver winds his way towards the edge of town. We come to a stop at a T-junction, the driver swearing under his breath as a cyclist pulls in front of him, almost hitting the car. I sit forward to peer through the windscreen at the same moment as the cyclist turns to raise a hand in apology. I only see him for a flash, but his huge frame hulking over the tiny bike removes any doubt it is him.

The man who I have handed £27,500 to is right in front of me, dressed in slim fitting joggers and a black windbreaker, no helmet to mess up his light brown hair. He stretches out his left arm, signalling his intention to turn.

"Could we turn left here, please?" I ask the driver.

"Sure." He turns to look at me. "Change of plans? What's the new address?"

I'm mortified, but I swallow it down. "Can you follow that cyclist?"

The driver shoots me a look and then shrugs. "Sure."

My blackmailer pushes off, gathering speed as we pass the cinema, barely looking as he shoots across the roundabout. The taxi driver tuts under his breath before shifting in his seat, hunching over the steering wheel in concentration.

The road starts to slope upwards and the bike slows down, the taxi slowing to stay behind him. My blackmailer motions for us to pass, but we stay in position. The car behind us flashes their lights in frustration at us for failing to overtake and the cyclist turns to look at us. I duck down in my seat and pray he didn't see me.

"Windows are tinted, love," the driver tells me with a chuckle. I think he's enjoying this a little too much.

"Oh," I say, and sit back up.

"Boyfriend?" he asks, nodding forward towards the cyclist.

"It's complicated," I reply.

"If he's going to see his fancy woman I could just..." he trails off, but claps his hands together softly.

I'm not entirely convinced he's joking and so I mutter something appropriately non-committal.

He turns right just before the railway bridge and picks up speed again, flying over the speedbumps like they're ramps in a skatepark, before turning into an area of low-rise flats. It's one of the less salubrious parts of the city, run down and shrouded in a cloak of despondency.

I feel stupid, unsure of what I'd hoped to achieve by following. Even if this is where he lives—and not a friend's place, or even a job—what exactly can I do with that information? I'm hardly going to knock on his door and ask for my money back.

"Can you take me home, please?" I ask the driver. I feel defeated, the rush of adrenaline from the chase has already dissipated, and my hangover has returned.

As we pull round the corner, something makes me glance into the little car park next to the flats. It sits out like a sore thumb, the sleek lines of the black Audi A5 incongruous among the colourful Fiestas and Golfs.

TAY 17.

The personalised number plate I bought him for his birthday last year. It cost almost five thousand pounds—which I agree is very expensive for a number plate—but he'd been thrilled that it combined his surname and birthday. "Now I'll never forget my number plate again!" he'd said.

What the hell is Edward doing here? Why is he visiting the man who is blackmailing me?

Chapter Twenty-One

2022
THEA

Jen rings, breathless and obviously excited. "Aberdeen," she tells me.

"Aberdeen?"

"It's where Ella moved to last month."

"Did you manage—"

She cuts me off. "Yes. I got it."

"Excellent. So now what?"

"Well..." she pauses for a moment, as if she wants to ask me something but she isn't quite sure how to phrase it. "I could...you know, go up there."

"To Aberdeen?"

"Yeah. It's just, the flights, you know? And I'd probably need to stay overnight."

"I'll come with you," I tell her.

"Haven't you been prepping for some huge meeting, some potential massive deal?"

"Shit. You're right. Look, Jen. I know it's a huge ask. But if I paid for everything, and for your time obviously, would you—"

"Of course!" she cuts me off, sounding thrilled at the opportunity. "Leave it to me."

Jen goes to Scotland on Saturday and sends me a constant stream of updates from her journey: the train to the airport, the latte she had while waiting for her gate announcement, the sad-looking toastie from the plane.

Once she arrives in Aberdeen city centre, she video-calls me. Buildings tower behind her, blending into the leaden sky. "Welcome to the Granite City," she says, as she turns her phone in a circle to show me the sights. "You have never seen somewhere so..." she gropes for the word. "Grey," she settles on, eventually.

"It's striking," I say. Helena and I spent a few days there when she was thinking about doing a masters at the university. There's a brutal beauty to the monotone when it's cloudy, but when the sun comes out the mica in the granite sparkles and the whole city glitters.

"Apparently Ella's place is about a mile or so out of town," Jen tells me. "It had better not rain." She tilts the phone upwards so I can see the sky more clearly.

"Call me when you leave her, OK?"

But two hours later I still haven't heard anything. Nothing, not even a text. I try to call her but it goes straight to voicemail. What the hell is going on? It would have taken her half an hour to walk to Ella's—if that, it's pretty flat.

I keep calling, but her phone remains switched off all afternoon and evening. In the end I call the hotel I booked for her.

"Can you put me through to Jen Alderson, please?"

"Do you have a room number?" the efficient receptionist asks me.

"Err, no. But she's definitely staying with you. I'm the one who booked the room for her."

I hear the clacking of a keyboard in the background. "I'm afraid if you don't have the room number I can't help you."

"She should have checked in today? Can you just confirm she checked in? I'm getting worried as I haven't heard from her."

"I'm sorry."

I hang up and start pacing. Where is she?

***

An hour later she Skypes me from her laptop. She's sitting in a hotel robe, her hair wet, little streaks of mascara running down one cheek.

"Jen! Thank goodness! Where are you?" I demand.

"Whoa. I'm at the hotel. Where else would I be?"

"Your phone is off and I called reception and they refused to confirm if you'd even checked in."

"Oh," she looks a little sheepish. "I used all my battery taking pictures and then video-calling you earlier. But everything's fine. I'm here." She motions around the modest but clean and modern room.

"What happened? Did you find her?"

"Yes. But I'll tell you everything in person when I'm back tomorrow."

"Did she talk to you? Do you know what really happened?"

"I'm waiting for her to fill in the final pieces of detail. But trust me, Thea. She knows what happened. You need to hear it in person though."

"Jen, please te—"

But she's already disconnected the call.

***

Jen's flight is due to land just before six p.m. and I'm waiting for her at Arrivals.

"I thought you might be waiting for me," Jen says. "Sorry I was so elusive last night. I didn't have anything concrete till this morning and even then..." She trails off and takes in my slightly crumpled appearance. I probably should have made more of an effort, seeing as we're in public. "Let's go upstairs, there's a bar we can talk in." She links her arm through mine and leads me towards the lifts.

Once we're settled in a high-back booth, a gin and tonic in front of us, she reaches into her little carry-on wheelie case and pulls out a plain brown A4 envelope. *Jen Alderson c/o Residence Inn* is written in loopy writing on the envelope.

Jen looks directly at me, her hand resting on the envelope possessively. "So," she says. "I found Ella. And let's just say that she didn't seem to appreciate how easily I'd tracked her down." Jen grimaces. "She slammed the door in my face. But I kept trying. I might have made a bit of a pest of myself and so eventually she let me into her house. I think she wanted to avoid her new neighbours witnessing a scene on her doorstep."

I nod. She drums her fingers against the brown paper absent-mindedly, but I can't help but allow my gaze to drift from her face to the envelope.

"She took a lot of convincing that I wasn't connected to what had happened, not trying to tie up loose ends by tracking down potential witnesses."

"But you were able to convince her? You told her you were my friend?"

"Well, that was the other issue. Apparently Helena hadn't really talked about you that much." She grimaces, as if it pains her to say the words.

Another small piece of me dies. Was I really that bad a friend?

"But," Jen says, her tone turning upbeat, "I worked my magic. Convinced her you and Helena went way back, that all you wanted was the truth, that you wouldn't involve her in anything, never divulge she was the one who gave you this information. And in the end, it was better that I went in your place." She takes a breath and looks at me. "You owe me big time, Thea."

"What did you do?"

"I told her if you did anything reckless, anything that would link her to this envelope here," she taps it for dramatic effect, "she can come after me." She sits back and holds my gaze. "So you'd better not do anything stupid."

I lean forward in my seat. "Thank you, Jen," I say.

She maintains eye contact for another beat and then she looks down at the envelope. Her voice is soft as she starts to speak. "She told me Helena was murdered. The accidental death verdict was wrong. There was someone else on the roof that day."

There's a low buzzing in my ears. The contents of that envelope will shape the rest of the plan. I'm so close now. So close to finally getting justice for Helena.

"This is the proof." Her fingers tap the envelope.

I swallow loudly.

"Are you sure you want to know who it was?"

I nod and pick up the envelope. Inside is a stack of papers and a handful of photos, obviously taken from a distance and then enlarged before being printed.

The first one shows a fancy looking A5 parked in front of the main door of The Grange. The number plate TAY 17 I know because Helena told me a million times how amazingly she was nailing Edward's birthday gift that year. Someone is getting out of the driver's seat dressed in a dark blue jumper and a navy baseball cap embroidered with the instantly recognisable rose of the English rugby union team.

In the next photo another car has pulled alongside Edward's. The driver's face is clear in the photo. "Who is this?" I ask.

"Ella told me he was someone Edward had met a few times. But he'd been cagey about who he was."

"So she doesn't know?"

Jen clears her throat and leans over to whisper: "He's a contract killer."

"A what?"

"Did you think he would have done it himself? This is why Ella is so terrified. It's not Edward coming after her she's worried about. It's the man Edward hired."

I flick to the next picture. The men are shaking hands, both their faces in solemn profile.

Then the next, a grainy CCTV image showing the contract killer inside The Grange. It is time-stamped 18:05 on 17 August 2018. Just five minutes before Helena died.

I sit back in the booth. I feel deflated. Disappointed. I'd hoped the evidence would be much more compelling.

"There's more," Jen says, her eyes on the envelope. "Remember Ella was Edward's PA. She had access to quite a lot of his stuff. Including his phone."

In the stack of papers, I find a printout of text messages exchanged between Edward and a guy called Kirk. At 18:15 Kirk had sent three simple words: *It is done*

I push down my desire to leap to action, to hunt him down and slit his throat for what he did. Instead I take a moment, push the rage back down. "Ella was sure that's what this was?" I ask.

"She was one hundred percent sure. Edward paid a contract killer to make Helena's death look like an accident."

Chapter Twenty-Two

2018
HELENA

Light streams in from the open window, burning through my eyelids even as I clamp them shut against the assault. My head is pounding and there's a taste in my mouth that is making me gag. I reach a tentative arm out of bed, groping for the bedside table to see if I remembered to bring a glass of water up with me, but I knock my phone off. Instead of a dull thud as it hits the carpet, there's a loud crash as it hits wood and my eyes fly open.

Where am I?

For a moment I'm confused, but then the memories of yesterday come crashing over me like a tidal wave. I'm in the spare room. I slept in here last night after I screamed at Edward not to come near me, that I hated him and couldn't bear to sleep in the same room. I groan and sink back against the pillows, wishing the duvet would swallow me up. But still the memories come, the images threatening to drown me.

After seeing Edward's car outside that man's house, I came home and opened the bottle of Glengoyne he'd been saving for a special occasion. Then I waited for him to come home. I waited and waited, topping up my glass with whisky. I don't even like whisky; it was always Thea's choice, not mine.

Edward woke me up from my position on the sofa. "Let's get you to bed," he said softly, holding out his hand to pull me up.

I looked at him and saw him clearly for the first time in months. The look on his face was part pity, part disappointment.

You're a mess, his eyes said as they roamed from my face to the crumpled dress I was wearing.

"I'm fine," I said, ignoring his outstretched hand and hauling myself up to a sitting position.

"You're far from fine," he said. The ugliness of his tone made me wince.

I took a deep breath and prepared to stand up. He rushed to grab me but I slapped him away. "Get off me," I hissed.

"Helena," he warned. That self-righteous, supercilious bastard.

"Leave me alone."

"Just let me—"

"Fuck off!" I screamed in his face and pushed him away.

The rest of my diatribe is fuzzy, as if my brain has tried to forget my exact words in a bid for self-preservation. But I remember enough to know it wasn't pretty.

I crawl into the shower, get dressed and eventually make it downstairs. It's gone nine a.m. and the house is empty. There's a little note on the kitchen island, his scrappy handwriting a sign of just how quickly he rattled off the words.

Helena. No pleasantries, then.

We cannot go on like this. I feel like I don't know you anymore. And the drinking is becoming an issue. Your head is probably killing you after drinking all the Glengoyne. Have some ibuprofen and take it easy. I'll be home this evening and then we will talk.

I do love you.

There's a packet of ibuprofen next to the letter and I wash a couple down with tap water and then read the note again.

I do love you. Some of the fuzziness from last night coagulates into a more concrete image. I'm at the top of the stairs, tears streaking my face, looking down at him by the front door. *"You don't love me!"* The memory of my high-pitched shriek makes me wince.

I need to get out of the house. Perhaps a walk will clear my head. I need to think about what I want to do next. Or at least try to figure out what the options might look like.

I don't head anywhere specific, just aimlessly wander around. But everything reminds me of him. The bench where we sat and waited for the locksmith the time I managed to lock the keys inside the house. The oak with the dilapidated remains of his childhood treehouse that formed a surprisingly romantic backdrop to his proposal. The bakery in the village where he buys us fresh croissants and pains au chocolat on Saturday mornings.

The whole place is imbued with our history, the vestiges of the life we have shared.

Of the life I know is slipping away from me.

I can't bear it and I hurry back to The Gatehouse, wiping the tears from my cheeks and praying I don't see anyone I know. If anyone stops to ask a polite "how are you?" I think I'll bawl my eyes out.

I grab the keys to my car, desperate to get away from here. Inside the safe confines of the leather interior, I breathe deeply. Then I turn the key and drive.

I don't know where I'm going, just somewhere. Anywhere. Perhaps if I keep driving and don't ever stop all of this will cease to exist, it will fade into the annals of time, becoming nothing more than a half-forgotten memory. I've always been a little bit obsessed with the idea of running away.

At the railway bridge I turn right, slowing as my Prius travels over the speedbumps. The car park is empty, the owners of the Fiestas and Golfs that had filled it yesterday probably at work. And of course my husband's A5 is no longer here; no doubt it will be in his dedicated spot outside his office. I need to know exactly what he was doing here.

Yesterday, my blackmailer had swung off his bike and opened a gate just off from the car park. I push the same gate open and find myself looking into a garden with possibly the world's smallest patio, barely big enough for a minuscule table and two folding chairs, shrouded from the road by some tall bushes. I can't picture him sitting out here, he would fill the whole space.

I take a few steps forward and the gate swings closed behind me. I know it's trespassing, but the gate wasn't locked and he should've been more careful. From the patio I can see into the single room that makes up the kitchen and living and dining rooms.

An estate agent would call this place "bijou." The reality is that it's just tiny.

There's a scruffy looking pot with a few sad-looking weeds growing in it, a series of cigarette butts pressed into the soil. Next to it is a rock. I look around, but it's the only rock in the garden and it looks incongruous, out of place. I pick it up and it emits a chinking noise as I give it a little shake. One of those fake rock key safes; the code showing is 1110. I turn the last dial forward one position and the little door clicks open to reveal the keys inside. He really needs to take security more seriously.

I glance around, checking I'm alone, that no one is watching me as I tip the keys out into my palm. I hold my breath as I slide them into the lock, heart thumping in my chest as I push open the door. What if there's an alarm? But the only sound is the creaking of the rusting door hinge. I step inside, recoiling as the stench of day-old curry hits me.

In the kitchen I find the source of the smell: three unwashed plastic takeaway boxes are sitting on the side, along with two plates smeared in a bright red curry and a jar of that hideous lime pickle stuff, the lid left off. He doesn't seem exactly house proud. And he doesn't seem to live alone.

Unless one of those plates was Edward's? Did the two of them sit in this little flat, eating curry and chatting like old friends? It just doesn't make any sense. I feel like my husband is as much of a stranger as my blackmailer.

Despite the mess on the kitchen counter, there is nothing else out of place, no other clutter accumulating in corners, or on surfaces, or piles of shoes and coats by the front door.

I go hunting round the living space, looking in every cupboard and drawer. There's a reason it's all so tidy; he literally has no stuff. Not like he just travels light, but *nothing*. In the kitchen there are four bowls, four plates, four mugs, four sets of cutlery; all cheap and looking like one of those student starter kits you can buy in Ikea for a tenner. There are no pictures, no trinkets, nothing personal at all.

The hairs on the back of my neck prickle. What was that noise? I search for somewhere to hide, my hand over my mouth as if to hold my panic inside. A shadow falls across the glass in the front door. But then a flier is stuffed through the letter box and the shadow moves away again. Just the local pizza place delivering menus.

Spurred into action and keen to minimise how long I spend here, I head upstairs to the bedroom. There I find a built-in closet with a handful of his clothes inside; mainly jeans and T-shirts and a couple of hoodies. I slide open the other side of the wardrobe and find some women's clothes: dresses, jeans, a few nice tops. And a skirt suit, one which would be perfect for a twenty-three-year-old to wear to an interview, classy and demure but with a clinging skirt. Why is the suit I lent Ella sitting in the wardrobe of the man who has been blackmailing me? Of the man who was blackmailing her too?

Except he wasn't. Of *course* he wasn't. How was I so blind?

I need to get out of here. I run back downstairs but my attention is caught by an alcove in the hallway, the kind of place you might store a vacuum cleaner or whatever. But instead it's home to a mini-safe. It's locked. I pick it up—it's surprisingly light—and give it a shake. Something shifts inside, it sounds like a stack of papers. Why does a twenty-three-year-old have no *stuff* but a locked safe?

I look towards the front door. I'm really pushing my luck staying so long. There's a combination dial and I spin it a few times, trying to feel the click as the right number is selected but it seems it's not that easy. I try a few obvious code combinations but none of them work. I'm forced to admit defeat, even as a little voice whispers in the back of my skull that there are answers to at least some of my questions inside.

I'm going to have to leave it. But then I remember something. Have you ever watched that show where they auction off the contents of storage units? It's really rather sad, people who have defaulted on paying for their units, and then all their stuff gets sold to some hipster to "upcycle" their worldly goods. Anyway, they often find safes in those units. Safes without keys. I remember this guy standing there with this smug grin on his face as his wife tried to break into one, dropping it on the corner over and over again as she got increasingly frustrated. And then he mansplained to her all about them. It was cringe-worthy and just awful to watch, but thinking about it there was a little nugget of gold in there. Most home safes aren't designed to stop a burglar; they're designed to stop a fire eating through your birth certificate and house deeds. They're also controlled by a four-digit code, one that people are rather prone to forgetting and so they need a mechanism to be overridden. All you need is a magnet.

I turn round and take the few steps towards the fridge. There is a chunky—and a little ugly—3D magnet of Brighton Pier stuck to the door. There's no time to waste, I contemplate moving the safe onto the kitchen counter, but it'll be quicker if

I just duck into the alcove. The safe pings open in seconds with the help of the magnet.

All that's inside is a simple purple plastic folder with a loop closure, full of personal documents. I open the first passport. Douglas Kirkpatrick Barnes. The giant, his handsome face more tanned in his photo than in the present day. I put it back and take out the other one. Katie Abigail Evans. The face looking back from the picture is Ella.

I'm still staring at it, trying to make sense of what I'm seeing when I hear the front door open.

"Katie?" a male voice calls out. I hold my breath and press myself backwards, deeper into the alcove, the magnet in my hand as if I could use it as a weapon.

I hold my breath as Douglas Kirkpatrick Barnes walks straight past my hiding place into the kitchen, my heart hammering, palms slick with sweat.

"There'd better be beer left," he says under his breath. There's a hiss as he opens a can from the fridge. He walks past me again to carry the beer to the living room, switching on the TV and huffing as he settles on the sofa.

I need to get out of here. Should I make a run for it? There are only about five steps between where I am and the front door. I creep out of the alcove, trying to remember if the sofa would give a vantage point over the front door. I don't think it does; maybe I can just slip out and no one will ever know I was here?

"Did you really think I didn't know someone was hiding in here?" He's crept up behind me. He reaches for me, but I duck from his grasp and fling open the door, narrowly missing hitting myself in the face.

And then I'm running. Running as fast as I can away from him.

My feet slap the tarmac and I can hear him behind me, his breath ragged as he chases me. I don't risk turning to look, that will only slow me down. Instead I search for a potential place to hide, but there is nothing, just more of the same low-rise depressing flats on either side of the road.

I keep running, pushing myself even as my legs begin to burn, my handbag banging against my hip. I loop my thumb around the strap to stop it bouncing. He's still coming for me, but he sounds further away. I close my eyes for a split second and focus my inner strength. Thea is a runner, she talks of runner's block, of swallowing your mental fears and powering through. I dig down and find a store of energy I never knew I had, my legs pumping harder as I speed up.

"Fuck!" I hear my pursuer shout. It sounds like it's half a street away and I sneak a look. He's stopped running, his hands on his knees as he doubles over to catch his breath. He's so huge he must already have run out of steam.

I keep running, turning right and then right again, heading towards the scrubby line of trees that runs alongside the train tracks. Once I reach relative safety I slow to a walk, heading back towards the car. I can't leave it there, but at least I can see it from the trees.

Unfortunately, he's standing directly next to it, his phone to his ear.

"Grey Prius," he is saying to whoever is on the other end of the line. "Yeah. So it's hers?"

There's a pause for a moment while he listens to something and I watch him physically bristle.

"Of course I chased her. For fuck's sake. She's surprisingly fast."
Another pause.

"You want me to let her go?" He sounds incredulous.
He listens again.

"You're the boss," he says, even though you can tell he doesn't really think whoever he's talking to should be the boss. He ends the call and walks back towards his flat.

I wait until he's inside and then I run to the Prius, flinging the door open and throwing myself inside. I lock the doors, feeling as if I'm about to have a heart attack. But he stays inside and I pull away, eyes glued to the rear-view mirror to check he isn't following me.

I desperately want to go home, have a long cold shower and try to figure out everything I've seen. Try to make sense of it. I don't know what is real anymore.

My phone buzzes with a message from Edward and I glance at it as I drive: *Where are you?*

I ignore him.

Please call me.

I'm getting worried now.

Are you going to make me come and look for you? Again.

I try not to cry. Let him come and find me. For fuck's sake, he can use Find My iPhone to track me if he's really that bothered.

I turn into Ofcombe St. Mary, The Grange coming into view at the top of the hill. I have an idea. Or at least the start of one, a place to begin to unpick this web of deceit. Two minutes later I'm standing outside the front door of The Grange. This was where I first met "Ella"—there must be some record of her employment, and how come no one noticed that the name on her passport wasn't the name she was using—and it's where Edward met Persephone. I'd hazard a guess there is more for me to find here.

I head towards Jamie's office, wondering if I should use the route where I will avoid being captured on camera. But when I get to his door, there's a *Do Not Disturb* sign hanging on the knob, his signal that he's conducting an important meeting inside.

To kill some time, I head up to the spot on the roof I've used for the last six years to hide from Geraldine when this place gets too much, when the obligations of this life press down too firmly on me and I need to suck nicotine into my lungs in defiance of her expectations of her daughter-in-law.

I spot his favourite rugby union cap, the vibrant red of the rose unmistakable. Edward has found me. I realise I'm calm, ready to have whatever conversation we need to have. And there's something rather fitting about having it up here. Over the years this is the place we've had all our most important conversations.

You need to climb out of a sash window in order to get onto the roof. And I move to the edge as I wait for him to make the awkward manoeuvre to join me.

The sun is starting to set on the horizon, streaking the underbelly of the cloud a brilliant salmon pink. It's really rather beautiful.

I feel his hand on the small of my back and turn to face him.

His eyes are dark, his face impassive.

The sharp shove forces me backwards, my feet desperately scrabbling for purchase on the slate tiles.

But then I'm falling, the ground rushing up to meet me. I try to scream but the wind rips the sound from my throat.

Part Two
Revenge

THEA
2022

Chapter Twenty-Three

How do you commit the perfect murder? It's quite simple really; you just need to make the world believe it was an accident.

Tens of thousands of people die unexpectedly every year. How many of them weren't what they seemed? How many spouses, relatives, friends—even strangers—saw an opportunity and...well, you know what I'm saying.

When Helena died everyone agreed it was such a tragic accident. A life cut short. Thoughts and prayers for her family.

But they were wrong; she was murdered. And I hold evidence in my hands that proves it. Edward paid someone to kill his wife. The proof is irrefutable, despite how ludicrous the idea is of mild-mannered Edward, who adored Helena, doing such a thing.

"Are you going to the police?" Jen asks me, her voice soft.

"No," I reply, my eyes meeting hers. "This was never about some lawyer making a fortune for getting a reduced sentence or even a slap on the wrist. She deserves more than that."

"You really loved her."

It's not a question, but I nod in answer anyway. Yes, I loved her. But I failed her; too wrapped up in my own life to see the danger she was in. "I should have saved her."

"So what are you going to do?" Jen whispers.

"I'm going to get revenge...And make it look like an accident."

***

There is even more evidence in the envelope from Ella.

"Apparently Edward agreed to pay this man after the event. There was a life insurance policy," Jen says. "The documents are in that pile."

I look at them, signed by Helena, her scrawled signature so familiar, she didn't change it after they were married.

"Ella managed to get copies of Edward's bank statements too," she says.

I shuffle a few papers until I find it. Details of multiple transfers from Edward Taylor to a series of numbered accounts.

"Seems like quite a lot of money." Her tone is dry.

"One million pounds." I look up from the papers. "It's a *huge* amount of money."

"Ella thought this guy had caught wind of the size of the life insurance policy and decided to increase his asking price."

I stare at the number for a few moments, trying to process just how cold-blooded it all was. How meticulous the planning must have been.

"Fucking bastard," Jen says, the disgust clear in her voice. The look on her face sends a shiver up my spine. It's the same look I remember from my own younger days, before I was taught to keep my anger under control, to channel it back inside myself so it didn't erupt. I'm thrown back in time to when I was ten years old, sitting on the whitewashed wooden steps of the folly on the edge of Uncle Jed's estate.

I call him Uncle Jed and describe him as my godfather, but the reality is totally Dickensian—at least that's what the girls at Ferndown said when they found out, describing it as the kind of thing you'd only hear in a Victorian novel. I was abandoned as a toddler with no idea who my birth parents were, and ended up in foster care. My foster mother, Pauline, did her best, but she didn't really know what to do with a girl like me. She'd drag me to work with her sometimes, cleaning the houses of wealthy families in our village. That was when I met Uncle Jed, and in me I think he found a kindred spirit. He basically paid for my entire education at Ferndown, allowing the other girls to think he was my rich uncle.

I had been suspended from the local primary school for punching a boy in the face after he told me I was so ugly even my mum had abandoned me. Uncle Jed had laughed when he heard the story, this huge deep laugh that I've learnt only stupidly posh men can pull off. Not wanting me to be alone, Pauline had taken me to work with her, and I was on the folly steps, eavesdropping. My foster mother and Uncle Jed were inside, thinking themselves alone and out of earshot.

"That school could be a godsend," Uncle Jed had said. "They'll make a lady rather than an outlaw of her."

"Do you think they can tame her?" Pauline replied.

"I hope so."

The next sentence from Pauline had been little more than a whisper, one I always wondered if I'd really heard correctly. "Sometimes she terrifies me."

"Me too."

But to my face Uncle Jed had never let me know he felt that way. He even gave me a nickname, called me the daughter he always wished he'd had. A nickname that means Gift of God. Thea.

"Thea?" Jen's voice sounds far away as she interrupts my reminiscence. She's reading the details of the life insurance policy. "Even after he paid that man a million pounds, he still had another million and a half left. I didn't even know you could get a policy for that much. The premiums must have been hu—" She flicks the page and stops herself. "Oh. Is that it?" She shows me the neat little table with the policy schedule on it, the monthly cost of a two-and-a-half-million-pound policy. "A hundred and fifty quid a month. How can that even be possible?"

"Well, I guess no one expects a healthy thirty-six-year-old to die." I do some mental arithmetic. I remember reading something during the pandemic that the probability for a woman in her thirties to die in any given year is like one in 2,500. On that basis, a £2.5 million pay-out on a one in 2,500 chance should cost about a grand a year; apologies, I know quite a bit about probabilities. So, the idea that you can get a multi-million-pound insurance policy for a healthy woman for a couple of hundred quid a month isn't as crazy as it sounds.

"There's one thing I don't get," Jen says. "And please forgive me for prying, OK?"

I nod.

"Didn't Edward own like a huge estate? Weren't his family *proper* rich?"

"They had no cash." I was so livid when Helena told me what Edwin had done with the estate. He thought he was sticking a finger up at Geraldine—theirs was a marriage based on far more hatred than love—but all he was doing was condemning Helena to a lifetime of Geraldine's meddling. All that "old-money, keep it in the family thing" just perpetuates the whole patriarchal women-as-chattel-and-baby-makers myth. Did you know, it was only in the last decade that the law was changed to allow the royal title to pass to the eldest *child* of the Duke and Duchess of Cambridge rather than the eldest *boy*. Like we were still living in the Middle Ages.

Chapter Twenty-Four

I drive us back to Brighton from Gatwick, a silence settling between us which is only broken as we pass Preston Park, a few minutes from Jen's house.

"What are you going to do next?" Jen asks.

"I want to go down there. To Devon."

"You're going to confront him?"

"God, no. I'm going to see what he's up to, see what his life is like."

"Would you like some company?" She says it so innocently, like I'm proposing an entirely innocuous road trip.

I pause for a moment, choosing my words. "I don't want you to get wrapped up in all of this, Jen." I don't say what *all of this* is; there isn't any need to clarify that any sane person might want to back the fuck away from my mission.

"But it's just a recce? I don't think you should be on your own."

I'm silent as I pull up in front of the little house she shares with a couple of other girls she finds utterly exasperating. "I would appreciate some company," I say, not turning to look at her. I don't want her to think I'm too needy, but there is a definite whiff of desperation in my tone.

"I'm coming," she says decisively. "But I'm driving though."

"You don't have a car."

"Have a little more faith, Thea. I'll pick you up at nine a.m."

***

Jen pulls up five minutes after nine a.m. in a pillar-box-red convertible Mazda MX5, the roof down and Maria Becerra blaring into my normally quiet street. She cuts the engine and the silence is sudden. The car is so conspicuous, such a poser's car. It'll blend in perfectly in Ofcombe St. Mary.

I hoist my bag onto my shoulder, check I've locked the front door for the hundredth time and walk down the steps to the kerb. "Umm. Whose car is this?" I ask, throwing my overnight bag into the back and opening the passenger door.

"Frannie's. My housemate. She told me I could borrow it while she's on some fancy weekend break with this sleazy guy she's been dating."

She drives too fast, overtaking when she really shouldn't, braking only at the last possible moment, never bothering to indicate. The stereo is turned right up, not leaving much opportunity for conversation. It's strangely cathartic; the threat of imminent death and blaring Latin rap stopping me from obsessing over what we'll find in Devon.

"Hey! This is where we were the other day," Jen shouts over the music, the wind whipping our hair. "That's the KFC you wouldn't let me stop at."

"We can stop now, if you'd like?" I don't actually want KFC, but I do want to take over the driving and this seems like my best opportunity.

She moves into the nearside lane without even looking, causing the person behind to beep their horn angrily. "Fuck you, arsehole!" she says, giving them the finger.

After we've eaten, Jen agrees to let me take over the wheel. "Just promise you won't crash Frannie's car, OK?"

"She *did* let you borrow it, didn't she?"

"I hack one little website to find an address and all of a sudden you think I'm a criminal mastermind who would steal a car." She's laughing as she says it, but she doesn't actually confirm she has permission. At least my insurance covers me to drive other vehicles. And I'm certainly the one less likely to crash.

We make it about half a mile down the road before the traffic grinds to a standstill.

Jen leans over me to shout at the driver of a dark grey car in the other lane of the dual carriageway. "Any idea what's going on?"

"Just Stonehenge, love. It's always like this."

She throws herself back against her seat and huffs loudly, fishing her phone from her bag. "Well, if we're going to be stuck in traffic, I may as well make good use of the time and do some research."

I take my eyes off the stationary vehicle in front of me to look at her. "Research on what?"

"Your friend. The husband. Didn't you say there was an awful mother-in-law in the mix too?"

"I used to call her Smaug."

"To her face?" Jen sounds incredulous.

"No! I never met her, but Helena would tell me these horror stories about Geraldine."

Jen falls silent as she begins to tap at her screen, reading and occasionally scrolling. But then she sucks in a breath.

"What?" I ask, glancing at her.

"Just reading some articles about Helena's death. It's so weird the way they reported it in the local press," she says, and then starts reading out loud, squinting at the screen in the bright sunlight. "The *Chronicle* regrets to report the tragic death of local woman Helena Taylor; business icon, philanthropist, and beloved wife of Edward Taylor. The Taylor family own The Grange, an exclusive members' club in the Devonshire countryside and the site of the terrible accident. It is believed

Helena slipped on a loose roof tile and plunged to her death on the cobblestones below. A witness at the scene described..." she trails off. "Sorry, Thea. You probably don't want to hear the details."

"I've read that article a hundred times," I tell her. The *Chronicle* had—for reasons I could never really fathom, except that they thought it would shift more copies—gone into excruciating detail about the scene and Helena's injuries. They had stopped short of printing pictures of her corpse but hadn't been shy about publishing the grainy image from a camera phone of the spot she had landed, the bloodstains blurry but unmistakable.

I look over and see that Jen is still scrolling through the archives of the *Chronicle*. "Why did Geraldine give them an interview a week after they published that..." She waves a hand as if unable to think of an adequate word.

"Accident-porn?" I offer her.

She grimaces and nods. "Accident-porn seems pretty accurate."

"As to why Geraldine gave them an interview? Just read it." The engine of the car in front of me starts rumbling and we move forward a few precious inches.

"The *Chronicle* is pleased to announce we have secured an exclusive interview with local legend, Geraldine Taylor." She stops reading from the screen. "Local legend?" she asks me.

"Oh, Geraldine really got into character as the grieving mother-in-law. Look at the picture."

"Wow." Jen exhales with the word, elongating the sound. "That is some outfit."

Geraldine had chosen to wear a high-necked dress—black, of course—with a vintage wide-brimmed hat. The hat had this long stiff net veil that covered the wearer's entire face, extending down to about the collarbone. It was utterly ludicrous. And even more so given she had worn elbow-length, black-lace gloves to complete the look.

"I am devastated by the loss of my daughter-in-law," Jen starts reading again. "Such an unexpected blow to the family, especially so soon after the death of my own husband."

"He died in 2014, so four years before Helena," I point out to Jen.

"Her passing is a tragedy, one whose repercussions will echo throughout the life of my only son. He is left both widowed and childless, their marriage having not yet been blessed with much hoped-for children." Jen frowns at her screen. "That's such an odd thing to say."

"All the Taylor money was put in trusts for Edward's future children."

"I don't get it."

"She tried to use Helena's death as grounds to overturn the trust. Said that Helena's death took with it Edward's chance at parenthood, and it was therefore unfair to punish him for something so far out of his control."

"How do you know that?" Jen asks.

"It's public information." I shrug. Of course I followed every scrap of available information into what happened after Helena's death.

Jen taps her phone a few times. "Oh, wow. It actually worked?"

"Are you looking at the *Chronicle* still?"

"Yep. Ooh..." she reads ahead. "So it did work."

I look at Jen. "I was almost convinced that Geraldine killed Helena to pull it off."

"But you don't think that anymore?"

"No."

"What made you change your mind?"

"You. And the evidence you found."

Chapter Twenty-Five

How far would you go for revenge? How far would you go to make the fucker who stole the one person you loved more than anyone else in the world pay for what they did?

Helena saw through the veneer of my apparent breeding within about five minutes of me setting foot in the grounds of Ferndown. "Thea Persimmon-West isn't your real name, is it?" she whispered as she showed me to my new dormitory, one I would be sharing with six other girls. I'd been stricken, would they all know who I really was? "I added the A to Helen to make myself sound more like I would fit in here," she confided.

"My real name is Becky," I told her. "Thea's a nickname from my erm...godfather." The title seemed so alien in my mouth; I'd never had a father, let alone a *godfather*.

"Which do you prefer?"

I thought for a few moments. Becky had been written on my arm in marker pen when I was found on the street as a toddler. It was assumed to be my name, especially as I seemed to recognise it. There was an investigation—of course there was, kids don't just appear as if from thin air—but my parents were never identified. "I think I prefer Thea," I said eventually. That name had been gifted to me by someone who seemed to care what happened to me.

"In that case, Thea Persimmon-West, welcome to Ferndown." Helena winked at me, keeping my secret and offering me a chance to reinvent myself at school. From that moment she'd been like a big sister. Keeping an eye on me, making sure I didn't get into trouble—not too much at least.

Helena would have killed for me.

I just hope I have the strength to do the same for her.

"Pull over," Jen instructs and I roll to a stop in a lay-by just before we drive into Ofcombe St. Mary.

"You OK?" I turn to ask. "How come we're stopping?"

"I want to put up the roof," Jen replies, leaning over to press a button on the dashboard. "We need to adopt a disguise."

"Why?"

"Err, in case people recognise you." She says it like I'm an idiot.

"No one knows me round here," I tell her.

"Edward would."

She says it so matter-of-factly, like it would be so obvious. *Of course your best friend's husband would know you.* The guilt stabs me in the chest again. All those times I should have flown over: her engagement party, the wedding, anniversary celebrations, even the funeral of her father-in-law. All those times I should have supported her, been a part of her life.

"Edward and I never met while Helena was alive. I wasn't the friend I should have been," I tell Jen.

"Photos? Helena must have had photos of you that he would have seen."

"Do you not remember how much I hated having photos taken for my social media?"

"Damn," Jen says. "So, err, are we going *into* The Grange?"

"It's a private club. Members only. And we're not members."

"Right . . ." she says and exhales, settling back into her seat for a moment. Then she leans forward again to rummage in the glove box, revealing two pairs of oversized sunglasses and two baseball caps. She hands me one of each. "Just in case."

"Did you bring disguises?" I ask.

"They were in the glove box already." Jen shrugs. "Who knows who Frannie's been stalking."

We drive through the village. Signs of the Taylor family are everywhere. There is obviously a Taylor Street, a small but impeccably maintained village green named after Edwin, flyers advertising the upcoming election to the local council with Geraldine evidently running as a Conservative candidate—no surprises there.

"It's like some kind of feudalist nightmare," Jen says as we pass a war memorial: *In memory of Stanley E. Taylor* in huge letters, before a list of the other poor boys from the village who had also lost their lives, in significantly smaller font.

We take the road up to The Grange, passing The Gatehouse on our right. "That was where Helena and Edward lived," I tell Jen, slowing to a crawl to get a better look. Despite the name conjuring a vision of a small square building converted into a tiny house, The Gatehouse is huge. Three double bedrooms, a massive open-plan living and dining room, an amazing farmhouse kitchen, and a garden with an incredible patio. At the front of the property is a neat box hedge and a few trees.

"Do you think he still lives there?" Jen asks.

"It belongs to the estate, so probably," I reply, picturing Edward rattling around that huge house on his own, squashed by memories of her.

The road winds onwards, manicured lawns on either side, bordering woodland where Helena often saw small herds of deer. "Helena saw a white stag here once," I tell Jen.

"Cool," she replies, as if it meant nothing. White stags are so rare, so improbable, that they're the subject of a thousand folktales and superstitions, considered messengers from other worlds. In Celtic mythology they are said to appear when taboos are being transgressed. Helena and I had laughed about it at the time. But we should have considered it an omen.

The Grange sits on higher ground, overlooking the entire valley below. The original house was built in the late 1890s and is quite frankly a bit of a monstrosity, all white stucco and ornamental flourishes. Gravel crunches beneath the tyres of the MX5 as I drive in a slow arc round the fountain in the centre of the front driveway.

A brass plaque on the wall by the main door is inscribed with the words *The Taylor family welcome you to The Grange.* "They still own the place," I tell Jen, pointing to it through the windscreen.

"If I were him, I think I would have sold the scene of the crime," she replies. "Although he probably thinks it's all over."

"Do you think?"

"He got away with it. It's been what? Four years? He probably feels pretty safe by now."

I pause for a moment. "I wouldn't be feeling safe if I were part of it."

She turns to me, a look of alarm flashing across her face at the tone of my voice. "Remind me not to get on your bad side," she says.

I take a final look at the house, the place where Helena was taken from me. *This is all for you,* I tell her silently. Then I put my foot down, sending gravel flying as the MX5 accelerates down the driveway.

Chapter Twenty-Six

We head to a quaint country pub we passed on the way to Ofcombe St. Mary, taking a corner table in the beer garden, tucked away from the other diners and surrounded by fragrant flowers. I choose a goat's cheese salad with balsamic dressing; Jen opts for a spiced lamb tagine with couscous.

"Shall we have some cocktails?" she asks.

"One of us needs to drive to the hotel," I say with a hint of sadness. "I could really do with a glass of wine."

"Is it far?"

"I don't think so, let me check," I reply, pulling out my phone and scrolling through my emails looking for the confirmation from the hotel. "Shit," I say under my breath, and look up at Jen.

"What?"

"Umm..." I grimace. "I think I've made a bit of a screw-up."

She raises an eyebrow, wanting me to elaborate.

"I booked through one of those cheap deals sites. But I didn't realise that the hotel rejected the booking as apparently there's some event in the area and everywhere is full. Fuck! Now what are we going to do?" I throw my phone back down on the table.

"Jeez, chill out a bit," Jen says with a laugh as she picks hers up and starts tapping. "Leave it to me," she says confidently. "I'm a whizz with this stuff. I should have been a travel agent." A few minutes later she has booked us into a hotel fifteen minutes' drive away. "I...umm..." she looks at me and pulls a face.

"I'll pay," I tell her quickly. "Just tell me how much and I'll sort it out."

"Thanks, Thea," she says. "Now, let's eat and then head to the hotel. They have a spa."

***

Once we've checked in and dropped our bags in the room—a two-bedroom suite with a huge balcony and incredible views— we head down to the spa. I didn't bring a bikini, but there's a small shop in the hotel foyer that sells me a swimsuit at a grossly inflated price. I dread to think how much this trip is going to cost me in the end. I hope it's worth it.

"This is a bit swish," Jen whispers as we are shown the outdoor pool and hot tub. "Sorry, I didn't realise it was quite this fancy."

"That's OK. It only seems fair given I dragged you all the way down here."

"You know I came to support you, not because we could stay in a swanky hotel." She sounds offended.

"That isn't what I meant, Jen." But she's not listening, distracted by a small gaggle of women sipping fizz and giggling loudly as they lounge nearby.

"Should we have a cheeky Prosecco?" she asks.

The spa only serves Champagne—Bollinger, no less—but I order a bottle for us. We drink it sitting on the edge of the pool, feet dangling into the water and the sun warming our faces. We barely speak. Did Helena ever come here? I should have brought her, used some of that crazy salary I was earning to treat us to more extravagant weekends away.

"This is nice," Jen says, topping up our glasses. "I don't really have a lot of female friends. Not the kind that want to come to spas and stuff, anyway," she adds sadly. "I imagine you do things like this all the time."

I swallow the laugh that threatens to escape, I'm afraid it would make me sound unhinged. "No. Not really."

"What about before?"

"Before?"

"With Helena."

"You know, I only saw her twice during the whole of her marriage to Edward. She came to see me in New York in 2015, a long weekend we had planned for years, derailed and postponed numerous times by one thing or another." Once more the guilt rolls in: I thought we had all the time in the world. So much time that if I just popped to the office for a few hours and left her to go shopping alone it wouldn't really matter. *There'll always be other trips*, I had justified my actions to myself. If only I'd known, I would have eked out every precious moment. Actually, that's a lie. If I'd listened to her instead of keeping half an eye on my emails, I might have seen that her perfect life wasn't quite so perfect after all.

We eat dinner in our suite, not wanting to have to shower and get dressed up to sit in the dining room. The restaurant specialises in Japanese fusion small plates and we order a huge selection. It arrives on a trolley, wheeled into the room with a choice of sake, the bottles clinking together.

I mix the sake with elderflower cordial and soda and, once the drinks are made, ice cubes cracking as they bob in the pale straw-coloured cocktail, we settle around the dining table.

I chink my glass against Jen's in a toast. "Thank you for coming with me," I say.

"Any time," she replies with a smile and takes a sip of the drink. "Especially if you carry on making cocktails this good." She laughs.

I don't laugh with her and she stops, clearing her throat.

"Are you OK?" she asks, concern in her voice.

"It's just...being here, in Devon...seeing where it happened..."

"It must bring back a load of memories."

"It's not that. Not really. It's more..." I trail off, trying to think of the right words. "It makes it real somehow. Like it did really happen and it's not simply a bad dream."

Jen nods. "I understand."

"Before, I could imagine she was still here, still living her life in that house, spending time at The Grange with Geraldine and *hating* it, messaging me to bitch about her, but still going back the next week because she always did what was expected. Well, almost all that was expected." I concede the final point. After all, she hadn't given Geraldine that elusive grandchild.

"Do you think he's remarried?" Jen asks.

"Now that is a good question. How would we find out?"

"Well, I'm assuming you already looked at his social media?" She says it like it would have been the most obvious thing in the world and I blush. "Seriously?"

I turn away from her incredulous stare. "I...I..." I clear my throat. "I just didn't think about it, OK?" I'm defensive, crossing my arms over my chest.

"What if we'd come all this way and he wasn't even living in the area?" she asks and then rolls her eyes at me. "Let's see what the internet has to say, shall we?" she says as she grabs her iPad and folds the screen cover down to make a stand on the table in front of us. "Let's start with social media. Twitter, Insta or Facebook? Which is most likely to be his preference?"

"Facebook. Helena said he wasn't really into social media. But every forty-year-old has a Facebook account."

It takes her about ten seconds to find his profile. His picture shows him sitting in the stands of some sports venue, a Native American chief in a headdress emblazoned on the chest of his rugby shirt. "Hmm," Jen says, looking at the picture. "He looks to be enjoying himself."

"He's wearing a ring," I say, pointing at his left hand which is holding a plastic cup of beer.

"Fucking bastard," Jen hisses.

"Oh, hang on," I say. "Can you zoom in? On his rugby shirt?" 2017 is stitched below the logo. "It's an old photo."

Jen looks impressed. "I would have missed that," she says.

"The Chiefs have changed their logo; thought they should step away from the whole Native American thing."

"I didn't peg you as a rugby fan."

"I'm not. I read it somewhere. I have this incredibly frustrating ability to remember stupid facts."

"But not names and faces?" Jen has been taking the mickey about my inability to recognise faces for months. "So," she goes back to business mode, "it's an old photo, taken while Helena was still alive. Makes me think perhaps he hasn't remarried. I mean, would you put up with your husband having a photo wearing his previous wife's ring as his profile picture?"

She points at his status, which says, "It's complicated." Remember that time when everyone thought "It's complicated" was hilarious? Like we were all embroiled in such interesting love trysts rather than going on a handful of awkward dates with people who looked nothing like their photos.

"I suppose 'I murdered my first wife' isn't an option in the drop-down box," I say.

"Not exactly Mr. Popular is he?" Jen says, gesturing at his "friends" section. He has sixty-five friends.

"Is that weird?" I ask. I mean, if you don't really use Facebook, you're not exactly going to have a ton of Facebook friends, are you?

"Is it weird that he's nearly forty and only has sixty-five Facebook friends?" She raises an eyebrow. "And I thought you were a fellow *Catfish* fan." Of course I watch *Catfish*, I have a teeny tiny—read massive—crush on the grey-haired one. It was one of the first things that Jen and I discovered we had in common, this mutual appreciation for a silver fox, but now is not the time to delve into that particular thirst-fest.

Jen starts to scroll down the Facebook wall. Edward has been tagged in a handful of photos, all at rugby grounds or occasionally the terrace of The Grange. Jen carries on scrolling and the tone starts to shift.

You're in our thoughts.

Sending condolences.

Just heard the news. There is nothing I can say to make this better, but know I will be praying for you.

She scrolls a bit further and a picture of a woman fills the screen.

Seeing her face hits me like a sucker punch. I try not to think about her too vividly, replacing my mental image with a fiery ball of hate about what happened. But sometimes she'll appear just as she was, alive and well and utterly, utterly perfect.

She is beautiful, that symmetrical, immaculate beauty that photographs so well. She sits on a sofa in a plush and tropical greenhouse, her blond hair loose around her face, the photo taken so it almost looks as if the breeze in the air is ruffling her fringe with gentle fingers. She wears only a hint of makeup, a sweep of brown kohl and a flick of mascara, but her lips are lacquered in post-box red. Her signature style, flawlessly applied the same way she has done every day since my sticky fingers pilfered that lip-gloss from the Clinique counter for her sixteenth birthday. She is looking directly down the lens of the camera, as if it's the eye of the person she loves most in the world, a relaxed and carefree smile tugging the corner of her mouth. There is a cocktail in her right hand, her left resting on her lap, the angle perfect so the light refracts on the large diamond ring on her fourth finger.

Underneath the photo is a short message.

RIP my darling Helena. I will love you forever.

"I will love you forever." Jen spits out the five words. "Did he really write that after what he did? Fucking bastard." There is so much venom in her words I'm momentarily taken aback. But something in me starts to stretch and uncoil.

We both sit in silence, the only sound the occasional cracking of the ice as our drinks settle. The air is bristling, crackling like static. Something is shifting. Taking root. Retribution is coming.

Chapter Twenty-Seven

I decide to cut the atmosphere in the room by ordering more drinks. The room-service waiter puts the ice bucket containing a very nice bottle of Gavi on the small table by the door and hands me the little leather wallet containing the signature slip. This single bottle is almost fifty pounds.

"Oh. I'm not the name on the booking," I say to the waiter. "Does she need to sign?"

"Yes, please."

"Jen!" I call to her and watch the waiter shift his weight from foot to foot.

"There you go." She signs with a flourish and he blushes as she smiles at him.

"Oh, err. Well, thank you," he says as he looks at the slip and sees the ten-pound tip she's added. "That's very kind of you." He almost falls over his own feet in his haste to leave before she changes her mind.

"You'd think no one had ever tipped him before," I say as the door closes.

"Maybe they haven't," Jen replies simply. "I've worked in places like this. The patrons are notoriously bad at even saying thank you, let alone leaving a tip for the people who serve them."

I stay silent as I open the wine. I never had a job while I was at school, Ferndown wouldn't even have entertained the idea of letting me off site to go to work. And then I got headhunted in my second year of university by J.P. Morgan, who paid me a stipend until I graduated and started working for them. Helena had worked very briefly as a chambermaid while she was a student, something she neither had the aptitude nor temperament for. She was fired on about day four and said it was the hardest job she could ever imagine.

"I think I might have to get a second job," Jen says, as I hand her a glass of wine. "I'll probably end up waitressing or working retail again." She sounds heartbroken. "It's just the business is crumbling. I've worked so damn hard for so long and it still just isn't enough." She brushes her tears away with the back of her hand. "Sorry. I don't quite know where that came from." She gulps her drink. "I think it's being here with you. You're so put together and in control, and I'm this kid who can't even make her little business make enough money to pay the rent on a crappy shared house."

"Hey, don't be too hard on yourself," I say. "It's not easy to get a business off the ground. Especially in the current climate."

"I thought I was finally moving forwards. Away from worrying about how I was going to pay for every little tiny thing." She puts her glass down and plucks a tissue from the box on the coffee table. After blowing her nose, she straightens her shoulders and flicks her hair back. "Sorry, I promise I won't moan anymore. Just pretend I didn't say anything, OK?"

I nod. "While I remember though, and only because I'm kind of prone to forgetting stuff—"

"You literally remembered an obscure sports team changing their logo earlier," she interrupts.

"Yes, well I'm prone to forgetting *important* stuff. Anyway, let me sort out the transfer for the room and things. I just don't want you to be out of pocket, OK?"

"Thank you, Thea. I appreciate that."

I pull up my PayPal and make the transfer.

Her phone beeps with an incoming transaction notification. "Umm, what's this?" she asks as she frowns at her screen. "The room wasn't anywhere near this expensive."

"Just in case there are any other charges." I shrug innocently. I transferred her three thousand pounds. At most the stay will cost eight hundred.

"Thea," she says seriously. "I can't accept this. It's very generous and everything but I just can't."

"Just take it, please. Pay your rent and treat yourself a bit. Take it as a little thank you for coming with me today. And...well," I smile, "you do kind of know a lot about my intentions." I try to keep my tone light.

I didn't know how she would react, but I'm not prepared for the anger that erupts from her. "You have to be fucking joking! Jesus Christ! We're friends. Or at least I thought we were before you..." she doesn't finish her sentence, her breath hard and fast, eyes burning into mine.

"I'm sorry. I just thought—"

"That you could buy me?" She finds her voice again. "Send me a couple of grand and I'd...what? I mean, seriously, Thea?"

"I just thought," I try again, "that you could use the money. Friends help each other."

"Friends help each other because they're friends. Not because one of them is planning something and wants to make sure the other doesn't..." she trails off again. "What the fuck did you think I'd do?"

"I don't know," I say softly. "I'm sorry."

"I'm part of this now. I just want to help you to find some peace."

"Peace?" This time I'm the one spitting my words. "Peace?"

"You don't think you'll find peace at the end of this?" Jen asks.

"It's not about me. It's about Helena. Making her killer pay."

"I'm going to send the money back to you. And then, you're going to let me help you."

The air around us is super charged as I look at her. "OK," I whisper. My voice is thick, the word almost sticking in the back of my throat.

"Do you trust me?" Jen asks softly.

"Yes."

"Promise?" She is holding out her little finger. I hook my own around it.

"I promise." I'm still holding her finger when I add, "Why would you help me, Jen?"

She looks at our hands and a tiny smile flickers across her face. "Do you have a sister?"

I shake my head. "No."

"Me neither." Her eyes meet mine. "But I always wanted one. I don't really have a family. But perhaps it's never too late to create something just as good." I nod. She adds, "We will need to trust each other to do what needs to be done."

"I know what needs to be done," I tell her.

Jen swings her eyes around the room, as if looking for a hidden camera. She scooches closer to me and leans in so her lips are almost touching my ear. The sensation of her breath on my neck sends an involuntary shiver up my spine. "An eye for an eye."

Exactly.

I can see Jen is waiting for me to say something. She has, in essence, just offered to help me kill Edward. I need to be absolutely sure she realises that is what she's saying. "Jen?" My voice is serious, a layer of gravity hanging heavy in the space between us. "Do you realise what you are suggesting?"

She nods, her eyes serious, but I can see a tug of a smile trying to break free. "Yes," she replies.

"I'm not sure even most blood sisters would help each other out like this."

She sits back a little, tucks her chin under and watches me. "Did I ever tell you about my Uncle Tommy?"

I shake my head.

"So, 'Uncle' Tommy." She mimes an air quote around the word uncle. "He stepped up and helped me and Mum after my dad died. I was maybe six or seven at the time. A big brute of a man, tattoos on his knuckles, chip on his shoulder, you know the type. He was nice to us though, at first at least. Dad had left Mum with nothing and so 'Uncle' Tommy helped out: paid the rent, bought the food, made sure I had a shiny new uniform for school. I remember asking Mum what he did for work, how he could afford all this stuff for us. I know now that he was a grifter. A conman. Someone who made his money from the backs of others."

She scrubs a tear from her cheek and swallows. "I grew to despise him." There is so much hatred in her voice I recoil slightly at the force of it. "I hated what he did. What he made Mum do to pay him back for all his kindness."

"What happened to him?" I ask gently, my hand on her shoulder.

"I wanted to kill him. To watch him hurt."

"Did you . . ." I leave the question hanging between us.

Jen huffs out and then lifts her face to look directly at me. "Some gang of Albanians or Romanians got to him first."

"So he did get what was coming to him?"

She laughs, but there is no trace of humour in the sound. "A single shot to the back of the head as he was walking down the street, nice as pie. One moment he was there, all swagger and self-righteousness, and the next just . . . nothing. You think that was fair? After everything he did? Bastard got off lightly. But maybe other people shouldn't, eh?"

I knew she had a fire that burned in her. But what I hadn't seen before was this anger that raged so close to the surface, the one that made her look at a guy and want to squeeze the very life out of him as slowly and painfully as she could.

She looks back at me and for a moment all I see is a kick-ass revenge warrior. "Thea, I'm here for you. For whatever you need. Let's make that fucker pay."

Indeed.

Let's.

Chapter Twenty-Eight

The next morning, Jen uses the TV in the room to check the final bill.

"You owe me seven hundred and twenty-six pounds. I'll let you off the thirty-nine pence." She laughs. "We are friends after all." She grins at me, but there's an undercurrent there, not of tension that I offended her by making the transfer, but of a mutual understanding of what comes next.

I send her the money. "Done."

"Thank you. Now, let's get some breakfast and then get on the road."

Get on the road is such a weirdly antiquated expression for someone in their mid-twenties, but I don't comment.

We're in the foyer, looking for the dining room where they serve breakfast. "I'll go and ask the concierge," I say and start walking towards a uniformed guy behind a small desk. But when I come back to where I left Jen, she has disappeared.

"Jen?" I call, turning in a circle as I search for her.

"Psst" I hear from behind a pillar, a hand motioning me over.

"What are you doing?"

"The concierge guy?"

"Yes, what about him?"

"You know I said I've worked in places like this before?"

"Yes," I reply.

"We worked together once." She makes a face.

"What, round here? In Devon?"

"Oh, no," she says quickly. "It was in Sussex." She doesn't elaborate further.

"But why are you hiding?"

"Because..." she takes in a breath, waiting for me to say something. "Arghh, am I going to have to spell it out for you?"

"Oh," I say.

"Oh, indeed. We dated for a few months before he shagged one of the guests. I found his wallet in her bedsheets when I went to change them."

"Ouch."

"Yeah, so we need to find a way to sneak past without him seeing me."

"We could just go out the other door?" I suggest. "I kind of want to head home anyway. It feels like this trip has been a bit of a waste of time. Shall we just get some breakfast en route? Ooh we could pretend it's 1994 and have Little Chef pancakes."

"I wasn't born until 1995, but I would still prefer throwback pancakes to having to make small talk with my ex."

It turns out there are no Little Chefs on the drive home, despite my halcyon memories of them every few miles on the route between Brighton and Ferndown. We settle for Starbucks instead.

"You sounded disappointed before," Jen says as she stirs her Strawberries and Cream Frappuccino. "Like you thought this trip hadn't been worthwhile."

I've just taken a bite of my breakfast wrap and I mull over my answer as I chew. "It's just...I didn't get to see him. Or talk to him. Or understand anything at all really." My tone is disappointed.

"You found out his family still runs The Grange." Jen points her croissant at me. "And that he isn't married."

"Both of which I could have discovered online." I sigh. "Sorry, I just feel bad about dragging you down here." I smile sadly at her.

She just shrugs. "Great hotel, amazing food, good company. It could have been a lot worse."

"Yeah. I just wish it had been fruitful." Although even as I say it I can feel my mind whirring through the possibilities of the plan to come.

We make good time on the drive back to Brighton and Jen drops me back at home a little after 3 p.m. The rest of the day yawns in front of me; empty, void of responsibilities. I need to start working on the final plan of action. I wish I could talk to Helena. Ask her advice and make sure she thinks what I'm doing is the right thing. In some ways I think she'd get a kick out of it. If she wasn't already dead.

In the end, I decide to head into the office. I may as well get some work done, stop myself falling behind in case I need to take some time away again to pull this off properly. Besides, I always feel better if I'm busy; it stops my mind from getting away from me, jumping from idea to idea and connecting dots that shouldn't be connected. To my surprise, the office is oddly busy for a Tuesday late afternoon. The building thrums with energy and the enthusiasm is catching, sweeping me up in the atmosphere despite the stresses of the last few days. The kitchen is the centre of all the activity and I head towards the noise.

"Thea!" One of the girls who runs a jewellery re-sale company on Etsy yells as I push open the kitchen door. "We're having a party!" She thrusts a beer into my hand.

"What are we celebrating?"

"One of the tech boys just sold his dating app for like a total fortune." She bashes her bottle against mine. "Now, where's that friend of yours? The hot one?"

Jen giggles when I phone her to say that the Etsy girl called her "the hot one." "The guys are buying the beer and pizzas," I tell her.

"I'll be there in ten minutes. Make sure you save me a slice of pepperoni."

Jen turns up in only eight minutes, she must have practically run down here. "What! I wasn't going to miss free pizza," she tells me with a grin.

The tech boy—I want to say he's called Justin, but I'm not a hundred percent sure—makes a speech about perseverance and following your dreams.

"It's always easier with a rich husband supporting you," someone behind me bitches. "The rest of us can't afford to work for free for three years until it takes off."

There's a smattering of applause as the speech comes to an end, but given the whispers around me I'm not sure if people are happy for the tech guy, or just pleased he's finished speaking.

I glance at Jen, but she's engrossed in her phone, a smile playing across her face as she reads something on the screen.

I lean over to look. "What are you doing?" I ask.

"Just checking out this dude's amazing new dating app. It's basically just like Bumble," she says as she scrolls. "Same guys on it too." She shows me a picture of an attractive guy in a bright yellow T-shirt.

"He's cute," I say, although my heart isn't really into Jen's dating, not after our trip to Devon.

"That's all you're going to say? Nothing about how I shouldn't go back for seconds?"

"Have you been out with him before?" I take another look.

"Seriously? Are you really that bad at recognising people? That's James, we went out a few weeks ago."

"Oh, maybe he looks a little familiar . . . you know how I am with faces."

"How can someone with your kind of memory not... well...remember?"

"The brain is a strange and wily thing," I reply. "Didn't he give you some lecture about dairy farming?"

She looks sheepish. "Maybe he has a point?" She shrugs. "Plus, I can hardly bear the thought of dating another random. Most of them are complete potatoes."

"Oh God. Like that guy with the pygmy rabbit he carried around in that special backpack?" I start laughing before I even finish the sentence. That was last summer, just after we came out of lockdown and everyone went a little crazy.

She snorts. "Oh, he was just awful."

I don't have a lot of personal experience with dating apps. But I do have an idea.

"Jen? Would you be able to find out if someone had a profile for one of these apps?"

"When you say 'you' are you meaning 'the general public' or are you meaning me specifically?"

"I'm meaning someone with your impressive skillset."

"Then yes. I'm fairly sure I could find someone's profile if it's on one of the main platforms. Is there someone you have your eye on?" She narrows her eyes at me. "I kind of always assumed you were, like not interested in that kind of thing."

I've had a few boyfriends, but none of them have ever stuck. "One day you'll find someone and fall head over heels in love," Helena had promised me. She and Edward had been dating for about a month and were still in that crazily intense honeymoon period.

"I'm not looking for a date," I tell Jen, looking at her intently until she gets what I'm asking.

"Ohhh." She nods at me a few times. "You want me to see if I can find Edward?"

"Bingo."

"And then what?"

"Well, then could you help me make a profile he would be interested in?"

"Ohhh," she says again. "Actually, I've got a better idea. He's even older than you, right?"

"Right..." I say, not quite sure where this is going.

"So, he's more likely to do internet dating rather than apps. Which is good because most apps are location-based and you guys don't exactly live that close. Plus," she holds up a finger to stop me interrupting, "I can probably hack into his profile so we know exactly what his preferences are, and then set you up a profile that is guaranteed to match with his."

I'll be honest, I was just going to make myself sound suitably appealing in a generic way—you know, good sense of humour, likes movies and walks in the countryside, that type of thing—but Jen's way seems much more rational. "Can you do that?"

"Of course. Right then, let's grab some beers and go make you into the perfect virtual girlfriend!" She sounds genuinely excited about this as she beelines to the fridge.

"Jen?" I say, forcing her to turn back towards me.

"Yep."

"Um. It's just...you're making me a little nervous." She seems so entirely nonchalant, like she's forgotten what I'm planning to do to Edward.

"I do understand the stakes, Thea. But after what he did I have zero sympathy for the bastard. They say revenge is a dish best served cold. But it's also a dish best served with a side order of fun to help you maintain your sanity."

Chapter Twenty-Nine

It takes Jen about half an hour to discover that Edward has a dating profile on Affinity.com, the favourite dating site for boring middle-aged men with rugby obsessions and a love of spaniels. His profile picture shows him relaxing in a cosy-looking pub, a real fire in the background and a glass of red wine in front of him.

"And the award for blandest profile goes to..." Jen says, tapping the desk in a mock drumroll. "I mean, he's not unattractive, if you like older guys, but he's really not selling himself."

Jen creates me an account and then starts to build my profile. "So, are you sure he doesn't know what you look like?" she asks. "Because we could just use some random photos from another account to be sure."

"And then I meet him and he thinks he's been catfished?"

"Yeah, you've got a point. Although this is technically still catfishing."

"Touché. Shall we use the ones on my website?"

"And risk him reverse image searching you and finding out exactly who you are?" She shakes her head. "It is very lucky you have me, you know. You are *bad* at this clandestine stuff. We'll need to take some new photos."

"Really?" I ask, but it sounds a little whiney.

"We'll do candid ones, like you don't know the camera is there so you're not just gurning down the lens."

I nod and try to remember that needs must and it's only a few pictures and I'm an adult for God's sake.

"And we need to think of a name for you; he might not know what you look like, but Thea isn't exactly a super common name."

"Becky," I say, without missing a beat. "It's my real name, or at least it was before Uncle Jed started calling me Thea. I changed it legally but kept Becky; well, Rebecca, as a middle name."

"Your uncle named you?"

"It's a long story." I wave my hand as if to say that it's not particularly important or very interesting. I've always been reticent to share details of my background, not because I'm ashamed or embarrassed or even that it brings up traumatic memories. But it sounds so fantastical and invariably people say that I should write a memoir detailing how I was found on the street with my name written on my arm. "You could call it *A Girl Named Becky?* With a question mark!" someone had told me more than once, like they were the only person to think of it. As if I'd want strangers dissecting the minutiae of my life—it makes me shudder just to think about it.

"Do you have a preference for a surname?"

I shrug and look around me for inspiration. The last book I read is still sitting on Jen's desk, despite me telling her it was fantastic and she should give it a go. "Clift?"

"That works."

"Actually, use West. Just in case."

"In case?"

"Well, if there's an investigation, it might look too weird that I'm using an alias. Becky West is just using part of my full name. No one would expect me to call myself Thea Rebecca Persimmon-West on a dating profile!"

"Cool." She types a few lines and then shows me the shell of the profile she's built. "Now all I need to do is break into his account—that might take me an hour or so—but then I can see exactly what search parameters he uses so we can guarantee you come up in his next search. And we need to get those photos sorted, but I think Becky West is looking like a pretty good catch for a widower in Devon."

"How are you going to break into his account?" I ask.

"I just need to guess his password." She says it oh so casually.

I pause for a moment. "Try TAY17, all capitals."

"O...K..." She draws out the word as she types. "It worked!" she spins round to look at me like I'm a genius.

"Edward's personalised number plate."

She makes a face. "Eughhh. Men are so predictable!"

***

The next day, Jen and I head to the beach during our lunch breaks and take a few photos. I try not to look directly at the camera or twist my face like a bulldog and in the end I'm not too horrified by the result. "They'll do, I guess," I tell Jen.

"You know you're actually quite pretty," she replies, apparently innocent to her totally backhanded compliment. I don't hate the way I look; I hate the way I look *in photos*. There's a significant difference.

Back at the office, Jen puts the finishing touches to the profile and then uploads everything. "You are now live, Becky West."

"So what happens now?"

"Now we hunt. Obviously I've made sure your profile is within his parameters, and your preferences would include him. But you've still got to match through the algorithm, I don't want Affinity.com to think you're a bot and delete you."

"OK, then," I say and we spend the next half an hour clicking no to most of the profiles that come up in my search.

"You need to accept a few of them, Thea. Make it look natural."

"Well, maybe Becky is picky."

"*No one* on a dating site is that picky."

Another half an hour passes and I dutifully accept a few profiles, looking for those that are closest to Edward in the hope the algorithm will learn this and send him to me sooner. "Jesus, this is soul destroying," I say, scrolling past the thousandth—or at least it feels like it's been that many—man with salt and pepper hair and a nice smile.

"Now imagine you are doing this for real, to find a half decent man to genuinely date in all this."

"I really don't know how you do it," I say, honestly.

Eventually my patience—I use that term loosely as I am about to scream and sack off this whole endeavour—pays off and up pops Edward Taylor.

"Got you!" Jen says in a sinister tone right in my ear.

"Now what?"

"Now we see if he likes you too."

"How will we know?"

She rolls her eyes. "I swear most grandmothers know more about internet dating than you do."

Edward is evidently not that busy as he matches with Becky within the hour. "Right then," Jen says, cracking her knuckles, "now the real work begins. So you need to make the first move," she tells me, her face expectant.

"What? Like I message him first?"

"Yes."

"What shall I type?"

"I don't know, what's the end game here?" she asks me.

I look around to check no one is listening. "You know what the end game is," I whisper.

"I meant from the dating site. Do you want to meet him? Lull him into a false sense of security and then go all *Fatal Attraction* on him?"

"It needs to look like an accident."

"So you need to get close to him. How fast will he run if he thinks IRL you and Internet you aren't the same person. Plus, you knew Helena; how did she make him fall in love with her?"

Her use of the past tense "knew" stabs me in the heart, but I nod and square my shoulders. And then I start to type a message to my best friend's husband. Helena didn't make Edward fall in love with her, she was just the kind of person you couldn't help but want to be around.

"Are you really going to open with *Hi*?"

"Err...what else would I open with?"

"OK," Jen replies, suggesting it is anything but.

He types back *Hi*.

Jen exhales an exaggerated sigh. "Well, at least he didn't send you a dick pic."

"Eww...that doesn't really—" But I cut myself off when I see the look on her face. "What do you do with them?"

"Block them, of course. But given how much work we've put into the creation of Becky West, you would have been sending him a compliment about it."

I make a face at her. "Oh, does that mean he's typing something else?" I point at the three little pulsating dots.

"Yep." She reads it out loud: " 'You look familiar, have we met?' " She turns to look at me.

I reply, *I think I just have one of those faces* 😊

"Emojis?"

I shrug and wait to see what he replies. *You have a beautiful face.*

Jen makes a face. "I guess Helena didn't marry him for his witty repartee?"

"To be fair, Helena did always say he thought he was funnier than he was. Love is blind and all that."

"Well it certainly made her blind to being married to a psychopath."

***

Edward and I continue to trade not very witty messages over the course of the evening and again the following afternoon. We talk about very little of any substance. And then he invites me out on a proper date.

I know it's a long way to travel, but my family owns a small private members' club and you would be more than welcome to stay in one of the guest rooms.

"Wow, he's a fast mover!" Jen exclaims. "I thought it would take longer for him to bite."

"Do you think I should go?" I ask.

"Like you haven't already packed a case."

The date with Edward is set for Saturday and I'm starting to feel the butterflies beating in my stomach. The plan is starting to come together, starting to feel like a real and tangible thing. I just hope I'm strong enough to pull it off.

"If you're nervous," Jen says, handing me a cup of tea she's just made in the kitchen, "then I could come with you."

"He wants me to stay at The Grange." I make a face.

"I think he's probably hoping he'll stay with you."

"Well obviously that isn't going to happen."

"Tell him that you're going to bring a friend and stay somewhere close by. I mean, that is what you're meant to do when you meet any stranger off the internet, let alone one who you know is a psychotic wife killer."

"I'm trying to lull him into believing I'm just a nice girl who wants to enjoy his company."

"OK. Let me turn this round. If I were planning on driving for four hours to meet a random dude I'd been chatting to online for a few days, and he'd invited me to stay at his 'family's hotel,' would you tell me to go? Or would you tell me there was at least a fifty percent chance I wouldn't make it home alive?"

"I'd tell you to run a mile," I concede.

"Exactly."

Chapter Thirty

On Saturday morning, Jen comes to pick me up in the MX5 again.

"Does Frannie realise the mileage you're putting on her car?" I ask.

"Apparently it was a gift from the boyfriend. They broke up a few days ago and he wants the car back. She practically begged me to drive it long distance just to piss him off."

"Fair enough," I reply.

We fall into a companionable silence as we make our way round the M25, somehow managing to run the gauntlet without hitting a traffic jam. This time Jen has settled on Taylor Swift for our musical accompaniment.

"I thought this might be more someone of your age's thing," she says, without even a hint of irony.

I'm not really into music; I use it to drown out the day-to-day noises around me that grate on my nerves and echo around my brain. You know, like a dripping tap in another room, or the sound of people breathing close by. But I don't process the music, it fades into the background as if it were white noise. Although, I will confess that Taylor Swift is entirely pleasant and curiously catchy. Perhaps I might become a fan.

Jen used her travel agent wizardry to book us into the Fullcroft Manor Hotel, about fifteen miles from The Grange.

"I chose it for their pool area. I mean, just look at it," Jen says, thrusting her phone under my nose. Given I'm driving this leg of the trip I barely glance at it, but she doesn't notice. "I'm going to lounge around and finally read that book you lent me. And then you're going to treat me to the six-course tasting menu in the restaurant while I'm on-call as your relationship consultant."

"Looks like you're getting a taste for the finer things," I joke.

"I could get used to staying in places like this," she says, awe in her voice as we pull up outside the hotel. The original Fullcroft Manor is a ruin, but the remnants have been integrated into the glass frontage of the hotel and the result is incredible. "See why I picked it?" She grins at me and then gets out of the car, standing on tiptoes to get a better view of the rest of the property.

"That old church," and she points to where the bell tower is just visible, "is where the spa is. The nave contains all the treatment rooms and there's a hot tub built into the apse."

"Well it sounds like *you* are going to have a lovely evening," I say.

"You have a hot date," she replies, with a wicked look in her eyes.

"Which I'd better start getting ready for. I don't want to be late."

***

Edward is hovering outside The Grange, looking nervous and uncomfortable as my taxi pulls up.

"I thought you might have changed your mind and decided not to come," he says as he opens my door and offers a hand to help me out.

"Of course not," I say, keeping my voice light and trying not to think about why I'm really here.

"What's your hotel like?" he asks.

"Lovely, thank you."

"A pal of mine runs it, so I took the liberty of arranging for a bottle of Champagne to be delivered to your room later."

"That was very kind, thank you."

"My pleasure."

The evening continues in similarly banal and slightly stilted politeness. Well, it *is* meant to be a first date. We have dinner on the terrace, tucked away in a corner so people don't bother him. "That's the problem with having your name by the front door, everyone thinks they can just come and talk to you when you're in the middle of dinner."

"We could have gone somewhere else," I say.

"I wanted you to see the place," he replies simply.

It doesn't work though, and we've been sitting for barely five minutes before the first interruption.

"Your mother will be ecstatic that you're dating again," an older woman with perfectly styled blond hair tells him with a smile.

"Well," he replies with a hint of shyness, "I don't want to get her hopes up. Perhaps this should be our little secret, Moira?"

"Oh. Of course." She pats him on the shoulder. "Good luck," she says as she walks away, before rushing back to whisper loudly—more than loud enough for him to hear—in my ear, "He's a catch this one." She scurries away and I laugh at Edward's creeping blush.

The next person to approach is a man in his early fifties dressed in a tweed waistcoat with huge pockets and suede patches at the shoulders. He looks as if he's just walked off a hunt. I excuse myself to use the bathroom, but really I'm desperate to avoid small talk. Plus I want to have a little snoop.

Conscious I only have a few minutes before my absence might be noticed, I move quickly through the main members' area, but the place looks like any other posh hotel, if I'm honest. There is very little of *them*—the modern Taylors, I mean

—stamped into the fabric of the building. It looks like it would have done in the 1950s.

I'm disappointed as I return to the table, although I don't know what I thought I'd find.

"Did you get lost?" Edward asks. "You were ages."

"Oh, sorry. I was just side-tracked by some of the artwork inside."

"You like art?" he asks, and we begin another insipid conversation as the main course arrives.

Jen messages me while we are waiting for our desserts. *How is it going.*

OK, I reply back.

You'd better be chattier when you get back to the hotel for the debrief.

After dessert, Edward offers to give me the full tour. "The Grange has been in the family for generations," he tells me, "first as the primary residence, and then my great-grandfather converted it into the members' club and the family moved to a newer property down the road." I follow him through room after room, making appropriate oohs and ahhs, but really I'm scanning for all the little details, things that tell me more about this man who Helena loved so dearly. There is one door left off the main corridor and I walk towards it.

"Oh, not that one. It's…" he trails off. "It was my father's favourite room. Let's go and have a nightcap in the bar instead." He leads me away from the mystery door and I follow him for a few moments.

"Actually, I'm just going to nip to the ladies' room. I'll come and find you," I tell him. As soon as he turns the corner out of sight I jog back to the closed door, praying it isn't locked.

The mahogany door swings open to reveal what must have been a smoking lounge, the air heavy and stale, a selection of leather wingback chairs clustered around small tables. But it's the walls that draw my eye. Covered in portraits, they tell the story of the Taylor family: of patriarchs, and graduations, and marriages, and children, taking over three of the four walls. But then they end, with a picture of Edward on the day he accepted his degree from Bristol University.

Helena had rung me a week before the wedding in a foul mood. "Fucking Geraldine has booked the portrait artist for three days after we get back from the Maldives."

"Sorry, what?"

"It's some stupid tradition apparently. But if he makes me look all sunburnt and bloated I will be livid."

"Surely the whole idea of an artist over a photo is they make you look even better than in real life," I replied. I was in the middle of writing a presentation for a client pitch—the one that would ultimately stop me from making it to the wedding—and I was only half listening.

"You'd better be right," she replied.

And I was right. The artist had done a great job and Helena looked radiant and beautiful. She sent me a photo of the portrait hung alongside Edward's graduation picture.

So where is the picture now? There is just a blank space where it used to hang, a very faint rectangle of discolouration on the wallpaper to show something missing. Had the Taylors scrubbed her from their history, as if she had never existed? That was always Helena's secret fear when she'd decided not to have children. "What if everyone forgets me?" she whispered one night during our Las Vegas trip, a little tipsy on too many Mai Tais.

"No one is going to forget you," I told her.

Now it was time to make good on my promise.

***

Edward and I call it a night after a quick whisky. He kisses my cheek gently before I get into my taxi. "See you soon," he says.

"You'll have to come to Brighton."

"Sounds like a plan," he replies.

Back at the hotel, I find Jen is still wide awake and desperate to comb over every moment of my visit.

"It was fine," I tell her, finally taking off the heels that have been pinching my toes all night.

"Fine? Fine is such a nothing word."

"Which basically describes the evening," I tell her. "We had a drink and a meal and he gave me a tour of The Grange and then I came back here."

"Did you kiss?"

"It was a first date."

"You will have to kiss him eventually, you know."

"Not if I kill him first." I say it with my back turned to her as I reach for a little bottle of water.

"Do you have a plan?"

I turn back round to look at her. "Look, Jen. I think maybe the less you know the better." I pause to sip my water, weighing the words. I need her to be part of this, but I don't want her to feel forced. "You could claim plausible deniability at the moment, say you had no idea what I was planning."

"Why would I need plausible deniability?" she asks, forehead creasing into a frown. "You're not going to get caught."

"But what if it goes wrong? I'm prepared to take the risk. She was my best friend and I *have* to do this. But you can still walk away."

"Or I can help you make sure you get away with it," she says simply.

I breathe a sigh of relief.

"Now spill the plan," she demands.

I take another swig from the bottle. "You're sure?"

"One hundred percent."

"Edward has terrible allergies. Like fatal anaphylaxis if triggered. Helena had to inject him with his EpiPen on their very first holiday together, completely ruined the romantic getaway she had planned."

Jen narrows her eyes in consideration. "But if he's that allergic, he'd have an EpiPen on him at all times, in a pocket or whatever."

"But what if he didn't? Or he couldn't get to it in time?"

"Now that could end in tragedy," Jen says, nodding a few times as if contemplating the veracity of the idea.

"A tragic *accident*," I reply.

Chapter Thirty-One

On Monday night, I invite Jen to mine for the evening so we can brainstorm some ideas. Edward is coming the weekend after this one, so we have about ten days to figure everything out.

She's due at seven p.m., but it's already ten past and I'm getting nervous. What if she's changed her mind? What if she's decided she doesn't want to be part of this? I can feel myself starting to spiral, catastrophising every tiny detail until the whole plan has crumbled into dust.

My phone rings and I snatch it up. It's her. "Sorry, I'm running late, I'll be twenty minutes tops. What's your poison?"

"Sorry?"

She giggles. "Sorry, that was probably a poor choice of words. I'm in Tesco. What would you like to drink?"

She arrives fifteen minutes later and smiles at me as she hands over a bag for life that is crammed with goodies. "Provisions," she declares. "I figured we would need appropriate drinks and snacks."

I take another peek: there's a bottle of that overpriced elderflower cordial I love in there and some big bags of Kettle chips, the lightly salted type which are my favourites.

"Right. C'mon, then. We need to figure this whole thing out," she says and sashays towards the kitchen. I follow her and find her already opening all the cupboards, obviously looking for something. "Glasses?" she asks.

"What type?"

"Ooh...well, aren't we fancy!" She throws me a theatrical wink over her shoulder. "For spritzes, of course!"

"In the island." I point to the large kitchen island where the glassware for cocktails is housed. I might have very little in the way of cooking utensils and appliances and all that stuff, but Uncle Jed made sure he left behind a veritable bar's worth of glassware and mixology paraphernalia. "There are some balloon glasses on the bottom shelf, next to the Martini ones."

"Oh, wow!" she exclaims as she throws the cupboard doors open. "How the other half live. I don't think I've ever met someone with this many different types and sizes."

"My godfather and his cocktail obsession," I tell her.

"Your godfather?"

"He trained me well," I add quickly.

"He certainly did."

"Shall we head into the garden?" I ask her. It's a gorgeous evening.

"Are you mad?" she asks. "Too many people could hear us."

We take our drinks into the living room. To be fair, many of the houses on my street have been converted into tiny little flats, people living right on top of each other. Crammed in. But the reality is that they are so close to one another they're blind, deliberately turning away from the detail to retain their own sense of privacy. No one would see or hear anything.

"So, I did have an idea," Jen tells me as soon as we're settled; her on the sofa and me on the oversized armchair I like to use for reading.

I tuck my legs underneath me and lean forward a little. "I'm all ears."

"Do you remember Hendrick?"

"Hendrick? Like the gin?"

"Exactly! We went on a couple of dates a few months ago. He thought it was ironic to take me to a gin bar on Union Street."

It's called The Gindependant and serves a hundred different gins and very little else. Helena would have loved the place. "OK. So what about Hendrick?"

"So, he's one of *those* types, you know. Skinny jeans, man bun, spends too much time in the gym. Totally hot though, if you can get past how ridiculous he is. Anyway, guess what Hendrick does in his spare time?"

"When he's not drinking overpriced gin, you mean?"

"Yes."

"Erm, does he work for an electric scooter company?"

"No."

"Campaign to save some rare type of sloth?"

"Nope."

"Alright, I give up."

"He keeps bees."

"How do you mean, he keeps bees?"

"Oh, come on, you must have heard of the plight of the bees? How we're ruining all their habitats and so there aren't enough left and we're hanging on an ecological knife-edge?"

Sometimes I wonder if she thinks I'm sixty, not mid-thirties. "Of course I've heard of the plight of the bees."

"So...there's this movement to create more urban bee populations. Some guys in London and New York started out with some hives on the tops of buildings and it's kind of grown from there. Hendrick is leading the charge here in Brighton."

"Right." I still have no idea where this is going. "So he has bees?"

"Millions of them. Well, I think that's hyperbole; he was trying to impress me, after all. But he has a lot." She pulls her phone from her bag. "Look at this."

She passes the phone to me, a YouTube video is playing. It shows a man sitting amidst the pieces of what I assume is a modern urban beehive; he's shirtless, wearing no protective equipment at all, thousands of bees just crawling over him. In the video, he looks down the lens of the camera and smiles lazily. "They only sting you if they feel threatened by you," he whispers.

"I'm thinking I could rekindle our relationship. Get him high, distract him." She gives a little hip wiggle, her distraction plan evidently not particularly intricate. "Then I'll borrow a few. We can Macaulay Culkin him. Edward, I mean."

"The guy from *Home Alone*?"

"Have you never seen *My Girl*? Macaulay Culkin gets stung by hundreds of bees."

"Nope." My foster mother was very much a "books before TV" type and then there wasn't much time for watching films and stuff at boarding school. "What happens to him?"

"He dies."

"Oh."

"Yeah, it was kind of dark."

"How are you going to get the bees to sting him?"

"Um." She crosses her arms over her chest, the irritation rolling off her in waves. "Well...I didn't think of that bit." She exhales with a little huff and I'm reminded of how much younger than me she is.

"I like the originality," I tell her, with a soft smile. "But I just don't think it would work. And there can't be any room for error."

Jen waits a few moments before she breaks into a grin. "You're right. It's ridiculous. I just got carried away. What else is he allergic to?"

I pause for a moment. It feels so callous, so cruel. I remember the panic whenever Helena thought about his allergies, the way she would second-guess everything she cooked, or every gift she bought him. And now here I am planning to use all that insight she gave me in such a calculated way. "Penicillin. Molluscs. Sesame seeds."

"OK. I'll think of something else," Jen says, as if we're discussing which film to watch at the cinema. A shiver runs down my spine.

"Shall we go for a walk?" I ask. "See if some sea air will clear our heads?"

She offers me an almost feline smile. "You sound like my grandad. He was always extolling the virtues of fresh air and exercise."

"A wise man, your grandad," I reply, standing up and going to lock the back door.

We walk along the seafront, the evening sun still warm. I love Brighton, especially at times like this, when the weather is good and the city thrums with life. Jen catches me smiling. "You look happy," she tells me.

"It's finally almost over," I reply. If this goes to plan and I manage to pull off what I've set out to do, will it be enough? Enough to erase the mistakes I made and let me start over. Build a life for myself, a real life instead of one based on lies and stories. A life with a future.

We buy Aperol spritzes in plastic cups filled with ice from a street vendor and head down to the seafront. We're sitting on the steps just by The Doughnut, watching the tourists and sipping our drinks when Jen goes white. Not just a lighter shade of pale. She is white, like a corpse. Like all the blood has been sucked from her by a malevolent force I can't see. Her eyes are locked on a man lounging on the pebble beach in front of the cafe. He's mid-twenties: attractive, well dressed in a preppy kind of way.

He's vaping, leaning back, a cloud curling from his lips to the sky. He looks relaxed, comfortable. Without a care in the world. His head swivels towards us, his mouth forming a lazy smile as he sees us watching him. A small squeak escapes from Jen's clamped mouth. It's the same noise my house mistress's dog used to make when she was trapped inside as Miss Thalis did her inspection rounds to ensure we'd all made our beds properly.

The squeak is quickly followed by a loud noise as her drink slips from her fingers, the contents exploding onto the steps, bright orange liquid spraying our feet. She's still watching the man, her eyes not leaving him for even a second to assess the damage to her Converse and light-wash jeans. I turn back to face him. But he hasn't moved either. His eyes are on Jen's face, the vape paused an inch from his mouth.

I hold my breath as neither of them move. Jen seems so...so...I'm grasping for a word. It's not fear per se that is holding her rigid. It's shock. This is someone who has seen a phantom. Someone from her past she never expected to see again, given form in front of her. Manifested. But if Jen is in shock, the man most certainly isn't. He looks like he's enjoying the effect he is having on her.

He brings the vape the final inch to meet his lips and takes a deep drag. It's almost sensual, the way he draws the cloud deep into his lungs, holding the breath for a few moments before opening his mouth a fraction to allow it to billow from his lips. He winks at Jen, slowly and deliberately.

The wink seems to break the spell that trapped her in place. "I've gotta..." she mumbles under her breath before she turns and runs. Away from the man. Away from me. I run after her, throwing my own drink into a bin as I run past so I'm not sloshing it over my hands as I chase her.

She's fast, weaving in and out of people as she runs towards the Pavilion Gardens, almost getting herself flattened by a bus as she rushes across the road towards the huge dome of the palace. I don't get anywhere close to her until she's in the middle of the little park that divides the palace from the theatre. There's a guy playing a song on a steel drum, the same singular song he plays every evening he's there. But he always has such a look of joy on his face.

"Jen!" I shout and I'm relieved when she pulls to a stop. The blood has certainly returned to her face; in fact she's bright red, sweat running down her forehead from her hairline. She's gasping for air, bending forwards so her elbows are on her upper thighs. I worry for a moment that she's about to vomit. "Jen," I repeat more gently as I reach her.

I can see that she's trying to decide what to tell me about the man. "Did he..." She's still gasping for oxygen.

I shake my head. "No." I'm assuming she wants to know if he followed us, but I'm looking over my shoulder and I can't see any sign of him. "Who was that?"

"No one."

"No one?"

She straightens up and looks at me. "No one." Her voice is firm, or at least as firm as you can be while still struggling to catch your breath after legging it from someone. "No one that matters anyway."

"An ex?" I ask.

"No. Just. Look, he's no one, OK? I don't want to get into it."

I take a step back from the harshness of her words. "OK." I put my hands up. "Noted. I won't ask anything else about him."

She suddenly breaks into a smile. "Thank you," she whispers in my ear as she loops her arm through mine. "Now, can we please go and get a drink to replace the one I dropped?" Her tone is light, as if there's nothing wrong, but every third step I can feel the slight pull on my arm as she steals a glance behind us.

The man on the beach has really freaked her out. I've never seen someone look so stricken, so completely vulnerable in the moment, so prepared to drop everything and just run as fast they can away from the threat.

Chapter Thirty-Two

The next few days pass relatively uneventfully. On Thursday I'm walking to the office, absentmindedly winding through the Laines. The pedestrianised area is quiet at this time in the morning, the shutters still pulled down on the windows of the jewellers and small antiques dealers who call this part of the city home.

I cut down an alleyway and the window displays turn more edible in nature. There's an artisan doughnut place, the dough-nuts as big as bricks, filled with vanilla custard and slathered in salted caramel sauce, a slice of candied bacon laid on top like a jewel. I debate getting some for the office kitchen. But then I spot a new place that must have only opened in the past week or so.

Lucille's. Why does that name ring a bell? I walk over to take a closer look. "Home of the cocktail cupcake." I read the sign under my breath.

That's why I recognise the name. Helena had sent me a photo of her and Ella in a branch in Exeter. She told me she felt so guilty about eating a Margarita-flavoured one, paranoid that she'd set off one of Edward's reactions because it had real tequila in it. But the expression on her face said pleasure more than guilt, Ella's smile reflected in the mirror behind her con-firming that these cupcakes were worth the risk.

On a whim I head into the shop and buy an entire tray of mixed cupcakes: Margarita, Espresso Martini, and Tropical Porn Star flavours. They look divine. And everyone loves cocktails.

I can't wait to see Jen's reaction.

***

"Join me in the kitchen," I whisper to Jen as I walk past her desk, holding the cake box carefully in front of me.

"What have you got there?" she asks, trotting behind me. "Please tell me it's something delicious."

I put the box down and spin it round to face her, lifting the lid with a flourish. "A Lucille's just opened in the Laines. Don't they look amazing?"

"They look good," she says after a moment's pause. "What flavours are they?"

"The ones with coffee beans are Espresso Martini, the passionfruit are Tropical Porn Stars, and the ones with lime slices are Margarita."

Jen stares at them for a few moments, jumping a little as I lean in to whisper in her ear. "I had an idea."

"I'm listening," she says and tips her head closer to mine to guarantee no one else can hear.

"Cocktails." I glance sideways at her.

"I can see that, Thea."

"No. I mean, what if Edward were to accidentally drink a cocktail made with tequila, like a Margarita?"

"Did he tell you he was allergic to tequila?" she asks.

"Does it matter? I can always claim I didn't know. It's only the second time we've met in person. Who would expect me to know everything about him? Just to be on the safe side, I can get something pre-mixed that I wouldn't necessarily know had tequila in it. It's clean and simple."

"And foolproof?" she asks. "I mean, is he definitely so allergic he's guaranteed not to recover?"

"Absolutely. Helena told me that his mother had one of his friends expelled because he snuck a bottle of Patron in after an exeat weekend and Edward had a terrible reaction to it, ended up in hospital for a week. He'd have died without his EpiPen."

"Ouch," Jen says with a theatrical wince. "What a thing to be allergic to, though. So many opportunities for an unfortunate accident." She winks at me and it finally feels like the pieces are falling into place.

***

The next morning, Jen arrives late to the office, looking really rather pleased with herself.

"So. Guess who I met last night?"

I shrug. "No idea."

"Well." Her grin widens. "His name is Jasper. Jasper works in a bar in town, but he considers himself something of an entrepreneur. He's setting up a postal cocktail company." She looks smug.

"A what now?"

"This company that will send you a box of pre-mixed cocktails in a convenient little package that goes through your letter box so you don't even have to be in for the delivery."

"And..."

"Well...how are you meant to know exactly which cocktails have tequila in them?" She sounds the epitome of innocence. "If you had a guest and you were having fun, would you really check the ingredients on the box?"

"I don't get it," I say, my voice tinged with confusion.

Her face drops for a moment. "It's simple." She makes it sound like I'm a little bit slow. "You get a trial box sent to the house, he's about to start sending them out and so all you need to do is sign up for one of the samples. Then you serve it to Edward, entirely devoid of guile at the dangerous contents and their deadly potential. Then bam!" She slaps her hands together.

"So I don't actually have to buy the tequila specifically. It's just part of this free pack?"

"That's the point. It's an accident."

"You are a genius," I tell her, because actually this is pretty clever. "But just be careful with this guy, OK?" I sound like a mum.

"Not too careful. Look at the body on him!" She giggles, but it soon bubbles into a salacious laugh as she shows me a picture of him on her phone.

"Just don't let him fall for you; the last thing we need is some guy moping about and somehow leading everything back to us."

"He thinks my name is Laura Green and that I graduated from Sussex Uni last year with an English degree and now I scratch a living tutoring kids while I work on my first novel."

The lies slipping from her tongue sound so convincing, even though I know who she really is.

Perhaps my plan can work after all?

***

The weekend crawls past. Every moment I spend in the house reminds me of what is going to happen next weekend. I have thought of every possible thing that can go wrong, replayed the scenario over and over, searching for flaws, for the weakness that might cause it all to collapse. I'm driving myself crazy.

I think it's the part with Jasper. Perhaps it just feels too easy, too much like the plan has landed in my lap. Murder isn't meant to be simple. It's meant to be messy and complicated and difficult. That is why so few people try to get away with it.

By Sunday afternoon I feel like I might explode, and so I organise to meet Jen.

We find a little cafe tucked down a side street, away from the main tourist routes and the hordes of students who are starting to return for the autumn semester. I'm jittery, but Jen is perfectly composed. It's as if someone has flicked a switch and activated her inner murder-bot. I almost envy her equanimity.

"I'm nervous about using the cocktails from Jasper," I tell her.

"Why? The plan is flawless. He doesn't know who I am. It's not like anyone would trace some guy I dated a few times to your boyfriend not checking the labels on some free cocktails."

"But what if they did?"

"Oh. What about some kind of poison instead?" She turns to face me, but her eyes are hidden behind the oversized sunglasses she thinks make her look like Jackie O. "We could slip arsenic into his food?" She pulls down the glasses so I can see the look of mock scandal on her face.

"I don't feel you're taking this seriously enough," I tell her.

She takes a deep breath and lets it out slowly. It's the same thing Helena used to do when she was tired of whatever I was trying to engage her in conversation about. "I'm just trying to lighten the mood. Don't be a bitch."

"Sorry. But we have to take this whole thing very seriously." She nods. "And we need to think things through very logically and methodically and make sure there is no chance that this goes wrong, OK?" She nods again. "When someone dies unexpectedly, there'll be an investigation. They'll do an autopsy and determine the cause of death. And then they'll try to figure out how the tequila got into him."

"So what's the issue with the cocktails?" She looks at me perplexed.

"We need to make sure that when they start asking questions, I can claim that I didn't know the cocktails had tequila in them." I take a sip of the gin—or rather it's an alcohol-free substitute, I've been drinking far too much recently—and tonic in front of me, still ice cold, condensation dripping onto the wooden table.

She glances around us, a final check that the coast is clear, and then takes a long drag on the straw served with her Daiquiri. "What if a sample box got sent to everyone on your street? No name on the box, just the address? Perhaps some other affluent areas in Brighton as well; you know, the kind of people who like to waste their money on that kind of shit."

"That could work. But how are you going to make it happen?"

"Remember, he thinks I'm Laura Green, English graduate? Perhaps I have a uni friend who studied marketing and had a *totally brilliant idea*." She affects a Leeds accent for this imaginary friend and then laughs. "Whatever. I'll figure it out. And then I'll hack his system to make sure your house is absolutely on the list."

"What if he catches you?"

She laughs again, louder this time. "You need to have a little more confidence in my abilities." She picks her glasses back up and puts them on, before pushing them up to use them as a hair band. The sea breeze whips tendrils into her face, sticking to her lip-gloss. She looks like a movie star, that casual elegance that comes from a place of absolute surety in the adoration of your audience.

Sometimes I worry that I might have underestimated her.

Chapter Thirty-Three

The next day, we go for a walk along the seafront at lunchtime. "So, here's the plan," she tells me. "Next Sunday—"

"Saturday," I interrupt her.

"You're right. Sorry."

"That's why we're going through this so many times. Carry on," I tell her.

"What time is he arriving?"

"He's with a friend in London on the Friday then coming here for the rest of the weekend. His train gets in at ten a.m."

"Right, so you go and meet him at the station. Then head somewhere for brunch."

"I'll take him to Cafe Coho for pancakes," I say.

"Wherever. Although it's probably best you take him somewhere you've been a few times, you want to look entirely innocent. Then, you guys go home, stopping off at a shop to buy some ice and other stuff you'd use for cocktails."

"Can't I just get them from the supermarket this week?"

"No. The idea is that it all looks spontaneous, like you've decided it's such a nice day and so you're going to have a few drinks in the sunshine. Nothing pre-meditated. No planning and scheming and making sure you have all the right ingredients in place. Besides, you're going to have to ostensibly run out of whatever you start drinking so you have an excuse to open the freebies that will have dropped through the letter box at some point during the week."

"OK."

"Right. So, you get home and you sit in the garden with a drink and you chat. Loudly. So all the neighbours will hear you. Perhaps you're a bit flirty, a bit suggestive?"

"In the garden?"

"The idea is that people witness you having a good time."

"Right."

"And because you're being a bit flirty, you suggest taking a little dip in the hot tub."

"I don't have a hot tub."

"You're going to buy one on Friday. One of those posh inflatable ones that look quite inviting. It means he can't possibly have the EpiPen in his pocket."

"Clever," I say and I mean it.

"So you're in the hot tub and you leave him to pop inside to fix you both another drink. First you find his EpiPen and hide it. Then you serve up a couple of cocktails from the free box that got delivered. Make sure you serve one without tequila in it as well. And get his fingerprints on both glasses, like he might have switched them by accident."

"Then what?"

"When you realise he's drunk the wrong one, you scream and run inside, shouting, 'Shit, where's his pen?' and other stuff. Whatever he brought with him you start rummaging through as if you're looking for it. After a few minutes of searching, you need to ring 999 in a complete panic that your date is having a reaction and you don't know what to do. There will need to be lots of wailing and gnashing of teeth to be convincing. But," she leans closer and puts her hand on my arm, "when you see him, I think you'll be able to react accordingly." She shivers a little.

"Have you seen someone have a reaction like that?" I ask, failing to mask the horror in my voice.

"A girl at school was allergic to orange oil. You know, the oil in the skin? Remember those Christingle candles we used to have to carry?" I nod. "It was the first year she was at our school. I mean, you'd think a nine-year-old would have seen a fucking orange before, but apparently her mum was a bit lax with the whole idea of fruit and veg." She rolls her eyes. "Anyway, a minute or so into the service, we're all carrying the candles down the aisle when suddenly she just collapses. Her whole face was swollen to the point you couldn't recognise her, these huge hives breaking out over the rest of her. She was gasping for breath, making this horrible wheezing sound, writhing on the floor in agony."

"That sounds horrible." The poor girl.

"You're not having second thoughts, are you?" she asks with a slight tilt of her head.

I swallow audibly. Shake my head. Needs must.

***

I don't want you to think badly of me. I know that what I'm planning is wrong. But don't tell me you wouldn't try to seek your revenge?

Helena was the innocent victim of a psychopath who must be stopped. I am haunted by the idea that the last thing she ever felt, the last vestige of human contact, was a hand on the small of her back, pushing her over the edge of the roof.

I cannot make it right. I cannot make it better. And I certainly cannot bring her back. But the architect of her suffering will pay for it. I will make damn sure.

***

There was one part of the plan I had failed to consider and the storm that rolls in on Friday afternoon threatens to derail everything. I fall into an anxious sleep as lightning rips the sky to pieces and the rumble of thunder shakes the foundations of the house.

But somehow Saturday morning is clear and bright. I feel vindicated. I'm not a superstitious person, but it feels as though fate is smiling on me, confirming that this is the right thing to do. Justice will be served.

I walk through the house, doing a final check of the scene, making sure nothing is out of place, nothing that would raise any suspicion at all. I collect up the framed pictures of Helena that are dotted around: the two of us in our school uniform, Helena's mane of blond hair half covering her face, my skinny legs sticking out from my too big skirt; Helena standing by the pool of the Mirage in Vegas, an almost comically large Piña Colada in her hand and a brilliant smile on her sunburnt face; Helena facing away from the camera as she stands on a tiny platform, her arms raised above her head as she prepares to bungee jump into the abyss below.

In the final photo she is sitting on the bench in a beer garden, tears of laughter streaking her face, mouth half open, face tilted up to the sky. I trace the outline of her with my finger, trying to remember her like this. Full of joy, of laughter, of love. She was the very best person I have ever known.

I tuck the photos into a drawer in the kitchen. *This is all for you*, I whisper under my breath as I slide the drawer closed.

I walk up to the station to meet Edward's train. The rising heat causes the pavement to shimmer slightly. Two people enjoying cocktails in the garden is going to be entirely plausible this afternoon.

He's waiting outside the entrance to Marks and Spencer, a bouquet of flowers in his hand that he presents to me with a flourish. My eyes meet his and for a moment I consider backing down and not going through with it. But then I think of that photo in the pub garden, of the life she could have still been enjoying. This isn't about me. It's about Helena.

And for her I *can* do this.

Part Three
Aftermath

KATIE
2022

Chapter Thirty-Four

I'm sitting in a cafe down the road, wondering if she'll go through with it. There's a waitress trying to carry too many cups of coffee: if she makes it without spilling, Thea will definitely do it. A woman with a buggy, her toddler riding the kick board, passes the window: if the lights stay green for her to cross the road, Thea will do it.

This is what Grandad always did. Asked the universe for signs that things would happen one way or the other. He believed in all that stuff, visions and omens and the like. I'm not so sure.

The waitress makes it. The light remains green.

I drain the last of my coffee and head towards Thea's stupidly expensive house.

"Are you absolutely and completely sure you want to go through with this?" I ask her, as I press a little stack of books into her hands. We had agreed I'd pop round before she ... well, we know exactly what she's planning to do to him. My visit is mainly to offer "moral support," and of course to make sure she isn't having second thoughts.

"Yes," she replies, a slight tremble in her voice. Her eyes meet mine; she looks terrified.

"You're sure?" I have to ask a final time, even as I'm willing her to just get the fuck on with the whole thing. Get it over with so we can all move on to the next part of the plan.

"Yes."

"Good luck." I don't even wait for her to close the door before I walk away, not even looking back towards the house. Just a friend dropping off a pile of books. Nothing to see, nothing for anyone to take notice of.

The ambulance arrives an hour later, screeching to a halt in front of the house, siren blazing into the quiet of the street. I'm sitting in a different cafe, this one has a much better view, and so I watch as the green uniformed guy runs towards the house, his huge bag thumping against his legs.

I realise I've been holding my breath. She really did it. There was a part of me that wondered if she would. I mean, to actually kill someone? There are not many people who have the guts to do it, even if it was by cocktail rather than a knife held in her hand or a bullet from a gun. And there's something almost sadistic about turning someone's allergies against them, after they've spent their whole life on high alert of a potential threat.

The other paramedic, the one who had been driving and was therefore a few moments slower than his colleague, gets out and rushes into the house. There's something a little familiar about him, something in the set of his shoulders as he runs. For a moment he reminds me of Johan, the tall blond Norwegian backpacker whose identity Kirk and I "borrowed" once. Well, actually, it was a few times but I wasn't really counting. I've probably just seen this paramedic around. Despite being a city, Brighton often feels much smaller, the same people popping up in your life over and over. It's time I moved on, found somewhere bigger to allow me to melt into the crowds. A few minutes later, he's back to collect the trolley. Another few minutes, and a crowd is starting to form as mums towing kids home from a morning at the beach stop to gawp at what might be happening. A few try to shield their children's eyes as they walk past. Although I imagine he's outside on the patio, or at the very least in the kitchen, certainly out of sight from passing pedestrians.

They wheel him out on the trolley, a huge plastic mask covering his face, one of the paramedics squeezing the attached bag rhythmically to keep the oxygen being forced into his lungs. I wonder if that is for Thea's benefit, so she thinks they are doing something to help him? His throat will be so swollen by now that they'll be finding it almost impossible to force any air into his lungs at all.

Thea hangs back as they load him into the ambulance, tears tracking down her face, hands fluttering from her mouth to her sleeves and back to her mouth again. She looks like the picture-perfect damsel in distress, caught in the midst of the type of crisis you pray will never come to pass. I always knew she was good, but I'm pretty impressed right now.

Edward had an accident. Going to hospital. The text message comes from Thea. She didn't know I was hanging quite so close around the corner, waiting to see what was happening, sipping a cappuccino as I waited for her "date" to die. The message is my cue, my call to action.

What can I do? I reply. After all, isn't that exactly what your best friend would ask?

Can you bring my handbag to the hospital, I left it in the rush? We'd agreed she would leave everything at the house, give me an excuse to go inside and get rid of the EpiPen she stashed before the police came calling. We'd made a bit of a thing last week, standing in the middle of the shared office space, about Thea losing her keys again and why didn't I keep hold of a spare set for her. We're not leaving any base uncovered here.

There's generally an investigation when someone dies suddenly. A couple of police officers will likely visit the house at some point later today, depending on how busy their shift is and what else is competing for their time. I was relieved when Thea suggested today; there's a football match between Brighton and Hove Albion and one of their bitterest rivals at the AMEX Stadium and little chance the match won't end in a riot. All the better to ensure that investigating what appears to be a tragic accident is fairly far down the priority list. There will be an autopsy that will corroborate death by anaphylaxis caused by the consumption of agave. Then, in one of the great idiosyncrasies of the British justice system, there'll be a court appearance so some guy being paid a king's ransom can proclaim the findings to absolutely no one. Because who gives a crap in the long run.

Or at least that's how this needs to go down. I've wasted too much time already, spent far too long making sure that everything is in place, that all the pieces are ready.

It's highly unlikely the police will do anything more than cast a perfunctory eye over the house, the kitchen and garden mainly, perhaps peek into the living room. Especially when they see that the house is obviously lived in by someone with money. The rich are so rarely suspects.

Might someone uncover that Edward was once married to Helena? That Thea and Helena were best friends since school? I mean, Helena died four years ago, and Edward is hardly exciting enough to pique the interest of the national press. His death should glide underneath the radar, his whole existence condemned to obscurity. Remembered only by his mother and a few rugby pals; such a fittingly mediocre end to his rather dull existence.

I let myself into the house, the scent of something I can't place hanging in the air. It's like a hospital but not quite, more like an old people's home. Whatever it is, it smells of death and despair. I move slowly towards the back of the house, not quite sure of exactly what I might find when I reach the kitchen. The smell is even stronger as I move further inside.

Silence wraps itself around me, a peculiar silence like a song was being played at full volume and then has been suddenly stopped. It's eerie and I can't stop myself from glancing behind me, just to check nothing is sneaking up on me in the quiet. An involuntary shiver passes across my shoulders.

He must have died in the kitchen. There are packages strewn all over from the paramedics, all that plastic used to keep the intubation paraphernalia sterile discarded in their hurry to try to save him.

As we'd discussed, the box containing the cocktails has been ripped, as if it was difficult to open, the tear cutting through the list of ingredients in each cocktail. Jasper had picked some more obscure options for the tasting box, not wanting to try to compete with every other similar service. So, there is no Tequila Sunrise or Tequila Sour, or even a Long Island Iced Tea that most people with a rudimentary knowledge of cocktails would know contained tequila. But would you know what was in a Cherry Paloma? Would you know that a Paloma is basically a Margarita but with a citrusy sharp profile instead of the sweet and sour of its mixological cousin? Such an innocent mistake to make. And one that wouldn't have been so catastrophic if only his EpiPen had been somewhere close by.

I head back into the living room. Pulling my cardigan over my hand, I open the secret drawer in the coffee table and extract the EpiPen Thea had stashed earlier. I will wrap it in a few dog poo bags and drop it in the bin at the park. No one will go rummaging for it there. And Thea will be able to tell the police he must not have had one with him.

On the floor lies the remnants of the cocktail, a pinkish-red puddle staining the tiles, shards of glass glinting in the afternoon sun. The oversized ice cubes still haven't fully melted; isn't it amazing how quickly things can change?

How one moment you can be sipping a cocktail from a stupidly overpriced crystal tumbler and marvelling at just how well your life is going and then you're on the floor listening as your new girlfriend fails to find the thing that could save you. Did he know? In that final moment that it was Thea who had killed him? That she had finally taken justice for Helena?

Or at least what she thought was justice?

Chapter Thirty-Five

Frannie is using her MX5, so I call an Uber to take me from the house to the hospital, the black handbag Thea normally totes around with her in my hand. She hasn't confirmed that he didn't make it. But that was the agreement. It looks kind of weird if you text people that your date died within an hour or so. Instead I act normally, as if he's just been taken to hospital but expectant of a full recovery. I even text her to say I'm on my way.

When I get to the hospital, she's waiting just down the road from the A&E entrance, a cigarette in one hand that she keeps dragging on nervously. I've never seen her smoke before, it's certainly not her usual style; she must have bummed one from a passer-by. I feel the familiar itch in the space between my throat and chest, imagine the sensation of the smoke pulling down into my lungs. The hospital's no-smoking policy is not exactly enforced around this area; it's full of other twitchy looking people, pacing up and down as they wait to find out if it is the very worst news they will ever hear.

Thea looks likes shit. Her hair is tangled and there are tracks of mascara staining her cheeks. One sleeve of her cardigan is misshapen where she has been plucking at it. She almost falls into my arms as I move towards her, burying her face into my hair. "They still haven't confirmed it," she whispers into my neck.

That's when I realise. She's not acting. She's terrified. Not that he'll die, of course.

But that somehow he will live.

We sit in silence in the waiting room, the smell of death and decay and stale smoke and burnt coffee all mixing together. We are waiting to hear the results of the scans they have been undertaking. This is what it all comes down to. Thea begged me to stay, imploring me in front of the entire waiting room and so I could hardly refuse. But I don't want to be here. This is all too close, too real. This wasn't the deal.

It's another hour before a man with the confident demeanour of someone important, pops his head around the door. "Um. Ms. West?" he asks.

Thea stands on shaking legs and throws him the most plaintive look I have ever seen. For a moment I feel genuinely sorry for her, before I remember exactly why we are here in the first place. "I'm Ms. West." Her voice breaks as she speaks.

The doctor allows a small smile that doesn't meet his eyes. "Could you come with me, please?" he asks gently. It's not going to be good news. I can barely contain my own smile, but I force it down, decorum must be maintained, for now. "Shall I..." I start to ask as I stand to join her.

"Stay," Thea tells me. "I already have only a tenuous link to him."

She has a point. At some point someone at the hospital might look a little more closely and realise that being on a second date doesn't really qualify you as next of kin, even if it was her house.

I wait another hour. Someone opens an internal door and the smells from the hospital kitchen begin to waft into the waiting area. Cabbage and burnt sausages seem to be today's offering. My stomach roils in protest. God, I'm hungry. There's a vending machine in the hallway; we passed it as we came in. How bad would it look for me to eat a packet of Mini Cheddars while my friend finds out the fate of the guy she thought might have boyfriend potential? I'm still debating when Thea appears at the door. If it's possible, she looks worse than she did when I arrived at the hospital. She looks like she's lost about a stone, her face lined and grey.

I don't say a word as I put my arm around her shoulders and lead her out of the hospital, away from the smell of cabbage and pour her into a taxi. No expenses spared for this journey, now is not the time to scrimp by ordering an Uber. We don't speak as the taxi takes us back to the house. The taxi driver is obviously not a rookie; he has taken people home from the hospital before and knows not to ask questions or attempt idle chit-chat. I wonder if he will go home tonight and hug his wife, thank the stars that she is alive and well and a complete contrast to the shell of a woman he drove home during his shift?

Once we are inside the house, she leads me into the living room and puts the TV on, the volume quiet. "He's dead," she says eventually, wiping her hands over her face. She grins and in an instant the pale and drawn woman is transformed back to her usual self. "Fuck!" she exclaims, dancing a little jig. "We did it!" She whirls around a few times, in the way that a four-year-old might to make their dress swirl out at a party.

I stride over to the bay window and pull the curtains across abruptly. I mean, Jesus, what if someone were to walk past and see her prancing about? "Thea!" I say, in my best impression of an old school governess.

She stops twirling immediately and looks at me, almost falling off balance. "Yes?"

"You need to get a grip." She looks momentarily surprised, but then again I've never spoken to her like this before. Things might be about to change. After all, I'm her ticket out of a life sentence for murder. She really needs to understand just how fucking serious this situation is.

It might have been all fun and games before, when we were just scheming and plotting and we could laugh it off and pretend like we were always joking. You might have thought I was being a bit blasé before. But it was all about maintaining that option of plausible deniability, as Thea was prone to saying all the time. My perfect alibi if it turned out she was playing me all along. "Of course I was joking, ha ha ha!"

But she was serious. We killed a man and no one can ever suspect us of that. "Sit," I command and she does, the twirling four-year-old replaced with a slightly petulant tween who doesn't quite understand yet why they are in trouble.

"Sorry. It's just..." She spreads her hands across her thighs, her fingers tangling into the fabric of her trousers. When she speaks, her voice is breathless, her speech fast, "We did it, Jen!" Two bright eyes shine up at me. God, her enthusiasm is almost infectious, I want to sing and dance and get drunk on expensive Champagne. But someone has to take responsibility right now and I guess it's going to have to be me. It feels like the roles have reversed. I can't say I don't prefer it this way.

"Look, Thea. I know you're excited. I know you've been planning your revenge on that bastard for weeks and you want to celebrate. But you need to think about the longer term. It's not worth it to have killed him if you are the one who ends up in prison, OK?"

She nods at me. "Sorry."

I have to stop myself from softening towards her, her contrition is so ridiculous but kind of adorable at the same time. There is just too much at stake and so I put on a strict voice to say, "There will be time, later, when this is all done and dusted to celebrate. But first, we need to make sure no one suspects a thing."

"OK." She takes a deep breath. "So what's next?"

"When the police arrive they need to see a woman who thought she was inviting an eligible bachelor to her house for the weekend and it has collapsed into a nightmare."

"OK," she says and nods as if she's psyching herself up for the next stage. "We've got this."

At least I'll be here to make sure she doesn't do anything stupid. Like confess to murder. Or implicate me in her plot.

Twenty minutes later, Thea's phone rings; it's a withheld number. "Hello?" she answers, infecting a sense of shock into her tone. Once again, she surprises me with her acting. There's a pause as she listens to the person on the other end of the call. "Yes, of course. I understand." Another pause. "First thing? No, no, that's fine. I'm not going anywhere." Another pause. "I . . . I . . . I can't even imagine going in there."

She ends the call and then double-checks the screen, I'm assuming to make sure it's fully disconnected. "The police can't come until the morning. They've said not to touch the kitchen."

Chapter Thirty-Six

I stay over in the spare room, just like any concerned friend would do.

She looks like a complete wreck the next morning when she finally wakes up and drags herself downstairs.

"Are you OK?" I ask her gently.

Her stare is haunting. "What we did..." she starts saying and then her voice fizzles out.

"Thea?" I say, moving towards her. She flinches away from me. "Thea!" Harder this time. She takes a full step backwards, almost tripping in her haste to get herself away from my touch. "Thea!" This final time is loud, but her name is almost drowned out by the crack of my hand across her face.

She lets out a strangled noise, her hand flying to the reddening mark on her skin. "You...you..." she shakes her head. "You fucking slapped me!"

I sigh with relief. "I thought you were freaking out." I shrug. I'm not going to apologise.

"I don't know what's wrong with me. I feel like I'm under one of those weighted blankets, but also floating just off the ground. It's weird. Difficult to explain."

"You need to get yourself together," I tell her. "What time are the police coming?"

"Oh. They rang a few minutes ago."

Weird, I didn't hear her phone. "And?"

"They said they would come around lunchtime."

"OK. Look, I'm going to pop home for a bit, have a shower and get changed. Will you be alright on your own for a few hours?"

She nods slowly and I see her settled on the sofa, some banal TV on in the background. She'll be OK for a bit and I need to get out of here before I start going crazy myself. Just so long as I'm back before the police arrive; I'm going to need to keep an eye on what she might tell them.

I head home, shower and get changed. Then I decide to treat myself to a little something, just to remind myself of how close I am to success. There is a place in Brighton that sells ludicrously expensive gelato. Not ice cream, but proper Italian gelato. In the height of the summer the queue goes out of the door, stretching down the narrow alley in which the shop is located. A little tub, with two small scoops inside is over five pounds. Last year my earnings—once you adjust for the actual hours I work, the late nights and weekends, all the periphery expenses for my endeavours—were approximately equivalent to four pounds fifty an hour. The idea that one ice cream would take me longer than an hour to earn means I have never been here before. As a kid, my grandfather taught me his "theory of economic relativity." He would say it in a deep and theatrical voice, like he was a mad scientist announcing his latest invention. But it was actually quite simple and really kind of clever.

"If it takes you longer to earn the money to afford it than it would take to enjoy it, it probably isn't worth it," he would say, as I sat at his feet with my brother and my cousins. "So, how quickly can you eat a bag of sweets?" he asked, pulling out a plain white paper bag from the local sweet shop from his pocket.

"Gimme!" my youngest cousin had cried, pudgy baby hands reaching for the bag. She was only two so I don't think she cared at all about the lesson.

My grandfather laughed and gave her a squishy pink sweet in the shape of a shrimp. Then he looked at me. "How long would it take you to eat these?"

"Ten minutes." It was an honest answer.

"So, let's say that you can earn six pounds per hour. How much should be the most you pay for a bag of sweets you would eat in ten minutes?"

"One pound."

"Which is a real shame, because these sweets cost one pound fifty." He shrugged and put the bag back in his pocket.

"But what if I made them last longer than ten minutes?" my brother piped up from the floor.

"How much longer?" Grandad's hand was resting just above his pocket.

"Fifteen minutes." My brother was smug at his mathematic prowess. It was embarrassing, he was almost ten and this was baby stuff.

"Very good. In that case you can—"

"What if I earned more?" I'd interrupted. I wanted the shrimps and I knew full well that my brother would only share them if forced to.

"How much more?"

"I know you want me to say nine pound an hour. But that's chump money. I'm going to be so rich I can eat the most expensive sweets in the whole world as quickly as I like."

"And that is the kind of attitude that gets you far, my sweetheart." Grandad had handed me the entire bag of sweets. I hoarded my prize, eating the little pink shrimps until my stomach hurt. But even then I didn't share them.

It might have taken me almost twenty years since then, but finally I am on the cusp—the real cusp this time—of being not just well off, but seriously fucking wealthy. Posh gelato wealthy. Six quid for five minutes of pleasure wealthy.

I walk through the Pavilion Gardens, minding my own business, trying to find a nice enough patch of grass to sit down for a few minutes and enjoy the gelato that is already beginning to melt in its little paper cup. Up ahead is a group of guys lolling on the grass, one of them quite blatantly smoking weed. They are probably eighteen or nineteen, most likely students. Next to them sit two rather dumb-looking girls in skirts that are too short, who are constantly flicking their hair towards them like some parody of *Legally Blonde*.

I see a flash of dark hair and turn towards it almost on instinct, catching just the profile of his face as he cuts across the edge of the park and ducks out of sight. Dressed in a pair of jeans that are a little too tight for a man of his age and a plain white T-shirt, I swear he looks exactly like the profile photo on Affinity.com.

I stand up to try to get another look at him, but he's already gone. It can't possibly have been him.

Edward is dead.

My phone ringing drags me back to the present. It's Thea. What the hell now?

"Hey," I say, trying to keep the frustration from my voice.

"They came early."

"Who came early?" But before the words are even out of my mouth I know exactly who. The police. Fuck! Which version of Thea did they find when they got there? I start walking, quickly picking up the pace, almost jogging in the direction of her house. Are they still there?

"The police," she confirms.

"And?"

"They looked in the kitchen and took some photos and asked me questions. So many questions."

"Have they gone?"

"They said they would be in touch. If they needed anything more."

"But are they still there?" I sound half strangled as I try to run and talk at the same time. Is it too late? Too late for me to get there and salvage the situation?

"No. They're gone." Shit! I stop suddenly; there's no point in running anymore and my ankle is already throbbing. "They told me I can clear up the...you know...in the kitchen. And that they were terribly sorry about my ordeal. They gave me the details of a group who provide support when you witness someone passing, it's really aimed at the witnesses of accident victims."

"Did they use that term?"

"Which term?"

"Accident victim." Is she really this slow? I thought she was clever; or at least she always proclaimed herself to be.

"Yes."

I don't even say goodbye, I just end the call. I need to sit down, the relief washing through me making me feel dizzy. The police think it was an accident. Unless there's something in the autopsy that suggests foul play, we are clear.

I get back to her house to find Thea finishing mopping the kitchen floor. I don't think I could have timed that better, I wasn't really looking forward to spending time in that room with its medical stench and the oppressive blanket of death. It's so easy to think we did nothing at all when we're celebrating in the living room, but in here it all comes crashing back to reality.

"Do you think he suffered?" Thea asks, leaning against the mop and staring at the patch of kitchen floor she's been scrubbing.

"I didn't see him." I'm trying not to think about his final moments of consciousness as he gasped for air right here in this very spot.

"The doctor said it would have been quick, that he was already brain dead when the paramedics arrived. He wouldn't have even realised they were trying to save him."

"That's good," I say, without conviction. I really don't want to get drawn into a long conversation about the reality of what we did.

"Did he really deserve it?" she asks, crossing to the kitchen table and picking up her iPad where she's already logged into Affinity.com, his profile on the screen.

"He killed your best friend." I keep my tone even.

"I can't see murder in his eyes. Look at him." She turns the iPad round to show me. He's wearing jeans and a white T-shirt. Exactly the same outfit as the man I saw in the park.

But that wasn't real. The world closes around me. *It wasn't real.*

"Jen? Jen?" Her panic breaks through the black. She's standing in front of me, her empty hand flapping in my face, the other still holding her iPad. "Jen? What happened?"

"I'm OK." I manage to say, eventually. *It wasn't real. He's dead. You just imagined him. You're safe. It'll be over soon.*

***

My grandad was a grifter, a chancer, someone who could needle his way into your life and turn it upside down. People called him a scam artist. And he was. An artist that is. There was a beautiful symmetry to his cons. I loved him. He taught me pretty much everything I know.

You know, I've just realised that I talk about him in the past tense. As if he's dead. Which he's not. Even though he always used to tell me that prison was a worse fate than death. "Go out in a blaze of glory," he would say to me when I was still a teenager. "Never get caught."

I can almost hear Grandad's words on the wind as I walk along the seafront. I know I should have stayed with Thea, but she kept talking about Edward and then the final straw was her knocking over that bottle of his aftershave he had left in the downstairs toilet. The scent of pine and spice pervaded every inch of the house, that rich cloying smell forcing its way into my nose, so strong I could taste it. I had to get out of there.

Scent is one of the most powerful memory recoverers, far better than an image or even a piece of music. The right scent can transport you to another place and time entirely, allowing you to remember even the tiniest of details. Grandad used aftershave to keep track of his cons. A different one for each of his "lady friends." The best way to make sure he remembered who he needed to be on that day.

I was thirteen when he bought me one of those Impulse body-sprays, a sickly floral monstrosity that I hated. At least it faded fast. For my fourteenth birthday he upgraded from body-spray to actual perfume. God, I felt grown up, swanning around the house. leaving a trail of Juicy Couture in my wake.

When I became Jen, I chose *Invisible* by Juliette Has A Gun. That name alone was just genius. But it smells great too: subtle, modern, crisp like fresh cotton. Perfect for a young woman who runs her own web-based company, who is working hard to build a future while still up for having a laugh.

Someone who you would never suspect.

Chapter Thirty-Seven

The lights and noise of the Pier clatter around me, making me wince. He's here. I can feel him. Smell the pine and spice of his aftershave. But I can't catch him. Just as I turn around one of the slot machines to get to him, he's already five steps ahead. Always just out of reach. Able to weave effortlessly through the crowds of faceless revellers so I can't get to him.

I jolt awake, the sheets tangled around me. It was nothing. Just a dream. But his scent lingers on, I can smell it here. So strong it's as if he's in the room with me. In my bedroom. In the little house share that was the only way I could afford to live in Brighton. I hate sharing with these up-their-arses, so-called young professionals who spend half their salary to commute up to London as there are so few jobs in Brighton itself.

Footsteps outside my door make me jump from the bed and yank it open. But it's just my housemate Frannie, shuffling towards the bathroom in the fluffy slippers she thinks are ironic. We're not friends exactly; I mean, if she's home in the evenings, she'll join me for a glass of wine and a cigarette in the tiny garden, and she did lend me her car a few times, but I don't go out with her and her mates or anything.

"Can you smell that?" I ask.

"Smell what?" she replies, narrowing her eyes as she looks at me properly. "Are you OK, Jen?" She's concerned, the syrupy sweetness of her worry irritates me. *Of course I'm not fucking OK!*

"Like a guy's aftershave." I try to be nonchalant.

"Do you have someone in there?" I think she has misplaced my nonchalance for guilt, my dishevelled state for a woman up all night having fun, not nightmares of trying to catch up with a dead man. "Because, you know, we need to respect each other." Her face wrinkles with a mix of disapproval and disappointment. "We need to tell each other in advance if we are bringing a guy back. It's only fair."

"I'm alone." The question, and the implication that I would try to hide it, really pisses me off. "What about Emily?"

"She wouldn't bring someone back without saying." Such conviction about our third housemate's morals. How sweet.

I push past Frannie and take the few steps to Emily's door, rapping my knuckles against it. The smell is even stronger here. "Emily!" There is no answer. "Emily!" I'm louder this time, the rapping on the door more forceful. "Do you have a guy in there, Emily?"

"Calm down, Jen, Jesus!" Frannie says behind me.

But I need to know if Emily has someone in there. If that is the source of the scent cloying in my nostrils. Making me think of him. "Emily!" It comes out as a strangled scream and for a moment it forces me to take a step back.

The door flies open. "What! For fuck's sake! I was asleep!"

I push past her, breathing frantically as I search for the origin of the smell. But Emily's room smells likes vanilla and freshly washed laundry. There is no one else in her bed. I turn on my heels to find two furious faces staring at me.

"You need to get a fucking grip, Jen," Frannie says.

"Sorry," I say quietly, willing the tears to stay hidden until I can make it back to my room. I don't want to fall apart in front of anyone, let alone these self-righteous women. I push past them and slam the door of my room behind me.

***

But the scent is too strong and so in the end I throw on some jeans and a hoodie. A walk will do me good. Fresh air will clear my head. I just need to get out of here for a while. I wait by my door, until I'm sure both Frannie and Emily are back inside their own rooms and creep out carefully, determined not to draw their attention. I'll have to apologise later, barging into someone's room is on the list of "worst things to do in a house share." Along with using the last roll of toilet paper, or the last tea bag, taking too long in the shower, cooking anything too smelly like microwaved haddock, leaving your laundry in the machine for longer than a half-hour after the cycle finishes, using someone else's shampoo. The list is fucking endless. I cannot wait to be able to afford to move out and live on my own. To not have to tiptoe around strangers. Grandad would be horrified if he saw where I live. But it's almost done now.

The house is only about a ten-minute walk from the train station, but there is a hill of almost epic proportions to struggle up. I hadn't noticed just how steep it was when I came to look at the house, but I guess at least it helps keep me fit. At the station, I treat myself to a takeaway coffee and a flaky, hot sausage roll. They've baked the ketchup into it so it's easier to eat one-handed. A genius solution, but it does burn my tongue. Thus fuelled, I take the main road down to the seafront.

It's still early, not even nine a.m. on a Saturday, but already the streets are bursting into life, a stream of day trippers already making their way down to the beach. I allow myself to be swept along by them. For so many months I practically hid away, going to work and then home again, waiting for things to get better. Freedom is close.

I'm passing the large bay window of a pub when the sound of a fist smashing against it causes me to stop so abruptly a group of teenagers crash into me, almost sending me flying.

"Watch it!" one of them snarls, but as I turn round and he sees my face, his anger turns to a lewd sneer. "Unless you want me to slam into you again, darling." His hand grazes his crotch as he thrusts it slightly towards me.

"Fuck off, dickhead," I tell him, hardening my stare.

"Oooh!" all his friends exclaim and pull him away and down towards the seafront.

As I turn back to the window, I can see him standing there inside the pub, watching the people walking past. Just like in his profile picture, Edward is wearing a plain white T-shirt and jeans. He waves and then his face breaks into a wide grin. He is impossible. He cannot be there and he certainly can't have made the noise that caused me to stop. Ghosts can't make noise.

The pub is closed, it's still far too early for it to be open. I try the door anyway, my fear rising; he cannot be real, yet he is standing there, still waving, watching me trying to pull open the locked door.

"Can you see him?" I grab the arm of a passer-by, pointing furiously at the window. "Please, tell me you can see him!" The stranger pulls their arm away from me and scuttles off. I pound the glass, as if I'm trying to break through it to get to him. My eyes dart around the floor, looking for a brick or something else that might smash the window, but when I look up, the window is empty. He's gone.

For a moment I stand stock-still, people pushing into me, jolting me, so I put my hand out to steady myself. There's an alleyway down the side of the pub and I turn into it, ignoring the stench of rotting vegetables and the sour smell of stale beer, blind to the huge seagull sitting on top of the bins until I almost run into it. But even then, I don't stop, rushing forwards, further down the narrowing alley. Ahead of me there's an arch of light, the pub must back onto a courtyard of some sort. As I emerge once more into the glare of the sun, I see a movement in the window of the pub's backroom. But then I blink and it's gone again.

There is no one there.

Chapter Thirty-Eight

Emily and Frannie are waiting for me when I get home later that day. There is a carrot cake—my favourite—and a bottle of Prosecco chilling in the fancy ice bucket someone bought Frannie when she graduated, which is engraved with her name and the symbol of her university. The Surrey stag is so badly rendered it's almost farcical. I know she has dug it out to cheer me up.

"We're worried about you," Emily says as she pours me a drink and motions at Frannie to cut a slice of cake.

"I'm sorry about earlier," I say and I realise I genuinely mean it. I might be a bitch sometimes, but these two girls haven't been the worst housemates and I think, in their own funny way, they do care about me. It's a strange feeling.

"Pfft," Frannie says, waving her hand in the air as if it was nothing. "Just promise me you're OK. Or talk to us. A problem shared is a problem halved and all that jazz."

"I'm OK."

"Is it that guy?" Emily asks, patting the sofa cushions to encourage me to sit instead of the awkward hovering I'm doing. "Your friend's boyfriend?"

I'm silent, keeping my focus on the cake.

"It must be so awful." Frannie wraps her cardigan closer around herself. "I mean, you like her, don't you? And then to watch her lose someone like that." She shivers despite the warmth of the day and the extra layer she's wearing. "Really makes you think about how short life is."

Surrounded by these girls and their concern and a glass of wine and a huge slab of cake, I start to believe that the apparitions are just the normal response to a stressful situation. It's easy to pretend I had no part in any of this. That I'm just another victim in this whole sorry endeavour.

My phone rings, a number I don't recognise. "Hello?"

For a moment there is silence on the other end and I brace myself that somehow it is him. Edward. Calling me from beyond the grave to tell me all the visions of him have been real. But then the caller speaks and I'm not sure if it's worse than I imagined. "Secrets and lies ruin lives, babe." Just that single sentence and then it clicks off, the line going dead.

Kirk's voice. I would recognise it anywhere. Especially the way he says "babe," somehow making my skin crawl and my heart beat faster at the same time.

I dial the number back, but it just rings and rings.

"Who was it?" asks Emily, motioning to see if I want a top-up.

I nod dumbly to the wine offer. "No one," I reply and down the wine in a long gulp. I want the peaceful oblivion. Kirk coming back is literally the last thing I need right now. He was meant to be out of my life forever; the bastard fucked off and I'm finally clawing my way out of the mess he left me in.

"You'd tell us if there was something wrong, wouldn't you, Jen?" Emily sounds so genuinely concerned. It's been so long since someone really seemed to care. For a moment I wonder what would happen if I told them the truth. If they knew I wasn't really Jen Alderson: social media guru and web designer. If they knew what I'd done. And not just this scheme with Thea and Edward. There have been so many others.

I'd been seven the first time. I remember the gentle knock on my door and his face appearing around the frame. "Are you awake?" he whispered, careful not to wake up the rest of the house.

"Yes." My fingers crossed under the duvet in the hope that maybe this was finally it.

"Do you want to come on an adventure?" You have never seen a little girl leap out of bed so quickly.

I don't remember all the details, but there are some parts of that night that are so indelibly inked into my memory they may as well have happened yesterday.

He brushed my hair out and fixed it into two slightly lop-sided pigtails.

"Do it properly, Grandad," I giggled, as I looked at myself in the mirror. My mum was just one of the seven daughters he'd had and so he knew exactly how to do perfectly neat hair.

"It has to be believable, Munchkin," he replied. "Most gran-dads would be useless at this kind of thing. Now, where is that dress you wore to the Jacobs' party last summer? The pink one with butterflies round the bottom."

I wrinkled my nose. "It's too small now, Grandad."

But he was already at the wardrobe, pulling it out. I stepped into it and he just about managed to zip it up at the back. It was far too short and the sleeves stuck out at a strange angle. "Is it too tight? Can you still breathe?"

I nodded. It was digging uncomfortably into my ribs, but the look of pride on his face was worth it. I always wanted to make Grandad proud.

"Perfect! Let's go, Princess."

He always had a hundred pet names for me. Munchkin. Princess. Darling Girl. He never used my real name though. Too easy to slip up and give up the con. I didn't care, back then. I *wanted* to be his Best Girl or Special One, I thought it was because I was his favourite. And I think I was, in a way. Because who can resist a pretty seven-year-old in a dress a size too small, tears suspended on her long lashes?

We made over a hundred pounds that night: the old man and the frightened girl at the train station, trying to get home, but without enough money for the fare. I knew it was preying on the kindness of strangers, but it showed me just how gullible people really are. We stopped at McDonald's on the way home and Grandad bought me a chicken nugget Happy Meal, with an apple pie for dessert. It was the best thing I had ever eaten.

Sometimes the cons lasted longer than a day; one even went on for well over a year. Carole was a widow who lived in the next city. Grandad had found her on a dating site for pensioners, which I remember finding hilariously funny at the time. I played his granddaughter, which I was, so it wasn't exactly difficult acting per se. But he used a new name and said I needed one too. Just to be careful. So I became Emmeline. "Just remember to listen out for your name, Peaches, OK?" He'd been nervous that first time he took me to meet Carole.

She was completely charmed by the earnest Emmeline, with her immaculate French plaits, dress almost starched in its perfection, carrying a little doll. Emmeline sat quietly and only spoke when spoken to first. She nibbled, daintily, on a biscuit so she didn't drop any crumbs and even offered to help do the dishes after lunch.

"You're good at this, Apples," he said as we drove home. "How did you know to act like that?" There was pride in his voice and a warm glow had spread through me.

"I thought that would be the kind of granddaughter she'd want." I shrugged.

"Is that what you think I'm doing? Courting her so I can marry her?"

I giggled. "Durr! Of course not, but you want *her* to think that's what you want. So, I thought I'd give her the dream granddaughter experience. Make her want you more."

"You're a good girl."

That time we'd stopped at KFC on the way home. Carole's cooking, although I'd obviously said it was delicious at the time, was shit.

I kind of liked being Emmeline for a while, and Carole invited me over a number of times. I even remember a long weekend in Weymouth or somewhere, staying in one of those static caravan thingies, Grandad and Carole letting me eat as many ice creams as I wanted. That holiday was when Grandad asked Carole to marry him. There were tears. Of joy at that time. A month later, when Grandad had racked up fifteen grand of credit card debt in her name, taken the ten thousand from her savings account and filled his friend's van with all her valuable artwork and knick-knacks, her tears were probably less joyful.

"It's easy to make someone think they have fallen in love with you, Angelface," he told me at a service station on the way back to my mum's. "Just make sure you're not the mark, OK. You need to be in control. Don't trust anyone." He leant over to dip his chip in my ketchup and I swiped at his hand.

"Except family, of course," I said.

"Oh, Angel," he replied sadly, elongating the "Oh." Then suddenly he grabbed the last handful of my chips and stuffed them all into his mouth. "Don't trust *anyone*. Especially family." His voice turned more serious. "If I would steal your last chips, just imagine what that brother of yours would steal if you had it."

"I don't understand." I was only a baby; maybe eight, no older than nine.

"You will one day." He refused to elaborate further.

I was fifteen when Grandad and I "convinced" the leader of my youth group that it would be better all round if he just wrote me a cheque for a couple of thousand pounds and I "forgot" that he'd been trying to chat me up on some dating site. In his defence, I'd used a fake picture and my profile said I was twenty-five, but he still paid up. Grandad and I split it fifty-fifty. I had big plans for the money. I wanted to use it to pay for a school trip to France the following year. My brother, my own flesh and blood brother who I'd grown up with and admired as if he were a god, told me I had to give him half as "protection money."

"Protection against what?" I sneered, hands on my hips as I tried to stare him down.

"Not what. Who."

"OK. Protection against who?"

"Chris. Petey. Jamie." He shrugged as he carried on listing his acquaintances—I couldn't call them friends, they were guys he knew from the streets where they ran significantly less sophisticated cons than Grandad and I did—until I interrupted him, my bravado diminishing with each name.

"You wouldn't..." I almost whispered.

"That a risk you want to take? *Cherub-Pie.*" He used Grandad's current pet name as if it were something shameful. Something wrong. I wanted to punch him square in the face. But he was over a foot taller and close to fifty kilos heavier, the hours and hours he spent in the gym had inflated his eighteen-year-old frame to an almost comical size. But I wasn't laughing then.

I paid him five hundred quid.

A few months later, Grandad and I pulled a similar scam. Again, my brother demanded his fifty percent. "Well, *Mon Cherie*, it isn't like you can run away from them, is it?" he jeered. "Not after your nasty accident." The pain in my ankle still flared occasionally, despite the three years which had passed since the break.

A few days later my brother got in a fight in a bar and someone thrust a broken bottle into his neck. It took him less than two minutes to die. I swore to Grandad that I had nothing to do with it. But it's amazing what Tony agreed to do for two grand and a quick grope round the back of the pub. There were rumours of course and I watched as people began to cross the road to avoid me. Being the psycho pariah suited me rather well, thank you very much.

But here in Brighton, with these lovely—if slightly posh and highly strung—girls stroking my arm and checking on my well-being, I don't want to be the pariah. I accept another slice of carrot cake and sink back against the cushions of the sofa, closing my eyes for a few moments. I might think it would be lovely to be more like them, but in a few weeks I am going to be exceptionally rich and able to finally leave all of this behind.

Chapter Thirty-Nine

The bus leaves from outside the Pavilion and takes just twenty-five minutes on a good day. There are at least five other visitors on the bus, I can spot them a mile off even though I only properly know Jimmy and his wife. We don't acknowledge each other, not on the journey into Lewes, no one wants the confirmation of why we are heading out of the city, winding our way towards the smaller town to the north. Away from the seafront and the breeze that has been helping to cool us, the temperature continues to rise. Why the hell a bus can't have functioning air conditioning I'll never understand. It's 2022 for Christ's sake.

Jimmy and Daria get off at the same stop, and my assessment of the other passengers proves to be correct. Everyone else left on the bus swivels their heads to watch the building as they continue their journey, although you can barely see any of it from the road; the high wall sees to that. Two women, dressed in their finest clothes, makeup impeccably applied, exchange shy smiles with each other. Their husbands or boyfriends are obviously new and this is one of their first visits. You can track the passage of time of a sentence by the amount of effort the other halves make on visiting day, waning as the months tick by.

"You alright, sweetheart?" Jimmy asks, his weathered face creased in concern. "Keeping well?"

"Hanging in there," I reply.

"Good, good. Your grandaddy will be pleased." He gently pats my shoulder with one oversized hand.

"We'd better get to it." Daria starts to steer Jimmy towards the gates. She rolls her eyes at me, we both know that if you let Jimmy get started he will never stop chatting. And visiting hours are preciously scarce and can't be squandered by small talk.

HMP Lewes was built back in 1853 and has housed some pretty awful people over the years. But now it is categorised as a Cat B facility; a proper prison but not home to high-risk prisoners; murderers need not apply to Lewes. In a way it's kind of amusing to think that I'm visiting the man who taught me everything and then forgot the most simple thing. Don't get caught. That is the only lesson you really need. But in the end Grandad did get caught. Even if all they could charge him with was extortion. If only they knew the real extent of his activities!

The visiting room is just like the kind you see in English soap operas and cosy crime series: a collection of metal-topped tables with those plastic chairs they use in schools. The men dressed in grey T-shirts or sweatshirts, hands held across the tables, whispered conversations as inmates and visitors huddle as close as they are allowed to extract the maximum amount of privacy from the set-up. Not that anyone cares what the person at the next table is saying. No one gives a shit about how the neighbours are doing, that Aunt Lydia has a new toy boy, that the car needs an MOT and there isn't enough money in the account to pay for it.

HMP Lewes allows inmates of my grandad's class to have visitors every week and there are options for weekdays or weekends. I try to come every week, alternating the days so that Thea thinks I'm just taking my poor sick mother to the hospital. She even gave me the money to take a taxi up here a few times. Idiot.

Over the past few years, I've got to know some of the guards, learnt which ones are likely to smile at the pretty dedicated granddaughter who diligently visits her grandad so regularly. These are the ones who tend to leave us alone, who don't worry about how close I huddle into him. Because while no one gives a shit about the neighbours, or Aunt Lydia, they might care about the details of my little plot to get rid of Edward. And I don't want to cause a scandal, do I?

At the gates I reach into my bag to bring out the worn and battered leather wallet the granddaughter of a convicted con artist might carry. The DVLA think I'm terribly careless with my possessions, I've had to replace my driving licence five times in the seven years I've had one. Each time I change my hair and get new glasses, or take to drawing on fake eyebrows, or whatever else I do to change the way I look. Obviously I also get a whole new set of IDs and credit cards in whichever name I choose for each job, but I still need my official ID. Otherwise I can't visit Grandad.

"Afternoon, Katie," the perpetually cheery woman who works on the gate says as she sees me approaching. My fingers close around the wallet, but when I pull it out it is sleek and black and made of real leather, a Gucci logo embossed ostentatiously on the side. The kind of wallet a woman named Jen who likes the finer things she can barely afford might carry. Shit! I manage to slip it back into the recesses of my bag as I fumble for the other one. I should have left the posh one in my desk, that's my usual plan. You don't want to be seen in a fucking prison with a wallet full of fake IDs and credit cards, do you?

"You good?" the perpetually smiling woman asks in a sing-song voice.

My fingers are still searching, fluttering over everything in the bag slung over my shoulder. It has to be in here! I need to see him today, I need his advice, his counsel. I need him to tell me everything will be OK and that he believes in me. I need him to be proud of me. I can't miss this visit. It can't be another week before I can see him. I can feel the panic rising in my chest, the little girl who had worried about every detail coming up to the surface. No. No. No. This isn't possible. It isn't happening.

Breathe, I scold myself. Just breathe and pull yourself the fuck together. There is not space for this shit. Not now. Not today. I can feel the panic railing against my attempt to calm it, the internal battle raging, pulling me back down towards the fear and the anger I have spent a lifetime trying to tame.

There! I pull out the battered purse, the pleather cracked and peeling away in sections. "Thought I'd forgotten my ID." I try to disguise the swooping sensation in my stomach as relief floods through me under the volume of my voice and the fake joviality. I brandish the purse at the smiling woman's face.

"Lucky you didn't, hun!" She flaps her hand at me so I pass over the driving licence. Katie Evans. My real name. The name my mother gave me. The final part of her legacy that I cannot erase, however much I would like to. At least I don't have her slightly wonky teeth anymore. Those Invisalign braces are a damn miracle.

I hold my breath as she takes a perfunctory look into my bag, and passes it through the metal detector. She knows that I know the drill. She won't look too hard. "Oh, Gucci!" she says, murdering the pronunciation—Gucky!—as she gives the bag a little shake.

Fuck. I scramble for a reasonable excuse. Anything to stop her from opening it up and finding another name on that driving licence, even though the picture is identical to Katie's. "Oh, that's my friend's. She left it at my place. I'm meeting her after." I try to sound casual, try to take the disappointment in myself out of my voice. I don't make mistakes like this. But all these sightings of a dead man have freaked me out.

"You know, I found a purse a few weeks ago. Had three hundred pounds in cash just sitting there in it, you could hardly close it for all that money." She leans in towards me. "You know what I did?" I shake my head. "I looked at the address on the licence and I walked to her house. This fancy one with a proper driveway and everything. She didn't even say thank you. 'I guess you already helped yourself to a reward,' she said, before she slammed the door in my face."

"You should have kept it," I tell her.

"Damn straight, I should. Ungrateful bitch." But the smile doesn't slip and there is no real venom there. She is watching me, waiting for my reaction. I don't know what she wants. She's holding my stare. Does she believe me about the friend or is she implying that I stole the wallet? Some kind of "apple doesn't fall far from the tree" test.

"Anyway, have fun," she says and hands me back the bag. She gives me a conspiratorial wink. I think she does think I stole it, or found it. But she obviously doesn't give a shit.

Now then, you're probably picturing a wizened old man, bowed by the years, skin paper thin and stretching over angular cheekbones. Or perhaps someone a little closer to a traditional Santa Claus, with a beard and white hair and a friendly demeanour.

You're wrong.

There's a reason my grandad was so good at what he did, why so many women fell for his charms. He looks like a Hollywood actor, one of those types that people go, "Oh my God, I can't believe he's seventy!" He's actually closer to eighty, but he looks like an attractive sixty-five-year-old. Salt and pepper hair, still thick and ever so slightly curly, no sign of any receding at the hairline. Straight white teeth—the wonky monstrosities afflicting my mother and me were a gift from my grandmother

—that are all still his own; I don't think he's ever had so much as a filling. His skin crinkles around the eyes and there are a few laughter lines around his mouth, but you would never describe him as wrinkled. He has kept his physique trim and athletic, even during his time in prison, and can often be heard proclaiming how he can still wear clothes from when he was a much younger man. The Silver Fox, the headlines had called him. Normally the level of crime he committed would pass the papers by without so much as a tiny by-line. But for Grandad there had been a circus.

We'd graduated from small-time widows in suburban middle England to women enjoying the spoils of their divorces from industry magnates. These women fell hard and fast for the debonair and sophisticated Benedict—Benny to his friends—who promised evenings at the theatre and trips to Lake Como and the French Riviera. Sometimes his granddaughter would accompany them on holiday and I loved playing the stuck-up rich bitch, eating lobster for breakfast and fucking some hot young waiter who thought I could rescue him from a life of poverty.

We kept it going for four years, scouring the *Sunday Times* Rich List and the obituaries for potential targets. Lisbet Hansen. Kristen Allaire. Geraldine Taylor. Sarah Loughty. I was careful to make sure they didn't know each other, that they wouldn't figure out they had all been conned by the same man.

But I messed up. Sarah Loughty saw right through "Benny" and went to the police. The papers splashed his face across the front pages and more women came out to say he'd duped them too. But only a few of the charges had ended up sticking, proba-bly adding another five years to his sentence. We're still working on that, trying to get the sentences commuted, suing the papers that had printed his photograph. Entrapment. That was what his lawyer had said. A deliberate ploy to sell papers with overly sensationalised reporting. There would be an appeal soon. But lawyers need paying. And Thea is going to pay for it all.

His back is to me, but his impeccable posture can't be mistaken. He was a dancer, back in the day, ballroom mainly, another thing he used to charm the ladies. My grandmother had taught him, suggested that it might help him, after she was gone, to find another wife to take care of him. But he had never wanted anyone else, not in the way he'd wanted her. A great love story, he'd called it.

He senses me as I approach, leaping up to gather me into his arms as if I were six years old again. He squeezes me tightly before finally letting me go, and taking a few steps back to appraise me properly.

"So..." he says, when we sit down. It's a question. He wants an update.

"It's done," I reply. I didn't come to visit last week, making sure my focus was kept on Thea. We'd agreed that, Grandad and I, a few weeks ago.

"And..." he waggles his eyebrows at me. To anyone looking at us, it would probably appear that he was gently quizzing me about a date or something.

"It was perfect." I don't tell him about the times I have seen Edward since we killed him. He would only see it as a weakness; compassion isn't a word in his vocabulary, nor is guilt.

"And your 'friend'?"

"She's playing her role. But I'm keeping a close eye on her. I don't want her to make a mistake."

"Not like before." His voice is brittle. My failings are what landed him here after all.

"That was—" But he cuts off my excuses, refuses to hear them once again. Failure is not part of the family rule book.

"That was because you got sloppy and you didn't take adequate precautions to protect us. And now look where we still are."

I feel as if he has slapped me around the face, his words sting-ing. I hate to upset him, hate to disappoint him, hate to feel his anger turn in my direction. "The ruling is already back," I tell him, sweetly. "Accidental death. Such a tragedy." I allow myself to grin.

He smiles back at me, blue-grey eyes twinkling, as he leans forward. "Really?"

"Really," I confirm.

His eyes dart around the room, just to be sure no one is lis-tening. "So she thinks she's in the clear?"

"Yep."

"When are you telling her about the cost of your continued silence?"

"Soon."

"And the rest of it?"

"Only when it's all mine, Grandad." I reach for his hand. "Only once nothing can stop us. Then I'll tell that stuck-up bitch exactly what I did."

"God, I wish I could be there for that."

"Me too, Grandad. Me too."

Chapter Forty

By the time I leave the prison the sky has clouded over, the heat dissipating quickly. I decide to get off the bus a few stops early and walk the rest of the way. Walking is a great way to clear your head, to think through problems and allow your brain to come up with a solution all by itself.

I'm halfway home when my phone rings. That same number that rang when my flatmates were feeding me cake and pouring wine down me in an attempt to get me to open up. I don't want to answer it, but I know that I must.

"I know what you're up to, babe," he says, laughter in his voice. The same tone he used before, when he said, "It's nothing personal, babe. It's just too much money for me to share."

The line goes dead. I vomit onto the pavement in front of me, a thick stream that splatters and causes the other pedestrians to cry out and try to leap away from me. "Sorry," I mutter under my breath before I turn and run. Away from them, away from the vomit, away from everything.

I keep going, legs pumping hard against the sea breeze coming off the water. I'm not dressed for this. Within minutes my jeans are sticking uncomfortably to my skin, boobs bouncing almost painfully, my bag banging hard against my hip. But still I run. I haven't run for years, not properly anyway. Twelve-year-old me thought running was my ticket out of my fucked-up family, away from everything they wanted from me. That if only I could win another medal, take another step towards the Olympic team, then I'd finally make it far enough away and they could never catch me.

My brother hated my running. Hated the medals that decorated my half of the poky room we shared, with the green swirly carpet that didn't quite meet the skirting board. Hated the attention I got, the article in the local paper that called me a hotshot and said I was destined for greater things than our local town.

As I run I can feel the sharp pain in my left ankle, even after all these years and the months of physiotherapy I had in the aftermath of the accident. But all the treatment hadn't been enough to allow me to run competitively again. And nor had it been an accident. I can still feel his beefy hand on my back as he pushed me, feel the fear as I realised the carpeted stairs were coming too fast towards my face, feel my shock as I heard the snapping of bones. There was no pain. For a second or more I laid at the bottom of the stairs looking up at my brother's hulking frame. "Now you're normal like the rest of us," he said with a cruel smile. And then the pain came, as if someone had taken a blowtorch to my ankle. "You should have been more careful."

And he should have known I would eventually get my revenge.

I make it as far as the Marina before I'm forced to concede to the pain in my ankle and stop running. Sweat runs in rivulets down my back and I can only imagine how red and blotchy my face must be. I duck into the car park to catch my breath, away from the crowds of people preparing for an evening of fun at the casino or the cinema or one of the waterfront restaurants. My phone vibrates. A text.

You can't run from me forever, babe. We need to talk.

I look around but there is no one here. Is Kirk sitting somewhere watching me? Laughing at me and waiting to take everything again?

I met Kirk a few months after Grandad went to prison. He thought I was a waitress and I let him believe I was penniless and struggling. I thought that was better than him knowing the truth about me.

Grandad didn't approve of me having a boyfriend, although it was nothing against Kirk per se. "Chasing boys will make you weak," he told me.

I laughed. "Are you jealous, Grandad?" I teased. "Jealous that you'll have to share my time with someone else?"

"Don't say I didn't warn you, Katie," he said—he was already in prison and so there were no more scams, no more need for cute pet names—and I should have listened to him.

But Kirk was beautiful and brilliant and I fell head over heels for him. He was my opposite: six foot five, broad-shouldered, muscular. He would pick me up and swing me round like I was a doll. God, it was sexy as hell. The first few months of our relationship are a blur of stolen moments, his lips hard on mine, his hands gripping my hips, the way he would make me beg for him, the look in his eyes as he came for me.

All the time Kirk thought I was working shifts for minimum wage, I was really trying to find a way to generate as much cash as possible. I needed enough to get by, but also enough to send Grandad to keep him in luxuries to trade and to build a fund for his appeal.

A friend suggested I found myself a sugar daddy. "You're pretty enough and these guys love a bit of an Eliza Doolittle challenge." It was an awkward backhanded compliment, but when Joni told me how much some of these guys would pay you just to hang out with them and let them take you shopping and whatever, I was tempted. "You don't have to fuck them, but they'll expect a blowie at the least." In the end though I realised I couldn't do it. I've done stuff I'm not proud of, but that felt too much. And Kirk would never have forgiven me.

Joni was obsessed with the idea of being a celebrity and an influencer. It was 2016 and this new world order was starting to spring up. "Imagine getting given all this stuff for doing nothing at all?" she would whisper as she scrolled through the Instagram feeds of those who had begun to make a name for themselves. "Look at this woman's house!" She showed me this incredible white stucco property in north London somewhere.

"There is no way she pays for that via Instagram," I said.

"I think she wrote a book. Something about her identical twin." Joni had screwed up her face. "Yeah, maybe Leah Patterson's not a good example." She tapped her phone a few more times. "What about this one. I know for a fact that she has done nothing else apart from start a fashion blog."

She showed me the Instagram feed for this woman called Natalia Ormerod; her wall was full of pictures of her and her husband cosied up together. It was all very staged, something false about the images, none of it rang true. But I guess that was kind of the point; people don't want to look at real life, at pictures of someone else's laundry and the reality of evenings spent doing entirely separate activities and the arguments about whether you really have to spend all of Saturday with the boring friend your other half thinks is hilarious. What was the truth of Natalia's life? What secrets was she hiding?

Because we all have secrets, don't we?

Natalia had just over a million followers. A million people who scrolled through the pictures of her perfect little life, salivating over her clothes and shoes and all the finishing touches in her pristine home. I started to wonder. She didn't create anything to get famous; she didn't write a book, or a song, or paint a picture, or star in a film. There is no product she built, no life-changing invention she manifested. *She* is the brand, an entire empire built on the sands of public opinion. On the *shifting* sands. How easily it could all crumble to nothing if the veneer was to crack.

It's easy to find someone's address, no matter how hard they might try to conceal it, especially if you are patient and methodical, two skills Grandad made sure I learnt from before I could even walk. At home that evening, I scrolled to the bottom of her Instagram account, right back to the first completely over-filtered images she had started with, and began making notes. Within ten minutes I knew exactly where she lived, her phone number, the name of her GP, her mortgage provider, and every member of her family who had a birthday in March. It is amazing how much of someone's life you can unpick from the things they leave lying around: a pile of post, a noticeboard in the background, a picture of your wall planner for the month #busyMarch #mightneedaholiday.

I cross-referenced those early posts and the people who liked the pictures, figuring out who were the friends and family tagged, and who were random people who had started to follow this pretty girl who liked to post pictures of herself in some fairly skimpy outfits. There was one account that was particularly intriguing, a guy who would always like her pictures, except those with her husband tagged in. I scrolled this guy's wall, assuming he was just a fan, until I came across a #throwbackthursday picture of him and Natalia, wearing the same uniform, arms around each other's shoulders, happy grins splitting their faces. #firstlove. So he was an ex. And he obviously still lived close to her and had never married. It could have been innocent. But what if it wasn't?

Secrets and lies ruin lives

That first note was designed to unsettle Natalia. To make her think that someone knew something.

Some secrets are buried deeper than others
How far do I need to dig before I find yours
We all have secrets . . . but you're going to pay for yours

She went to the police but they thought it was just a prank, some jealous fan trying to unsettle her. She changed the locks on her fancy house, put up some motion-activated cameras around the perimeter. Then she got a dog, a rescue collie cross who, according to an Instagram post, was "the world's best guard dog." Natalia and Lily met a lovely young woman in the park one day and got chatting about the pros and cons of rescue dogs. "Lily is the most placid thing you've ever met; literally just snoozes all day and occasionally asks for cuddles," Natalia told "Claire." So much for being a good guard dog then.

Natalia and her ex were having an affair, meeting in a hotel a few towns over. I managed to get a picture of them kissing in the underground car park as they said their goodbyes after one such tryst. I sent it to Natalia with a demand for five thousand pounds. She paid it immediately. So I asked for more, ten thousand that time. It took her a few days, but she still paid.

The next week, I paid cash for a room in the hotel, booked under a fake name and found the perfect place to hide a tiny camera. The next night, Natalia and her ex checked into the room they always requested and that camera streamed everything over the hotel's slightly dodgy wi-fi connection.

But then Kirk found out what I was doing. He didn't run; he wanted in, and I wanted to impress him. I asked Natalia for more. On my own, I had instructed her to leave the money for me to pick up. But Kirk wanted to meet her. "I want to see the look on her face when she hands it over," he told me, eyes shining at the thought. Natalia paid over twenty thousand pounds to stop us from posting the pictures screen-shotted from the video.

"I think she'll pay more," Kirk said the next morning when we were half asleep, the warmth of his body against my back.

But she had given us all her savings, and taken out a loan for the twenty thousand. She refused to pay any more.

"Are you going to let her get away with that?" Kirk asked me.

So I made an example of her.

Do I feel guilty for destroying her life?

It's not like I killed her.

I need to get home and rest. My ankle is so swollen that putting any weight on it is almost impossible. There's a queue for the taxi rank and I almost squeal in frustration. I pull out my phone and bring up the Uber app. Thank God there's a driver only three minutes away who will accept my ride, and he somehow makes it to me in less than two.

I sink into the back seat, trying to breathe through the pain, a trick I learnt very young.

"Big storm coming in," the driver tells me, nodding his head towards the sea and the black clouds gathering on the horizon. "Looks like it's gonna be a bad one," he adds, but I'm barely listening to him, too engrossed in looking out of the window for signs of Kirk.

But it isn't Kirk I see as the Uber passes the entrance to the Pier. Edward raises his hand in a tiny wave as the car crawls past him. I squeeze my eyes shut.

He is not real. He cannot be real. I know he is dead.

But if he's dead, then he must be a ghost.

Or perhaps I really am losing my mind.

Chapter Forty-One

Do you believe in the wrath of God? I don't. I've been an atheist since I was nine years old and realised I had a choice. But an hour later the storm breaks. It's so powerful it knocks out the electricity and I peer out of the window at the darkness of the other houses as the lightning flashes and thunder booms overhead.

He is standing in the middle of the street, staring at the house and seemingly unaware of the rain lashing down on him, water streaming down his face, his white T-shirt and jeans moulded against the contours of his body.

I jump back, some primeval defence mechanism screaming that he must not see me. That if he does it will be the end of me. The end of everything. I take deep breaths, willing my heart to slow back to normal.

After a few minutes, my curiosity overrides my primitive self-preservation and I peek out of the window again. He's gone. I instinctively turn, half expecting to find a dripping spectre behind me. But the house is empty. Silent. Dark.

I grab my phone to use it as a torch, but the battery is dead. I howl in frustration. Kirk always had a supply of fully charged battery packs, but I've never been that organised.

Instead I pick up my laptop and wedge myself into the corner of the room, ensuring no one can creep up behind me. Every rumble of thunder makes me jump, every burst of lightning convinces me it will illuminate his ghost in front of me.

I've always been logical, the kind of person who thinks about things rationally. I do not believe in ghosts. I need to see the evidence for myself, I need to prove that he really is dead. My laptop screen casts a greenish pallor across the room, turning to a brighter white as I pull up a browser page. I type *Edward Taylor death* into the search bar and wait for the inevitable pages of local press coverage, blogs from his random friends distraught at his passing, photos from his memorial service.

But nothing happens. The screen remains blank. Fuck! There's no internet! Of course, the router needs electricity.

Frannie has left the keys to the MX5 on the side; I grab them and my phone. At least I can sit in the car and charge it, I could even tether my laptop to use the internet. I slide into the leather driver's seat and slam the door shut. The car starts to steam up so I turn the key and switch on the heating. I'm not even aware that I'm driving until I get to the end of the street and pull onto the main road. I need physical proof; it's so easy to fabricate a whole life online. I need to see for myself; I need to know he really is dead.

I take the A23 northbound, feeling the water on the road threaten to take control of the little car as I press the accelerator even harder. Adrenaline is pumping through me, and I feel alive, all my concentration consumed by driving.

I stop at the Fleet services on the M3 and treat myself to a Burger King, cramming salty chips dipped in mayonnaise into my mouth as if no one is watching. To be fair, the only witness is the pimply-faced teenager who served me. It's almost midnight and I can feel my energy levels dipping so I buy a huge coffee and take advantage of a 2-for-1 deal on Haribo, hoping the combination of caffeine and sugar will keep me awake.

As I turn off the motorway onto the A303, the weather starts to worsen, the rain coming down in sheets that almost obscure the road ahead. Light refracts through the water on the windscreen, the wipers unable to cope with the deluge. In the end I'm forced to concede defeat and pull into a petrol station, too rural to still be open at this time of the night. I feel like the only person left in the world.

At three a.m., the rain has eased off enough for me to continue and the rest of my journey is uneventful. I pull into the village just as the sun is rising, spreading vivid orange and red across the thick cloud still hanging in the sky. The village is quiet as I drive through, taking in the once so familiar sights. It's such a strange place, Ofcombe St. Mary, the locals split into two distinct camps: those who would smile and wave and ask how you are, and those who would brand you an outsider and subsequently refuse to acknowledge your existence. I wonder how many of them would remember me. Well, Ella anyway.

There is something different about the village as I look more closely. As if a shroud is hanging over the place. Gone are the flyers for Geraldine's election that were everywhere when Thea and I did our recce. The village green looks unkempt, the grass uncut. The flag outside the pub flies at half-mast. Black ribbon flutters on the trees surrounding the war memorial.

I turn onto the road up to The Grange and find the gates are closed, a padlock strung across them. *Closed Until Further Notice*, a large sign announces. There are a few bouquets in front of the gate and I step out of the car to take a closer look.

RIP Edward Taylor says the note attached to a bunch of lilies.

Edward, you are forever in our hearts says another on a bunch of red carnations.

Getting back in the car I let out a deep sigh. Everything points to Edward being dead. The village is in mourning, even The Grange is closed.

I should leave before anyone recognises me. But then I realise. So what if they do? Ella left Devon after Helena's accident, but why shouldn't she come back? She did nothing wrong.

The newsagent is just opening as I pull into a parking space out front. I vaguely recognise the shopkeeper, who gives me a friendly wave and calls out, "Morning!" in that overly chirpy way early risers do.

"Morning," I call back with less enthusiasm.

"Do I know you, love?"

"I worked round here once. A few years back. At The Grange."

"Such a shame," he replies sadly.

"A shame?" I ask, as if I have no idea what he's talking about.

"About the Taylors."

"What happened?"

"Edward passed. A couple of weeks ago." He shakes his head. "And it has destroyed Mrs. Taylor. You'll remember Geraldine from The Grange, I suppose?"

I nod.

He leans closer to me, as if to impart a juicy titbit of gossip. "She's closed down the club. Refuses to leave the place. No one has seen her since it happened."

"Is she alright?"

He shakes his head. "Edward was all she had left."

So he really is dead. Absolutely, definitively dead.

***

I try to grab a few hours' sleep in the car before I drive back to Brighton, pulling into a lay-by behind a man selling strawberries and raspberries to passing families on their way home from holidays on the Cornish coast.

For the first time Edward isn't wearing the T-shirt and jeans combination. He's dressed entirely in black. Black shoes, black trousers, black shirt, black jacket. His hair is slicked back neatly as if he were going to a funeral. His own perhaps. He stands in the lay-by on the other side of the road. Watching. Waiting. This time he does not ignore me. He raises one hand and points, deliberately, right at my face. Then a lorry drives past and when the view is clear again he is gone.

Did you see him? I want to ask the strawberry seller or the other people in the handful of cars who have also stopped. I step out of the MX5 and head towards them. But suddenly the near black clouds split open and there are shrieks as huge fat raindrops start to fall, forcing everyone to run for the safety of their vehicles. I spot a car edging out of the opposite lay-by. He's sitting in the back seat, eyes boring into mine as the car starts to inch forward, slowed by the potholes in its path. For a few moments I am frozen in place, but then I am running. Running full pelt towards the car and his impassive face staring at me. I need to reach him, to touch him and find there is nothing to him but air and guilt and the fuel of nightmares.

The screeching of brakes fills the air as the van tries to avoid me, the driver leaning out of his window to scream expletives at me. Somehow I make it across the road, but the car has already accelerated away from me and he has gone.

Chapter Forty-Two

I ignored the pain in my ankle on the drive down to Devon and back, but now I am suffering the repercussions. For the past week I have barely left the house as I rest it and give it time to heal. Or at least that's my excuse for hiding away. But I'm kidding myself.

I see Edward everywhere.

He's on the bus that passes my house. Just sitting there, waving at me.

He's the man I see walk past Tesco as I scan a loaf of bread and a pint of milk.

He's the man ducking into the loos by the Pavilion.

He is everywhere and he is nowhere and I think I might be going mad.

I want to tell Grandad about him. Tell him that I keep seeing him everywhere I go, that he is following me and haunting me and I'm scared and anxious and worried and what the hell does it mean? But I can't say anything. He's not real; I know he's not real.

I wake up on the sofa in the living room, the TV still blaring out some American sitcom I was watching before I dozed off. I can smell him. The scent cloying in my nostrils.

On the screen the sitcom goes to a break, advertising a new series called *The Guilty*. Is that what my visions of Edward are? Some gothic manifestation of my guilt? Some way that my subconscious is trying to tell me that I'm culpable and need to repent my sins, open my mind to the possibility that I did something awful? Again?

It's all bullshit though. I feel nothing at his death.

A key scrapes in the lock of the front door and I jump off the sofa, wincing at the pain in my ankle. "Jen, Jen!" Emily squeals before she pitches forward and collapses in a heap in the hallway. I can smell the alcohol from here. There's an embarrassed-looking taxi driver standing behind her.

"Thank you," I say to him. He's obviously a good guy, making sure she gets back safely.

"Don't envy you, love," he replies and motions at Emily, who is now trying to stand up, foal legs collapsing beneath her.

"I met a man!" Emily tells me. "We drank too much wine!"

"I can see." I close the door and try to grab her under the armpits to at least drag her into the living room.

"He was fit as fuck. Older though and, damn, he was sexy." She giggles and hiccoughs.

"But he let you take a taxi home by yourself? Sounds like a proper gentleman." I'm sarcastic, but I guess at least he didn't try to take her back to his place.

"He's so fit. You're gonna be soooo jealous." She attempts to crawl onto the sofa, grinning as she just about manages it. "Here, look!" She starts digging around in her tiny clutch bag, before pulling out a strip of photos, like the ones you used to get for passports, or that are used at parties and stuff. "See how gorgeous he is."

I take the strip of photos; you can't see his face in the first two, she's straddling him and you can only see her. The third and fourth are blurry, out of focus, as if he had moved at the exact moment the shutter clicked. But there is something so familiar in the hazy shape of his features.

He looks like Edward.

***

The next morning Emily wakes up on the sofa; I'm still sitting in the oversized armchair, legs tucked underneath me, the strip of photos in my hand. I hadn't wanted to go to sleep, not trusting the nightmares that would inevitably haunt me.

I've been waiting for her to wake up and now I pour a can of Diet Coke into a glass and use a long spoon to knock all the bubbles out so it's almost flat. This is Emily's drink of choice when she's hungover and I've watched her do this a hundred times over the past year.

"OMG! You are an angel," Emily says, voice dull and monotonous as she takes the glass. She gulps it down greedily before wiping the back of her hand across her mouth and smacking her lips loudly. "Delicious!" The proclamation is a lie; flat Diet Coke is foul. But I guess when you consumed as much booze as she did last night, any liquid is golden.

"What did he say his name was?" I ask, waving the photos towards her.

"Hmmm?" She squints at me.

"The guy in the photos. What was his name?"

"Oh, the hot one?" Well, at least she remembers him, so that's a positive. "Erm...something boring and terribly pedestrian. Chris, or Paul, or Nick, or Dave."

Or Edward? But I don't want to prompt her, I need the memory to be organic so I know it's real and not just her agreeing with my suggestion. "Anything more specific?" I ask.

"Why?" Emily screws up her face and so I open her another can of Diet Coke.

"I'm just interested." The lie sounds hollow.

"Oh God!" she wails. "Is he, like an ex, or something? Please tell me I didn't..." She trails off as she makes this weird waving motion.

"You didn't sleep with him, did you?"

"Of course not. We were in a *bar*!" She says it like she didn't fuck the DJ in the disabled loos that one time she and Frannie made me go clubbing with them.

"But you don't remember his name." I can feel my irritation rising, replacing the dread and fear that consumed me through the night.

"Umm..." she giggles and shrugs. "He gave me his number though." She grabs her little bag from under the sofa and turns the contents out into her lap. "Here!" It's scribbled on a flyer for some nineties revival night. Then she leans forward, almost falling off the sofa.

I jump to catch her. "Woah, there! Let's get you to bed, shall we? Before you hurt yourself?" She's like a child as I help her to her room, tucking her under her duvet to sleep off the hangover.

Back in the living room, I begin pacing, wincing every time I hit the floorboard that creaks. It sounds like nails down a blackboard. But at least it reminds me every tenth step that I'm awake and this isn't all a dream.

It must just be someone who looks like him. A trick of the light in the photo. It isn't even that clear. It could be anyone. I take a deep breath and stop pacing, hovering for a moment as if suspended in time. Eventually I sit down on the sofa. I don't believe in ghosts. That is all there is to it.

But I can't help myself and the flyer is just sitting there, the number scrawled across it. There is only one way for me to know that the man in the photos is definitively not Edward.

Before I can change my mind, I grab the paper and punch the number into my phone.

It rings five times. Then, "You have reached the voicemail of Edward Taylor."

No, no, no, no.

I throw the phone away from me as if it's on fire. This cannot be happening. I slump forward, my hands moving involuntarily to cover my ears as I curl into a ball and squeeze my eyes shut.

There's a knock at the door and a whimper escapes from my mouth. Is it him? I pull the blanket from the sofa over my head, my phone falling with it. I call the number again, expecting to hear a phone ring outside the front door.

Instead I am greeted by a woman's voice. "Welcome to the EE voicemail. I'm sorry but the person you have called is not available."

What the hell? I ring it again and get the same message. And again. And again.

No Edward Taylor.

I emerge from under the blanket. Did I just imagine it? Am I going mad? I pick up the photos again and squint harder. It still looks like him. But I suppose it could be another fairly attractive man of a similar age.

My head aches and I feel dizzy, wrung out like I'm only just recovering from an illness. I can't go on like this. Feeling like I'm going crazy, like I'm being watched, followed, like someone is waiting in the wings to devour me.

There is no one at the door. I must be seeing and hearing things that aren't real. Is it paranoia? Some form of paranoid delusion in which I conjure the man I helped kill, like he's the manifestation of my guilt?

But why would I feel guilty now?

Why when I killed Edward?

Why not when I killed Helena?

Chapter Forty-Three

It was all Kirk's idea, his appetite for the finer things in life whetted by us spending some of the proceeds of the Natalia scam.

"How many of the women your grandad scammed never came forward?" he asked me one evening.

"A few," I replied, shifting closer to him on the sofa.

"Why wouldn't they all come forward? Try to get compensation for the money they lost?"

I wasn't sure if he was asking for an answer, or if he already knew and it was entirely rhetorical. I answered him anyway. "I'd be too embarrassed, too worried people would think I was stupid enough to be played like that."

"Yeah."

"And some of these women were pretty high profile, you know, the kind of women who think they're important. Who would do anything not to have everyone know they fell for a conman."

"Anything?" he asked with a raised eyebrow, one finger tracing a line down my arm, something he knew would break me out in goosebumps.

I turned to him and smiled. "You have a plan?"

He leant in, his lips millimetres from my ear. "I think we should find out what our silence would be worth," he said before he began to kiss a trail down my neck.

***

Geraldine Taylor had met "Benny" at the 2014 Cheltenham Festival. It was just a few months after she was widowed and her friends thought a few days of horse-racing might cheer her up. She was certainly happier when she left, having been wined and dined and promised a trip to the Grand-Hôtel du Cap-Ferrat. There, the new couple were met by Benny's nineteen-year-old granddaughter, Ella, and the trio had a *thoroughly splendid time*—Geraldine's words not mine—eating, drinking and languishing in the opulent surroundings of one of France's premier hotels. But on the day they were meant to check out and head home, Geraldine woke up to find herself alone. Benny, his granddaughter, and the contents of the safe had disappeared in a puff of smoke. Oh, and left Geraldine with a bill totalling almost a hundred grand.

When I took a job as a waitress at The Grange in 2018, I wondered how Geraldine would react to seeing "Ella" again. It was a huge risk, but Kirk convinced me she wouldn't go to the police, and he was right. She was livid, but kept her cool in public, waiting until we were alone to unleash her particular brand of ice-cold fury on me.

"You little bitch," she hissed at me. "Do you have any idea of the bind you left me in?"

"Grandad and I really did appreciate that wonderful holiday," I said sweetly in return, putting on the same cut-glass accent I'd adopted in France. "And it really was *thoroughly splendid*." I'd smiled at her, a cocky cat-who-got-the-cream smile I knew would really piss her off.

"What do you want?"

"You never came forward," I say, reverting to my usual dialect. "So I'm assuming your sordid trip with the Silver Fox wasn't the kind of thing you wanted your friends to gossip about."

Then she laughed. This deep, throaty laugh like she was a twenty-a-day smoker, which morphed into a cackle the longer it went on.

"I don't think you should be laughing," I told her.

"You want money, I presume? For your silence?"

"I expect my silence is valuable."

"It may be, Ella. Or whatever your real name is. But you already took everything."

Then it was my turn to laugh. "You really expect me to believe that?" I motioned around me, the artwork on the walls, the heavy furniture, the cut-glass decanter on the sideboard. The whole room screamed of wealth.

"All this belongs to the bank. I've mortgaged The Grange twice over to try to keep it running." Her face was impassive.

"But your husband—"

"Left everything to my son," she interrupted. "Or more accurately to the children he hasn't had."

I sat back in my seat. "It looks like we have a problem then, doesn't it, Geraldine?"

"It does look that way." She met my gaze, her expression unreadable.

I stood up. "Well, I suppose I have some rumours to spread," I said, as I turned to leave.

What she said next shocked me, and given the life I've lived I'm not easily shocked: "Unless I can tempt you with an alternative target?"

I sat back down. "I'm listening."

"My daughter-in-law runs a successful business."

"It can't be that successful if you've had to mortgage this place," I replied.

"I don't want my son to know how much I lost to your grandfather, so I can hardly ask his wife for help."

"OK. So what do you suggest?"

Geraldine smiled. "Everyone has secrets. Secrets they would pay to protect. How about I help you to exploit Helena's?"

I laughed. "I've done this before, Geraldine. If she has secrets I am perfectly capable of making use of them without your assistance."

Her smile widened. "Where is Benny these days?" she asked. "Because I think his current *predicament* is rather testament to the fact that you're not always as capable as you think."

The bitch actually tried to table-turn me and I have to say I respected it. Enough to agree to a deal anyway. "Alright. Help me get close enough to her, and *if* she pays up we will call our relationship finished," I told her and she offered me her hand to shake.

"I suggest I allow you to unite in your mutual hatred of me. She is joining me for lunch a week on Monday. You will work that shift and then I will fire you. She loves to help out the waifs and strays and she won't be able to resist."

Getting Helena to like me was effortless. She wanted an ally against "Smaug" and it never occurred to her to question who I was or where I had suddenly appeared from.

And then I saw that huge life insurance policy. Enough for us to retire. To run away from this life of grifting and never look back. No more small scams, no more bargains with decrepit old witches like Geraldine Taylor. We'd be free.

Kirk and I brainstormed all the possible ways to get our hands on that pot of gold, but in the end it proved to be so very easy. I ingratiated myself into Helena's life, made her think I was her friend, her only confidante, even as I chipped away at her confidence with the notes. It took a while to break her down, to make her paranoid and jumpy and desperate to share all her secrets with the only friend she thought she had. And then when I discovered her big secret was that she was the source of all the Taylor financial issues, I twisted the knife, made her believe her whole world was on the brink of collapse.

Of course she paid her blackmailer—people always pay up eventually—and £27,500 was more than enough to get us through the next few months until the final payday. Could I have just had Kirk kill her without all the theatrics? Perhaps. But it suited us to have a load of people who had witnessed her disintegrating mental state, who thought there might be something rotten at the core of the Taylor marriage.

As soon as she was dead we celebrated by moving out of that poky little shithole of a flat. We took a suite at the Lympstone Manor Hotel, almost a grand a night, but it had twin brass clawfoot tubs in the bathroom where we sat sipping Champagne and planning the next phase.

"This really is the life, babe," Kirk had said, topping up his glass with Krug.

I held out my own flute, giggling as Kirk overfilled it. We were frivolous, already so sure of ourselves and our future. But Grandad had trained me to go over a plan a hundred times to make sure it was watertight and you can't go against your upbringing, however hard you try. "One more time," I told Kirk.

He rolled his eyes and huffed softly. "Alright!" he said eventually and downed the Champagne. "Tomorrow you will go and have a little chat with Edward." He paused for a moment, his brow creasing as if deep in thought.

"What?" I said.

"Explain why it's you and not me going to talk to him?"

"Fuck's sake, Kirk!" I necked my Champagne and motioned for him to top it up again. "I'm his PA, and his wife's friend. I have reason to see him. No one will even bat an eyelid if they see me going to The Gatehouse." I said it like I was explaining something to a toddler.

"But I want to see his face when you show him the picture," he replied with a petulant edge.

"Tough shit." I wasn't sympathetic. The plan was designed to give us the best possible chance of success.

Kirk paused for a few moments, watching me intently. "You're sure this is the best way?"

"Positive."

"What if he refuses to bite?"

I laughed and stood up in the bath, water dripping down my body. "What would *you* pay to avoid a lifetime in prison?" I asked, stepping out of the tub.

His eyes roamed over me and a hint of a smile flicked at the corner of his mouth. We had repeated this conversation over a dozen times. "The evidence wouldn't hold up in court," he said.

"So?" I shrugged. "He'll still pay."

"Promise?" Kirk asked as he hauled himself out of his bath.

"Promise," I whispered, stepping closer to him, my breath catching as he pulled me against him.

***

It went perfectly. Edward—poor, distraught Edward who had loved Helena so very much—welcomed me into the home they had shared.

"I can't believe she's gone," he said, his voice raw from crying so hard. He showed me into the living room and motioned to the sofa.

I didn't sit down as I replied, "Such a tragic accident," putting all the emphasis on the word "accident."

He narrowed his eyes and looked at me warily.

"How well do you think you knew your wife, Edward?" I asked, voice unnaturally light so it grated on him. He could tell something was off, but he didn't know exactly what.

"I..." he started, unsure of the answer I was looking for.

In four strides I was standing in front of Helena's desk. "She had plenty of secrets," I told him, opening the drawer and lifting out the stack of cards with their beautiful calligraphy. "Secrets she was terrified you would uncover." I turned to look at him. He stood with his mouth slightly open, shock and confusion etched into his features. "She paid a lot of money to keep her secrets." I smiled a feline grin.

"I don't know wh—"

"Oh, Edward." My voice brimmed with fake concern. "Perhaps you should sit down and I can explain everything. And then we can figure out where to go from here."

He nodded and perched on the edge of the sofa, looking distinctly uncomfortable.

"Right then." I handed him the cards from the desk and watched his lips move as he read them.

"What is this?"

"This is your motive." I enunciated each word carefully, slowly.

"Motive?"

"This is why you killed your wife."

He jerked back, as if I had physically slapped him. "Wh—"

I didn't let him speak. "You killed your wife because she was keeping secrets and then she used all your savings to pay her blackmailer." There was a singsong quality to my voice. "But you found out and went crazy. Pushed her off the roof of The Grange."

"She fell."

"Did she?" I looked puzzled as I leaned forward a little. "How many times had she been up there, Edward? She wasn't stupid, she knew not to stand too close to the edge."

"But..."

I reached into my bag and took out the photograph. The one that apparently showed Edward climbing out of the window onto The Grange roof at 18:15 on that fateful day, Helena already standing there. Of course it was really Kirk in the picture, wearing the same stupid England Rugby cap Edward loved. "You pushed her," I said emphatically.

"That isn't me." He sounded strangled.

"It looks like you," I said, pretending to peer more closely at the picture. The angle was clever and it looked convincing. "A few minutes before this was taken your security card was used to scan entry to the building," I added.

"But..." He slumped forward, resting his elbows on his knees.

"What's the penalty for killing your wife, Edward?" I asked softly.

"I didn't—"

"Life in prison, Edward. Unless..." I let the word hang in the air between us.

"What do you want?" He sounded resigned, defeated.

"Half of that lovely big life insurance policy."

***

I thought he'd come after me, seek retribution. After all, the photo that made it look like he had killed Helena was proof she didn't just slip, proof it wasn't an accident. But he was so busy covering his own arse and making sure he didn't end up in prison, he didn't stop to think his blackmailer was the real murderer.

Kirk and I disappeared the day Edward paid, almost a million pounds transferred into a series of accounts.

It was all so perfect. Until fucking Kirk pulled the oldest trick in the book.

I left him in the apartment we'd rented in London and took the train to Brighton to visit Grandad. On the way home, I thought I'd pick us up some wine. My card was declined. I checked my online banking for the account it linked to, expecting to find a balance of about ten grand. It was zero. I checked another. Also zero.

I ran back to the apartment and found him sitting astride a motorbike, the panniers stuffed full of his belongings. "What's going on?" I asked, trying to keep the panic from my voice.

"It's nothing personal, babe," he said as he pulled on his helmet. "It's just too much money for me to share." He shrugged, as if he hadn't taken it all and ripped my heart out in the process.

"Did you ever love me?" I asked, horrified at my whining desperation.

"What do you think, babe?"

"I told you," Grandad had hissed at me, when I finally plucked up the courage to tell him everything was gone. I had never seen him look at me that way, like he actually hated me with a deep, dark passion, at least for a few moments. It went beyond anger—anger burns like a fire and then fizzles to nothing—no, this was pure and unadulterated. It had been both terrifying and abhorrent at the same time. Terrifying that maybe, at least in that moment, he didn't love me at all. Abhorrent that I even considered that he didn't love me, that I wondered, just for those seconds, if he would leave me as soon as I wasn't useful anymore.

I tried to find new targets, people to blackmail, those with reputations to uphold. But no one bit. I had to set up a legit side-hustle, but even that floundered in the dust.

Then Thea swept into that overpriced shared office.

Chapter Forty-Four

I could smell the money rolling off her, despite her efforts to appear casual. Saint Laurent tote bag, Golden Goose trainers that probably cost over £300, brand-new MacBook, Varley Eland water bottle. I had to look that one up, £38 in case you're wondering. For a fucking water bottle.

"I'm Thea," she said as she slid behind her brand-new desk.

"Jen," I replied with a smile.

"What kind of business are you in?"

"IT," I said, not expecting any further questions on the specifics. "You?"

"Wine," she smiled. "I have a vineyard in New Zealand, Harris Bay. I'm setting up an import company."

"Cool," I said. "Let me know if I can help you settle in at all."

"Thank you."

I flashed her a quick smile, but my fingers were already tapping "Thea" and "Harris Bay" into Google. Thea Persimmon-West was once considered something of a wunderkind in the investing world. The youngest ever director of a top investment bank, she caused a furore when she suddenly quit in the winter of 2018 citing "personal reasons."

My interest firmly piqued, I opened Instagram and searched for her. It's such an unusual name and I found her immediately. I scrolled through a handful of pictures of the vineyard, including a rather fat Labrador who featured repeatedly. There were no pictures of Thea, not even caught in the background of a landscape shot or as part of a group. I scrolled backwards through time.

Her smiling face had almost made me drop my phone. Blond hair framing her features, lips that exact shade of red she always wore. What the hell was Thea doing with a picture of Helena Taylor on her Instagram? I looked sideways at Thea as my mind combed over every moment since she had walked into the offices. There had been no moment of recognition when she saw me, no flare of the pupils. I spend my whole life watching people, analysing their every movement, expression, tone of voice. Constantly searching for their weaknesses to exploit, or for the moment they realise I am scamming them. But with Thea there was nothing. She had no idea who I was.

I searched Thea Persimmon-West and Helena Taylor, eventually finding a webpage for the alumni of Ferndown School for Girls. So that was the connection. Old school friends. Thea was the friend Helena had occasionally mentioned.

I knew immediately I would make a mark out of Thea, but I needed a plan. So I cultivated a friendship with her, waiting for inspiration to strike. Then the pandemic happened and I thought I should wait until things went back to normal. I ended up waiting quite a long time.

A few months ago I found the first tentative questions Thea had posted on Reddit. She was looking for someone. She was looking for Ella Hazelwood. Not that she would ever find her, I had buried Ella completely. But then inspiration struck. What would Thea do to the person who had taken Helena from her? Would she want revenge? There was an anger burning in her that could only be extinguished through retribution of the most permanent type.

If Thea thought Edward had murdered Helena, would she kill him?

And if she did? Well, I'd already proved how willing people are to keep their murders under wraps. She wouldn't be any different. Another payday was coming. And this time I wouldn't mess it up.

***

How much money would you need to leave your life behind and start again? I suppose it really depends on what you want your life to look like. And how much you can squeeze out of the rich bitch you witnessed kill someone.

I need enough to pay for a decent lawyer, one who can get Grandad's case to appeal and then win it, and then enough for us to live in complete luxury on a beach somewhere. I have been dreaming about the Maldives for over a decade, the pristine beaches and shallow, warm waters brimming with multi-coloured fish. Although maybe not as a permanent place to settle with rising sea levels. I'll let Grandad decide, he knows what is best.

Five million should be enough. What? You don't think Thea has that kind of money? She spent almost a decade as an investment banker, making huge bonuses and building a serious share portfolio. Last year she earned a little over two million. And that's not what her wine business was making, that was just the money she had sitting about making even more money for her. It will take her a few days to liquidate some of her assets, but I have no qualms that she can do it with relative ease. And it's not like she had to work for it, so I'm not going to feel particularly guilty for taking it.

"I'm concerned about loose ends," Grandad says when I visit, his eyes meeting mine.

I look away before giving a tiny nod. I've always known it would come to that, but I've been trying not to think about it. Don't think I'm soft, but there is a small part of me that quite likes Thea. She has guts. *Chutzpah* as my grandmother would have said. Perhaps if our lives had collided in a different way we would have been genuine friends.

"Katie?" His voice is stern. "Look at me and tell me you will do what is needed."

"I promise."

"Good girl," he says and smiles at me in a way that makes me feel warm inside. All I've ever wanted is to make him proud.

***

I'm in Thea's kitchen, sipping a large G&T from one of those balloon glasses, you know those ones you get served in fancy gastropubs who want you to take photos of your drinks and post them to social media, tagging them in to raise awareness. The glass is so fragile the ice cubes don't clink, they rattle in this high-pitched way that makes me think the glass could shatter in my hand at any second.

"What are you going to do now?" I ask casually.

She looks contemplative for a moment. "You know, I have no idea." She laughs softly.

I take a long sip of the freezing bitter drink and watch her face for any sign she knows what's coming. But she remains oblivious. I've rehearsed my speech in my head a thousand times, but my heart is still beating too fast, my tongue heavy in my mouth. "I think I might leave Brighton."

"Where would you go?"

"Somewhere with better weather."

"That sounds like heaven." She smiles at me.

"I could use your help," I say and wait for her response.

All she does is shrug a little and say, "Sure. I've lived in a few places; Singapore is nice, Australia too. And Australia might be better for you in terms of work. Plenty of beach-based influencers." She says it like she's offering me genuine advice.

"Oh, I don't intend to work," I reply, putting down my drink. "That's the kind of help I'm after."

Confusion ripples across her face. "I don't..."

"Of course you do, Thea. You offered me a couple of grand once, because I—and I quote here—'knew about your intentions.' I turned you down, pretended I was offended because we were friends and I wanted to help. And you bought it." I pause for a moment and allow myself a smile. "And then you bought some story about an uncle and a desire for justice. You told me everything, kept me right at your side as you plotted to murder a man. You never even stopped to wonder what was really in it for me."

"You're blackmailing me?" She sounds affronted. As if someone like me would have the audacity to blackmail someone like her.

"Yes, I'm blackmailing you," I reply.

"Jen, I'm not going to pay you for your silence."

I grin and lean forward towards her. "But Thea, of course you are." I inject a distinct business-like quality into my tone. In fact, it's exactly the voice I've heard her use on the phone to an errant client who is taking the piss with how long they are taking to pay an invoice. It's always useful to watch people carefully, to draw these little caricatures of their behaviours that you can mine for future endeavours.

"No."

"Thea." I wait until she is looking at me. "You will do it."

"I don't th—"

"No, you didn't think, did you. Don't you realise I could just go to the police? Tell them about your little mariticidal plot?"

"Mariti-what?"

"Mariticide, it means murdering your husband. Or boyfriend in this case. Anyway, I could do that, you know."

"But you found the cocktail box guy. You hacked his system to send it to me. That was your idea. You are just as complicit in this as I am," she says.

"Why would I murder *your* boyfriend, Thea? I never even met the guy. The police would have no reason to think I had any motive at all."

"I'll tell them you're blackmailing me."

"No, you won't. I have all the proof I need that you're a killer, Thea. More than enough to ensure you would spend the rest of your life in prison. Is that what you want? Or do you want to simply pay me to walk away?"

She takes a deep breath, exhaling slowly as she thinks about the next move she might make. I take a sip of gin and wait for her to come to the only viable conclusion.

"How much?"

"Five," I reply.

"Five grand?" She's already reaching for her iPad, no doubt to make the transfer.

I laugh in her face and she recoils from me. "Do you really think I'd ask for five *thousand* pounds? From a woman who is currently wearing a pair of Tiffany earrings that cost almost twice that?" She reaches up to touch the offending earrings. "Seven thousand, four hundred and twenty-five pounds, to be exact."

"How do you know that?"

I grin. "Let's just say I've been doing my homework on your financial situation."

"You hacked my credit card bill?"

"And your current account, your savings, your stock portfolio. All of it. I assumed you were rich when I saw this house. But this," I motion around the kitchen, "is a drop in the ocean."

"Just spit it out. How much do you really want?" She's getting irritated now.

"Five."

"Hundred thousand?"

"Million. Five *million*, Thea."

"You have to be joking."

"You would be given a mandatory life sentence. That is twenty-five years. I think five million is a really rather good deal."

She looks at me, a hardness in her gaze. "It'll take me a few days to get that much together. And we'll need to think about how we transfer it. That kind of money changing hands might raise a few flags."

I nod. "You'll figure it out, Thea."

"I should hate you," she says.

I laugh. "You should."

She will hate me. Once the money is safely in my accounts and I finish the final step in the plan. But for now I am happy for her to think I will simply disappear into the night.

Chapter Forty-Five

He is sitting on my doorstep when I get back to the house, a cigarette in one hand and a stupid smile on his handsome face.

"Did you miss me, babe?" he says, pushing himself up to standing.

"What the fuck are you doing here, Kirk?" I hiss at him. "How did you find me?"

"You're hardly good at covering your tracks, *Jen Alderson*." His tone is mocking, as if there is something in the alias itself he finds ridiculous.

"What's wrong with Jen Alderson?"

"It just doesn't suit you, babe."

"Don't call me babe." He used to call me babe just before we drifted off to sleep. *Sweet dreams, babe* whispered into my ear as we lay entwined. It was my favourite moment of the day, but now the endearment is sullied.

"Oh, don't be like that." He takes a few steps towards me. "I don't like it when you're mad at me," he adds petulantly, like a child who has been ticked off by his mum.

"I'm not mad." I try to keep my voice level. "I am livid. You took everything, Kirk. Or have you forgotten that part?"

"It wasn't personal, babe. And I'll admit what I did wasn't right. OK? I apologise."

"And you think I'm going to accept your apology?"

"I still love you, Katie. And I know you still love me." He takes another step towards me, his face neutral.

What does he want? I take a quick step backwards, trying to put more distance between us.

"We're good together, babe." His face breaks into a sly smile. "You know that. Just think of everything we managed to achieve."

"I'm doing plenty well on my own, thank you," I reply tartly. "So you can fuck off and leave me alone." There is more conviction in my words than I feel, a traitorous part of my brain already asking if letting him back into my life would really be the worst thing in the world. *He fucked you over.* Rational thought takes control for a moment.

"You don't mean that." He flashes me an overconfident smile and my stomach flip-flops.

"Yes, I do." But my conviction is waning and I hate myself for it. I take a small step towards him, drawn like a moth to a flame, even though everything screams I will get burnt.

"Please, babe." He changes tack again, this time his voice is gentle and he reaches out a hand to touch my cheek. "I missed you."

"I missed y—"

But I'm interrupted. "Are you OK, Jen?" I look up to see Emily leaning out of her bedroom window.

"Who is that?" Kirk hisses under his breath, the harshness to his tone making me recoil slightly.

"My housemate," I tell him. Emily's interruption brings me back to my senses.

However much I once loved him, he never loved me and he hurt me more than I ever thought possible. I won't put myself through that again. I wave at Emily. "I'm OK," I call up to her. "He's just leaving."

"No, I'm not," Kirk says. "Not without you, anyway." He puffs his chest a little, his physical bulk blocking access to the door.

"Shall I call the police?" Emily calls.

"Shall I tell her to?" I ask Kirk. "Or are you going to walk away?" There's a tremor in my words and I pray he doesn't notice it, doesn't use it to try to break me down, I need to keep my resolve.

"Babe, think about it? Think about how good we were. I beg you. We could be brilliant. Legends even! A modern-day Bonnie and Clyde."

"We could have been. But you ruined it, Kirk. I don't need you anymore."

His face breaks into a lazy smile. "You have something, don't you? Something good?" His eyes flash and he raises an eyebrow slightly.

I want to tell him that I'm on the cusp of a payday bigger than he could ever imagine. I want to rub it in his smug bastard of a face. But instead I mimic his smile. "I have something good. I'm assuming that as you're sniffing around you have fuck all. How did you spend it all already?"

He opens his mouth to answer, but I cut him off.

"You're a fool, Kirk. I can't believe I ever thought you were a catch."

He stares at me for a moment, I can feel him debating his next move. His eyes are hard and an involuntary shiver passes up my back.

I take a deep breath. "Leave me alone, Kirk. I don't need you."

"Yes, you do, babe." It sounds like a warning.

"No, I don't. I never needed you." I take a step towards him, my bravado rising. "You're nothing." I say it with such venom he recoils.

I watch as he clenches his jaw, his eyes boring into me, the vein on his forehead starting to pulse. I hold my breath, not really knowing what he's going to do next. I used to think his unpredictability was sexy. Now I see him for the thug he really is.

"Fuck you, bitch," he growls and pushes past me. He turns back as he reaches the end of the driveway. "You think I can't figure out whatever the hell you're up to? Just remember that I found you, *Jen Alderson*."

"Who was that?" Emily asks as I close the door behind me.

My legs are weak and I'm worried I might be sick. I might have called him a fool, but Kirk is far from stupid. What if he does figure out what I'm planning? I wouldn't put it past him to either blow the whole thing up to spite me, or find a way to get to the money anyway. I rest my forehead against the cool PVC of the door frame.

"Who was he?" Emily asks again.

I stand up straight and turn to face her, swallowing my emotions. "Just an ex," I tell her.

She nods and a look of understanding crosses her face. "I had one of those. The type who wouldn't leave you alone. Who turned up on the doorstep at all times of the day and night."

"What happened?"

"I got a restraining order."

"Did that stop him?"

Her smile is sad. "Of course not. In the end I was forced to move to a different city."

"I'm sorry," I tell her, and I realise I am genuinely sorry. "And I'm sorry if this brings back painful memories."

"Do you think he will stay away? Your ex?"

I want to tell her he's gone for good. But I think we both know that would be a lie.

Part Four
Reckoning

THEA
2022

Chapter Forty-Six

Was I surprised when Jen turned on me? No. I'd been waiting for it. I was a little surprised she waited as long as she did before she broached the subject of a significant pay-out. Mind you, she's obviously been going through some shit, so I'll cut her a little slack. She looks terrible, as if she hasn't slept properly for weeks. In fact, if you'd put the two of us next to each other and asked a stranger to tell you who had recently watched their new boyfriend die in front of them, they would almost certainly have said her not me. And that isn't because I'm a bad actress; I deserve an Oscar for this.

It takes me a few days to pull together the money, but on Friday I call her. "I have it." I listen for the sound of her sucking in a breath on the other end of the line. I don't need to explain to her what the "it" I'm referring to is, she's been waiting for this call. "Now what?"

"We need to meet," she says.

"Meet me by the running man in an hour? I need to know how you want me to start getting the money to y—"

"Not on the phone!" she says and disconnects the call. As if anyone would be listening to us.

The running man is this weird statue on the seafront between the Pier and the Marina. It's some runner called Steve Ovett who was kind of a big deal apparently, back in the day, but whom I'd never heard of before moving to Brighton. Anyway, it's as good a place as any for a clandestine meeting and it'll work perfectly for what I have planned.

Five million pounds. That's what she wants. Five million or she'll make some accusation that I murdered Edward. Go to the police and tell them I plotted to kill him and she's somehow an innocent bystander. She insinuated she has proof, something that will irrevocably point the finger in my direction and let her skip away unscathed.

Two days ago we met in the office, a nice safe space and somewhere that no one would think twice about us chatting, playing the radio in the background as we huddled together in one of the meeting rooms. She's already given me the outline of the ways in which I am to transfer the money. Lots of small transactions to various accounts which can be routed and re-routed until no one can trace them.

She really has not thought this through. She will need to find a way to launder it before she can touch it. I know a little bit about this kind of stuff from Ada. Growing up in the shadow of the São Paulo mafia gave her a bird's eye view into a world of washing vast sums of money. Ada spent her childhood skipping between the ice cream parlours, cafes, restaurants, and salons whose owners helped her father. They would lavish treats on her while they inflated their takings and charged erroneous expenses to shell corporations to make everything look above board. Jen is going to get a rude awakening when she tries to get her hands on that five million: unless she is going to try to convince HMRC that someone wants to pay her millions to optimise their crappy Instagram feeds?

Plus, there's the other side of the equation. Something that I *definitely* know about. My Uncle Jed has been trying for years to find ways to squirrel away his earnings to avoid them ending up in the control of the various ex-wives who still sniff around. Hiding money is even more difficult than laundering it. I have already removed five million pounds from a moderate-risk share portfolio that has been giving me pretty poor returns over the last few months, but that raised a number of questions about why I was divesting so much in a single period. When that money actually leaves my accounts the questions will intensify. Although I suppose she's assuming that is just my problem. Like no one is going to try to chase the money and find her at the other end of the transaction.

"Won't people wonder where my money went?" I ask when she arrives at the statue, keeping my voice low and furtive, eyes darting around as if to make sure we can't be overheard. I want her to think I'm still a bit clueless, that I'm just having last-minute jitters and we're almost ready to hit that transfer button.

"You just have to tell everyone you made some bad investment decisions. That you bought a wedge of bitcoin and messed up your exit strategy or something," she tells me.

"Do you really think people will believe I bought bitcoin? I worked for prestigious investment banks for over a decade, I'm hardly going to screw up with crypto." I raise an eyebrow and she looks at me with barely concealed disgust.

"I don't really care what people believe, Thea."

But she will care. Soon enough. Although there's plenty that needs to happen first.

"Are you alright?" I ask her, my hand on her shoulder as I peer at her face. She looks even worse than she did two days ago. I mean, I'm hardly looking my best, it's been a stressful time recently, but I don't think she's slept at all these last couple of nights, her eyes are rimmed in red to the point she looks like she's suffering from hay fever.

"I'm fine." She moves away from my touch. But there is the smallest tremor in her voice.

"Are you sure?" Pretending to care is oh so easy.

"Yes," she replies angrily. But her eyes widen and her mouth drops open. She is staring at something behind me, her eyes widening even further as they track its movement down the road. "I..." she continues to stare as it passes us.

As *he* passes us, face pressed up against the passenger door of the taxi, staring.

"Do you..." She sounds like a child. A small child who believes there is a monster living under the bed but whose parents think she is being silly.

"Do I...?"

"Do you see him?" she whispers. "Edward?"

"All the time. He's in the house with me. In the kitchen when I cook. In the living room when I watch TV. Sitting next to me in the garden while I try to relax."

"I see him too," she finally says, taking a few steps backwards until her back is against the stone sea wall. She drops to her knees, head hanging downwards as if to stop herself from fainting. I slide down against the wall until I'm sitting next to her. When I take her hand in mine it feels almost cold to the touch.

There's a heaviness in the air, an oppressive feeling as if the dark grey sky could cleave open at any minute. Almost as if the weather knows a reckoning is coming and has decided to treat us to its capricious way. "Here." I hand Jen the half bottle of whisky I had concealed in my handbag. A little nip might help her. She almost chokes as she takes a huge swig. "Woah! Woah!" I try to take it from her, but she shoots daggers at me.

We sit in silence for a few minutes. Neither of us quite sure what to say to the other. But it is Jen who speaks first. "We killed him."

"You feel guilty?"

"Don't you?"

"I'm not a monster," I reply. I don't need to ask her the same thing. It's written all over her face.

"He's dead. Because of us."

Just then a car passing us beeps its horn and we both look up. I resist the urge to wave.

"It's him!" She jumps up, pointing her finger towards the vehicle as it continues its slow journey down the street and out of sight. "You saw him." She looks almost wild as she paws at my arm.

And then something inside her breaks and she's sobbing in my arms. "Oh my God, oh my God," she repeats over and over under her breath.

"I think we should go for a drink. You don't look like you should be alone right now," I say, smoothing her hair away from her face. "There's a place over the road, OK?"

She nods dumbly at me. I hold her arm tightly as we cross the road towards the pub. Late at night it's a popular spot for stand-up comedians testing new material and bands on the brink of breaking out; normally it's heaving with people. By day, it's open for a quiet sandwich and a pint, but it's rarely busy, and at this point in the afternoon it's basically dead.

An air-conditioned chill hits my face as I push the door open. But then I feel someone grab the back of my T-shirt, pulling me back into the street. "What the—"

Chapter Forty-Seven

A hand clamps over my mouth, the scent of stale cigarette smoke making me gag. "Keep your mouth shut," a man's voice instructs me.

I try to bite him, twisting and turning as I struggle to get free.

"Kirk!" I can hear Jen's panic. "What are you doing?"

"Taking your golden goose, babe." His laugh sends ice down my back. "Stop struggling," he says to me, "or I'll cut you." He releases his hold on me and I take the opportunity to whirl round to face him, letting out an ear-piercing scream into his balaclava-clad face. But he's faster than me, and reaches to grab my wrist, twisting it behind me, the knife he pulled from his pocket glinting in his hand. "Scream again and I'll cut out your tongue."

"Kirk! Let her go."

"Just shut up, babe. And get in the van."

Then he pushes me towards the rear doors and I stumble into the dark interior, tripping over something on the floor.

"Sit!" Kirk demands. He proceeds to tie my ankles together and then does the same to my wrists. He stuffs a rag in my mouth and ties a strip of fabric to keep the gag in place. I'm wearing one of those cross-body handbags and he uses the knife to slice the strap, opening the bag to check the contents before tucking it under his arm. "Can't have you making a phone call, can I?" he sneers, and then jumps out of the back of the van, grinning as he slams the door shut and I'm plunged into blackness.

"We're going on an adventure," I hear him tell Jen. "Oh, cheer up. Jesus Christ. I told you I'd figure out what you were up to. You only have yourself to blame."

In the darkness I scream into the gag. It's part fear and part rage and part sheer fucking frustration. I'm so close. So close to finishing this final part of the whole plan. So close to it ending the right way. The way I had planned for so long.

I try to slow my breathing down, stop the panic that is threatening to consume me. Eventually my head starts to clear and I become acutely aware of the way the gag has sucked all the moisture from my mouth and how the binds are making my wrists burn.

Calm down, Thea, I tell myself. Panic is pointless.

He called me his "golden goose." So he wants money from me. And he's taking me somewhere he thinks I will give it to him. But where? Surely he realises that all I need is a laptop and an internet connection, it hardly requires an elaborate set-up.

But he needs a way to make me pay. The thought hits me with a blinding flash of clarity.

He needs somewhere where no one will hear me scream.

***

We drive for hours without stopping. So far four hours and thirteen minutes to be exact, the face of my watch showing me the minutes ticking past. I'm desperate for a pee, but I refuse to relinquish my dignity. Another twenty minutes and we roll to a stop. I hear the creak of the driver side door opening; a minute later it slams shut and we move forwards again.

I try to take deep breaths, the gag making it difficult to pull the air into my lungs. We are almost there, wherever *there* is, I can feel it. Don't panic. Breathe. Don't panic. Panic is pointless. But no matter how many times I say it, I can feel the sweat running down my back, the stench of my own fear filling my nostrils.

Kirk opens the rear doors of the van and the thin light of dusk seeps in. He has removed the balaclava and I stare into the face of the man who really killed Helena. The last person to ever touch her as he sent her to her death.

"Nice journey?" he says, grinning. He grabs the binding around my wrists and hauls me up to standing, pins and needles shooting up and down my legs as the blood starts to flow again. "I'm going to take the gag off," he says, grabbing the knot at the back of my head. "It doesn't matter if you scream, there's no one around to hear you."

I don't scream.

Instead I silently promise that before the end of tonight I will kill him.

With my ankles bound I can't walk and so he throws me over his shoulder in a fireman's lift. I try to pummel him with my hands, but he just chuckles to himself under his breath, as if I'm a child who entertains him with her futility.

"Where are we?" I ask, trying to twist myself to see what's around me. I can smell mud and petrol.

He ignores me and instead calls out, "Babe! For fuck's sake. Get out of the van and come with me."

"No." She sounds like she's sulking.

He drops me on the ground and I find myself sliding down a bank—I was right about the mud, it's slimy beneath me—fingers clawing to stop myself. I roll onto my back. There is still enough light in the sky to allow me to make out the hulking shadows of heavy machinery. Where are we? On some kind of building site? I try to use my feet to pivot round to face the other direction and then I see it.

The Grange rises in front of me, her white façade looming from the shadows, all her windows black, dozens of sightless eyes reminding me how alone I am. Edward had told me the plans to create a new swimming pool in the grounds; the mud pit I now lie in must be part of the build. It isn't that deep, maybe a metre from the lip to the bottom where I now lie, and about ten metres across.

I hear Kirk stomping back to the van and the sound of the door being wrenched open. "Get out of the van, Katie," he demands.

"Shhh!" she says. "Jesus! She doesn't know who I am."

But that is where she's wrong.

I know exactly who she is. Exactly the role she has played.

There is no such thing as coincidence. I didn't choose to take shared office space at Q for the occasional free yoga and pizza night. I tracked Ella Hazelwood to Katie Evans and then to Jen Alderson. I've known the truth for years.

Chapter Forty-Eight

"Hold the torch," Kirk tells her from the top of the pit and I squint as the beam of light hits my face in the twilight.

I struggle to get my shaking legs underneath me and stand up. I lift my bound hands in front of me in an awkward wave. "Hi, Katie."

She thumps Kirk on the shoulder. "Fuck's sake. You couldn't keep your mouth shut," she hisses at him.

I debate speaking up and telling her I already know everything, that her real name is far from the secret she thinks it is, and that unpicking her aliases was easy as pie. But however smug I have felt about my detective skills, *I* am the one in a muddy pit with my ankles and wrists bound; it's an impossible place from which to maintain the high ground. Instead I'm going to see what they do next. I almost said, "What they have planned." I don't think much of this was planned, and certainly Katie has been dragged into this unwittingly. A quick aside, but calling her Katie after years of calling her Jen is a bit of a head fuck.

The seconds tick past. They have now begun a whispered— yet obviously heated, from their body language—conversation at the top of the mud pit. Eventually it gets so heated they forget to whisper and the words tumble down to reach me.

"You idiot!" Katie shouts at him. He takes a tiny step back, his hand wiping across his face. "She was going to pay up. I had a plan for her to transfer me the money."

"To transfer it to *you*, yeah. But this is my plan now."

"Like hell it is!" She rounds on him as she says it.

"Oh come on, babe. Can't you see that I've won here. That I'm the one who is calling the shots."

"She was going to make the transfer tomorrow. Thea and I had the whole thing planned out. And now you've ruined it." She shoves him, but his huge frame doesn't budge. "She can't make the transfer from here. Unless you have her laptop, and mine, and a stable internet connection."

"Why would you need those for her to make a bank transfer?"

She throws her head back and laughs. "Are you serious? Do you think you just log into NatWest online banking and transfer millions of pounds from one account to another?"

"Isn't that what happen—"

"Of course it fucking isn't! Jesus, no wonder you managed to lose it all so quickly."

"I didn't lose it all." He sounds pissed off. As well he might. I'd be pissed off if all my money disappeared from my accounts overnight. The idiot should have bought *something* with it. Anything. I would have gone for gold or even diamonds if it were me, or possibly some kind of complex financial instrument. I certainly wouldn't have left it in a handful of accounts in my own name.

Syphoning all the money was the first thing I did after I found him. Edward had paid Kirk and Katie a million pounds, but almost one hundred thousand of it had been frittered away by the time I found him. I spent a few days breaking down the remaining nine hundred thousand into tiny increments and donating it to a load of charities set up to help Ukrainian refugees and animal shelters across the country.

I wanted him to come crawling back to Katie. Leaving him penniless and then dropping the trail of breadcrumbs to Jen Alderson had worked like a dream. Although I have to admit I'd assumed she would take him back. I underestimated her.

"What happened to it then?" Katie asks him.

"It disappeared."

"Almost a million pounds doesn't just disappear." She sounds serious.

"It did. But then I decided to look for you, and I found you, *Jen*. Maybe it was fate?"

"How did you find me?" There's an edge of suspicion in her tone.

"Someone sent me an email." He shrugs.

"Who sent it?" The edge hardens.

"I dunno. They said they were a friend." He shrugs again.

Katie turns slowly to look at me, but she continues to talk to Kirk. "So this friend just appeared and told you where I was?"

"Yeah."

"Kirk?" She's still staring at me. "Do you think it's a little strange that she isn't more terrified?"

He looks at me. "I guess..." He grabs the torch from Katie and shines it on my face. "Hey!" he calls. "You know you're in deep shit, right?" His tone suggests I'm not more terrified because I don't understand the situation. "We know exactly what you did to Edward. We have the proof you're a killer."

"I'll transfer you the money," I call back up to him. I was always planning to transfer whatever demands were made. It will leave an electronic trace no matter how many accounts they try to route it through, but they won't even realise until it's too late. Whatever happens, Kirk and Katie will be punished for what they did to Helena, even if the only charge I can guarantee to stick is blackmail. It still carries a potential sentence of fourteen years.

I hear a rustle behind me, on the other side of the mud pit. The torch is still shining on me so I resist the urge to sigh in relief. He's made it.

The sound of a shotgun cocking makes me spin around. Kirk raises the beam of the torch to the source of the noise. "What did you do to him?" Geraldine demands, the barrel of her shotgun pointing directly at me. "What the hell did you do to my son?"

Fuck! Geraldine is meant to be on a cruise somewhere in the middle of the Caribbean, entirely unaware of what has been playing out in Ofcombe St. Mary.

Her voice bounces across the mud and erupts into the night sky. "What did you do to Edward?"

I'm frozen to the spot, the wet mud seeping into the bottom of my jeans, heart hammering my chest.

Now I'm terrified. Nothing is more frightening than a bereaved mother with a shotgun pointed at you. Especially when she obviously thinks I killed him.

"Geraldine," I call up to her, trying to put my hands up into a placatory gesture that is foiled by the binding at my wrists. "Geraldine? Put the gun down."

But she doesn't listen. Instead she takes a few steps towards me. I hear Kirk do the same thing from the opposite bank. "You're sure it was her?" Geraldine asks, the muzzle twitching as she gestures with it.

"Positive," Kirk says. "She plotted to kill him. He died in her house."

"*Kirk,*" Katie says with urgency. "What the hell is going on? What did you do?"

He walks in a wide arc around me until he's side by side with Geraldine. "You had your golden goose, babe. I just found someone who would pay an even higher price for her." He sounds smug, cocky even.

My breaths come in shallow quick gulps as I try not to let the fear take control of me. I underestimated Katie when I assumed she would go back to Kirk. And I underestimated Kirk. I thought it was my money he was after. I was wrong.

Geraldine had the trust overturned after Helena died, citing the punitive nature of the terms given Edward was now a childless widower. It meant she regained access to all the cash and various valuable heirlooms the Taylors had amassed over the years. Geraldine is a very wealthy woman.

"You're a fucking cretin, Kirk." Katie spits the insult at him.

"No, babe. You're just jealous because you didn't think of it. You could've taken Thea's money, and then Geraldine would have paid you to take care of the loose ends, just like your grandaddy would have told you to do anyway. If you'd only thought that little bit harder you could have taken it all. Or if you'd come back to me, we could have shared it."

"You two are irritating me," Geraldine says, her eyes still locked on me. "I have already transferred the first tranche. The rest will follow, assuming you uphold the rest of your bargain." She flicks her eyes to Kirk. "Now fuck off." Her tone is sharp, like a headmistress dismissing a detention. "You and your ditsy bitch of a girlfriend."

Kirk shrugs in my peripheral vision and crosses the pit back to Katie.

"What are you going to do to her?" I hear the panic in Katie's voice and then I realise she's talking about me, about what Geraldine is going to do to me.

Geraldine's face is hard, and for the first time I notice the bags under her eyes, the grey of her skin in the torchlight. She looks like someone who hasn't slept for days. But there is no trace of exhaustion when she speaks. "I'm going to make her suffer. And tomorrow this pit will be filled with concrete and no one will ever find her body."

This has gone far enough. "Geraldine?" I say, trying to keep my voice level. "Geraldine, please listen to me." I take a step towards her. All she does is raise the gun half an inch to hold her aim steady. She knows exactly how to use that gun. I remember how horrified Helena was by all the hunting trophies in the living room of the main Taylor house. "This isn't what you think."

"You killed my son."

"I know that's what Kirk told you..." I trail off and look again at what she's wearing. It's almost dark, but the print on her outfit is still distinctive: a zebra print kaftan over crumpled white linen trousers, her sandals sinking into the mud. She was meant to be on a cruise and she looks like she just stepped off the ship. "Look, Geraldine—"

"Just shut up!" It's almost a screech, and it stops me mid-sentence. "Nothing you can say will change things. You can't try to sweet talk your way out of this. You killed him and you're going to pay for it." She sounds completely unhinged, the combination of shock and rage and grief has pushed her over the edge. She is incapable of listening to any logic.

Cold tendrils start to wrap themselves around my organs, squeezing the air from my lungs and forcing bile into my mouth. It wasn't meant to end like this. I was meant to win. I raise my head to look into the eyes of a woman driven mad.

***

The light is blinding, like a nuclear bomb being detonated, and then there is nothing but white.

For a moment I wonder if she shot me, if the white is the infinite oblivion of death. But shapes start to form in the void as my eyes start to adjust. Geraldine is still pointing the shotgun at me, but she isn't looking at me anymore. She's staring at something behind me.

A piercing scream fractures the silence, the sound taking on an increasingly unearthly quality as it echoes around the mud pit. I spin to face the sound. Katie has collapsed to her knees, mouth open as the shriek continues to pour from her. She raises a finger and points at him as her wail dissolves into a whimper.

He ignores her as he walks down the side of the pit, both hands held in front of him in a gesture of surrender. "Jesus Christ, Mum! What are you doing?" his voice booms across the space. "Put the gun down so we can talk."

Part Five
Revelation

EDWARD
2019 to 2022

Chapter Forty-Nine

2019

My friends have decided six months is the allowable grieving time for a widower of my age, which is why in April—seven months and twenty two days after I lost her—I find myself in some hotel in Bristol city centre on a "boys' trip" to celebrate Josh's fortieth. Everyone else is already gathered in the bar for an afternoon of drinking and making a nuisance of themselves. Later on there is the promise of more drinking, a curry, and the ubiquitous trip to a strip club. I feel physically sick at the idea.

I miss Helena every moment of every day. It feels as if part of me has been surgically removed, leaving me only part of a person.

A fist thumps on the outside of my hotel door. "Come on, Ed! We're all waiting for you!" It's Rob, the mastermind of this particular torture.

I take a deep breath and call out, "Coming," the fake joviality in my voice making me feel even worse. Helena used to think these weekends were funny, used to take the mickey out of a bunch of guys pretending to still be in their early twenties. I'd ring her before I was dragged into the clubs, not because I felt guilty or because she needed reassurance that I wouldn't do something stupid, but because *I* needed a pep talk.

"You're going to go in there and have a drink," she'd tell me and I could tell she was smiling, "and then get a dance, being nice and respectful and leaving a good tip for the dancer. And then you're free to call it a night and go back to the hotel. OK?"

"OK," I'd reply with a level of machismo I didn't feel.

"You've got this," she'd add. "I love you."

"Love you too."

But there's no one to call today.

I make it down to the bar about half an hour later to find the guys are already a little tipsy and a shot of what smells suspiciously like sambuca is thrust into my hand.

"Cheer up, Edward," Rob's younger brother tells me and hands me another shot, this time it's black as tar and smells disgusting.

I knock it back. Perhaps alcohol-induced oblivion is the optimal strategy to get through the rest of the day.

A few hours later we spill out of the curry house, weaving through the streets towards the Kitty-Kat Klub. Rob performs a half skip to catch up with me, his heavy arm draping across my shoulder and almost pulling me over. "I'm going to do you a favour," he says, and then laughs loudly in my ear, pulling me closer to him. "Some of these girls, these Kitty-Kats," he elongates the "s" into a hiss, "some of them are open to an invitation, if you catch my drift?" He pokes me in the ribs with his elbow.

"Absolutely not." I'm emphatic.

"Oh come on! It's been months and months. You need to get back on the old horse."

"No," I repeat.

"Is it because they're professionals? We can go to a normal club if you want. Pick up some girls. Here, look," he makes a big deal of taking off his wedding ring and putting it in his pocket. "Now I can play proper wingman." He laughs loudly. "Just don't tell Charlie."

"No, Rob!" I stop dead in the street. I'm angry and flustered and frustrated and all I want to do is go home to my wife and curl up in our bed and pretend the rest of the world doesn't exist. But the rest of the world *does* exist. It's Helena who's gone and I can't bear it anymore. I can feel my eyes are filled with tears and I turn away from the group, knowing they'll only mock me. "I'm going back to the hotel," I say over my shoulder and walk away.

"Edward!" Rob calls after me, but I ignore him. He has no idea how lucky he is to have Charlie waiting for him in Exeter.

***

I don't sleep, spending the whole night sitting on the window seat in my room. By two a.m. I had drunk the rather paltry contents of the mini bar, and have been drinking water ever since, my mind racing like a skittish horse. As the sun rises, the space heats up and I open the sash window to let in some air.

The buzzing induces a visceral reaction and I jump off the seat as the striped body of a bee lands on the inside of the window. It's still early and she's lazy, lethargic as she takes a leisurely meander across the glass. I stand and watch her, transfixed. I could just...my hand reaches out as if operated by another. Perhaps it would be for the best.

If only I'd been better. A better man. A better husband. A better confidant to my wife who was struggling with a host of demons I couldn't even imagine. I could have helped her. I could have saved her. Instead, Ella had wormed her way into my wife's life, twisting her against me. Helena died hating me because of Ella. I should have killed her instead of handing over that money.

But I was so weak. I could barely fathom the loss of her, all that joy and love just...gone. And then when Ella accused me of killing her? Told me she had concrete evidence I was the one on the roof that day, I couldn't bear the idea that people would think I'd killed her. So I paid Ella and sank even deeper into my despair.

A gentle breeze lifts the edge of the curtain. I touch the bee, taunting her. I want her to sting me. Fast and clean and ... well, shameless. As suicide goes.

But then my phone rings, dragging me back to the present and I pull my hand back, stepping away from the window.

"Edward?" The voice on the other end of the line is clipped and formal. "It's Thea. We need to talk."

Chapter Fifty

2019

Thea refuses to talk on the phone. "I'm in Malaga, but there's a midday flight to Gatwick. I arrive at four p.m. Meet me in Joe's Coffee in the South Terminal." She's matter of fact, no hint of emotion or anything I can use to determine just what she actually wants to talk about.

I don't even say goodbye to Rob and the others, just pack my weekend bag and get a taxi to the station. Two trains later I'm at Gatwick, but I still have three hours to kill before Thea's flight lands. I'm brimming with nervous energy, having spent the entire journey running through every possible reason she might have for wanting to meet.

Does she know something about Helena she wants to tell me? Does she have something of Helena's she wants to give me? Those are the positive ones. But of course my brain is quick to discount those and move to the more catastrophic.

What if she thinks I killed her? What if Ella decided a million wasn't enough and has sent her the photos? Ella made a big thing of burning the picture, but we all know she will have kept a digital copy; it's not the 1990s when you could feasibly have destroyed the negative and the picture would cease to exist for ever. I keep circling back to this scenario and I can feel my panic starting to rise.

I need to get out of my own head for a while and there are two ways I can do that: alcohol or exercise. For once I take the sensible option and start walking, leaving the terminal and discovering there's a lake just a few minutes away. It's almost idyllic, the sun glinting off the water and the scent of spring in the air. As I walk I feel Helena's presence next to me. Not in a weird way, I understand she isn't really there. There's no such thing as ghosts, but it's a comfort, a connection back to her.

Thea's flight arrives exactly on time and I'm waiting for her in the coffee shop. It's awkward. We've never met in real life before. I am simultaneously terrified to meet this woman who knows almost all my secrets and overjoyed to meet someone who knew my Helena so well.

We have barely sat down when she hands me a stack of pictures printed from various social media profiles.

"Ella," I whisper as I see the first picture and the fear in the pit of my stomach coils as I realise Thea knows at least part of what happened. Does she think I killed Helena? I raise my eyes to meet hers, expecting to find anger flashing there. But it's pity I see reflected back at me.

"I know you didn't kill her, Edward," she says softly. "You know this woman?" She taps at the photo.

My fear evaporates and my face turns pink with shame as I nod. "Her name is Ella Hazelwood," I confirm.

"Well, that isn't her real name." She sits back in her seat and looks at me in a way that makes me feel like an errant child. "You fucking idiot," she hisses.

I swallow and avert my eyes from her disapproving gaze. "You know?"

"That you paid her off? Yeah, I know." She sounds almost as disappointed in me as I am in myself. "She's a con artist. She was born Katie Evans."

"How do you—"

"Just look at the pictures."

They have been taken from about a dozen different social media profiles. Thea taps each one, showing me how El— sorry,

Katie, appears in every single one. She's normally in the background, or at the edge of the shot, turning her face away from the camera. Doing what she can to not be seen in full as she moved through their lives.

"Are you sure they are the same person?" I ask softly. Some of the women are blonde, some brunette, glasses and different makeup styles obscuring their identities further.

Thea blushes. "There are tiny little details that connect them." She lays out two pictures side by side, both showing the subject in profile. "These two women have the same ears." She pulls over another. "This woman has the same little birthmark above her left eyebrow as the woman in the first picture." On and on she goes, pointing out the minuscule details that connect one image to the next. "The only conclusion," she says at the end, "is that all these women are the same person. This Katie."

"How did you..." I stare at her in awe.

"My brain is weird. I notice things, details that other people don't see, patterns that most would just ignore." She shrugs as if it's nothing. Helena would always talk about Thea's brilliance, how she had scored so highly on an IQ test when she was eleven they made her take the test three times just to be sure it wasn't a marking error. It was why she's the youngest director her huge swanky hedge fund has ever had.

She sits back, and as if reading my mind, says, "I quit my job."

"Oh." I'm not quite sure what I'm meant to say. She sounds both sad and excited.

"I have a plan." My eyes meet hers. "Are you in?"

Chapter Fifty-One

2019

We start by gathering as much information about Katie Evans and all the other girls she has been.

"So she was this Lara girl in 2016?" I ask Thea. We're on the terrace of a pub on the River Wey in Guildford, eating roast beef sandwiches. We tracked one of Katie's aliases to the area.

"She was twenty-one. Please don't call grown women 'girls,'" Thea tells me with an overexaggerated grimace.

"Sorry. So she was this Lara *woman* in 2016?"

"Yes. Running some kind of scam targeting students at the university." She nods towards the inside of the pub. "The barmaid was a fresher in 2016 and had a friend who fell madly in love with a Lara Stephenson. He's meeting us in ten minutes."

Once again I'm impressed by Thea's ability to track people down and get them to talk to us. She's so much better at this than I am. "How do you find them?" I ask, my tone tinged with awe.

She gives me a shy smile. "I can't explain it in a way that would make sense to you."

"Ouch!" I say with mock hurt. "No need to rub in my intellectual failings."

She turns bright red. "That's not...I didn't mean...I..."

I put up a hand to stop her. "I know it's exactly what you meant, Thea, and it's fine." Helena had told me Thea could sometimes say the wrong thing, that sometimes her brain didn't think through the full implications of what other people might infer from her words.

"Sorry," she says and returns her attention to her sandwich.

377

Todd Leadbetter arrives five minutes later, dressed in chino shorts and a white linen shirt.

Thea takes one glance at what he's wearing and says with authority, "Grad scheme junior banker." Luckily he's too far away to hear.

"Hi, Todd," I say, standing up to shake his hand. "Thanks for meeting us."

"You wanted to know about Lara?" he asks, pulling out a chair and sitting down. He has that easy confidence that comes with youth and privilege. I was like him once.

"You dated for a while?" Thea asks.

"Yeah." He laughs before pulling out a vape and taking a long drag, throwing Thea an apologetic look as the vapour cloud drifts towards her. It is sweet, like the raspberry laces I used to buy for Helena when we were still students. "I was a second year and she told me she was a fresher. I was crazy about her. But then I took her home to meet my family in the Christmas hols."

There's obviously a story there. "What happened?"

Todd clears his throat. "We went for lunch with my grand-parents. Well, my grandad and his new wife, Patty," he corrects himself. "She's cool though," he adds quickly. "Anyway, as soon as we walked into the restaurant I knew something was wrong. Patty went white; I thought she'd had a heart attack or a stroke or something." He shifts in his seat a little and runs his hand over his face. "My grandmother's death hit Grandad hard, I was terrified he'd lose Patty too."

"But she was fine," Thea says, her tone suggesting Todd should hurry up and finish his story.

"Thankfully. She was just shocked. Patty recognised Lara, she knew her from years back."

"But not as Lara?" I ask.

"Ashley," he confirms. "The granddaughter of a man she had dated."

"What did you do?"

"Lara... Ashley... Whatever her name was ran from the restaurant and I never saw her again. She left her overnight bag at my parents' house and didn't even come back for it. After the Christmas break, I went back to university and discovered my girlfriend had been scamming loads of people." He looks heartbroken. "Plus she'd been asking all my friends odd questions about their families. Like if their grandparents were still alive and stuff."

"She was looking for new targets," Thea says, matter of fact. "She and her grandad had been running relationship scams."

"I know. Patty told me everything. He stole her entire life savings." He puts the vape away and gets out his phone. "If you have any other questions, I'm sure she'd talk to you. We could video-call her."

"Thank you," I say, "that would be great."

He calls her and they chat for a few moments, then he passes the phone to me.

"Hello," Patty says with the tiniest trace of an Essex accent.

"Thank you for talking to me, Mrs. Leadbetter."

"Call me Patty. This is about Ashley?"

"Yes. Although that wasn't her real name."

"She was just a child." There's sympathy in her voice, a tinge of sadness. "That poor girl was just as much a victim as I was."

"She isn't a child anymore," I scoff.

"Imagine her childhood." Patty has a gentle face and kind eyes, every inch the stereotypical loving grandmother of old story books. "Imagine how hard it must be for a young girl to be dragged from pillar to post as a prop for a man she adores. And that girl really loved her grandaddy, worshipped the ground he walked on and would've done anything to make him happy."

I have to concede that she has a point, but it doesn't excuse the things she's done as an adult. Plenty of people have terrible childhoods, much worse than being dressed up and paraded past unsuspecting lonely women who would lavish her with attention and gifts, dote on her as if she were their own flesh and blood. Those people didn't go on to become murderers.

Thea leans over and grabs Todd's phone from my hand, she shoots me a look as if to ask me what the hell I'm doing.

"Mrs. Leadbetter, Patty. I'm Thea." She turns on the charm in a way I hadn't realised she could. "I don't suppose you ever found out who he was? The man who stole from you?"

I hear Patty laugh. "He was arrested in 2017, a year after Todd introduced us to his new girlfriend. Michael Wood. But the press called him the Silver Fox."

After Todd leaves us, we start searching for more information.

"Michael *Wood*," Thea mutters under her breath as she picks up her iPad. "Different fucking surname. Must be Katie's maternal grandfather." She sighs loudly, clearly frustrated with herself. "Here," she says less than a minute later. "Michael Wood, arrested September 2017 on charges of fraud, theft and forgery. Damn..." she trails off and then turns the tablet round so I can see what she's looking at. "I guess that's why they called him the Silver Fox."

He is undoubtedly attractive and looks much younger than his almost eighty years. He has a full head of thick grey hair. My hand creeps to the back of my own head and the thinning patch I can no longer ignore.

Thea turns the tablet back round and continues to search. "Apparently he was targeting rich women who often had no one else, who were estranged from their own children, or hadn't been lucky enough to have them, or in a particularly cruel phase, women who had lost not just husbands but sons and daughters too." Thea makes a face.

I use my own phone to look up related news articles about him. The papers had gone crazy for this handsome con artist. But there is never any mention of the granddaughter. "Is it odd that no one ever named Katie?" I ask Thea. "She was old enough in the later scams to be named as an accomplice, but no one ever mentioned her."

"Perhaps they all thought she was another victim, like Patty did," Thea says with a shrug, as if it isn't important.

"Do you think she was a victim?"

Thea puts down her iPad and stares at the space above my head for a few moments as she contemplates her answer. "Perhaps. At least at the beginning, when she was just a little girl." She tilts her head a little. "But then she grew up. She can't claim immunity for the things she did as an adult." She looks directly at me and something in her eyes makes me shiver. "Do *you* think she was a victim?"

I take a deep breath and exhale slowly, my eyes still locked on Thea's. I keep my voice quiet to avoid being overheard but there is no mistaking the fury I feel. "Katie helped to kill my wife. Without her, Helena would still be alive. There is no excuse for that. She must be punished."

A slow smile spreads across Thea's face. "Good. At least now we have a clue about where she might be."

Chapter Fifty-Two

2020

Michael Wood was being held in Lewes prison, just outside the city of Brighton, and so that was where we started hunting for Katie. But we couldn't find her. With no idea what name she might be using or how she might have disguised herself, it was like searching for a needle in a haystack.

Thea had just one complete photograph of her, one picture where you could see her entire face front on. It was a selfie taken by Helena in a cupcake shop in Exeter. There is a wicked grin on my wife's face as if she's up to something. My heart breaks every time I look at it, that I will never know what she was thinking at that exact moment. "Ella" was with her that day, her face reflected in the mirror behind Helena.

For the rest of 2019, I spent hours and hours trawling the internet looking for signs of Katie, combing through thousands of social media accounts of people who lived in Brighton and the surrounding area, hoping for a glimpse of her.

But on 1 January 2020, Thea wakes me from my New Year's hangover with a phone call.

"I found her!" she almost shouts down the phone, making me wince. "I fucking found her!"

"Where?"

"You know I've been running this import business for the vineyard?" she asks.

"Err...I guess." To be honest I have no idea what Thea does all day. I just assumed she was living off the proceeds of the vineyard and any accumulated savings from her career.

"Well, my New Year's resolution is to make a proper go of it. While I'm here in the UK, anyway. I've been looking at office spaces in Brighton. Uncle Jed has said I can move into his house for as long as I want but working from home in silence will give me a headache."

"OK…" Perhaps I should have paid more attention to Thea's life.

"Anyway, there's a shared office space in the city called Q. It's a bit funky; I was going to dismiss it as an option, all free ping-pong and pizza and whatever."

"So…" I wish Thea would just get to the point, my hangover is crystallising and my head is pounding like a drum.

"I'm sending you a picture from their Instagram. They had a New Year's Eve party last night."

My phone beeps as the picture comes through and I squint at it. "Is that…?"

"Yep."

"Fuck."

"She's calling herself Jen Alderson and running some social media optimisation company. I'm assuming it's a cover for her to find other people to extort."

"What now?"

"On Monday, Harris Bay Imports Ltd will take a contract for space in Q. I think it's time I met this Jen."

"But what if she recognises you?" I ask.

Thea laughs. "You know how there were so few pictures of Katie? She was trying to slip through people's lives without leaving a trace, but we still managed to find a few of her."

"Yes?" I'm not quite sure where this is going.

"That's because she wasn't very good at hiding. I'm much better at it." There's a hint of pride in her voice.

"There aren't *any* photos of you?" But as I ask I remember Helena's exasperation with just how much Thea hated the camera. Even when they went to Vegas just before the wedding Thea wasn't in any of the pictures. All Helena had was an old photo, slightly discoloured with age and bleached from years on display; she and Thea from their time at Ferndown.

"None except the school one. But anyway, the issue isn't that she will recognise me. The issue is that she might not."

"You want her to know who you are?" I'm struggling to follow her logic.

"I want her to befriend me. Wealthy Thea Persimmon-West will be very tempting as a potential mark. But she won't be able to resist once she realises my connection to Helena."

***

Thea and "Jen" become friends, having lunch and coffee and partaking in those pizza evenings Thea had been so derogatory about.

But then lockdown hits and the whole country is closed.

"This is a disaster," I tell Thea over the phone as I pace The Gatehouse, the walls closing in on me and the ghost of my dead wife following me from empty room to empty room, demanding I get vengeance for her murder. I think I'm losing my mind.

"This is a godsend," Thea corrects me. "Jen is so lonely and bored at home that I've set us up with daily Zooms. We talk more than we ever did in the office. She thinks we're friends. Proper friends."

"Do you feel a little guilty, lying to her like this?" I ask her.

"She killed Helena." Thea's reply is cold as ice.

Chapter Fifty-Three

2022

Our plan was to wait until things started to return to normal after lockdown. We thought it would be a few months and we'd be ready to launch the next phase in the summer of 2020.

But things didn't return to normal. 2021 started with yet another total lockdown, this one lasting even longer than the first.

"Be patient," Thea told me during the weekly Zoom sessions we set up to stay in contact. "It's not like anyone is going anywhere, and we have more time to plan this way."

She was right—she has this habit of always being right, not that I tell her that very often—and she found more and more people who wanted to help us pull off a revenge plot that became more audacious as the months trundled on and 2021 turned into 2022.

It's the Tuesday after Easter and I'm trawling the grounds of The Grange looking for stray chocolate eggs that got missed during the hunt we host every year for the village children. Helena used to organise it all, noting all the locations where she hid the treats on a little map to make the clean-up quicker. I should have done the same but I thought I'd remember. I can almost hear her gently mocking me as I crawl through one of the flowerbeds in search of an elusive flash of coloured foil.

My phone rings in the back pocket of my jeans and I wipe a long smear of mud down my thigh before pulling it out. "Hey, Thea."

"It's time," she replies.

"Are you sure?"

"Everything's ready. It's all in place."

I swallow. "OK." I feel a crackle of nervous energy ignite in my veins. "Let's do this."

"No second thoughts?"

"No." I am steadfast. This is it. It's finally going to happen. "Good luck, Thea." I tell her.

"Luck is for people who fail to plan appropriately," she says sniffily.

"Just say thank you, Thea." Some of her social foibles have been exacerbated by lockdown. I just hope she can act well enough that "Jen" doesn't see through her lies and tricks.

***

Thea begins to spend her evenings dropping breadcrumbs all over the internet that she's looking for Ella Hazelwood. It doesn't take long for someone to make contact with her via DM.

"You're sure it's Katie," I ask her.

She rolls her eyes.

"You know we're on Zoom, so I can see you, right?" I ask.

She repeats the action. "You worry too much, Edward," she tells me. "Yes, of course it's Katie. Now I'm going to ask Jen to help me find out who's sending the DMs."

This is the part of the plan that has worried me the most. I think Katie will realise that Thea is laying a trap and run. Thea is convinced she won't.

Once again Thea is right.

"So Jen has traced the DMs. Guess who they are coming from?"

It's obviously a rhetorical question, but I answer anyway. "Ella Hazelwood?"

"Bingo. Jen is going to help me find her and see what she knows about Helena's murder. It's absurd."

"Just be careful, Thea. Please. Remember Katie's dangerous."

"You need to have more faith in me, Edward."

***

I book my mother on a month-long cruise with some of her old friends. They've been talking about doing the trip for years and they can't make any more excuses once the tickets are in their hands.

"Oooh, an outside stateroom," coos one of them.

"It had better have a terrace," grumbles Mum.

"Of course it does, only the best for the Taylors," I tell her with a wink, even though I have begun to see through her façade to the real woman beneath. I know that love is unconditional, and I do love her. I just don't really like her all that much.

With Mum out of the way, Thea and I move to the final phase. Luckily my list of allergies is so long there is a plethora of options when it comes to the thing that could kill me.

Thea rings me one evening after she and "Jen" have been brainstorming. "She actually suggested we use bees." She's laughing as she says it, like it's the funniest thing in the world.

I try to join in, but all I can think of is that morning in the hotel, stretching my finger towards the yellow and black striped body, wondering if it wasn't the way out of all the pain.

"Oh," Thea says. "I almost forgot to tell you about Todd!"

"What happened?" We had asked Todd Leadbetter from Guildford to help unsettle Katie a little and he was more than happy to oblige.

"He was absolutely brilliant! Just stood there, staring at her. Then she freaked out and ran. I wish you could have seen her face."

***

A few days later, Thea calls me. "Cocktails," she tells me proudly. "I can't believe I didn't think of it right at the beginning, it's so obvious and so simple. All we need to do is smash the glass on the floor so it looks like you drank some of it."

"When?"

"Next weekend."

"And everything's in place?" I ask, even though I know she wouldn't be suggesting the date otherwise.

She begins to reel off a list of the people whom we have convinced to help us, a combination of people whose lives were torn apart by Katie's scams and some trusted friends of ours. "Daiki is a little nervous."

"I'm not surprised," I reply. "He'd get into serious trouble if he got caught." Ada's husband, Daiki, is a paramedic and will fake taking me to hospital. "Are you sure we need him to do it?"

"I know Katie, Edward. She will be watching the house. It's the only way this works. Johan and Timo are ready to play the second paramedic and the doctor at the hospital."

"So we're ready, then." It's a statement not a question. This is happening. I just hope it works.

***

My apparent death goes off without a hitch, not that lying on a trolley for five minutes was particularly taxing. I slip out of the ambulance as Daiki takes it back to the hospital at the end of his shift. "Thank you," I tell him, as I call for a taxi to take me to the hotel. I need to lie low for a day or so.

I've already checked in and left my car in one of their underground spaces, but now I collect my case and take it to the room to unpack. Five identical white T-shirts and three pairs of identical jeans. An entirely black outfit, like you might wear to a funeral. An iPad with the app for the tracking device we've placed inside Katie's mobile phone case.

My plan is brilliant in its simplicity. All I will do is hang around Brighton, dressed in the exact same outfit as my dating profile photo on Affinity.com, iPad tracking her every move. Occasionally I will put myself into her line of sight, just a glimpse of me, enough to make her question what the hell is going on. I want her to suffer, to think she's losing her mind.

Is it cruel? Petty? Maybe it is. But what she did to Helena was a hundred times worse.

***

I've started to go a little crazy, just me on my own in a hotel and randomly stalking the streets of the city. Eventually Thea capitulates and agrees to meet me for dinner in the hotel. "I have something to tell you anyway," she says.

I'm so excited about some human company that I don't consciously register the way she said she had something to tell me until she knocks on the door to my room. "Is everything OK?" I ask, worried that something has gone badly wrong with the plan and it's all starting to collapse around us.

"Everything is fine." She clears her throat. "It's just, well I wasn't sure if it would play out so I didn't want to tell you before."

I pour us both a drink from the mini bar and motion for her to continue.

"Thanks," she says, taking the glass of whisky from me. "Do you remember the photos from the evidence envelope?"

"Of course." Thea had sent me a copy of the evidence Katie had fabricated against me. She'd done a good job, to be fair. It certainly looked convincing that I had hired a contract killer to murder Helena.

"There was one I didn't send you." She reaches into her bag and pulls out a picture, handing it to me without another word. It shows a perfectly clear shot of Kirk's face. Up to that point we hadn't been able to find him, having to content ourselves with only punishing Katie. "You found him?" I whisper, staring into the eyes of my wife's killer just moments after he had pushed her.

"Look at the tattoo on his neck," Thea instructs.

I squint at the picture; it's a barcode, the words *made in 1992* written underneath. "Classy."

"It tells me the year he was born. Now look at the one on his upper arm, you can see most of it."

"Is that a sheep?"

"A ram. The mascot for Derby County FC."

"Right..." I wait for her to connect the dots as she no doubt already has done, always at least five steps ahead of me.

"Douglas Kirkpatrick Barnes was born on the third of February 1992 in Derby. He went to Allestree Woodlands School. Here is a copy of his leaver's photo, he's the tall one at the end of the back row."

"And you know where he is now?"

"Southampton. Idiot is still using his birth name."

"Wow," I say, in disbelief that the guy who blackmailed me for a million pounds is so brazen he hasn't even tried to hide. "Why didn't Katie go after him? If he was that easy to find, surely she would have tried to get her share back."

"She probably did try," Thea says and I can't fault her logic.

"So what shall we do about him?"

"Well..." she sounds reticent.

"What have you done?"

"Don't be mad..."

"OK. Just tell me what you've done." For a moment I worry she's done something reckless and compromised the whole plan. But Thea doesn't really do reckless.

"I know it was technically your money, once upon a time. But I donated the entire contents of his bank accounts to charity."

I laugh. I don't give a shit about the money. "A good one I hope."

"I parcelled it out into tiny increments for a load of smaller charities. Mainly to help Ukrainian refugees and animal shelters."

"Fine choices." At least now some good might actually come from the money. "So, now what?"

"I've told him where to find a certain Jen Alderson."

"You think they'll get back together?"

She did. It was the only mistake she made.

And if I hadn't been tracking Katie's phone, I might never have found her.

Chapter Fifty-Four

2022

The floodlights illuminate a scene from a nightmarish fever dream. My mother is dressed in animal print, pointing a shotgun at Thea who stands bound at the bottom of the quagmire, Kirk and Katie stand watching.

Katie screams, filling the air with a sound that echoes the pits of hell. She collapses into a wail, but I ignore her as I run towards Thea, screaming at Mum to put the gun down. But Mum remains frozen, her face twisted in a mask of anger and disbelief.

"What the…" I hear Kirk say as I reach Thea, standing between her and my mother.

"Move!" Mum demands. "She needs to pay for what she did."

Can she not see me? "Mum!" I turn to face her, pushing Thea further behind me. "Just listen to me."

I walk slowly towards Mum, her eyes boring into me as I get closer, hands raised in front of me in the same way you would approach an animal caught in a trap. Eventually I reach her, pushing the gun to one side to wrap her into a hug. She slumps against me, my weight supporting hers.

"I thought you were dead," she whispers.

"You weren't meant to be part of this, I'm sorry," I whisper back to her. That was the whole point of the cruise. Four weeks at sea with her friends, sunning themselves on deck, getting pissed on the all-inclusive premium drinks package, gambling away part of the inheritance in the on-board casino. A few of the villagers had helped me to stage the scene round here in case Katie needed proof I really was dead and I thought it had worked like a charm. Everything would be back to normal by the time Mum came home and she would never know what had happened.

"Why did he tell me you were?"

"Who?"

"Him." She pulls away from my hug to point at Kirk on the opposite side of the pit. "I came back as soon as he called and told me what had happened."

"But why the gun? Why here, on the building site?"

"He told me *she*," she hisses the word and motions to Thea, still bound and now on her knees in the mud, "had killed you. That he would deliver me your killer."

I sigh. This is all such a mess.

It was meant to be so simple. Thea just needed to transfer the money to Katie and then she would go to the police. Tell them all about Katie's scams, all the evidence she had gathered, Katie's aliases she had found. That transfer would be the final piece of proof.

"Mum, Thea is innocent, OK? She's done nothing wrong. I'm here, aren't I?" I leave Mum and slide down the bank back to Thea. After I untie her, I stand up and address Kirk and Katie. "I think it's time we all had an honest conversation about what has brought us here."

Katie takes a step forwards, raising a finger at Mum. "If we're going to be honest," she says, "you should know this all started with her."

"Me?" Mum says, completely incredulous. "You are the little con woman who crashed into my life and messed everything up."

"Really, Geraldine? *That's* how you're going to play it?" Katie laughs. "You're really going to claim that your life got messed up? You got *everything* you wanted. Everything!"

"That's no—"

"That's exactly what happened. You got the inheritance, and kept The Grange, and that daughter-in-law you hated so much didn't just die, she died and left you with *even more* money."

"I had nothing to do with what happened to Helena," Mum says, but it sounds hollow. Thea sucks in a breath next to me.

"You started this, Geraldine. You told me Helena had money. You painted a target on her back."

"Oh, shut up, you silly little girl. You have no idea what you're talking about."

Katie raises her voice. "Tell him the truth, Geraldine. Tell your darling son what you d—"

But her words are cut short by the crack of the shotgun as Mum fires at her.

Kirk throws himself in front of Katie, taking the full force of the bullet to the chest.

Katie's scream rips through the night.

Blue lights on the horizon announce the arrival of the police. I had called them before I arrived, as soon as I'd been able to track Katie's phone to The Grange. If only they'd got here a few minutes earlier.

The gun slips from Mum's hands and she sits in the mud, staring at Kirk. I don't know if you've seen what a shotgun can do. It's not pretty—don't Google it—and at this range it's probably fatal.

Katie lies across him, tears streaking her face. "Kirk, Kirk, Kirk," she whispers under her breath, as if she can hold him in this life if only she can say his name enough times.

Thea gives Kirk and Katie a wide berth as she climbs up to greet the police.

Chapter Fifty-Five

2022

Thea only made one mistake and it almost ended in disaster. I, on the other hand, made a catalogue of errors, more than I can count. One of them will haunt me forever.

"Do you really think Mum wanted Helena dead?" I whisper to Thea. We're in the living room of her house in Brighton. The events of the last few days are etched into Thea's face; she looks as exhausted as I feel.

She takes a deep breath and looks at me. "I don't think she wanted her dead, no. But she wanted her out of your life," she says sadly.

"Really?" I ask, but I know she's right. I have always been blind where Mum was concerned. Always far too quick to jump to her defence no matter what she did, always assuming she was misconstrued or misunderstood.

"She was truly horrible to Helena."

"I know."

"No, you don't. You think she was 'just a bit difficult' or 'their personalities clashed sometimes' or 'she was doing what she thought was for the best, even if she was occasionally wrong.' She made Helena's life a living hell, constantly undermining her, eroding her confidence, nit-picking at every single thing she did."

"Was she really that bad?" I ask.

"For fuck's sake, Edward!" She shakes her head. "I was going to save you from this, you know. I was going to keep this part from you, but you're going to keep making excuses for her for the rest of your life. Even if she's convicted of Kirk's death, you will still try to visit her in prison every weekend like the dutiful son."

She stands up, heads to the drinks trolley and pours herself a huge slug of whisky. She knocks it back and then pours another. "Could I have one of those, please?" I ask. I think I'm going to need it.

She hands me the whisky and then sits on the coffee table so she's facing me directly. She waits for me to take a mouthful. "Right. Ready?" she asks, not unkindly. I nod as the Lagavulin burns the back of my throat.

"You were meant to marry Cecily, and when you married Helena instead your mother blamed her for it. Helena might have been your idea of the perfect wife, but she wasn't your mother's. And then there was the will and the inheritance and you not wanting to have children, but not having the balls to tell your mother that it was your choice. You let Geraldine torture Helena because you were too weak to stand up to her. All she wanted was the Taylor money, and the status that came with it. Helena told me how she became more and more obsessed with getting the will overturned."

"You make it sound so..." I grope for the right word.

"Fucked up? Your mother is a sociopath, Edward. She doesn't give a shit about who gets hurt as long as she's happy. Katie wasn't lying when she said Geraldine painted a target on Helena's back. Geraldine *owed* Katie. And she paid her debt by giving Katie a new person to blackmail."

"Why did Mum owe Katie?"

Thea sighs and pulls out her phone. She taps the screen a couple of times before turning it to me. It's a photo, taken in a beachfront restaurant. Mum is smiling, leaning in to the man who has his arm around her shoulder. I look at Thea. "Is that...?"

"Yes, Edward, that is Katie's infamous grandfather, the so-called Silver Fox. Do you remember when you had to bail your mum out the first time?"

"Mum fell for him?"

"Fell for his charms. And for his con. That was 2014, just after your father had passed."

"I didn't know anything about it," I say, the shame at my lack of awareness flaring.

"Then Katie showed up in 2018 and demanded Geraldine pay her to not go public."

"But she didn't have any money..." I stand up and help myself to another measure of whisky, putting my hand out to take Thea's glass to refill hers too. It's all becoming clear. Mum gave her Helena. She started all of this.

"You see it now?" Thea asks gently.

"So Katie was telling the truth."

"Your mum literally fired that gun to stop Katie from talking. Jesus, Edward! Did you not see that?"

I remain silent for a few moments gathering my thoughts. "Did you know? About Mum, I mean, before that night?"

Thea says nothing as she drinks her whisky.

"If you knew about Mum... knew that she started it all, that she was part of it..." My words are stilted. I know what I want to ask but it's almost impossibly hard to say. "If you knew, why would you let her walk away?"

The colour spreads across Thea's cheeks and she looks away from me.

My mum faces a murder charge for killing Kirk, she'll probably spend the rest of her life in prison. She shouldn't have been there that night, she should have been safe on that cruise, oblivious to our plan.

Thea stands up, walks over to the collection of photographs of Helena on the mantelpiece. Her fingers trace the outline of

Helena sitting on a bench outside a pub. She looked so happy that day, so full of life as if her future was one endless stream of possibilities. Thea whispers something under her breath, so quietly I'm not sure if I hear it correctly. *This was all for you.*

Looking at Thea, right at this moment, I know there is one final question I need to ask.

"Thea, how did Kirk know how to contact Mum, which cruise she was on?"

Epilogue

2023
KATIE

I hold my breath as I loop each letter carefully in the perfect copperplate script. This has to work. I've wasted too much time already, spent far too long making sure that everything is in place, that all the pieces are ready.

You are dead to me

There is no punctuation at the end of the sentence, no need for the drama of an exclamation mark or the severity of a full stop. I pick the card up to inspect my penmanship in the glow of the setting sun. Satisfied, I slip the card into the envelope, the one with his name already written so precisely in a beautiful cursive.

"Now what?" I look up at her.

She smiles and picks up the envelope, turning it over in her hands, the perfect red gloss of her manicure in contrast to my own bitten nails with their cracked skin and ragged cuticles. She reaches into her drawer and brings out a rectangle of bright pink plastic, flicking the spark wheel to produce a brilliant flame. "Now you burn it and send the message into the ether." She hands both things to me, and then pushes a large metal bowl towards me.

I have been in here for almost a year now. Only another four more to go. Unless I can prove just how rehabilitated I am, how I really was just his pawn. Coercive control has become a bit of a buzzword recently, heaping the blame for all my wrongdoings onto my famously sociopathic grandfather. Plus I added an abusive mother, a psychopathic brother and a scum-bag of an ex-boyfriend, painting myself as a thoroughly tragic victim.

Grandad would be so proud.

In the end the police struggled to make a case against me. Thea never transferred me anything so there was no blackmail charge, and the whole story about the cocktail and the plot to kill Edward was just all a little bit farfetched. Plus, no harm, no foul, right?

Helena's death was not investigated. It remains just a heartbreaking accident.

I turned Kirk's death to my advantage, pinning everything we had done together onto him. Well, he wasn't around anymore to call me a liar.

It was actually my flatmate Frannie who fucked me over. I might have taken a credit card out in her name when I got a little desperate and she went to the police. Bitch. Some clever shit went digging and discovered a few more identity theft scams I'd run. The maximum term is seven years, but the judge was "lenient" and only gave me five on the condition I also attended therapy. How generous of him.

"It's OK, Katie," the woman tells me as I pause, the lighter in my right hand, the letter in my left. "This is the final stage. The one where you finally break free from his control and can move on with everything." My therapist has had me spend months writing little letters to my victims, apologising to them and asking for their forgiveness. Each one drips saccharine sweet missives about my regret and how "I would take it all back if I could" and how "I've been able to meditate on the pain and hurt I've caused them."

The final stage of my "treatment" is to release the control my grandfather had over me. The other letters will find their ways to the victims. This one though, he will never read. Because it isn't about him, it's about me.

"You can do this, Katie." Her words are gentle, her eyes expectant. "And then we'll see what we can do about getting you moved somewhere a little nicer for the next stage in your treatment."

Good behaviour will take at least six months off my sentence. Good progress in therapy might shave off another year. I'll be out before I'm thirty. Grandad will still have plenty of years left.

I hold the lighter against the letter, watching the flames take control, roiling like waves as they turn the paper to ash.

I don't mean it, I whisper inside. *I promise I will find a way.*

And at least I have a couple of years to think of the most perfect and most flawless of plans.

A few years to let Thea get comfortable again. My revenge will be so perfectly sweet.

Acknowledgements

Everyone says that second books are the hardest to write and I think there might be some truth in that. But no one ever mentions how difficult second acknowledgements are! So I'm going to try to keep this short, even if that's not normally my forte...

Firstly, thank you to my wonderful agent, Hannah Sheppard. I feel incredibly lucky to have such a brilliant advocate for my work and I am so excited to see where the future takes us!

To Sara Adams for your editorial genius in helping to take this book from the mess of that first draft to a story I adore. To Beth Wickington for taking over the baton and guiding me through the final edits (and not killing me for last minute tweaks and random emails asking for urgent changes!). To Kate Keehan and Callie Robertson for being such brilliant champions of me and my books. To Katy Aries for your production wizardry, Ellie Wheeldon for the audio, and Lewis Czismazia for the gorgeous cover. Plus everyone else in the wider Hodder team who has worked to bring *Her Sweet Revenge* out into the world.

To Alex Logan, Leena Oropez, Lauren Sum, Jeff Holt, and all the rest of the incredible team at Grand Central for your hard work in getting *Her Sweet Revenge* to US readers.

To the Brighton Write On group: Alex, Ericka, Helen, Jodie, Steve, and Wayne. I feel so grateful to have found such a wonderfully weird bunch of writing pals. We might not always get much work done, but our sessions are always one of the highlights of my week!

To all the authors I have met this past year or so: your friendship and support has made this writing journey 100% less lonely and I feel utterly privileged to be part of the community.

To all the bloggers, reviewers, advocates, and generally book-ish lovelies: your enthusiasm for my writing has blown me away and I am so thankful for everything you do to raise the profile of authors and our books.

To Doug Barnes for your generous donation to Book Aid for Ukraine, and to Kirk Barnes for the use of your name. Your dad requested you were a villain, but apologies for just how villainous your character turned out to be!

To all my friends and family for your continued support. Special thanks to Mum for being my first reader, for your proof reading, and for all your encouragement and cheerleading.

To my husband for supporting me through this crazy journey. And to Lily for cuddles, being my plot walk companion, and for not minding the hundreds of pictures of you sleeping I post to social media.

And finally to all the readers. Thank you for everything.

About the Author

Sarah Bonner grew up dreaming of a career as a writer and performer. Instead, she became an accountant. The pandemic gave her the opportunity to answer her original calling, and she completed her first novel, *Her Perfect Twin*, which was published in 2022. *Her Sweet Revenge* is her second novel. She lives in West Sussex, United Kingdom, with her husband and very spoiled rescue dog.